# The Dark Side of Blue

# The Dark Side of Blue

Colin Doyle

ISBN 979-8-52433-769-6

*For Oscar*

# One

"Hello?"

"Trench, you hear the call over the radio? The body at Oldbury Hill?"

"Just heard it, Chief, yeah."

"I want you to get down there asap," said Detective Chief Superintendent Nick Lewis. "I spoke with Harris in Kent. He agrees we should take it, given the circumstances. Lock it down. Don't let the uniforms trample all over it. And for fuck's sake don't let anyone else near it. Keep it tight as possible."

Detective Chief Inspector Trent Chambers thought he sounded tense. He was speaking faster than normal, and slightly louder than was necessary. He rarely swore.

"On my way, Chief. Do you kno—"

"And don't let any media types get within an arse's roar if any of them turn up. Last thing we need."

"Okay. We'll get goin—"

"Take a look, see what you think. Secure it 'til Forensics gets there. I've told them to send Wharton as well."

"Understood."

Trench waited. No point trying to talk. He knew what was coming next anyway.

"And Trench?"

"I know, Chief."

"If it's her, if it's the Osbourne girl, don't bloody tell anyone. Not a soul. We need to manage this. And the family needs to hear it directly from us. That's the priority, okay?"

"I know, Chief, understood. On our way."

"Right. And Trench? I want you leading on this, that's official. Report back to me directly. And do it quick. I want to be ahead of this. I'll need to brief the Commander first thing. Get back to me as soon as you can. And *only* me, Trench."

"Will do."

Trench waited to see if there was anything else, but Lewis hung up. He wasn't normally so abrupt but this was shaping up to be anything but normal. Lewis was relatively new to the role of Detective Chief Superintendent, in the job only a couple of months. This was by far the highest profile case the Met's Criminal Investigation Department, CID, had had since his appointment. Or at least it had the potential to be. As he hung up the phone, Trench thought to himself that he'd learn a lot about the new Chief in the coming days.

He turned to his partner.

"Correct. Keep going."

Detective Inspector Jasmine Zaveri gave a quick told-you-so pout and hit the accelerator. She'd started toward Oldbury Hill as soon as they'd heard the call over the radio. They were already well beyond Westminster Bridge. She'd been in no doubt they'd be the ones getting the call.

Trench had been less sure. He thought he'd noticed a change in Lewis's demeanour in recent weeks, since the resolution of the Nassor case. Trench wasn't sure if it was just some worrying controlling tendencies emerging or if there was more to it. But a missing person case always put the squad on red alert. Especially this missing person. And Lewis was assigning him the lead. Trench decided he'd give Lewis the benefit of the doubt for now.

They were silent for a few minutes, Zaveri driving as fast as she safely could through the urban streets of South London. Most streetlights were already on, despite the fact it was not yet five pm. The gloomy November afternoon was cold and dank. Though at least it hadn't started raining yet. Deep, dark clouds brooded across the skyline, looking almost black at their highest point. Like smoke rising from the flame-orange hue of the street-lights, the whole city simmering.

Zaveri flipped on the siren and blue lights as they approached a queue of cars at a red light near Elephant and Castle. She gently swerved onto the wrong side of the road to get past the queue and hit the accelerator again as they sped down New Kent Road.

"So we're in charge of this now, right?" she asked.

"That's what he said."

"Then as soon as we're done here, we need to go and speak with her family. We need to get the full picture from them. We've got sod all to go on so far. We'll take over the incident room for starts...if you can even call it that. I had a quick look in there after the morning briefing. Flimsy would be a flattering description of what they've got," she said, eyes on the road.

She was short, so had the seat at its highest setting and pushed close to the steering wheel. She was leaning forward so she could keep her arms bent for optimal high-speed driving.

"Uhm," Trench responded, deep in his own thoughts.

"It's only been forty-eight hours, they're not even taking it seriously yet. The Chief had Higgins give a short update at this morning's briefing. Sounds like all they've done is take a statement from the parents. And whaddaya know, the boyfriend is now the prime suspect."

She kept her eyes on the road and her foot hard on the accelerator. They passed through New Cross and were heading into Blackheath.

"*If* she's even missing, that is," she added.

After a few seconds of silence, she glanced over at Trench. She was used to him being preoccupied with his own thoughts. They'd been partners for a few years. Initial wariness had given way to trust, as they each recognised that the other shared an appreciation for privacy and personal space – traits painfully rare across the squad. Over time trust had evolved into firm friendship. Trench could count the number of firm friends in the squad on one finger.

"Hello?" she said in a slightly raised voice to get his attention.

"What?" he replied, snapping back to the present. "Sorry, Jazz. I'm thinking we'd probably be better off starting from scratch. They won't have done much, and we'll want to talk to everyone ourselves anyway."

Trench knew the police officers taking the parents' statements will have felt to some degree like they were just going through the motions. At 22-years old, their daughter was a grown woman. She was perfectly entitled to go missing if she wanted to. Or missing from her parents, anyway. He'd experienced countless situations where young adults felt stifled by their family's attention and chose to simply disappear for a while. Someone with the means of Vanessa Osbourne would certainly not find it difficult to do so.

Knowing this, and the fact she was gone less than forty-eight hours, the officers would probably consider it their main priority in taking the statement from the parents to make a show of providing them comfort. We're the police, we care, we're here to help. This would be especially true in this case. Police responded more quickly and more urgently when those calling were from the more prominent, wealthy contingent of London's populace. Money talks. Or in London, more like money screams and shouts. And you didn't get more prominent, nor wealthy, than Vanessa Osbourne's parents.

But if this body was indeed that of Vanessa Osbourne, Trench knew, then everything was about to go ballistic.

"And let's speak with the boyfriend, Sheldon, as soon as possible too. I don't think the lazy bastards have even spoken with him yet," Jazz continued, rolling her eyes. "Anyway, if it's her, it's our shitshow now."

Trench nodded. Shitshow was probably right. He thought about the prospect of informing the Osbourne parents that their daughter was dead. No matter how many times he'd done it, it never got any easier. Probably the opposite. Each time he knocked on the door to shatter the lives inside, he could feel the weight from the memories of all the times he'd done it before.

As they merged onto the M25, Jazz moved straight into the outside lane and floored it. It wasn't quite rush hour yet but there were lots of cars on the main southern route out of London. Plenty of people stealing a head start home, leaving work as early as they could get away with. The rat race started earlier as the week got later. By Friday, every vein out of London was clogged up virtually all day. Commuters hoping they weren't the ones trapped by the inevitable failing rail signals or stuck for hours in static traffic.

The cars in front swiftly moved out of the way of the siren and blue lights. As the evening gloom descended, the brightness of the flashing blue lights was sufficient to make drivers aware of their presence. Jazz flipped off the siren.

Her train of thought had obviously followed Trench's.

"We're going to be the ones notifying the family too, guarantee you," she said. "Chief's not going to want to do that." Then she added, "Can't blame him, I suppose."

Trench glanced over at her instead of responding. She took her eyes off the road for barely a split second to look at him.

"What?" she asked.

"I didn't say anything," replied Trench.

"No, but you're looking at me with your seen-it-all-before face. You know, the patronising one, when you're expecting me to catch up with your think—"

She broke off for a second before continuing.

"That's it, isn't it? You think he's only making us lead in time for the notification?" she said.

"I didn't say that," said Trench.

"But that's what you're thinking," insisted Jazz. "You still think he's got a beef with you?"

"I don't know. Forget it."

"Because I was just thinking that if he's assigned us to this case, it means he's over whatever beef he may have had with you. He's a stats junkie, Trench. You've closed more cases than anyone in the squad, so he wants you on it."

"Maybe," said Trench. "But none of that matters. We've got more important things to worry about now."

# Two

Ten minutes later, Jazz eased off the accelerator as they approached the junction for Sevenoaks. She indicated left and exited onto the Westerham Road. Traffic was lighter in this suburban, almost rural area. Jazz kept the blue lights on anyway. Some heads turned as the unmarked car sped through the streets.

After passing through the outskirts of Sevenoaks, they turned onto the Maidstone Road and were soon surrounded by fields on both sides. After a couple of miles these gave way to woods, which gradually became more dense. There were less streetlights, so it felt darker in the encroaching evening. Bleak, black sky nestled above the dark green and brown woods.

As they approached the turn off for Oldbury Hill she slowed right down, then turned left onto Styants Bottom Road. Although just off the main road, this was no more than a thin country lane, traversing the woods. If two cars were coming in opposite directions, one would have to pull aside to make way. The lane continued straight, but there was a dirt road leading off to the left. Jazz slowed down, unsure whether to go straight or take the dirt road. The dirt road seemed to turn right after a few yards, but any further view was obscured by the woods. A thickening mist settling in amongst the trees didn't help.

"There," said Trench, pointing to the dirt road.

He could just see the back of a grey Ford Mondeo. The number plate was familiar. Typical, he thought. Grubby bastard couldn't stay away from something this high profile.

Not even policing could escape the seedy allure of media and celebrity these days. Trench was convinced that an unhealthy number of recent recruits were drawn to the police largely by the prospect of becoming celebrities on one of the many reality TV cop shows. And it wasn't only new recruits. He suspected some of his own squad even lobbied to be appointed to the cases most likely to attract the cameras. Getting their mug on telly meant a lot more to them than solving cases. He'd seen some of them talk directly into the camera, trying to sound urbane as they issued some rehearsed line about delivering justice or catching bad guys. They hadn't seemed to notice the tongue-in-cheek voiceover was often designed to take the piss. The TV producers knew their audience.

Jazz turned left. As she drove slowly around the grey car she nodded at it.

"I think that's Callow's car. What're they doing here?"

"Who knows, who cares," Trench mumbled.

They followed the dirt road around the bend. The mist tumbled determinedly down from the woods onto the road. The beam from their headlights bounced back brightly off the mist, making it hard to see beyond a couple of yards. The dirt road only went about another twenty yards, before opening into a gravel car park in the woods.

There was only space for about a dozen cars. Two of those were taken up by marked police cars. The front passenger door of the one on the left was open, the interior light on in the car. Jazz pulled in behind the car on the right, leaving space for the numerous other vehicles she knew would be arriving shortly.

Trench got out and went to get a couple of torches and some latex gloves from the boot. The little remaining daylight would not last long, especially in the woods. As he moved to the back of the car, he kept his eyes on the squad car with the open door. He could see movement in the front passenger seat. Someone was hunched down low in there.

As Trench closed the boot and moved back toward the front of the car, the figure straightened up. Having heard them arrive, he stepped out of the car. They could see it was Police Constable Donny McCloskey of Kent Police. They recognised him because the Met police had regular interaction with their colleagues in surrounding police districts. This was especially true in recent years. Deep budget cuts across all regional forces had devastated resources. You took whatever help you could get.

McCloskey was a young, relatively new recruit to Kent Police. From their occasional dealings to date, Trench had not had any reason to doubt him. McCloskey started walking toward them slowly, but stopped before he reached the end of the car.

McCloskey suddenly lurched forwards, grabbing onto the car with his hand. He wretched loudly and dramatically. Trench and Jazz exchanged glances and waited a second to give him a chance to get himself together.

"Sorry…", he spluttered, straightening up, "I just…fuck's sake…"

"Nice to see you too, McCloskey," said Jazz.

McCloskey looked up at them, his reddened eyes looking puffy, with tears rolling down his cheeks, now blotchy from the exertion. He pointed off to his left, where there was a pathway leading away from the car park into the woods.

"Couple of hundred yards down there," he said, "over a small hill beside the path."

"Thanks," said Trench, as they started in that direction.

"Jazz, it's bloody horrible, I'm telling you," McCloskey stammered after them. "Seriously, what the fuck! Why would someone…"

"Okay, thanks," said Jazz. "And McCloskey, next time your tummy gets excited at a crime scene, don't spit. Swallow."

As they walked off toward the path she turned to Trench.

"Didn't have to warn *you* how horrible it is, did he? Prick."

Trench ignored the barb, used to Jazz's semi-faux indignation at being treated differently because of her gender. They each put on a pair of latex gloves and made their way slowly down the path, taking short, deliberate steps. They shone the torches in wide arcs to take in their surroundings, instinctively scanning the path itself for anything out of place. A small hill rose gently on both sides in line with the path. The further they progressed, the higher the hill rose alongside the path.

As they walked down the path, they could just make out through the dark and mist that it turned sharply to the left about ten yards ahead. The hill beside the path was now around head height, obscuring any view into the woods on either side. Only the top halves of the surrounding trees were visible. They seemed to net at the top, creating a ceiling above the woods.

As they approached the turn they could hear voices, murmuring softly. Right around the turn, three uniformed Kent Police constables were standing on the path. Two of the three were gently stamping their feet and bobbing from side to side, attempting to ward off either cold or boredom. They stopped talking as the torchlights approached. One of the faces was familiar but Trench couldn't recall her name. Each wore a solemn, weary looking face. They all exchanged nods by way of greeting.

"What've we got?" said Jazz.

"Horrible scene, just over this hill," sighed one of the constables, gesticulating with a thumb. "Pretty sure it's female. Ripped to shit. Tied up to some trees too. Brutal."

"When did you get here?" asked Trench.

"Got the call about two hours ago. We were first here, probably within twenty minutes or so. Adams and McCloskey got here shortly after that. McCloskey is back at the cars. He's uh, callin—."

"Have all of you been on the scene?"

"We had a butcher's of course," replied the constable in a prickly tone. "Had to see what we're dealing with, didn't we? But we kept our distance, don't worry."

"Who called it in?"

"Local lady, walking her dog. That's what this place is used for mostly. Dog walkers and the occasional mountain biker. She came from this direction," he said, pointing in the opposite direction from the way Trench and Jazz had just arrived. "She says that's the most popular route for dog walkers. They go from the other side of the car park and loop around on the path in the other direction. Means they're going uphill at the start, and it's easier coming back this way because it's downhill. Mostly old birds out walking their dogs, you know. Midweek it is, anyway. We got a full statement from her."

As he spoke he reached into his pocket and took out his notepad. One of the other constables shone a torch on it as he flipped through the pages.

"Did she say anything else that could be useful?" asked Trench.

The constable stopped flipping through the notepad and looked up. He considered for a second before responding.

"No, not really. She doesn't think the dog got at the body or anything. Seems it started yapping but didn't go too close. She had the usual near-heart-attack of course, and pretty much fell down the hill before running back to her car. She reckons there were no other cars here when she got here."

"How long did it take her to get home before calling it in?" asked Trench.

After a very short pause, the constable replied.

"You're right, she did go home first. Said she was too freaked to hang around here. Less than ten minutes. We met at her house and took her statement before coming here. No-one else has been here since she discovered it, far as we can tell." After a fraction of a second he added, "Except for your lot, of course," again waving his thumb in the direction of the scene. "They got here about half an hour ago."

Trench did not return the slight sideways glance from Jazz. He responded to the constable instead.

"Right. I presume you've given them the details of the woman who found the body?"

"Yeah, I did," replied the constable.

"Including her address?" asked Trench.

"Of course," said the constable.

"Right," replied Trench. "Can you guys go back and tape off the entrance to the road into the Woods, what's it called? Something Bottom Road. One of you stay there to make sure only police vehicles get through. No exceptions. And also tape off the other end of this path, where you said the lady who called it in came from. And man that end too. No-one is to get within a mile of the scene."

The constables nodded and Trench continued.

"And if anyone comes and starts asking about the police presence here, don't confirm it's a body. Just tell them we're investigating dodgy activity or something. Tell them it's suspicious material even. No harm at all if the grapevine thinks it's terrorism at this stage. Better that than a body, you know what I mean?"

The constables mumbled agreement and began moving back to their cars to get more tape. As they left, Trench and Jazz turned and began moving up the hill, silently preparing themselves for the scene they were about to face.

# Three

The hill wasn't especially steep, but it was muddy and slippery, so they needed to put their hands out to keep their balance. The darkness and mist were thicker in the woods than on the path. But from the top of the hill, they could see police tape and the light from two torches about thirty or forty yards in front of them. Although they couldn't make out the faces, they knew who was holding the torches. They appeared to be standing to the side of the taped-off area, in discussion. Or more likely, Trench thought, waiting for someone else to come along and do the actual police work.

They silently made their way toward the tape, moving with the same slow, short steps. When they reached the police tape they stopped walking and shone their beams at the ground just inside it. The mist seemed a little thinner here, possibly because of the body heat of the two men inside it. Their torches illuminated some fresh scuff marks in the mud, but they looked generic and it would be impossible to say who or what had made them.

"That's the way we came in, it's fine," called out DCI Nigel Callow, one of the two men standing within the taped-off perimeter.

Neither Trench nor Jazz gave any indication they'd heard him. Completely blanking Callow was by now just instinctive. Just as they both knew without needing to say it out loud, that they wouldn't say anything of note in front of him. They would wait until they were alone before discussing anything they'd seen. Callow didn't seem surprised at being blanked, but Trench noticed him roll his eyes in an exaggerated manner.

When they were done examining the ground inside the taped-off area, Trench raised the tape to about chest height. Jazz ducked under it and Trench followed. They resumed their torchlight examination of the ground as they inched forward. After a few yards, in the centre of the taped-off area, the torchlight illuminated the body.

It could only be partially seen from where they were standing. It was on the far side of a tree trunk about a foot wide. On closer inspection, they could see rope around the base of the tree, pulled taut, about a foot or so from the ground. There was also some grey duct tape wrapped around the tree, about a foot above the rope.

Angling their torches slightly, and moving a little to either side, it appeared as if the naked body was kneeling on the other side of, but facing away from, the tree. They very slowly made their way toward the body. They stopped a few feet from it and focused their beams.

"Hogtied," said Jazz.

She moved around to the right as Trench moved left, both keeping their beams trained on the body. They could see that the hands were pulled back behind the kneeling victim. They were tied together at the wrist by thick plastic cable ties. A rope was wrapped tightly around the hands and fed through the cable ties. The rope was tied fast to the tree, meaning the victim was held rigidly in that position.

The duct taped was wrapped multiple times around the upper half of the victim's face and head. It completely covered the eyes and most of the forehead. It too was then wrapped around the tree, having the effect of keeping the head jerked up to face forwards. The mouth hung open. A sharp chemical smell seemed to be emanating from the body.

"Shit," Jazz uttered, as she shone her torch on the victim's back.

It was covered in criss-crossed incisions. None looked especially deep. Certainly not fatal. But they would be painful as hell if administered when the victim was still alive.

"Yep, we've got a fucking psycho on our hands, Jazz," bellowed Callow. "A proper ripper. Enjoyed it too, he must've. See those knife wounds? Pre-mortem, I reckon. What'd be the point of doing that after?"

No one responded, but he went on anyway.

"I'd say the cause is strangulation too. Neck's bruised like a plum in the sun too long. Knives were just for kicks. Poor bitch."

After a few seconds of still not getting a response, he gabbed on.

"Though I'm sure Inspector fucking Clouseau there will have it wrapped up by tea-time. Won't you, Chambers? And you can have the pleasure of letting the goodly Osbourne folks know what's happened to their princess."

Callow gave an exaggerated tut, turning to his partner, DI Clive Burgess. He spoke under his breath but still loud enough for everyone to hear.

"Right up his alley that, spreading the gloom. Miserable bastard."

Burgess looked down at the ground and kicked at something with his foot.

Having scoured around the body with their torch beams, Trench and Jazz now huddled as closely to it as they could without disturbing the immediate vicinity. The whiff of chemicals definitely grew stronger the closer they got to the body. In addition to the knife wounds, there were numerous fresh-looking blisters on the back and buttocks. The knife wounds also covered the buttocks, as well as the upper arms. Trench also ran his torch down the inner arm, inspecting it closely.

With the head held in place by the duct tape, they could see a ring of dark purple bruising most of the way around the neck, about an inch in diameter. Hunching down, Trench very delicately leaned forward and used his torch to raise the victim's light brown hair so that they could see the back of the neck, also exposing the ears. He could see there was some chafing amongst the bruising on the neck.

On the back of the neck, almost indistinguishable amongst the bruising, was a small tattoo. It was a simple black cross, with a loop as the upper part. Trench had seen the symbol before. It was a common enough tattoo. He knew that it was called ankh and was an ancient Egyptian symbol meaning life, or immortality.

Not quite, he thought grimly. Poor soul.

Each ear had multiple piercings, but there were no earrings. Scratch marks around the piercings suggested any earrings may have been torn out. Still crouched down, they gently stepped around to examine the body from the front. They could make out further knife wounds at the top of the chest. These continued down onto as much of the breasts as they could see.

In turn, they each hunched lower, shining the torch fully underneath the body to get a closer inspection of the front of the body, though they couldn't see much more given the position the body was in.

After a few minutes, they were done. They exchanged nods and without a word stood up, Jazz subconsciously blowing out her cheeks as she considered the horror inflicted on this poor woman. The darkness had by now claimed all visibility beyond a few feet. The torches had provided sufficient light for their initial cursory examination of the body. But it made sense to wait for Forensics before moving around too much, to avoid potentially contaminating the scene or missing something important.

As they stood beside the body, they scanned their torch beams around the rest of the taped-off area to see if there was anything else of obvious interest. Not seeing anything, they started slowly walking out the same way they had come in.

Just as they were ducking under the tape, DI Burgess also ducked out under the tape where he'd been standing, letting out a small grunt as the movement challenged his girth. It was the reason that behind his back in the squad room, Clive Burgess became Five Burgers. He walked over to them.

"Hey guys. So, what do you reckon?" he said, in his usual half-jovial, half-apologetic manner.

He was the type of guy who needed you to nod along when he was talking, otherwise he'd lose momentum. Might run out of confidence altogether.

"Burgess," nodded Jazz. "Been here long?"

"Not really. Just a few minutes before you got here. We, uh, weren't too far away when the call came in. We figured we'd come by and, you know, see if we could help."

Both he and Callow would have known that if they hadn't got the call to lead, someone else had. But they had come anyway.

"Right," said Jazz.

There was a moment of silence, as neither Jazz nor Trench felt inclined to discuss anything material. They didn't have anything against Burgess particularly, but the presence of Callow always hung heavy in the air. Their contempt for him was strong enough to trump any inclination to be civil to Burgess.

After a few seconds, the silence risked becoming long enough to make Burgess feel awkward, though Trench only began to feel impatient.

"Great, thanks for coming. Couldn't have done it without you lads," said Trench deadpan.

Burgess looked a little unsure how to respond. Trench let it hang there for a moment, looking at Burgess. No harm in creating a vibe that wasn't worth hanging around for. Eventually, Trench continued.

"I presume you guys didn't get a chance to talk to the lady who called it in yet, did you?" Before Burgess could answer he continued, "We're going to head over there now to take care of that. Get her account directly. Can you make sure the uniforms don't let anyone other than Forensics onto the scene."

Trench turned slightly as he said it, as if to head back to the carpark. Having been listening in, Callow began moving in their direction. Right on cue.

Burgess replied hurriedly.

"Oh yeah, we were actually just about to go see her. We didn't want to leave the scene unattended, you know. So we waited for you. But we can go there right now."

Trench paused and made a brief show as if considering this.

"Well, thanks, but we're leaving now anyway so can take care of it. We'll keep you posted," he said.

"We'll go now," declared Callow loudly, as he approached. His usual grand, authoritative delivery. "We've already lined it up, so she's expecting us. Apparently she's pretty upset. Best not make it any harder on her by introducing loads of different police to her."

Callow stood just over six foot tall. Whereas he'd probably been in good shape once, despite his height it was getting more difficult to hide the burgeoning belly. The new beard was currently sufficient to hide the increasingly swollen jowl, but that wouldn't work for much longer.

As he spoke he tucked his hands into his pockets and leaned slightly backwards on his heels. He raised his eyebrows and after another second remembered to try to smile too. Half his mouth remembered, anyway.

This, Trench marvelled to himself not for the first time, was his attempt at appearing genuine. So blatantly duplicitous, yet with maximum self-belief in his ability to dupe others. The mind boggled. Trench had long ago concluded Callow had that unique form of sociopathy that only the truly solipsistic possess.

Still, at least it made him predictable.

Trench didn't believe there would be much additional value in speaking directly with the witness who'd found the body, beyond what the constable had already told them. Or at least, he'd much rather get rid of Callow from the scene, so that they could discuss openly with Forensics when they arrived.

"Right, okay. If you've got it in hand, then we'll stick around here," he replied as if persuaded. "We can compare notes later then."

Everyone gave half-hearted nods by way of lip service to something they all knew would never happen. Callow and Burgess walked off toward the path. Soon all but their torch beams was lost to the darkness of the woods.

# Four

"Nicely done," said Jazz. "Fucking head on him though. How the hell is Private Pyle so suckered in?"

She used the nickname that Chief Superintendent Lewis had already been assigned by someone in CID, despite his short tenure. It remained a constant source of both exasperation and incredulity that Lewis seemed so entirely taken in by Callow's duplicitous behaviour.

He was always first into Lewis's office in the morning, usually carrying two cups of coffee. Publicly, he was blatantly sycophantic, enthusiastically voicing agreement with Lewis. There was already far too much of that in the squad as far as Trench was concerned. Failure by consent. It seemed to be getting worse lately.

But whereas he'd agree to Lewis's face, Callow was constantly undermining him behind his back. He'd even been known to tell people from other regional forces that Lewis wasn't up to the task and was only a temporary appointment. He himself was a shoo in to take over from Lewis in the not-too-distant future.

Virtually everyone in CID had been on the receiving end of Callow's deceitful behaviour at least once. He was roundly despised as a result. Lewis's constant public showings of support for Callow therefore only served to chip away at morale across the squad.

"Managing up, I believe they call it," replied Trench.

Jazz raised an eyebrow.

"Didn't know you were aware of the concept."

"Speaking of which, he said he wants me to update him as soon as possible on what we've got here. Hard to say if he'll be relieved or not that this isn't Vanessa Osbourne."

"Yeah. The duct tape doesn't make it any easier, but this woman looks older. And a bit…." she thought for a moment, then added "…more worn out than I'd expect Osbourne to be. It's a cheap hair dye job too. And see the nails? Tatty."

Jazz was clearly better placed to distinguish a cheap manicure from that you'd expect to see on the hand of an heiress.

Trench nodded. This supported the conclusion he was forming about the victim.

"I was going to say scrawny, rather than worn out, but both probably fit," he said. "Track marks too. Old. She's a long-term user. And despite the duct tape, she's got the sunken cheeks, tight lips, patchy dental work…"

"Think she's a Tom?" said Jazz.

"Almost certainly," Trench nodded. "Hopefully she's in the system. There's a small tattoo on the back of her neck. Pretty blurry, so not recent. If we're lucky we can use that for the ID."

"Brutal though. Hard to imagine a worse fate," said Jazz sombrely. "All that cutting. Looks like bite marks on her chest too. And her left nipple is missing."

"It's not likely to be around here though," replied Trench, waving his torch around the area. "She wasn't killed here. No blood, no clothes. This is just the dump site. Or more like display site."

"Why would he do that?" said Jazz, shaking her head. "Sick bastard. She was already dead. What did he gain from doing this?"

Trench didn't respond immediately. He'd been thinking the same thing and had loosely formulated a few thoughts. But he wanted to keep an open mind. Too much speculation at this stage could introduce bias into their investigation. That ran the risk of trying to fit their theory to the facts, rather than the other way around.

He decided he would get expert opinion on what may have driven the killer to display the body in this way. And any other help such experts could provide, such as a profile of the killer. He was now SIO – Senior Investigating Officer – and so it was on him to deploy the appropriate resource to the investigation.

"Maybe it's a statement. Or maybe he couldn't help himself," he said. "Or maybe it's not about him. It could be about her, what she meant to him. Either way, let's not jump to conclusions. We'll get the Psych Unit on it and get their take."

As Trench fished his phone from his pocket to call Lewis, they became aware of increased signs of activity from the path behind the hill. They could see the beams from numerous torches bouncing off the tree-tops above the path. He put his phone away and both he and Jazz headed over there to help the Forensics Unit with their equipment.

As they got to the hill, the first of the Forensics Unit was just reaching the top of the hill from the other side. Daniel Kenner, dressed in a full-length white plastic protective suit and wearing blue plastic shoe coverings, greeted them.

"Ah, of course. Where there's a murdered body rotting in the woods, there's you two skulking about to look forward to," he said. "Every cloud and all that. Or every mist, as the case may be."

"You guys finally decided to make an appearance," replied Trench. "Happy to stand aside and let the fetishists at it."

"That's the spirit, Trench. You guys have my permission to stand quietly far away from the scene, and to speak when spoken to," Kenner continued in jocular tone, though in doing so confirmed that he was the appointed Crime Scene Manager, CSM.

"All yours," Trench nodded.

The CSM was responsible for leading the CSI team of forensic specialists at a murder scene. Technically, they were one of the resources the SIO deployed. Their role was to make sure the investigation got everything possible of evidential value from ground zero – the crime scene. They decided which particular forensic specialists should attend a scene, such as blood spatter experts, biologists, forensic archaeologists etc.

Some, such as Daniel Kenner, also liked to decide who did not attend a scene. That sometimes included the SIO, depending on the circumstances. Trench believed those circumstances tended to depend on who the SIO was. He figured he was not on Kenner's shit list on that front, based on their previous interactions.

"Why, thank you," said Kenner. "Though I'm sure you've managed to take a look already."

"We made good use of the last of the daylight when we got here," confirmed Trench. "And just as well."

"Well, we can talk more about that later," said Kenner, deflecting Trench's comment.

Trench knew this was because Kenner didn't want to hear Trench's thoughts, prior to his own examination of the scene. He preferred to draw his own conclusions, then compare notes afterwards. Trench had not intended to share his thoughts at this stage, but he did want to subtly remind Kenner that, joking aside, he as SIO was ultimately in charge.

"Need a hand with your gear?" said Trench.

Kenner indicated back down toward the path and confirmed his colleagues would appreciate the help in getting set up. Trench headed back toward the path while Jazz stayed to highlight the way over to the scene with her torch.

Soon the scene was lit up by numerous specialist lamps set up around the perimeter. It made for an obscenely bright oasis of near-daylight amongst the darkness of the woods. The mist within the perimeter had almost completely dissipated given the heat from the lamps.

Kenner was joined by other members of the Forensics Unit, and also by forensic pathologist, Doctor Paul Wharton. All wore the standard full-length white plastic suits with blue plastic shoe covers. Some of the Unit were crawling on all fours from just inside the tape, in decreasing circles toward the middle. Wharton had exchanged brief greetings and then gone straight to the body. He too would not want any meaningful discussions until he'd examined the body for himself. He was soon doing so with specialist magnifying equipment.

Trench and Jazz observed the team's analysis from outside the perimeter. They didn't need their own torches because they were close enough to the scene. But it felt like they were standing in pitch darkness, as compared to the brightly lit interior.

Jazz had been using the time to study Vanessa Osbourne's social media accounts, occasionally showing Trench a video from Instagram or Facebook. They mostly involved bland updates about mundane activities in her daily life or funny clips of animals. The attraction was lost on Trench, but Jazz reckoned she had an impressive number of subscribers.

Jazz now clicked her mouth in acknowledgement.

"Okay, it's out. First rumour that Vanessa Osbourne is missing. Just hit in the last few minutes."

"Where? Mainstream?"

"No, Celebscene-dot-com is the only place I can see it right now."

"Right," said Trench, then added, "Never heard of it."

"It's a local site, mainly London-focused gossip. Just reading it though, the tone is definitely pretty pointed. It says, and I quote, '... *VanOz is certainly known to be partial to the odd rollover. But despite this her family and friends are said to be concerned she hasn't been in touch for at least a couple of days. According to a close friend, she has not been home since attending the Leadership 2030 bash at Grosvenor Square on Tuesday evening. Get in touch girlfriend, not cool!'* Pretty accurate information, in terms of timing anyway."

Trench was about to respond but felt his own phone vibrating in his pocket. He reached into his pocket at just the same time as Doctor Wharton got to his feet, muttering "Righty-ho. All done."

As Wharton straightened up, he squinted through his glasses against the brightness of the lamps. He looked around outside the perimeter, searching for where Trench and Jazz stood. He raised his hand above his eyes to shield the light, and seeing them, ambled the short distance.

Trench got the phone out of his pocket and glanced at the screen. Caller ID told him it was Lewis. He decided he could wait. It was more important to get Wharton's thoughts following his initial examination. He would fully brief the Chief after that.

"Well?" he asked Wharton as he put the phone back in his pocket.

"Well, indeed. A pretty awful mess, I must say. By any measure. Must be over a hundred different wounds in total," he said, shaking his head. "You'll have noticed the knife wounds, and probably also the cigarette burns. Pretty much everywhere. Definitely pre-mortem. Those were deliberate. Their only purpose was to cause pain."

He paused, as if contemplating the implications for the first time, having said it out loud. At sixty-two years old, Wharton had attended a huge amount of crime scenes, entailing varying degrees of barbarism. Whereas all the experience of death and suffering may have desensitised, Trench had noticed that in his advancing years, the doctor seemed to be less able to detach himself than previously. Trench knew he had two grown up daughters of his own.

Wharton took off his glasses and subconsciously began cleaning them on the sleeve of his plastic forensic suit. Trench waited for him to start speaking again. Wharton eventually cleared his throat.

"She wasn't killed here, as you'll have noted. This," he motioned toward the scene with the hand holding his glasses, "is just for show. I'd guess the torture would've lasted many hours. Possibly a day, even two. And the body's been cleaned thoroughly. At this stage I'd guess bleach, or some kind of industrial cleaning agent. Something like that. If he's been as thorough with that as he was at torturing the poor soul, there may not be much left for us to go on."

"What about cause of death?" asked Trench. "Strangled, obviously. But I couldn't figure out if it's manual or ligature. Looks like handprints, but there's chafing too?"

"Yes, good question. I'd say both. You're right there's handprints, but definitely ligature as well. Manual wouldn't cause chafing of course. At this stage, I'd be willing to guess he was using his hands to strangle her out during whatever game he was playing. It's more…personal to be hands on during the torture itself. That's what he's getting off on, the torture. It's not unheard of for a victim to be strangled beyond the point of consciousness. But then he stops. He wakes her up and it starts all over again. Impossible to say how many times, or how long this has gone on for. But when he's done, he uses the ligature for the final kill."

Trench was about to ask before Wharton raised his hand.

"And before you ask, no, I doubt there'll be usable prints. We'll certainly check, but bodies don't normally hold fingerprints well. Skin changes a lot, moves around, gets sweaty and so on, so it's not normally receptive to fingerprint transference." He glanced over his shoulder toward the scene. "And of course, in this instance the body's been washed down, so that makes it even more unlikely."

"What about the bite marks? Those are definitely bite marks, right? And human too, judging by the shape. The killer must've made those. Surely they're too localised to be made by a fox, or whatever else is in these woods?"

"Oh, I'd bet they're human alright," replied Wharton, before sighing. "But don't get your hopes up. Breasts are not a very good surface for retaining an identifiable bite pattern. Too soft, too much flesh. They move around a lot. Suffice to say, it's not common to be able to ascribe bite marks on fleshy areas of the body to a particular person."

None of what Wharton said provided Trench with much confidence there would be workable leads from the scene. He was about to ask the doctor the only other question he could think of when Wharton again seemed to read his mind.

"Sometimes with bite marks we can test for saliva, extract some DNA that way. But," Wharton again gestured toward the body, "The chances of that seem slim, given the clean-up job here."

Trench mulled all of this for a moment, then glanced at Jazz who looked similarly at a loss. He turned back to Wharton.

"So basically Doc, in summary, we've got nothing. Fuck all to go on."

"'Fuck all' is a police technical term Trench, not a medical one," said Wharton, adding after a brief pause. "But borrowing police parlance, then yes, I concur. We've got fuck all to go on."

They all just looked around for a moment, each trying to think of a way to make the best of the situation.

"Of course I'll do the full postmortem and you'll have my conclusive findings," said Wharton. "But that strikes me as a reasonable summary, I'm afraid. I think you should brace yourselves for that."

Trench glanced at their surroundings, barely able to see beyond a few feet into the darkness of the woods. The thick mist now felt damp and cold. No point staying out here any longer. They said goodbye to Wharton, who agreed to call as soon as he had preliminary results from the postmortem. Trench went over to Kenner to confirm he was leaving, and that Kenner could move the body to the coroner's office once he had Wharton's agreement. He and Jazz then headed back toward their car. As they reached the path, Trench could feel his phone buzzing. It was Lewis again. This time he answered.

"Just finished with Wharton at the scene, Chief," he said as he answered.

"Trench, about time. I've been calling," he sounded irritated. "What's your report?"

"One female victim, tortured and strangled. Definitely looks like a sex crime. But at this—"

"Yes, so I've heard," he interrupted. "Jesus, what a mess. We've got to tell the parents as soon as possible. Are you on your way back here now?"

Before Trench could respond Lewis added, almost to himself, "I'll have to tell the Commander now."

Trench felt a sudden rush of annoyance at how Lewis was constantly interrupting him when they spoke, and didn't appear to be listening very intently. To him anyway. Clearly Callow had already briefed him.

"It's not her, Chief," he said bluntly. "At least we're pretty sure. Wharton will confirm asap, but I'm certain it's not Vanessa Osbourne."

"What? Why?"

"This victim is older. My guess is a prostitute. Wharton should know more after the postmortem. But we definitely don't want to be saying anything to the parents yet."

There was no reply for a minute as Lewis considered this.

"Right. Okay. Get Wharton to confirm that officially as soon as possible. Tonight if he can. Tell him to do it tonight."

"Will do," lied Trench.

"See you back here shortly. We can agree next steps then. I'll update the Commander in the meantime."

Trench was about to hang up when Lewis spoke again, earnest.

"Trench, one more thing. I understand you may have gotten a little too close to the body, before Forensics arrived."

Trench didn't respond. What the fuck?

Lewis didn't say anything else for a minute. Trench didn't fill the gap either. Classic fucking Callow. Whispering snipes against other detectives, while at the same time trying to ingratiate himself with command. The fact that Lewis seemed to tolerate this kind of snide behaviour struck Trench as worse than the behaviour itself.

Having gotten no response, Lewis must have decided that whatever message he was sending had been delivered. He spoke as if to move on.

"See you when you get back here then."

Trench hung up and opened the car door. Jazz had been watching him during the call and now also got into the car. As she started the engine she turned to Trench.

"All good?"

"Yeah, fine. Just that arsehole up to his old tricks. Hope it takes him hours with that witness."

Jazz shook her head in understanding.

"Hard to say who's worse. That horrible bastard, or Pyle for letting him away with it."

They didn't dwell on the subject. They'd debated this particular question countless times, but it never achieved anything other than getting themselves more worked up. They let it slide and lapsed into silence. Soon the petty politicking wasn't the only thing bothering Trench.

"Let's go straight to the Osbourne parents' house," he said. "Hopefully we can figure out if she's really missing or not. Whoever's responsible for that is out there somewhere," he said jerking his thumb back at the scene they'd just come from. "The less time we waste looking for a grown woman who's probably off sunning herself on a beach in Marbella the better."

"Sounds good," agreed Jazz. "Can you get the exact address, I know it's in Highgate somewhere."

Trench reached into his pocket to get his phone. After a couple of seconds Jazz turned and glanced at Trench, then back to the road. She spoke as innocently as she could.

"You sure you can go tonight? Don't mean to pry."

"No, it's fine. Thanks." And then because it was Jazz asking, "Texting her now."

Trench appreciated the thought in her checking and knew it was genuine concern. But he always felt instinctively defensive on the subject. He hated to be drawn on it, always wanting to shut it down, no matter who was asking.

He got his phone out and sent a brief text. Always to the point, sometimes courteous, depending on the prevailing climate. This time he typed, "*I won't make it tonight, big case just blew up. Working all night. Please tell him I'm sorry and I can't wait for the weekend.*" He paused to recall what the current climate actually was, and not remembering anything particularly hostile, added, "*Thanks.*"

He then made a call to the station and spoke with one of the young constables on the incident team, who gave him the Osbourne parents' address. While he was on the phone he heard a ping, indicating he'd received a message. He thanked the constable for the address and hung up. He relayed the address to Jazz, who nodded.

He then checked his messages. He must have misremembered. Or maybe just the wind had changed direction. The message simply read "*Same old. FUCK YOU.*"

He looked up and glanced out the window, not focusing on anything in particular as the evening's orange-grey scenes of urban London blurred past. He had long ago developed immunity to the endless onslaught of hostility. But he would never escape the momentary pangs of guilt that he may have just created an environment from which he couldn't now rescue Milo tonight. Still, he thought genuinely, there's no reason to believe it wouldn't have been like that anyway.

Which just made him feel worse that he couldn't get there this evening.

# Five

They made the decision to go to Highgate too late to take the M25. But they made good time back into central London anyway because rush hour traffic was thinning out. They were also going against the flow, heading north as most people were heading south, out of town toward home.

It was slower going once they hit the centre. The usual Thursday night throngs were bolstered by revellers enthusiastic enough to be celebrating the Christmas season already. As good an excuse as any to hit the bars and clubs. As they crossed Westminster bridge, the revellers were replaced by the seemingly permanent protestors. Those waving red, white and blue hurled abuse at those waving blue with yellow stars, who hurled it right back. Where any of them got such ferocious passion for something as nebulous as sovereignty, Trench would never understand.

Revellers reclaimed the streets as they moved away from Parliament Square. There was even the occasional Santa hat, the odd Christmas jumper. The added numbers from office Christmas parties meant a greater number of taxis were out hustling each other for fares.

Trench couldn't recall whether Uber was currently barred from London or not. The long-waged campaign from black cab drivers to fend off modernity meant Uber coverage was patchy. City Hall didn't care that industry lobbies always meant higher prices for citizens. Either way, they both remained stubbornly challenged by the ubiquitous mini-cabs, easy to spot as mostly Asian men drove semi-electric Toyotas, looking unsure as to whether they were definitely going where they were supposed to be going.

As they passed through the centre of town heading north, they were forced virtually to crawling speed. The seemingly permanent road works all over London inflicted single lane traffic around every second corner. After sitting in static traffic for what seemed like hours, Trench was getting restless.

"Jesus, it'll be Christmas before we get there. Just hit the lights," he said. "And the siren. Max volume."

"Not quite an emergency," replied Jazz.

Trench turned to argue the point but Jazz got there first.

"Anyway, where're they supposed to go?" she said, pointing at the queue of cars ahead. "Roadworks on our side of the road. The paths are rammed with people so we can't use those. It'll take the same amount of time to get through, only everyone within half a mile will have their heads ringing."

Trench let it drop. They like everyone else were at the mercy of the stop/go lollipop sign being spun randomly by a bored looking youth in a hard hat.

They eventually made it out past Euston. Gradually the London hallmark corner stores with neon off-license signs gave way to concertedly leafy streets. The houses began to be set further back from the road, behind yards-wide grass strips. Those few yards of separation added zeros to the house prices.

A larger number of cars wore protective covers, their owners deciding they were still close enough to the rabble to warrant being hidden. Before long the cars didn't need covers. There was no longer anything exceptional about Porsches or Aston Martins. Construction work in this area was confined to private houses. Though much of it still seemed to involve cranes.

As they drove past Witanhurst, Trench vaguely recalled hearing something about one of London's most secretive ever property deals. Rumour had it that an anonymous buyer had paid £50 million for a house in the area, replete with a private ballroom and more bedrooms than a decent size hotel. Having spent about a decade doing construction work on it, including a multi-storey subterranean extension, it was now said to be worth over £300 million, and London's largest house after Buckingham Palace.

No doubt the constant works didn't endear the owner to his supermodel or hedge-fund tycoon neighbours. The owner eventually turned out to be yet another shadowy Russian billionaire. With funding for British political parties rumoured to be financed largely by Russian money, doubtless he couldn't care less what the neighbours thought.

They eventually arrived at the Osbourne's address. It was on a cul-de-sac with only a handful of gated entrances. It was impossible to see any of the houses. Each lay behind walls, beyond which were huge, thick trees which obscured any view. As they peered at each of the gates, Trench pointed at the one in the far-right corner. He could just make out the house name on a plaque on the gate. No mistaking this house for a Russian anyway, he thought, it being named after the birthplace of Churchill.

Jazz pulled into the kerb near the gate. Before opening the door, Trench checked his watch and saw it was after ten pm. He considered how long they may be inside with the family. Emotions would be running high. It would be completely inappropriate, and most likely counter-productive, to try to rush the interview with the parents. There was no telling how long they might be here.

"Just a sec," he said as opened the car door. "I'm going to call the Chief, let him know we probably won't be back there tonight."

As he pulled out his phone, he decided to send a message rather than having a conversation. He didn't want to give Lewis the chance to tell them to come back to the station instead of interviewing the parents. He'd hit send and then leave the phone in the car. The joys of modern technology.

He typed a text message but then decided to send it via Whatsapp. That way he'd know when Lewis had read the message. Always handy for tactical communication. If Lewis's response showed that he was pissed off with the decision, Trench would give him enough time to cool down before contacting him again. Or just avoid him for as long as he could. As he hit send and threw the phone into the glove box, it occurred to him that this is what passed for his own attempts at managing up.

They got out of the car and walked over to the solid-panel entrance gates. Spotlights suddenly burst on, glaring on them from somewhere high up just the other side of the gates. It drowned them in light, and dazzled them so they had to shield their eyes from the glare as they looked around the gate area.

The cast iron gates were painted black and stood well over ten feet tall, prohibiting even a gaze from getting past. They eventually found an elaborate panel on the wall beside the gate. It included numerous buttons, a screen and a microphone/speaker panel. It wasn't obvious which button to press so Trench started with the one on the left. He gave it about five seconds and was getting ready to hit the next one when a voice came crisply out of the speaker.

"Yes?"

"Detectives Chambers and Zaveri, Met Police," he said curtly. "Here to speak with Mr and Mrs Osbourne." Then, just in case, he added, "It's urgent."

He assumed they were on camera somewhere, so he stepped back slightly from the gate and looked around. Sure enough, he spotted at least two discreet cameras, one above either pillar. Despite having to squint from the light, he glared straight into one, looking police-business serious. And hopefully a little impatient.

After a brief pause, the voice came back.

"Okay, someone will be down to you shortly. Thank you."

Instead of speaking, in case it was picked up by the mic, he and Jazz exchanged raised eyebrows. Someone was coming down to the gate rather than simply buzzing them in. Seems they were definitely on guard anyway. Fair enough.

Looking around, Trench briefly wondered if the personal security guards hired by families living in these neighbourhoods would be armed. It was illegal for anyone – security guards included – to carry weapons in the UK since 1997. The legislation was passed following the murder of 16 school children in a mass shooting at a primary school in Dunblane in 1996. The ban was wide enough to include pepper spray, CS gas and other similar weapons classified as firearms. So strictly speaking, they shouldn't be armed.

But as he considered it, he found it hard to believe that people around here would not seek armed protection. London was currently awash with crime. Someone was stabbed to death nearly every day, and the trend was only getting worse. The terrorist threat remained persistently at the highest level, as attacks continued to happen routinely – nearly always resulting in fatalities. And that wasn't even counting the thousands of burglaries, car jackings, muggings and acid attacks constantly taking place all over the city, the numbers for which raged on unabated.

Politicians had made savage cuts to police budgets for over a decade, signalling to criminals that anything short of attempted murder was effectively decriminalised. The politicians seemed to assume that they weren't likely to be victims themselves, and anyone paying attention had realised that they no longer even pretended to care about the city's inhabitants.

Social housing budgets had been savaged just as much as police budgets, creating pockets of deprivation that rivalled anywhere in the world. Looking at the monumental wealth on display around here, and knowing that nowhere in London is more than a few blocks from the nearest social housing project – as a matter of town planning policy – Trench felt it would be difficult to *not* feel paranoid living around here.

Yes, he concluded, the use of armed private security must be rampant. Certainly if the friendly neighbourhood Russian billionaire is stormed by an armed gang, he won't be relying on PC Plod and his very-loud whistle.

The sound of approaching footsteps beyond the gate brought him back to the present. It sounded like two sets of footsteps. Both he and Jazz stepped to the side of the gate, in case they opened outwards. Instead, a door panel within one of the gates opened inwards. Neither of them had even noticed there was a door panel. They moved toward it just as a head popped out.

"Detectives, hi," said a woman, with a friendly but professional smile.

Trench immediately took her for police. Probably the family liaison officer. He nodded at her, stepping forward so that he was standing full square to the doorway. He wanted to establish control at the outset. He was in charge and wasn't going to leave anyone in doubt. Doesn't matter if other police had been here before, or for longer, he was now in charge.

The woman seemed to read his signal and stepped fully out through the door. She then motioned with her hands for them to step through.

"Cheers," said Trench, as he and Jazz stepped through the doorway.

There was another man standing a few yards away, not quite in the shadows but far enough into the darkness that Trench couldn't clearly make out his facial features. Trench stood facing the man and waited for the woman to step back through the door. It was darker here, especially having been standing under the floodlights outside. A lamplit driveway extended around to the left and out of sight behind the trees.

As he waited for his eyes to adjust, he glanced toward the woman and again introduced himself and Jazz, using their full names and titles. He did not turn his body away from the man.

Instead he added simply, "We're leading this investigation."

"PC Helen Barker," the woman replied, "Family liaison. I've been here since last night. They're pretty stressed out, particularly Mrs Osbourne. She's in and out of hysterics. It's really intense for them, they're extremely worried."

She seemed genuinely pleased to see them. Understandable, thought Trench. Reinforcements. And someone in charge. He pointed at the man in front of him.

"Who are you?"

The man stepped forward slightly, giving Trench a better look at him. He wore black slacks, a black bomber-jacket over a black shirt, open at the collar. At around six foot five or six he was a few inches taller than Trench. Probably a few years younger too, mid to late thirties. He had close cropped black hair – stubble really – a square jaw and the lean cheeks of someone who made a habit of sweating frequently. Trench kept himself in pretty good shape, but this man looked in peak physical condition. No doubt it made selling personal security services easier, Trench figured.

"Krige," said a thick South African accent. He held out a hand, "Family security."

He didn't smile, but didn't seem unduly hostile either. Trench shook his hand. Krige had to bend down slightly as he reached down to then shake the hand of Jazz, who was a good foot or more shorter than he was. As with all men, he did smile at Jazz. Who smiled back.

Introductions over, Trench turned to Barker.

"We need to speak with the Osbournes. Who else is here? You can fill us in on our way to the house."

He turned and walked briskly up the driveway.

## Six

"Both the Osbournes, the parents, are here," said Barker.

"How are they doing?" asked Jazz.

"Not good, as you can imagine. She's been spending most of the time either in her bedroom or the lounge," replied Barker. "Mister, or rather Doctor, Osbourne asked that we leave her alone unless she comes into the Library, which is where we're set up."

"We?" said Trench.

"That's me and PC James Walker. He was here yesterday afternoon and came back this morning. They wanted to make sure someone active on the case is here and available to the family at all times. Normally it would be just me, as Family Liaison, but I think HQ wants to give them comfort that we're going all out on this. You know how it is."

Trench nodded. He well understood the importance the brass placed on appearances. Especially when the appearances were made in front of those with powerful political connections.

They followed the driveway as they spoke. As it turned to the left, the Osbourne home came into view, brightly lit against the evening darkness. It was a huge, stately looking, three-storey Victorian house. It extended back nearly half the length of a football pitch. A huge, multi-car garage sat off to the left at the end of the drive, separate from the house. Outside the garage, two Range Rovers with blacked out windows were parked in front of a silver Bentley and a sports Mercedes Coupé. A little further back and pulled into the left was a marked police Ford Focus, and in front of that a two door Renault Clio.

"Who else is here now?" Trench asked, "Do they have staff or anything? Looks like they could just about squeeze them in somewhere."

"There's definitely a chef and at least one other in the kitchen," replied Barker. "Plus there's uh, a server, I suppose you'd call her," continued Barker. "She's been bringing us food and tea the whole time. And doing the same for the Osbournes, as far as I can tell. Plus there's the Osbourne's PA." She thought further for a moment. "There's definitely been some other staff coming and going, but honestly I'm not sure what they do. Or who is here at any given time."

She sounded a little annoyed with herself, but Trench thought it was fair enough. How could anyone know how many people would be servicing a place like this? He wondered vaguely if the Osbournes themselves knew, or if they had people to manage the other people.

"Any other family? Or friends, visitors?"

"No, I don't think so. They have three children altogether. A son, a bit older than Vanessa, and another daughter, a few years younger than her. But neither are here, and I've not seen them since I got here yesterday."

Trench turned to Krige, having assumed the Range Rovers were for his people.

"How many people do you have on site?"

"Right now, four including me. I'm not always here, but special circumstances, you'll understand. We always have at least one doing the perimeter, often two. And always at least one inside. They rotate throughout the shift and are in constant communication, with each other and with HQ. And for the record, Barker is about right. Currently there are nine members of staff on site, including our four. That's in addition to Doctor and Mrs Osbourne."

Trench glanced at him and for the first time noticed he had an earpiece in one ear.

"Four guys onsite. I presume that's only when the family is at home?"

"Right. Maximum two when the Osbournes are not home."

"Do you drive them?"

"We can do, but they don't ask for it very often. Doctor Osbourne drives himself to his office most days and Mrs Osbourne usually likes to drive herself as well. Though she rarely goes very far. Mostly social events, lunches, the occasional spa day, stuff like that."

"So you're mainly home security?"

"Correct, that's what we mostly do. But if they're attending any high-profile or public event where there's likely to be a crowd, then we do the driving for that too. Or even if they just both want to drink, they can ask us to drive. That happens, sometimes."

Assuming the service didn't come cheap, and that actual security incidents were rare, it sounded like a pretty expensive glorified taxi service to Trench. But money was hardly a problem, and perhaps there was some deterrent effect from having visible security around. No doubt it gave the Osbournes some peace of mind at least. Or did until now, anyway.

"How long have the Osbournes been using your firm?" he asked Krige.

"Years. I've been with the firm for six years, and they've been an important client since well before I joined. Probably around ten years altogether."

"What about the kids? Do you cover them?"

Krige sighed very slightly as he responded. He knew where Trench was going.

"Ja, we've had a detail on each of them at times. But to be honest with you, they've each rejected it as they got older. It's quite common. As kids get older they think either we're there to spy on them, or we're their servants. We're not their servants, we make that clear to them," he snorted slightly. "Either way, it usually ends in them telling Mommy and Daddy that they don't want us around."

Then, as if realising that he may have betrayed that the customer is not actually king, he added, "Understandable though, right? What kid wants someone like us following them around and watching every move, ay?"

"So you don't cover them at all?"

"No. Not even at public events anymore. They always think they can take care of themselves. Every kid does. It's normal," he said with a shrug of his shoulders.

They were nearly at the house now. Trench abruptly stopped walking, causing the others to also stop. They each looked at him as he turned to Krige.

"Let me ask you something. You know Vanessa Osbourne, right? You've known her for a few years." Krige nodded so he went on, "What do you think is going on here? Cock on the block, is she missing voluntarily. Or not?"

Krige looked up into the night sky, squinting and screwing his face as if deeply considering the question. He took about ten seconds before taking a deep sigh and looking back at Trench.

"Honestly, I don't know. I couldn't say. I want to say yes, she's gone off voluntarily and she's having a party or meeting some dude or something. She's a head strong girl, I'll tell you that. If she wanted to disappear for a while to suit herself, then I'm pretty sure she wouldn't think twice."

Krige stopped talking, so Trench pressed him.

"Right, you want to say yes. But what are you actually saying?"

"Well, I mean head strong in a good way, you know. She's not a stuck-up bitch, like you might expect her to be." He glanced slightly apologetically from Jazz to Barker. "Good looking girl, all that money, pretty famous, I guess. But no, she's pretty decent. Funny, even. She's always polite to our people, often chatting, cracking jokes. She's easy to be around. But when she disagrees with her parents she doesn't back down. She doesn't throw tantrums, like her sister does. I've definitely seen her parents get pretty steamed with her in the past, but she usually stays calm and lets them rant at her. Don't think I've ever seen her back down though."

Trench nodded appreciatively but didn't say anything else and didn't resume walking. Instead he looked expectantly at Krige. After a few moments Krige seemed to realise that Trench still wanted a direct answer to the question.

"But would she put her parents through this?" He seemed to wince slightly, before saying, "I don't see it. She's not a bad sort. I haven't really considered it, cos it's only been, what? A day or two? But I guess if she doesn't get in touch in the next day or so, then...maybe yeah, there is something to worry about it."

"Okay, thanks for the insight. Good to get perspective," said Trench.

It would provide useful context for their conversations with the parents, and then the boyfriend. These would inevitably be loaded with emotion and bias. Those closest to a missing person were sometimes too close to provide constructive information. They would naturally be trying to sway the investigation, to persuade police to jump to conclusions, to rush to action.

This often had the effect of actually slowing progress down, or even being counter-productive, sending the police down blind alleys that lead nowhere. So Trench knew it was important to get as wide a perspective of Vanessa Osbourne as he could, as quickly as he could.

"No problem, mate, I understand," said Krige.

When they got to the house Krige opened the door with a key. He led them into a huge reception area, made almost entirely of white marble. The ceiling was three floors above them. A huge, solid marble staircase swept into the middle of the reception area. It came from both sides, meeting in the middle. It was wide enough to easily fit two London buses side by side. Two large corridors trailed off either side of the stairs.

Krige excused himself and walked over to the security office, which was the first door to the right of the stairs. Barker lead Trench and Jazz down the corridor on the left. All of the doors along the corridor were closed. The far end of the corridor seemed to open into another reception type area. Before they got there, Barker stopped outside one of the doors on the left. She knocked gently before opening it and going inside.

As they walked in, a young constable in uniform jumped up from the large table where he'd been sitting.

"PC Walker, sir," he said enthusiastically, almost before they had made it into the room. "Uh, I mean Ma'am."

Jazz had walked in first, so gave brief introductions. She explained that they would be leading the investigation from now on. Walker's superior at CID, Sergeant Chris Higgins, had been leading on the preliminary investigation to this point, including having set up an initial incident room. The instruction from Lewis earlier this evening when the body had been found had changed that.

Trench noted there was nothing on the large table in the middle of the room except Walker's pocket notebook, in front of where he'd been sitting. His phone currently sat on top of it. Although the screen was locked, the background light was on. It went off as Trench glanced at it.

Probably bored out of his tree, Trench figured. And he couldn't exactly start reading one of the many books from the shelves covering the walls in the room. Be tough selling that as vigorous investigative work if the Osbournes walked in.

"At ease, Walker," he said, shaking the young man's hand. "Barker here's given us the lie of the land. Anything else happening with you? Has Higgins been on to you with any update?"

"No, I haven't spoken with the Sarge since this afternoon, guv. We still hadn't gotten hold of the boyfriend by then. So I'm assuming still nothing on that front. In fact," he made a show of looking at this watch, "I was just about to head off, guv. I'm not expecting anything else to happen tonight. I presume I'll be back here after the morning briefing tomorrow."

"Fair enough. Here's my number," Trench handed him a card. "We may not be at the morning briefing. And we probably won't be here either. Call me if anything comes up."

"Will do, thanks, guv."

Walker gathered his phone and notebook off the table and hurried out of the room. Trench turned to Barker and asked her to let the parents know they were here to talk with them. Barker set off to find the Osbourne's Personal Assistant. After about ten minutes, the PA came to tell them Doctor Osbourne was on his way. She explained apologetically that Mrs Osbourne was in bed and was unlikely to join them.

Barker sat down at the seat Walker had been sitting in. The furthest from the door on the far side of the table, though not at the head of the table. Trench and Jazz remained standing.

Eventually the door opened and Doctor Clarence Osbourne walked into the room.

"Any news?" he asked tensely as he entered, his gaze moving from face to face.

"No, Doctor Osbourne, nothing to report I'm afraid," replied Trench.

He needed to manage the Doctor's expectations. And his emotions. He continued to speak quickly to clarify why there were there.

"I'm Detective Chief Inspector Trent Chambers, from the Metropolitan Police's Criminal Investigation Department." He motioned to Jazz, "This is Detective Inspector Jasmine Zaveri. We're leading the team investigating the whereabouts of your daughter."

Doctor Osbourne had already spoken with police officers, so Trench wanted to make it completely clear that it was worthwhile doing so again, this time with a more senior officer who was leading the case.

"Oh, right," said Doctor Osbourne, his posture visibly changing, the tension giving way to something that made his shoulders seem to slump.

He seemed taller than he did on TV. Aged mid to late fifties, he was smartly dressed in a light grey suit, with a very faint pinstripe in a slightly darker grey. Underneath was a matching waist coat over a plain white shirt, open at the collar. His wavy hair looked more grey than black, and was currently less well attended to than on his occasional TV appearances.

Trench had always thought he looked more ambassadorial than scientist whenever he'd seen him on TV. Always authoritative, but with a confident, easy manner. But tonight he just looked drained and weary. Deep, dark bags pulled at the skin around his eyes.

Trench had initially planned to let him lead on the formalities – it was his house after all – but instantly realised that he was distracted enough by the situation to not be considering formalities.

"We should sit," said Trench.

He gestured toward the seat at the head of the table. He himself stepped toward the seat nearest to that. He pulled it out and angled it so that it was away from the table, but facing the seat at the head of the table. He did not sit down, waiting for Doctor Osbourne to sit first.

Doctor Osbourne stood there for a moment, looking blankly at him. Clearly the passage of time without any news was not making this any easier on him. It was unlikely he'd taken in their names, but Trench hoped he sounded authoritative enough to give the man comfort that they were taking the case seriously.

After a few seconds Doctor Osbourne blinked a few times, then rubbed his eyes with the thumb and forefinger of his right hand.

"Yes, indeed," he said absent-mindedly as he followed Trench's gesture and moved toward the chair.

He pulled the chair out from under the table and sat down. He leant forward, resting his arms on the table. Trench sat down and took out his notebook. He kept the seat pushed out from the table. He didn't want to crowd Doctor Osbourne. Jazz sat down in the same seat on the opposite side of the table. She did lean in closer, and spoke in an empathetic tone.

"Thank you for speaking with us, Doctor Osbourne," she said. "We're hoping to ask you a few questions that may help us to locate Vanessa. We understand this is a very difficult time for you, but any information you can provide could help us to do that."

Doctor Osbourne looked at Jazz, and then nodded.

"Of course, I understand. Ask whatever you want."

"Thank you. When was the last time you or your wife heard from Vanessa?"

"She was here at Blenheim on Sunday, for dinner," he said quietly, looking from Jazz to Trench as he spoke. "That's what we do every Sunday. It's tradition now, you see. Since the children moved out, their mother insisted we always get together as a family at least once a week. Sunday seemed to suit everyone best, and over the last couple of years Sunday dinner has become our tradition. She's devastated now, her mother."

He paused and stared off into the distance for a moment. When no one else spoke, he seemed to snap back to the present. He composed himself and carried on.

"She left here on Sunday, early evening. I was in my office but she came down to say goodbye. That's the last time I saw her. She was here on Tuesday afternoon though, to see her mother. I was at my office in town. They had lunch. Then she left to get ready for the gala dinner. We haven't heard from her since."

"The Leadership 2030 dinner?"

"Yes, that's the one."

"Can you tell us about that?" asked Jazz.

"Oh, it's all hogwash if you ask me," he tutted. "An excuse really, for those that feel important to hob nob with each other. Or rather, those that feel they *will* be important. The next generation, you see. Those that will be leaders in 2030 and so on. They get to mix with the current Tory leadership. Gives them a taste for power, supposedly."

"Is that Vanessa's crowd then?" asked Trench.

"No, not really."

"But she attended the dinner anyway?" Trench prodded.

Doctor Osbourne paused for a moment and seemed to be reconsidering.

"Actually yes, you're right. I suppose it is her crowd. She was President of the Oxford University Conservative Association in her final year at university. Though to be perfectly honest, I doubt she's ever had any intention of going into politics. She's far too clever for that."

"So it was purely a social occasion for her?" asked Trench.

Doctor Osbourne looked at him for a second and then sighed ruefully.

"Yes, probably. To be honest, Detective, I sometimes believe she does these things, these high-flyer events and what not, simply because she can. As in, she's able to. How do I put this? You see, things other kids have to work hard at tend to come easy to Vanessa. Even her own siblings. Academically she's always been a high achiever. Without much effort. She gets that from her mother. She has breezed through every exam she's ever taken, and I've never seen her study more than a few hours. Her siblings are cursed with my own academic aptitude. I've had to work bloody hard over the years," he said, conviction growing in his voice. "From school to university and ever since, it's always been about putting in as many hours as possible in order to achieve. And I have never shied away from hard work. Indeed I enjoy it, it makes the rewards that much sweeter, I dare say.

"But everything came easy to Vanessa. Not just academically. She's been very popular wherever she's been. Everyone warms to her, male and female alike. It's been that way since she was a baby. She has a gift, for how she interacts with people. She's very confident, precocious even. She's the life and soul of any room, or gathering or what have you. And dare I say, she's an attractive girl – or woman, now."

He had seemed to gain momentum, perhaps forgetting for a moment the context in which he was talking about his daughter. But as he paused again, a harrowing look flickered across his face. Trench and Jazz had been giving slight nods of understanding as he was speaking. Neither now tried to fill the silence. Better to let him talk freely if he was inclined to do so. More information was definitely better than less at this stage of the investigation.

Soon Doctor Osbourne gave a short shake of his head and continued.

"So, where were we? Yes, the gala dinner. As I say, she was President at university and the natural follow on to that is to get involved with the party-proper, once you graduate. To be perfectly honest, I didn't think she'd have much stock with them. Full of Eton and Oxbridge hangers on, it seemed to me. Frankly speaking, I thought she'd have far too much about her to be spending much time with those one-dimensional types. She's said as much herself on the rare occasions she speaks openly to me and her mother these days. I don't know if you have children, but they stop telling you much as they get older. Stop asking for advice, thinking they know it all. But every now and again she opens up a little.

"We want to know what she's going to do with herself. She has a law degree – first class honours! But seems she doesn't want a legal career. And she won't let me use my contacts to get her set up. She wants to make her own way, she keeps saying. I don't doubt she could, but she's stopped telling us anything about her plans…."

He trailed off again and was quiet for a moment. Trench was keen to get him back to the last couple of days, but all of this was useful context. Plus, if Doctor Osbourne was talking freely, that was better than having him overcome with emotion. That usually drastically limited the ability to get useful information.

He glanced over at Jazz, who also remained silent. She caught his eye, and gave a very slight nod, indicating she knew she had to get him back on track. After another few seconds, she gently cleared her throat.

"Doctor Osbourne, you mentioned Vanessa left here on Tuesday afternoon to go to the gala dinner…."

"Sorry, I'm rambling, aren't I? Yes, that's right. Her mother seems to think she was looking forward to it. She was trying on a few dresses and what not. She left here late afternoon to get ready for the dinner. Neither of us have heard from her since."

"Is it out of character for her to be incommunicado for a few days?" Trench asked.

Doctor Osbourne looked at Trench with what seemed like a bit more resolve than previously.

"I know what you're saying, Detective. And I appreciate you must ask your questions. The honest answer is no, not entirely. She has her own life, of course. She can do as she pleases. It's not a regular occurrence that she wouldn't be in contact for a day or two, particularly with her mother. But it hasn't happened often, and on this occasion her mother is worried."

"More so than on previous occasions?" asked Jazz.

"Yes. She'd promised to join her mother and sister for their planned spa day yesterday. It's been in the diary for months. When she didn't show yesterday and didn't return their calls, they went around to her home. She wasn't there, and her mother says her bed hadn't been slept in. They were concerned enough to call police right away. And obviously we still haven't heard anything from her."

"Is there anyone Vanessa may have willingly gone away with?"

"I don't know," he said, shaking his head. "She's had a boyfriend, Mathew Sheldon, though I'm not sure how serious it is. Her mother called him yesterday. He denied being with her. He said he hasn't seen her since the weekend."

"Right. Can you tell us a bit about him?"

"Mathew? Oh, he's…okay. He's been hanging around since University, but we've always felt it wasn't that serious. He hasn't been around much recently anyway. And uh, I never really got to know him much, after the first few times I met him."

"Why is that?"

"To be blunt with you detectives, we just don't think he's good enough for her. Nowhere near, in fact. He's not going to amount to much. Average education, bland job, few prospects. I don't wish to sound conceited, but we'd have rather higher hopes for Vanessa. But she has seemed smitten. I suspect she may have just stopped mentioning him to us. We probably haven't hidden our feelings very well. Her mother can be a bit of a snob."

"When was the last tim—"

"He just seemed a bit, what's the word, clingy. Or possessive," Doctor Osbourne interrupted, perking up slightly as if the thought was just occurring to him. "I think he was the jealous type. He let Vanessa know on more than one occasion that he wasn't happy with her being so publicly affectionate to others."

"Okay, thanks. That's very useful. We—"

"Have your people spoken to him yet?" he asked, almost hopefully.

"He's certainly on our radar," responded Trench, not wanting to get drawn into answering any questions. To further deflect he added, "Is there anyone else? Anyone she may have mentioned recently, or was expecting to meet at the dinner event?"

"I don't…I'm not sure," pondered Doctor Osbourne.

He leaned in further and rested his head on the points of his fingers, his hands clasped together as if in prayer. After a brief moment he shook his head. He remained in that position and stared blankly ahead. Trench decided to change tack. They would speak with the boyfriend, but for now they had little else to go on.

"How is your business doing, Doctor Osbourne. Futurnautics, isn't it?"

Doctor Osbourne pulled himself back to the present and sat back in his chair. He sat more upright and rubbed his face in his hands, a futile effort to wipe away the exhaustion and fear that remained etched into his face.

"What's that?" he said distractedly, before the question seemed to land. "Oh, fine. Good. The business is strong, sustainable growth each year for the past decade. Shareholder value is the highest it's ever been, and we have some deals in the pipeline which mean we should be in a very healthy position going forward."

"What exactly does your company do?"

"Aeronautics, mostly. And electronics."

He looked at Trench as if to check whether this answer was sufficient. Trench understood he'd be cagey on the subject, so sought to reassure him.

"We appreciate the sensitivities with your business Doctor Osbourne. I don't pretend to understand exactly what you do, but we need to explore whether it may have any link to Vanessa's disappearance."

"Yes, I understand. We make electronic components and operating systems for commercial and also military clients. Both aeronautic and ballistic components. My organisation comprises mainly scientists and engineers. Put simply Detective, we contribute to the manufacture of military aircraft and weaponry."

This description added little to what Trench already knew about Futurnautics. Although the armaments industry was naturally subject to a certain level of secrecy given the nature of work, the company itself was well known. It was lauded by British media and politics alike, often held up as a shining example of British ingenuity at its finest. Doctor Osbourne himself was often cited as one of Britain's greatest innovators, with the well-honed commercial acumen to go with it. In just a couple of decades since he had founded it, Osbourne had turned it into one of the leading players in the global defence industry. It was rumoured to be supplying technology to many of the world's leading arms manufacturers.

As Trench was considering his next question, aware that Doctor Osbourne would most probably be guarded about providing too much detail about its operations, Doctor Osbourne continued talking.

"And we're bloody good at what we do, even if I say so myself," he said in a more lively tone, seeming to find it easier to talk about something less painful. "We can compete with any company globally for the biggest contracts in the sector. With a damn sight less resources than most of our competitors. Most of the American and European companies we compete against have many times the number of people we have. And research budgets that dwarf ours. But we are just as good as any of them. Better, in fact. That's my honest opinion. And I've seen what they do, how they do it, and the Americans? Huh," he almost snorted, "They get endless grants and tax breaks, and all manner of favourable treatment when it comes to tenders from the US government. But still we can beat them."

Doctor Osbourne had perked up as he spoke, displaying considerable passion, even pride. The line of questioning was clearly providing him with distraction from the fraught topic of his missing daughter. Trench was keen to use this to his advantage, to continue getting as much information from him as he could before he inevitably became overwhelmed, as he knew he surely would.

"I see, thank you. Is Vanessa involved with the business?" he asked.

"No, not really. I've asked her many times to join. And not for nepotistic reasons either. Or not entirely, anyway. I genuinely believe she would be of great value to our business. As I mentioned, she's extremely smart. She spent a couple of summers during university working with the company. But she has declined to join permanently. I understand, of course. She's headstrong. She'd much rather make her own way in the world."

"And what does she do, career-wise?"

"She hasn't settled on that yet, is how she puts it. She's not that long out of university, so it's understandable I suppose. She's been talking about getting herself an agent. Seems being in the public eye can be a career in itself these days. I know she's been paid a couple of times just to appear at certain events." He waved a hand dismissively in the air. "It's not something I understand, frankly, but I offered to have some of my people review a contract she'd been offered."

Doctor Osbourne turned in his chair and looked expectantly at Trench. He had spoken a little faster as he answered the last question. He began shifting in his seat. Trench took it as a sign he was beginning to run out of patience.

He was used to it during missing persons cases. There was usually some initial grace time, during which the family would answer questions. But soon they would become overwhelmed with emotion or run out of patience with the process and start demanding answers of their own. Trench believed they had probably now reached that point with Osbourne, who at that moment straightened up in his chair and frowned.

"So what's the process here, Detective? What are you doing to find out what's happened to my daughter?"

"Right now we're gathering as much information as we can, particularly around her last known movements. We're trying to pinpoint exactly when and where she was last seen. We have a team back at headquarters reviewing CCTV as we speak – the city is covered by thousands of cameras, as you'll know. We're also monitoring her social media activity, and will soon have her bank account and mobile phone records. We'll determine a timeline as to when exactly she went missing, and narrow down approximately from where. That will put us in a strong position to work out what the potential scenarios are."

Doctor Osbourne nodded.

"Of course we'll speak to as many people as we need to in gathering information," Trench added.

He didn't bother bullshitting Doctor Osbourne with empty promises about doing whatever it takes to find her. He doubted someone of Osbourne's disposition had much time for bullshitters, and he didn't want to patronise him.

With that, Doctor Osbourn suddenly stood up.

"I must get back to my office. The only thing I know how to do at times like this is to work. We have some important deals coming up, and to be frank, I need the distraction. It helps. I hope you understand that. Vanessa's mother may not, but we all have our own ways of coping. Hers is to seek refuge in a bottle, and that's fine, I understand that. But that doesn't work for me. I need to focus on my work."

Trench stood too and confirmed he did indeed understand. Perhaps more than Doctor Osbourne would ever know, though he didn't say that. Instead he thanked him, and explained they would keep him posted. He also explained they would want to speak with Mrs Osbourne at some point. Doctor Osbourne distractedly agreed and offered any support and help his considerable resources could bring to bear.

As they all stood, Doctor Osbourne then floated the idea of offering a reward, asking how much they felt was appropriate to incentivise people to come forward. When he opened the bidding by suggesting a million pounds, Trench was quick to suggest they hold off on that approach for now. He didn't want every crackpot and self-appointed armchair warrior calling the station every time a young woman with brown hair was spotted on the streets of London. He delicately explained that a reward at this stage would turn the whole thing into a media circus. It would certainly hinder the investigation, as already limited police resource would inevitably be wasted chasing wild geese and red herrings.

Doctor Osbourne initially pushed back on this. He seemed at first sceptical and then frustrated that his considerable wealth could not be readily deployed to fix the problem. Trench realised it was probably rare for him to encounter a problem that his wealth couldn't overcome. Eventually Doctor Osbourne seemed to accept this. But he didn't try to hide his vexation.

"Well if you say so, Detective," he said, with more than a hint of scepticism in his voice. Then added more forcefully, "But I demand that you keep me fully informed at all times. I mean it. I want regular updates on whatever you've got, and what you're planning. I'll make whatever resources you need available to help you. I can – and will – make calls further up the line if needs be, but I insist that you report directly to me, regularly. I don't want to be kept in the dark on this. I want to know what's going on with the investigation at all times."

"I understand that, Doctor Osbourne, and will of course keep you updated. What's the best number to get you on? I will call you directly myself with any update. And here's my mobile number as well. Call me whenever you want," said Trench as he handed him a card.

Doctor Osbourne took it and studied it for a moment, before putting it into his pocket. He gave them his mobile number, which Trench wrote down in his notebook. Doctor Osbourne then nodded curtly and left the room.

Barker then dropped the detectives back to their car, because her Renault Clio was parked at the house rather than out on the road. As they got out of the car, Trench gave her his card and asked her to call him if anything of note happened.

As they approached their own car, Jazz tossed Trench the keys. Trench unlocked it and Jazz got into the passenger seat. She immediately reached down to adjust the seat to bring it forward and higher. Trench had to reach in to adjust the driver seat before he was able to get into the car, because it was too close to the steering wheel. Only when they had closed their doors did Jazz speak.

"So what did you make of the good doctor? Would've been better to get 'the mother' as well," she said, rolling her eyes at how Doctor Osbourne had continually referred to his wife.

"He's not exactly oozing emotion," said Trench, starting the car. "Clearly the stiff upper lip type. But he seems to genuinely believe she's not just gone off on some jolly somewhere. There's one avenue we need to check out. If she's not there, then we're going to have to give this priority over the body at Oldbury Woods. The brass will make sure of that."

"The boyfriend," said Jazz.

Trench nodded.

"It'd hardly be the first time a kid's taken off with someone their parents didn't like," said Trench.

"I know all about how that goes," sighed Jazz. "She's, what? Twenty-two? It's right about now she'll be deciding she no longer wants to pretend she's Daddy's little princess. She's probably been dropping subtle and not-so-subtle hints for years. Which have probably been ignored. Sneaking off and staying with a boy Daddy doesn't approve of is one of the more considerate ways of making the point. A much less rude awakening."

Trench frowned.

"Less than what?"

"Than letting him catch her in the act," said Jazz matter-of-factly.

"I see. Well let's hope she'd drop some pretty hefty hints before choosing that option."

"That's my point," said Jazz. "Odds are good that she's at her boyfriend's place right now."

Trench glanced at the car's clock.

"It's too late to go there now though," he said. "Let's get there for six-thirty tomorrow morning. Sounds like he won't have left for work, based on what Osbourne says about his job."

Jazz nodded.

"Let's hope she's there and not in Marbella," she said, before adding after thinking for a moment, "Assuming she's not actually missing, that is. The security bloke seemed to think there might be something to it too."

"Well if she is, Osbourne just offered to put all his resources at our disposal to help us find her," said Trench. "Fine by me, let's keep that in mind."

He was silent for a moment before speaking again.

"Although he got a bit feisty at the end," said Trench. "A million pounds?! Jesus, can you imagine the shitshow. It'd turn the whole thing into a fucking reality TV show."

"Well that's going to happen anyway, soon as it's out."

That reminded Jazz and she took out her phone. Before she'd even unlocked the screen she spoke.

"Shit. Looks like mainstream has it."

The screen was filled with notifications from various news sites that she had set up to alert her whenever Vanessa Osbourne was mentioned. She unlocked the phone and flicked through various different news sites.

"They've pretty much all got it now. Some are even quoting an unnamed source, saying the parents are devastated, really worried et cetera. Guess there's downsides to having a house full of paid employees."

Trench remembered his own phone.

"Can you get my phone from the glove box. See if Pyle messaged me back. Whatsapp."

Jazz reached in and got his phone. She unlocked it using her own thumb print and opened Whatsapp.

"Uhm," she said in pleasant surprise. "He checked it a few minutes after you sent it, but didn't respond."

"Fine. Let's take that as a good sign. We can give him a full debrief in the morning. But we'll speak with Sheldon first thing, that's the priority."

Traffic was much lighter at this time of night. The residential streets around Highgate were deserted. The freezing wind tore at trees, their shadows jerking violently. There seemed to be more foxes than people, skulking out from behind bins or scurrying across the road in the headlights.

The greenery retreated as they neared Camden, the urban jungle reasserting itself. It wasn't foxes skulking here. Central London was the domain of legions of the homeless and the hapless. They huddled in doorways, having succumbed to the dubious charms of their preferred liquid or pharmaceutical seductress. As common a feature of the city as the buildings themselves, they were invisible to any revellers still out on the streets, who simply stepped over them.

They drove in silence for a while, Trench allowing himself to be absorbed by their surroundings. He enjoyed driving in London at night. Enjoyed the distraction, losing himself in it. It was better than any movie. Any show or play. It was life. Raw, urban and real. He loved this city, and most of all at night.

During the darkest days of the broken chapters of his own life, it had provided solace when nothing else could. He hadn't succumbed to his own demons. Not liquid, not pharmaceutical. Instead he'd found whatever it was he needed on the urban streets of night-time London, as he drove around for endless hours, just watching. Quietly feeling alive and a part of something. It seemed to imbibe in him a sense of belonging. Of purpose. Maybe it even saved him.

He wondered what the city knew of Vanessa Osbourne. Was she out there somewhere right now, living large and enjoying some private freedom? Or was she yet another tragic lost soul consumed by its demons?

# Seven

Trench turned onto Agar street and pulled the car up to the gate of Charing Cross Police Station. Despite being well past midnight, all the dedicated spaces on the street marked 'Police Vehicles Only' were already occupied, as they always were. There was nowhere near enough of these spaces, so the surrounding streets were always full of police vehicles. The gates opened and he drove under the archway in the building, into the small carpark.

Jazz didn't need to go inside because she was going straight across to Charing Cross tube station, just a few yards across the road. Trench locked the car as they got out.

"See you back here at six?" he said.

"Yep. We can sleep when we retire, ay."

They said good night and Trench went inside to get changed. The Desk Sergeant's head was buried in a log so they just exchanged cursory hellos. He was tempted to not stop by his own desk, but then figured it would be better to check for any messages now rather than in the morning.

Then he remembered he'd be in and gone by the time Lewis got in tomorrow morning. So he decided to write up a quick report of the day's activities and email that to him now. That way his feigned look of innocence tomorrow if Lewis decided to have a go at him for not coming back to the station after being at the scene in Oldbury Woods would be slightly less contrived.

Managing up.

He made his way upstairs to the CID squad room. It was a large open plan office with rows of desks through the middle of the room. They were in banks of five on each side, with a walkway down the middle. Senior commander offices or meeting rooms lined either wall. Some of the meeting rooms were occasionally designated as 'incident rooms', depending on the cases the squad had at any given time.

Trench's desk was in the first row on the left, in the aisle by the central walkway. All the desks near his were empty, though some other detectives were scattered in seats around the room. He smelled fresh coffee and was tempted. But he decided against, instead picking up the water bottle he kept on his desk. The department's small kitchenette was to the right of the entrance doors. He walked over and filled the bottle. He went back to his desk before anyone else came to use the kitchenette.

He didn't want to end up in a conversation with one of those people who thought being in the office late meant you wanted to socialise.

He logged onto his laptop and began typing up his report. He realised as he was writing that it would also be a useful reminder to himself. It therefore took slightly longer than he'd intended, despite being mostly bullet points. He described the scene where they had found the body and a brief summary of their initial examination, including Doctor Wharton's early opinions.

He then summarised their conversation with Doctor Osbourne, and also with Krige of Imperium Security, the private security firm used by the Osbournes. He started this section with "*Given the urgency associated with a missing person's investigation…*" to explain their decision to speak with the parents rather than go back to the station. But it bothered him that he felt obliged to offer an excuse for what he judged to be the right course of action. It felt like he was pandering to Lewis's pettiness, so he deleted it.

The final section was on their planned next steps. The primary focus was on retracing her last known movements, which he intended to pick up from Higgins, the sergeant previously leading the investigation. He toyed with the idea of leaving out their intention to go see Sheldon in the morning. But he couldn't think of an excusable reason for leaving it out. The real reason was that his instincts were always to be noncommittal about his future intentions, in case someone told him not to. Forgiveness always trumped permission. He initially left it out, but then included it, figuring the early start tomorrow meant they would be with Sheldon before anyone could tell them otherwise.

He then sent the mail to Lewis and cc'd Jazz. Just before he sent it, he also included his own email address in the cc box. When he saw other people do that it pissed him off, because he couldn't figure out why they did it. But it always seemed to be people who took themselves too seriously. Maybe Lewis would interpret it that way. Or maybe it would just piss him off.

Once done, he shut down his laptop, drained the rest of the water then left the squad room. He went downstairs to his locker and changed into his leather jacket and Kevlar jeans. The November night was cold enough to require the full insulation from both, despite the ride home taking less than fifteen minutes.

He hung up the suit he'd been wearing in the closet, alongside a few other suits he kept at the station. They were mostly all the same cheap suit, just in different colours, all of them dark. No point in spending time or money buying suits that invariably ended up in the bin, having been ripped in a tussle or covered in someone's blood. He couldn't remember the last time a suit had made it to old age. He was wary of detectives who turned up in expensive clothes. They were either stupid or lazy.

As he passed the front desk, the sergeant looked even more consumed than before. He walked past silently and only after he'd opened the back door did he shout a good night. He walked straight over to his Yamaha MT09, put the key in ignition and sat on the bike.

Not for the first time he was grateful for the spot inside the station carpark. It meant he didn't have to carry the huge, 3-stone, chain lock that he'd need if parking on the streets of London. Motorbike theft had long ago blazed the trail of activities decriminalised by budget cuts. YouTube was full of clips proving the thieves no longer even bothered trying to conceal what they were up to, often using angle grinders in broad daylight in the heart of the capital to cut security chains on motorbikes.

As he left the station he noticed more tents than usual on the street. Those homeless looking to avoid their more lively neighbours had recently begun setting up camp right there, their wafer-thin tents almost touching the police station. Trench found himself once again wondering whether these desperate souls found the added security they sought. They were barely a stone's throw from those lively neighbours.

There was an underground walkway of pedestrian tunnels right underneath where they were, linking Trafalgar square with Charing Cross tube station and the Strand. This large, covered space provided some respite from the harsh elements above ground. But the various nooks and crannies of darkness also provided cover to those wanting to shoot up or hit the pipe. It could be hostile territory. And inevitably it doubled as a toilet for the area's destitutes. So they pitched their tents beside the police station like barnacles.

Despite spasmodic campaigns by police chiefs to keep the area relatively clean, commuters and tourists seeking London's most splendid sights were just as likely to step in urchin's piss and shit or a dirty needle. Try as they may, they could never shoo the vagrants on. Where could they go?

Trench turned onto Victoria Embankment and opened the throttle. He was soon passing New Scotland Yard. It reminded him of Lewis continually saying he needed to update the Commander. Thinking about it, Trench wasn't surprised Commander of Front-Line Policing, Leroy Campbell, was demanding regular updates.

Trench had worked for Campbell before his promotion to the role of Commander – a move which created the vacancy in CID now filled by Lewis. He figured that if Vanessa Osbourne remained missing much longer, Campbell was certain to involve himself in the investigation.

Barbadian-born Campbell came up through the ranks in Brixton around the time the 1989 McPherson Report found that the Met suffered from 'institutional racism.' That is, a time when a black officer wasn't sure if he had to watch his back more on the streets or in the station. His recent promotion proved he wasn't just a survivor, but also a canny political operator. Trench figured the potential lights from the coverage of this case would be too bright for him to ignore.

As Trench turned onto the long, straight stretch of New Camberwell Road, his mind turned to the body in Oldbury Woods. Vanessa Osbourne would get priority. Trench knew that a missing, and therefore potentially alive, person should get the full focus of police resources. Just as he knew Met command would make sure the well-connected Doctor Osbourne was in no doubt about this.

But he could not shake images of the body from his mind. It was a savage killing. He had not often encountered such a degree of sadistic torture. The horrors humans could visit upon each other seemed to know no bounds. He had experienced that first-hand on more occasions than he cared to remember.

But keeping her alive, possibly for days, while repeatedly strangling, cutting, burning and almost certainly raping her was a level of psychotic depravity he had rarely seen before. And why display her like that? It must have taken considerable time and effort. Why take the risk? The only answer he could come up with was that the killer gained some kind of satisfaction from doing so. Was he flaunting his handiwork? Trying to terrorise whoever found it? Or taunting the police?

Each answer was just as disturbing as the next. Whatever the reason, and whatever motivated him to kill in the first place, Trench was ominously certain of one thing. This was not a one-off crime. Either they would catch him, or they would encounter his macabre handiwork again.

# Eight

By five thirty the next morning Trench was back on his bike heading back to Charing Cross Police Station. Across Westminster Bridge, both sides of the euro-wars had retreated at some point during the night. The temporary truce afforded Parliament Square a dusk tranquillity almost reminiscent of its long-gone glory days. Big Ben leered on from within its scaffolding cage, looking unsure whether it was safe to come out and reclaim pride of place, but thinking better of it. The marauding protesters would be back in their droves in a few short hours to sully the aura.

Trench parked his bike and went into the station. He exchanged a few words with the Desk Sergeant, the customary recap of lowlights from the night's misadventures in the metropolis. Nothing beyond the perennial drunken scuffles and the occasional mugging. Still, all the station's cells were full, as they were almost every night. Though less than usual had been soiled by their current inhabitants, so not all bad according to the Desk Sergeant.

In the locker room Trench grabbed one of his suits from the closet. He changed quickly, without checking whether it was the same suit as yesterday. When he went upstairs, Jazz was already at her desk next to his.

"Got Sheldon's address?" he asked, without sitting down.

"Yep, he owns an apartment in Shoreditch. Columbia Road."

"Columbia Road?"

Trench knew it well. But he was surprised, based on what Doctor Osbourne had told them last night.

"Not the kind of place you'd get with a dead-end job," he said.

"You used to live around there, right?"

"Pretty close, yeah. Did you do any background on him yet?"

"I've just run him through the databases," said Jazz. "He's clean. His Driver's License is clean too, not so much as a speeding fine."

"Okay, well let's go and see what he has to say for himself."

Jazz stood up and picked her jacket off the back of the chair.

"How do you want to play it with him?" she said as they left the squad room.

"First, we need to find out if he's involved. If he is, it's one of two things. Either he's helped her to disappear for whatever reason, or he's caused her to disappear. That probably means he's killed her. Let's find out which one it is."

"Just ask him, right?" said Jazz.

They had interviewed many suspects together, and occasionally would prepare a particular tactic for specific situations or suspects. Usually though, they stuck to the simple process of asking direct questions and watching for any tells in the reaction. They had spent enough time interviewing the dregs of society to have honed their approach. They would each ask questions alternately throughout, on different subjects, probing for any inconsistencies or signs of deception. It was effective because most people were bad liars.

"Ask him and read him. If he's involved, it's a bloody big lie he's chewing on," said Trench. "Any developments on the web?"

"No, not really. It's the same story as last night on most sites. Still pretty low on the 'most read' headlines, but moving up."

"Okay, we've probably got at most another twenty-four hours before they're all over it."

"It could help, though," said Jazz. "The publicity could bring out witnesses, make it easier to put together her last movements."

"Yeah, but it'll also mean the brass are all over it. All over us. Too many people making decisions, and not always for the right reasons. And anyway, Higgins should've put together a pretty firm picture of her last movements by now."

He gave Jazz a sceptical look, which she returned. They both knew it was by no means certain Higgins would have done so. A combination of uncertainty around whether she was genuinely missing and Higgins' reputation for being more of an armchair detective meant it was at best fifty-fifty. Trench knew that was something he was going to have to tackle later in the day.

They left the station and headed out toward Sheldon's place with Trench behind the wheel. Jazz switched on the radio, flicking between the news programmes to see if the story was being discussed. It wasn't, with the eternal debates about EU trade deals continuing to dominate. Politicians on all sides continued their infantile name calling and self-indulged ranting that went nowhere. For reasons lost on

Trench this was all reported as news by the various broadcasters, each slipping further toward betraying their own bias. The only other main story providing any respite from the domestic squabbles was about a new, deadly strain of flu affecting some provincial city in China.

Embankment was already quite busy but most traffic was going in the opposite direction. Though it was just after six am, the City, London's financial district, was already teeming with commuters. Absenteeism was not the City's main problem. Here it was presenteeism that eroded productivity.

Bleary-eyed staff tried to outdo each other by turning up earlier and leaving later than their arch competitor – in the very next cubicle. Scrambling to stay one step ahead of the redundancy sickle, half the workforce was too stressed or sleep deprived to function properly. Like any jungle, to stay out of death's clutches you didn't have to outrun the lion, just your neighbour. So still they'd turn up for countless hours on end, six or seven days a week.

Jazz leaned over and turned the radio volume down.

"I also looked into Futurnautics this morning," she said.

"Good, I was going to do it last night but never got to it," said Trench. "Anything?"

"Can't say I understand any more about what they do," admitted Jazz. "But their client list is pretty impressive. Bit of a who's who of countries with dodgy military records. Saudi Arabia, Israel, Turkey, America, bunch of the Caucuses, a few African countries. I'd say their client dinners are pretty tetchy."

"And Blighty of course?" asked Trench

"And Blighty," confirmed Jazz. "Looks like we're their biggest client. There's even some client testimonials from a couple of ministers. If I didn't know better, I'd say the company had written them themselves…"

"They're a great British success story, aren't they," said Trench. "The government are probably their most important sales people."

"Looks that way," nodded Jazz. "There's a gallery page on their website. Mostly Osbourne and other company execs pictured with military guys or government people from all over. Plenty from our own government. He's definitely well connected."

"Right," said Trench.

He didn't want to think about the likely implications for their investigation.

"I checked recent news articles too," Jazz went on. "It was kind of hard to tell the difference between them and the company's website. All praise and glowing stories about how successful they are, how many jobs they've created. I'd heard of Osbourne before obviously, but don't think I'd realised just how big the company is."

"Me too," said Trench. "Let's just hope that doesn't mean all his minister mates want to stick their oar in."

It only took a few minutes to pass through the City and into the assertive bohemia of Shoreditch. Too rough for the City's workforce just a couple of decades ago, it had gentrified so emphatically in recent years its hipster residents were now fighting a losing battle to claim it still retained some of its harder, cooler edge.

With gentrification had come exponential property price rises. Homes here had increased by four or five times in the years since the financial meltdown of the late noughties. Trench knew first-hand all about the property price boom in this area. As a junior officer he had lived in nearby Bethnal Green. He had always wanted to buy a home in the area but there was no chance of that on a copper's salary.

They turned onto Columbia Road and pulled up outside Sheldon's address. The ground floor on this stretch of road was mainly shops, but there were doors beside many of the shop fronts. Judging by the buzzers, these were for residences in the three or four storeys above the shops. They got out and found the number they were looking for. There were only two buzzers on the door, despite the building being four or five storeys high. Neither buzzer had a name, so they couldn't tell which one was Sheldon's.

Trench was about to press one of them when the door opened inwards. Trench's hand was still hovering in mid-air in front of the buzzer when the young man coming out of the door looked up. He gave a start and instinctively jolted backwards, bringing up his own hands in defence.

"Mathew Sheldon?" asked Trench.

"Who are you?" he responded, straightening up.

He still looked a little wary, but more confused now than surprised. He was dressed in cycling gear and carried a helmet in one hand. Trench put him at early to mid-twenties.

"Met Police. Can we have a word?"

Sheldon didn't reply for a moment. He looked from Trench to Jazz, his face beginning to soften. Trench thought he looked tired, or resigned.

"It's about Vanessa, isn't it? I've been waiting for you. She's on the news now."

Sheldon glanced briefly at a large wrist-watch, then said "Come in."

He ushered them inside, to what was just a stairwell. He started up the stairs, saying, "I'm on the third floor."

They stepped past an impressive looking bicycle with *SPECIALISED* written in large font across the frame and followed Sheldon up the stairs. There was another door on the first floor, then the stairs continued straight up to the third floor, meaning no entrance on the second floor. Trench did a rough estimate in his head for the price of a two-storey apartment in this area of Shoreditch. He wasn't getting much change out of seven figures.

When they reached a sturdy looking door on the third floor, Sheldon used two separate keys on two different locks before opening the door and stepping inside.

"Please, let's go into the kitchen," he said, pointing the way.

The door opened into a surprisingly wide, if short, hall area. It had high ceilings, with doors to the right and left. Straight ahead was a stairs, with an open door to its left, in which was a small bathroom. The wooden floors in the hall looked expensive, rather than the cheaper faux wood in some modern buildings.

Sheldon put his helmet on a hall table and went into a large, open plan kitchen-diner, with an island rather than a table in the dining end. Sheldon sat on a tall bar stool at the island and motioned for them to sit down. As they did, he stood up again as if remembering his manners and offered them tea or coffee. They both declined as they sat down.

Trench glanced around the room, impressed at a very well-appointed kitchen. It was a bit flashy for his tastes, all white and stainless steel, but it was tastefully done and certainly did not appear to be cheap. When they sat down, neither Trench nor Jazz said anything for a moment. This was their well-established tactic, to test whether their interviewee displayed any signs of excessive nervousness or guilt. Sheldon simply looked at them, waiting for them to say something.

When they didn't, Sheldon spoke first.

"Maybe a glass of water?"

"No, thank you," said Trench. First test passed.

"You're right," he continued, "We're here about Vanessa. Do you know where she is?"

"I have no idea," said Sheldon. "I haven't heard from her since Tuesday. She texted me saying she was going to see her Mum for lunch. I know she was going to that stupid dinner on Tuesday evening, but I haven't heard from her since."

"What exactly is your relationship with Vanessa?"

"She's my girlfriend."

"Still?" asked Jazz.

"Still?" repeated Sheldon, appearing genuinely confused. "What does that mean?"

"Is she still your girlfriend? There seems to be some confusion as to whether you're still dating," Jazz asked, deliberately provocative.

Trench noticed a flicker of surprise before Sheldon's face hardened into what might have been anger.

"Yes, still. I take it you've spoken with her parents, then?" he said, some bitterness in his tone.

"Why do you say that?" asked Trench.

Sheldon let out a sigh.

"Nothing, it's not a big deal. I just don't think they like me very much."

"What makes you say that?"

"It's a long story," said Sheldon. "We've been seeing each other for nearly three years, but they've never really accepted me."

"Any idea why?"

"I don't know. And to be perfectly honest, I've stopped caring. I just assume it's because they don't think I'm good enough for Vanessa. We've talked about it, and that's basically what she's told me. I'm sure it's not that uncommon, for parents not to like their daughter's boyfriend."

"That must make things hard for you and Vanessa though?" Jazz pressed.

"No, not really," replied Sheldon calmly. "It took a bit of getting used to at first, but we deal with it. Vanessa knows he's a pompous ass. She tells him often enough. I haven't done anything wrong. It's his problem, not mine, if he wants to treat me like that. Vanessa's told him that too."

"Doctor Osbourne, I presume you mean?" asked Trench.

Sheldon nodded.

"What about Mrs Osbourne?" said Jazz.

"I get on okay with her Mum. She's pretty decent. She's called me the last couple of days, by the way, asking if I've heard from Vanessa. I told her no."

"Where do you think Vanessa is?"

"Like I said, I have no idea."

"Is it normal for her to go a few days without making contact," asked Jazz.

Sheldon thought about this for a brief moment.

"No, not really. It's probably not the first time, but we haven't had a fight or anything. I would've expected to hear from her by now. I'm surprised I haven't to be honest."

"Are you worried?" asked Trench.

Again, Sheldon took a second before responding.

"Yes, I'm getting there. It's strange she hasn't called, or at least texted. I….I'm not sure right now if I'm angry or worried."

Trench nodded. He could understand that.

"Where do you think she could be, if she's missing of her own accord?" he asked.

This time Sheldon paused for a little longer. He looked from Trench to Jazz, then lowered his head with a little shake.

"It's possible she's uh…I've started to wonder if she's seeing someone. I'm not sure, and I don't want to be the paranoid boyfriend. It's not just because she's stopped me from being around her parents. She's just been a bit more…distant recently."

"In what way?"

"I've just seen a little less of her. She hasn't been staying here as much, and I haven't been over to hers as much as I usually would. She's also cancelled a couple of things we were supposed to do together in the past month or so. Her excuses were pretty lame. I haven't been reading too much into it. I suppose it's normal after a few years." He shrugged his shoulders. "And I'm not going to sit around and worry about our relationship. I've got my own life, you know. But the thought has crossed my mind that we've been drifting. Only ever so slightly, but as I say, the thought has occurred to me."

Trench was about to ask if Sheldon might have an idea as to who she may be seeing, but Sheldon went on before he could say anything.

"Also, I think she got a new phone," he said.

"You think?"

Sheldon looked a little on the back foot for the first time.

"No, sorry. She's definitely been using a different phone at times recently. I asked her about it and she was pretty dismissive. Just said she needs it for something she's working on at the moment."

"Any idea what that is?" asked Jazz.

"No idea. I've tried to ask her but she shuts me down. I didn't pester her about it. I trust her. It's her business and I respect her space. She's always got loads of stuff going on, and I know she's been thinking about getting into the whole It girl thing. We've chatted about it. I assume it's to do with that. She can tell me when she wants to. I'm okay with that."

Judging by his tone, Trench thought he was probably trying to convince himself he was okay with it. But he could understand Sheldon not wanting to force the issue.

"But now you're saying it might have been because she's seeing someone?"

"Look, it's possible. I don't know, okay? But given she hasn't called, and we've been spending less time, my mind has just started wandering these past few days. Plus there's other signs, you know?"

He looked from Trench to Jazz, slightly pleadingly, as if hoping they'd understand and wouldn't press him to go into detail. No chance.

"What do you mean, exactly?" Trench asked.

He shifted slightly in his seat as he responded.

"Well, like I said, we haven't been spending that many nights together, you know what I mean?"

They looked at him blankly. Although they understood, they needed him to spell it out.

"Sex, okay?!" he said, slightly exasperated. "That's always been important to her. Uh, to us. And recently, when she's cancelled our plans and we haven't seen each other…well, there hasn't been much opportunity. That's been different to normal."

Trench considered this. Both in their early twenties, he could certainly understand this being an issue. Despite the fact they'd been dating for a few years, they should probably still be at the stage of thinking they had invented sex. Enjoying everything and believing they were pioneering in their adventures. In fact, knowing that their libidos were probably just about as chemically rampant as they would ever be, it was definitely possible – probable even – that even if they weren't enjoying each other, either one could be doing so with someone else.

As he looked at Sheldon, having watched his demeanour throughout, he was becoming increasingly confident that he was just as in the dark about Vanessa's disappearance as they were. He couldn't be certain yet, but based on his experience of interviewing all manner of people over the years, his instincts were that Sheldon was telling the truth.

"Have you lived here long?" Jazz asked, switching to a less embarrassing subject for the young man.

"Only a few months. I bought it earlier this year and moved in during the summer. It was a bit of a mess when I bought it, so I had to do quite a lot of refurb." He glanced around, adding with a bit of self-satisfaction, "I did a lot it myself."

"Is that what you do? For a living, I mean?"

"No, no," he let out a slight laugh. "I work in financial services. But I enjoy doing this stuff myself. I'm pretty handy. I get it from my Dad, I think."

"Where were you on Tuesday evening?" asked Trench.

"I play 5-a-side on Tuesdays, in Bow. I got back here around nine o'clock for a shower, then went out with a few mates. It wasn't a late night, just a few pints. We went to a couple of bars around here, on Shoreditch High Street. I was home before midnight. My mates can, you know, corroborate that."

"Does anyone else live here?"

"Not at the moment," Sheldon said. "One of my mates is supposed to be moving in after Christmas. There's a third bedroom too, but it's a bit small. More of a box room really. I could rent it out in future if I need to, but hopefully won't have to."

Having spoken for a few moments about more comfortable subjects, Trench felt they'd established a decent enough rapport, so moved back onto what he suspected would be the most useful input Sheldon could provide.

"You mentioned about Vanessa's other phone," he said. "Do you have any thoughts about who she may have been seeing, if that's what she was doing?"

"No. None at all," he replied, but Trench thought it was a little too quick. Probably denial rather than dishonesty.

"Look, I know it's not the happiest thought, but it could really help. Any possibilities even?"

Sheldon shook his head as he responded, more slowly this time.

"I honestly don't. I haven't given it a huge amount of thought, because, you know, she may not be. I mean, probably isn't. But I couldn't think of anyone. But she has loads of her own friends. She moves in a few different circles, so I really wouldn't know."

"How come you didn't go to the dinner with her on Tuesday?"

"Me? No way! That is *really* not my scene," he looked almost aghast. "Vanessa knows that. She doesn't even ask me to get involved in that stuff anymore. We agreed that a long time ago."

"What do you mean?"

"That whole crowd is a bunch of wankers. Uh, excuse my French. But they're horrible. I was a couple of years ahead of Vanessa at Uni. I had already learned to steer well clear of the self-entitled, wannabe brigade. I used to tease her about it actually. And she knows it, too. She's not really into it. Not sure why she still goes, but she got involved at Uni and just goes along out of curiosity now, she says. I thought she was over it, but she started getting a bit more involved again during the summer."

"So you don't know any of the people she'd have met up with on Tuesday?"

"No, sorry. I might know one or two of the faces, from Uni. But, no, I don't really know any of them."

"Okay," said Trench.

He glanced at Jazz. He had no further questions and from her facial expression in response he knew she didn't either. He thanked Sheldon and gave him his card. He asked that he call if he could think of anything else that might be useful. They all made their way downstairs.

As they left the building Sheldon wheeled out his bicycle behind them and pulled the door closed. They said goodbye and got into the car. Sheldon got onto his bike and cycled away in the direction they had come from, towards the City. Trench didn't start the engine, and purely out of instinct they both watched him in their side mirrors without saying anything.

As he got to the top of the road, he slowed slightly, stuck his left arm out then turned out of sight. A black cab coming from the right seemed to suddenly speed up as he turned, then pressed hard on his horn for an angry few seconds, even though Sheldon was well clear of him. Another silly skirmish in the daily battle for London's streets between black cabs and cyclists. Trench started the car and did a U-turn.

"Either he's a better liar than Bernie Madoff, or he's not involved," he said.

"Agreed, he's a decent kid. Seems like he's got a solid head on his shoulders too. I'm thinking the good doctor is being a little harsh on him."

"And sounds like Vanessa takes her boyfriend's side on that. We need to go to her flat. Check out her home. I know her Mum has been there, so she's not likely to be there. But looks like we're going to need to dig into her background, find out more about her. Maybe that'll help—"

He was interrupted by a high-pitched buzzing sound from the car's speakers, signalling an incoming phone call via the car's Bluetooth hands free set up. It was too loud, as always. Because both of their phones used the hands free set-up, they could never tell whose phone was ringing. They both began rummaging through their pockets. They could see on the screen in the car's panel on the dashboard that it was a mobile number, but neither recognised it.

"Not me," said Jazz, looking at her phone, so Trench hit the answer button on the hands free screen.

"Hello?" he said.

"DCI Chambers? It's PC Barker, at the Osbournes' house."

She sounded breathless.

"Morning Barker, what's up?"

"They've received a ransom demand. For Vanessa," said Barker urgently. "Someone put a letter into their mailbox during the night. It says they're holding Vanessa and they want two million pounds to release her. I just got here. Krige told me."

They both sat bolt upright.

"Did they get him on camera?"

"I think so, yes. He said the cameras by the gate got him. He said it wasn't much use though, he couldn't see a face. But they've got a pretty good view of him dropping it in."

"Okay, we're on our way. Don't let the Osbournes act on the letter. We'll agree the right way to respond when we get there. Make sure they understand that."

"Game on," said Jazz as she reached around and pulled on her safety belt.

# Nine

Trench flipped the blues and twos and stepped on the accelerator. They had travelled barely a hundred yards when the buzzing sound started again. This time they did know whose phone was ringing because caller ID on the screen said 'The Borg.' The station switchboard.

"Trench here."

"Trench, it's Lewis. I got your report this morning. After you didn't come back to the station last night."

Although his tone was neutral, the delivery made it feel like he was at least hinting at a rebuke. Trench felt a flash of annoyance but decided to ignore it. He focused on driving and didn't say anything. After a couple of seconds Lewis continued.

"Did you get the boyfriend, Sheldon?"

"Yes, we've just finished with him. My read is that he's not involved, Chief. He seems like a decen—"

Lewis interrupted, raising his voice.

"How can you be so sure? You've only spoken with him for, what, half an hour? In his own home? When are you bringing him in for questioning?"

Trench felt a burst of anger. Not just because Lewis was again interrupting him and failing to listen. He was also second guessing Trench's call without any knowledge of the situation. Jazz scrunched her face into a what-is-he-talking-about? look.

"Uh, sure we can do that, but it's not the prior—"

"Do it, Trench, today. Right now!" interrupted Lewis. "We can't just let suspects off the hook based on hunches and gut—"

"*They've received a ransom note!*" Trench practically shouted at him. He then added, only slightly softer, "The Osbournes. Posted into their letterbox last night. They got the guy on camera and we're on our way there right now."

There was silence for a brief moment. Trench's anger subsided slightly. He caught Jazz's eye and shrugged. He decided to try to repair any potential damage.

"We've got the sirens on here, I'm shouting, can you hear me?" he shouted, slightly less aggressively than before.

After a moment Lewis spoke.

"Okay. That's probably good news. At least she's alive. When you're done there let's meet back at the incident room to take stock. We'll plan the next move. As a team."

He hung up before Trench could respond. Probably just as well, he thought to himself, turning his focus to the drive.

Traffic was getting heavy, but thankfully the school run hadn't started yet. It still took them nearly thirty minutes to get to Highgate. When they were a couple of minutes from Blenheim the car speaker buzzed yet again. It was Trench's phone again and he recognised the number.

"Morning Doc."

"Trench, we've just completed the postmortem," said Wharton, before pausing for a second. "What's that sound, are your sirens on? Can you talk?"

"Not really, Doc. Can you give me the headlines?"

"Right. Firstly, it's as we feared. A very thorough cleaning job. He used industrial grade bleach and probably soaked the body in it for a considerable period of time. A day at least, quite possibly longer than that. So there's no traceable DNA. No blood or semen, and no saliva around the bite marks.

"However we did find a couple of things. Firstly, the duct tape was wrapped around her face premortem. We found evidence that it was at some point also used to cover her mouth, as some kind of gag. Second, we picked out some identifiable fibres, mainly from inside the mouth. They're quite distinctive, bright green or yellow in colour. Most of them were caught between her teeth, and a few more between the lips and gums. They're quite coarse, so unlikely to be from clothing. More like carpet or rug fibres I'd say."

As Trench processed this, Wharton continued.

"Also, she has a tattoo on her left hand. Three small, blue dots in a triangle formation on the skin between the thumb and index finger. We only found it after we cut the bindings on her hands."

Trench knew this was usually a prison tattoo. His immediate thought was that it further reaffirmed their initial suspicion that she had been a prostitute.

"The trauma to the body is as we speculated last night," Wharton went on. "Cause of death was definitely ligature strangulation. Judging by the marks and chafing on the neck, I'd say we're talking about some kind of wire. In total, there's one hundred and seventeen separate injuries, mainly the flesh wounds we saw last night. The left nipple was bitten off completely. The right nipple shows signs of burning, probably from a cigarette."

They turned into the cul-de-sac where the Osbourne's house was. Trench pulled in to the kerb and killed the lights and siren as he waited for Wharton to continue. But Wharton didn't say anything else.

"Is that it? Anything from toxicology tests," asked Trench.

"No, I'm afraid that's it. The toxicology tests didn't show anything particularly suspicious. We tested the blood, liver, stomach contents, even the vitreous humour in the eyes. There were trace elements of alcohol and recreational drugs, cannabis, cocaine etcetera, but nothing significant. She'd probably used some of these, what I suppose you'd call party drugs, in the days before her death, but that's not unusual as you'll know. Certainly nothing that played a factor in her death. I'll send you the full report shortly."

He was speaking more matter-of-factly than he had appeared last night, but then his voice took on a more forceful tone.

"Trench, we need to get this bastard, fast. This level of violence is…exceptional. It's rabid. I'm struggling to see how someone who could do this is just going to go back to living a normal life."

"Understood," said Trench.

He had already had the same thought. Nobody spoke for a moment as they thought about the implications. Trench then voiced another idea that had occurred to him last night.

"It's also unlikely he's started at this level. Too deliberate, too methodical. He must have been building up to this. We'll go through all known freaks in the system. If he has any kind of history with rapes, abductions or any kind of deviancy then hopefully he's in the system. Looks like me and Jazz are going to be tied up on something else for a while but we'll get started on the database search immediately."

Jazz nodded silently as Wharton mumbled agreement. Trench thanked him for the call and hung up. As they approached the gates of Blenheim, they noticed two cars parked nearby. They were both facing Blenheim, and both were occupied. A man stood beside one of them, smoking a cigarette. The equipment dangling around his neck made it clear what they were doing here. In the quiet, affluent cul-de-sac they blended in like cockroaches on caviar. And were about as welcome.

As they watched, the smoking man dropped his cigarette and raised a camera with a huge telescopic lens and pointed it at them.

"Suppose it was only a matter of time before they started showing up," said Jazz.

"Wait until they hear there's been a ransom demand. It'll be like Glastonbury around here."

"Size of that thing," said Jazz. "If we hear there's been a burglary at Greenwich Observatory at least we know where to start."

The gates opened as their car pulled up to them. Jazz turned to Trench as they drove through.

"The body in Oldbury Woods won't be our case, you know. We're on Vanessa Osbourne. Probably be that meathead given he was at the site yesterday."

"Uhm," was all Trench could respond with. He knew she was right.

It bothered him that Callow would be put in charge of finding the killer. Time was a factor in reducing the chances he would strike again and he had no faith Callow would be up to the job. It would be all media appeals and TV interviews. Trench made a mental note to assign a constable to begin searching through the system before Lewis made any formal decision about who would be leading on it. At least that way he could be sure it would get done.

After a few seconds he thought better of it and took out his phone. He'd make the call now.

"Hang on a sec," he said to Jazz as he dialled.

When he was put through to the incident room, he recognised the voice as the same young constable he had spoken with the previous night to get the Osbournes' address. He was impressed that the constable was there again this early, so asked his name.

"Tony Barton, sir", the constable replied.

"Okay Barton, we need you to drop everything and run the databases. Compile a list of all known male sexual offenders with a history of sadism against female victims. Or any form of violence, especially torture, rape, stuff like that. Abducting in the commission of, also."

He paused to think how else to structure the search parameters.

"Location, guv?" asked Barton.

"London. And also the South East."

"Right," said Barton.

Trench could tell he was writing it down, because he was quietly repeating the words to himself as he wrote them.

"And for victim profile, I presume I should use Vanessa Osbourne?" Barton asked.

"Correct."

Technically, Barton was part of the incident room for the Osbourne case. Trench didn't tell him the search was for the unrelated body in Oldbury Woods to avoid any pushback. He told Barton to prioritise checking the Police National Computer, PNC. This held the records of arrests, warnings and convictions for over twelve million people in the UK.

He told Barton to then also check the Police National Database, PND, a controversial database which held countless more records of 'soft' information about individuals. People didn't have to commit crimes to end up on this database. They didn't even have to be suspected of committing crimes. It was simply any information police found out about people that they wanted to keep for future reference.

Politicians justified this database as 'intelligence.' It included information passed on from over two hundred different systems, including housing authorities and social services. It could even include information from state schools that someone had seen fit to pass on to police. It had so far amassed over 3.5 billion searchable records on the population – more than fifty for each person living in the UK.

Civil liberty groups decried that this essentially boiled down to criminal profiling via the rumour mill. In fact, their claims the country was becoming a nanny state fell far short of the reality that it was by now much closer to an all-out 1984-esque police state. A project to combine both the PNC and the PND into a new advanced system was already well underway, effectively giving up any pretence that police profiling would differentiate between criminal records and entirely subjective, randomly held information.

The government had even given the new system the kind of bland name that any totalitarian secret police would be proud of – the Law Enforcement Data Service, or Leds. The brainchild of an insidiously ultra-right Home Secretary, ultimately this system would hold biometric data, passport photos and automatic number plate recognition data on as much of the UK population as police could get their hands on. Evidence of the effect of the Home Secretary's tenure was demonstrated during scandals such as the Windrush enforced deportation of British citizens or the revelation that the then-Home Secretary had instructed officials to create a 'hostile environment' for immigrants. But the scandals weren't sufficient to stop or even slow the changes.

Ironically though, the Home Office's tyrannical ambitions were continually undone by its own persistent incompetence. The project was miles over budget, the deadline kept being pushed out by years and the whole thing was racked by the blame game. This was compounded by a continuous onslaught of briefings from numerous senior police officials that the government's budget cuts meant its plans for these changes were not credible.

This meant that for the moment at least the databases remained separate. Using the information in each to search for potential suspects for a crime of this nature would require a degree of creativity on behalf of the searcher. And the systems were not straightforward to use. User training for the PNC alone took at least five days. The search parameters had to be specific to ensure they were neither too narrow nor too generic. Trench was making this point to Barton, when he interrupted him.

"Guv, with all due respect, I know this. I know how to search the databases. Leave it with me and I'll give you a call a bit later."

"Okay, fair enough. Good man," he said, but couldn't resist adding, "And more names are better than less at this stage."

He hung up as they arrived at the house. PC Walker was waiting at the front door.

"Morning. Barker's with the parents, in the kitchen I think. They know you're coming," he said.

He then waited, looking a little unsure of what to do next.

"Let's see the footage first. Then we'll go and speak with the parents," said Trench, walking over to Krige's security room.

He knocked on the door as he opened it. Krige was behind the desk, with two people dressed in the same all-black outfit seated in front of him. Krige made the introductions. One was a Latina woman called Ayala and the other a huge man with a Yorkshire accent called Doherty. They were both long term members of the Osbourne's security detail so Trench and Jazz exchanged cards with both.

Krige then got straight down to business. He didn't need to be asked to show the footage. He turned the monitor on his desk around as much as it would go, so the detectives could easily see it. They stepped closer and huddled around the screen.

It showed the empty street immediately outside the gates of Blenheim, in darkness. Trench noted the footage was in colour, rather than in the black and white more commonly used by security cameras. The timer in the bottom corner read 03:44.

There was nothing for a few seconds, then a figure dressed all in black emerged into the scene. He was on a bicycle, rolling slowly along the footpath toward the gate. He wore dark gloves and had a baseball cap under a black hoodie which had been pulled tight around his face. He was also wearing a black bandana or scarf around the lower half of his face. It was impossible to make out any facial features. All they could tell was that the figure appeared shorter than average height. He looked to be either stocky or fat, but it was hard to tell which.

As he got closer to the gate, the security lights burst on, causing a momentary whiteness on the screen as the cameras adjusted. This also caused the figure on the screen to suddenly stop his bicycle. He put both feet on the ground and just stood for a moment, frozen to the spot. He began urgently glancing around, both at the gates and also back over each shoulder.

After a few seconds, he sat back on his bike and pushed forward, right up to the gate. He stopped again, putting his foot down. He leaned in closely and began examining the gate. The figure's head movements got a bit more animated as he looked around, before finally seeing that the letterbox was built into the wall, just underneath the intercom.

He dragged his front wheel sideways in that direction, then reached inside the pocket on the front of the hoodie. He took out what looked like a brown envelope but then dropped it on the ground. Trench was surprised to hear a muffled voice, saying what sounded like 'guvnor.' The figure then laid the bike down flat as he picked up the envelope. He stuffed it straight into the letterbox, picked up the bike then peddled furiously out of screenshot.

"The cameras have audio?" Trench said to Krige, as everyone straightened up.

"Ja, it's heat-motion activated. When it's triggered it starts recording sound too. Here, I've made you a copy."

He handed Trench a datastick.

"Thanks. Have you done any kind of analysis on the voice? Is there any enhancement on here?" he asked, nodding at the stick.

He was hoping Krige might have access to better equipment than they had. Or that he had worked on it more rapidly than police resources would be able to.

"Sorry, mate. We don't have that gear onsite."

"Okay. But you do have that capability, right?"

"Ja, we have some equipment available at HQ, but it takes a bit of time mate, you know." He smiled apologetically, holding his hands out.

Trench could appreciate that he'd be a little reluctant to simply hand over such analysis to police proactively. They would at least want their client to know they were providing solid assistance to police.

"Understood. But do me a favour. Whenever you get to it, can you send me a copy of what you come up with. It'd be really helpful. Police resources aren't what they used to be. And second opinions are always welcome. I'm sure the Osbournes would be happy to know you guys are providing valuable help in all of this."

"Absolutely, mate, of course. We'll send it on asap."

"Thanks. Can you play it again. And turn the sound up."

Krige hit play again, though explained the volume was already at maximum. This time everyone instinctively leaned in closer to the speakers. When it was finished, Trench glanced first at Jazz, then Krige.

Trench again thought he heard 'guvnor.' It was common enough for Londoners to refer to each other as 'guvnor.' It was a kind of colloquial slang alternative to 'sir' or 'boss.' But in this context it didn't make any sense to him.

"What did he say? Sounds like 'guvnor,'" he said, looking around at everyone for their thoughts.

"Could be," said Jazz. "Or 'good now' maybe? Neither make much sense."

"Yes, we think 'guvnor' when we saw it," said Ayala in a South American lilt. "London guy talk to himself."

"We've watched it a bunch of times and can't come up with anything that fits," said Krige. "Maybe 'give more,' but again that doesn't really make sense. But we'll get the enhancement to you when we get it done. Hopefully that'll be more clear."

"Let's hope so," said Trench. "What about the note, do you have that?"

"No," interrupted Walker. "Barker has that. Or at least the parents do."

"Right, let's go see them."

Walker led the way deeper into the house. He knocked on a door before they stepped into a large kitchen-diner. The room was bigger than many central London restaurants Trench had been in. To the left was the conventional kitchen area, with cooker, fridge and a range of other appliances, some of which Trench didn't recognise. They turned to the right.

Barker was seated at a dining table near the window, as was Mrs Osbourne. Doctor Osbourne was standing on the far side of the table. He was dressed again in a suit, but no waistcoat or tie. It did little to disguise the fact he looked more weary than the previous evening, almost certainly after another sleepless night.

He was in the middle of what appeared to be a heated conversation with his wife, his voice raised and his hands gesticulating out in front of him. His face was reddened by exertion. Or was it anger? Barker's expression suggested she was close to stepping in to try to calm him down. He was talking with exaggerated slowness, as if addressing a child.

"But how do we know?" he was saying. "It could be bloody anyone!"

"We don't know!" screamed Mrs Osbourne, rising to her feet and banging her hands on the table. "But what the bloody hell else are we going to do?!"

She collapsed back down into her seat and started sobbing into her hands. As they walked over, Trench noticed that the slippers Mrs Osbourne wore were similar, but didn't match. She had a dressing gown pulled loosely over a light night dress.

Doctor Osbourne turned to stare out at the garden, hands planted on his hips. Neither he nor his wife had shown any sign of having noticed the detectives entering the room. Trench cleared his voice as they walked over to the table. As they reached it he noticed a piece of white paper lying on the table, on top of a brown envelope. He could see it contained scrawled handwriting in blue ink.

"Good morning," he said solemnly.

Barker nodded at him but neither of the Osbournes replied. He motioned to the letter, and Barker nodded again. He slipped on a pair of latex gloves and picked it up. He held it out so that both he and Jazz could read it. The handwriting was a mix of block capitals and joined writing.

WE HAVE your daughter. Vanessa

you must pay 2 MILLON POUNDS

SEND Email to VANESATHERANSOM@hotmail.com and get some Instrucsions

Not police

The handwriting looked childish, almost unreadable in parts. The turn of phrase was odd. He re-read it, swiftly concluding it gave at least some information about the kidnapper. He put the letter back down on the table and cleared his throat again.

"I know this is an extremely difficult time for you. We will do everything we can to ensure Vanessa's safe return. But for the moment we need to ask some questions so that we take the right actions to achieve that."

Again there was no response from either Osbourne. He gave it a few moments and eventually Doctor Osbourne turned around. He kept his hands on his hips as he spoke.

"What do you think of this?" he gestured toward the letter dismissively with his head.

"Can you confirm please that no-one has sent an email to the kidnapper yet?"

"We've just been discussing it. How do we even know whoever sent this actually has Vanessa?"

He glanced at his wife. She remained sobbing into her hands.

Trench could appreciate that their emotions were running high. But it was important he remained in charge and he wasn't going to let the doctor dictate the discussion. He also wanted to demonstrate to Mrs Osbourne that the police were in control of the situation, given they hadn't yet spoken with her. He didn't want her to think the police would take sides in any disagreement between the parents.

"Can I take that as a no?" he asked calmly, looking at Doctor Osbourne.

The doctor stared back for a second, then spat out, "No, we haven't responded."

"Thank you. We'd like to get your consent that the police respond. We'll respond as if we're Vanessa's parents, and will let you know at all times what we're planning to do. We'll consult with you to the extent possible before taking any action. But it's important there's only one line of communication open with the kidnapper. Could you please confirm you both agree with this?"

"Fine," said Osbourne, "That makes sense. You have our agreement. Uh, I mean my agreement."

He glanced again at his wife, looking impatient. She had stopped sobbing but hadn't taken her head out of her hands. After a moment's silence she looked up. She wore no make-up and her brownish-blonde hair was matted onto her face, which was streaked with tears. She looked at Trench with the haunted expression he'd only ever seen on a broken parent who doesn't know where their child is. He'd seen it before, but it never failed to send a shiver deep into this soul.

He held her gaze for a moment, trying to demonstrate solidarity. Hoping he showed resolve and confidence that they would share her plight and do whatever they could to return her daughter to her. Which was true, he knew that. He would put everything he had into trying to find her. But for that split second, he wasn't proud to admit to himself, all he could think was that he truly hoped he would never feel what she was feeling right now. He wasn't sure he'd survive that.

"Just do whatever it takes to bring Vanessa back," she croaked. "Pay the bloody money, it doesn't matter. Don't mess these people around. Don't try to be clever. Just make sure you do whatever it takes to bring Vanessa home."

Her face collapsed back into her hands. Barker went to put a hand on her shoulder but she shrugged it off with a violent lurch.

"Thank you," said Trench. "We have an incident room already set up at the station. We'd like—"

Mrs Osbourne suddenly shot up out of her chair, sending it keeling over backwards behind her.

"I can't take this," she shouted, panting for air, one hand clasped to her chest. She turned to Trench, jabbing a finger at him. "Just do whatever they say, okay. The money doesn't matter, you hear me. Just do whatever they say, and bring my baby home." She turned and pointed at her husband. "Give them fucking ten million pounds if they want it. *WHAT DOES IT BLOODY MATTER?*" she screamed.

With that, she stormed out of the room. Barker sat up, as if torn between following her or staying put. No-one moved or said anything. Doctor Osbourne just stared at the closed door his wife had stormed out of. For a second he looked like he was about to apologise on her behalf, but Trench was glad that he seemed to decide against it. He then blew out his cheeks and his head dropped to stare at the floor.

Barker sat back in her chair, seemingly deciding there was little comfort she could provide Mrs Osbourne. Trench felt that was probably the right option. There was silence for a moment, Trench letting a few seconds pass before continuing.

"Doctor Osbourne, we'd like to respond to the email at the station. We can use our technology there to more quickly trace the email traffic and any phone calls we may have with whoever sent the letter."

Trench paused to let Doctor Osbourne respond, but he just continued staring at the floor. He looked completely lost in his own harrowed thoughts. Trench decided to give him more time. Then Doctor Osbourne seemed to wince, and brought his hand up to pinch the bridge of his nose, his eyes shutting even more tightly. He held out his other hand to steady himself against one of the chairs.

Trench slightly bowed his own head, out of solidarity or sympathy, he wasn't sure. There was urgency in responding to the ransom demand, but these people were at breaking point. Or perhaps beyond it, in the case of Mrs Osbourne. He knew he had to make room in their investigation for these moments of sheer despair. It was always this way with missing persons cases. Especially for the parents, for whom a 22-year-old was still very much a child.

But he also had to keep the investigation moving. He would do whatever he could to provide solace or comfort along the way, but his only true priority was finding their daughter. He lifted his head to face Doctor Osbourne and was about to speak when Osbourne himself spoke. He did not open his eyes and continued holding onto the chair. He spoke slowly and clearly, but his voice was close to cracking.

"You heard her, Detective. My wife speaks for us both. Respond to them. Do it at the station, that's fine. I understand. But make it absolutely clear it is our full intention to pay their ransom demand. We will do whatever they want."

A stifled sob escaped as he finished speaking and he abruptly turned fully away from the detectives. He put both hands onto the windows to steady himself, then raised his head to stare out into the garden. Again Trench waited, giving the man a chance to compose himself.

"Thank you," he said after a few moments. "You're more than welcome to join us at the station, or I'll call you directly to advise you as things develop."

"Thank you," Doctor Osbourne responded after a moment.

He took a deep breath and turned back to face them. His voice sounded stronger, but his eyes were red and moist.

"I'll stay here for the moment, but do call me to discuss any plans. As I made clear to you last night, I hope, I want to be kept fully abreast of how your investigation is proceeding."

"I'll call you directly with any update. PC Walker will continue to remain here, as will PC Barker," confirmed Trench.

He then followed up on what had first struck him when he saw the ransom letter.

"Who is best placed to provide us with a list of people who have been at your house over the past year or two? We'd like to get details of any employees, workmen, anyone who has spent some time at the house. I presume Krige would keep their details?"

"Krige?" replied Doctor Osbourne, looking confused.

He clearly wasn't on familiar terms with the staff.

"You mean the security people? They take care of all of that. There should be a few of them in the security office at the front of the house."

"Thank you, we'll speak with them. Also, we'd like to search Vanessa's home. It could be important in helping us find her. Can you supply us with a key?"

Doctor Osbourne hesitated, looking at first confused then sceptical. It was a common response. People were naturally reluctant to let police poke around in the intimate settings of loved ones. It created another pull at already fraught emotions. Trench knew people often felt like they were betraying their loved ones by allowing an untold number of strangers to rummage through every personal and private possession.

Although police endeavoured to perform this as sensitively as possible, realistically there was a limit to how sensitive they could be. Ultimately, their investigation had to be calculated and clinical. They would methodically go through everything in a person's home, often focusing on the more secretive and hidden aspects of a person's life. Police knew that secrets frequently held the key to unlocking cases. It was therefore necessary, and Trench would have to insist if Doctor Osbourne was reticent.

Trench could see the doctor mulling all of this and was about to delicately make the point, but Osbourne eventually responded.

"Yes, I suppose I can understand that. But I don't want to see leaked details of my daughter's private life splashed all over some fucking tabloid rag, do you understand me, Detective?"

Trench nodded solemnly.

He truly did understand. The Doctor's concerns were not unfounded, he knew. There were plenty of cases where personal details or secrets had made their way into the media, generating sordid headlines and adding further anguish to bereaved and forlorn families. He would do everything he could to control such leaks. But he knew there were no guarantees. It was an ugly dimension to the nature of police investigations. Like any other walk of life, the force had its own fair share of bad apples willing to sell out victims' integrity for a few slimy quid.

"I'll get you a key, just a moment," he said.

He walked over to a cabinet on the far wall of the kitchen and opened a drawer. Trench could hear him searching through various sets of keys before picking a set out. There were two keys on a chain, attached to a small, fluffy, pink pom pom keyring. Doctor Osbourne then picked up a pen and wrote an address on a notepad on the cabinet. He tore off the page and handed both it and the keys to Trench. He glared at Trench as he did so.

"I'll hold you personally responsible for any leaks, Detective. I have enough contacts amongst your superiors to make sure you'll regret it."

He managed to put considerable menace into his tone. And Trench saw the sincerity behind the words in Osbourne's eyes. There was a hardness there, a steely, determined rage despite the genteel exterior. The man was a fighter, Trench felt.

No doubt it had helped him get where he was today. But now someone was attacking his family and he looked intent on fighting back. Trench held his stare for a moment and then gave a curt nod to show he understood.

"Thanks for the address," he said. "I'll be in touch as soon as there's any developments. You're free to call me at any time."

He picked up the ransom letter and envelope and put them into the plastic evidence folder. Having seen the amateurish nature of the ransom letter, he was beginning to feel hopeful they'd be able to get fingerprint or trace DNA from either it or the envelope. As they turned to go, Trench remembered something else. He looked at Doctor Osbourne.

"One last thing," he said. "You've got a few paparazzi outside your gate. You can expect more, probably a lot more, when news of the ransom demand brakes. I presume you've got connections to senior editors in the media. If you want to keep this out of the press, and avoid your quiet street turning into a campsite, then I'd suggest you use those connections."

"Editors, and owners," said Osbourne. "I've already made some calls myself, and my people are doing the rest as we speak. Those wretched leeches won't get a penny for any of their miserable pictures."

They said goodbye to Doctor Osbourne, who immediately then turned to resume his forlorn gazing out at the garden. Barker joined them as they left the kitchen, probably to give Doctor Osbourne some space. She and Walker then headed back to the library.

On the way out they again stopped by the security room, to request the list of visitors. Neither Ayala nor Doherty were in the room by now, with Krige sitting alone behind the desk.

"How are they doing?" he asked, as they entered the room.

"He's holding up okay, all things considered," said Trench. "His anger seems to be keeping any more destructive emotions away. Can't say the same about Mrs Osbourne though. She's not in great shape."

"Yeah, he's been pretty fired up since the letter arrived," said Krige. "I brought it in to him myself this morning. I thought he was going to take a swipe at me when he looked at it."

"I think I know what you mean," replied Trench.

"Poor Mrs Osbourne, though, shit," said Krige, shaking his head. "She's close to those girls. Her daughters. She nearly collapsed when she saw the letter. She was already in a bad way, but I thought she was going to keel over."

"She pretty much did when we were discussing it," said Jazz.

"Shit," repeated Krige, shaking his head.

Nobody said anything for a moment. Trench broke the silence.

"Krige, do you keep a log of who comes and goes here?"

"Yeah, daily. Everyone has to sign in and out. Every visitor, that is. Family members don't have to, obviously."

"How long do you keep the records for?"

"Years. Here, I can show you."

Krige motioned them over to his desk and again turned the monitor around so they could see it.

"I think legally we're obliged to keep them for five years," he explained as he tapped on the keyboard, "But I don't think we ever delete them. Can't think of a reason why we would."

"GDPR?" suggested Jazz.

"What?" Krige looked at her blankly. Clearly he wasn't the admin guy.

"Nothing," she said, not wanting to go down that warren hole if she didn't have to.

After a few seconds Krige pointed at the screen.

"Here, see? This shows all visitors on a daily basis going back to…2012. That's when we started transferring the written logs onto this system."

The screen showed a long list of names, dates and other information in what looked like a web-based format. It was a more impressive set up than Trench had been expecting. He'd been thinking they'd have to spend hours painstakingly going through handwritten logs.

"Nice," he said, straightening up.

Rather than look at the information now, he wanted to get back to the station and get moving on the ransom letter.

"Can you send us a list of all visitors here over the past couple of years," he said.

Krige paused, but only for a second.

"Yeah, sure. I can do that," he said. "For the record, we wouldn't normally just send client related information to the cops. No offence. But this situation is obviously not normal. We're happy to help."

"Thanks," said Trench. "And the sooner the better. Our email addresses are on our cards."

He could see both of their cards still sitting on the desk from when they had given them to Krige the night before.

"No problem. I'll send it right now," said Krige.

Trench and Jazz thanked him and turned to leave.

"Hey," Krige called after them.

They both turned. Krige had a conspiratorial look on his face.

"What, you think the guy might be in there?" he asked pointing at the computer, a sly grin forming on his face.

"Just covering the angles," replied Trench, wanting to deflect his interest. "We're casting a very wide net. We always do. That has to include everyone she may have come into contact with over the past couple of years, wherever that may be. This list is just a small part of that."

"I get you," said Krige. "You'll have it asap."

"Make sure you include your staff on there too," said Trench, trying to dampen his interest further.

Krige nodded. They thanked him again and headed out of the house.

"Pretty sloppy letter," said Jazz, after they were back in their car.

"Were you expecting different coloured letters cut out from magazines and glued on with Pritt Stick?"

"Very funny. You know what I mean. Scrawled in biro. And '*Vanessa the ransom*' at Hotmail? Creative...," she said sarcastically.

"It probably explains why we couldn't figure out what he says on the CCTV anyway. He's got to be foreign. '*...get some instructions'... 'Not police.*' Weird way of putting it. The foreign language experts in Linguistics should be able to confirm where he's from when they see the footage. Assuming the Home Office still permits us to use foreigners, that is."

"Well it's not Urdu anyway," Jazz replied.

"Excellent, now we're getting somewhere."

"But you think they're on the list, right? They've been here before."

"Just covering the bases," repeated Trench.

"It could make sense," she said, nodding to herself. "It looked like a pretty long list, though."

"But it's online. Better than sifting through a thousand pages of illegible signatures."

"True dat."

Trench took out his phone.

"I'll call Lewis. See if I can help him untwist his knickers about not being kept updated every time someone farts."

Before he dialled Jazz spoke again.

"It's painful, you know. Seeing the mother like that. Poor woman."

Trench nodded. It was painful. But he knew they had to use it to help them keep fuelled and focused, for what were certain to be long, gritty days ahead.

"I really hope we find her," said Jazz.

Trench nodded.

"We will. At least he's holding it together, though. It'll make it easier for us when it comes to decisions."

"About the ransom exchange?" Jazz asked.

"Yeah. But even now. How we respond to the letter, what we say. It's better to have their agreement and permission. And then yes, when it comes to the ransom exchange, it'll make it easier if we can discuss it with one of them and we all agree the strategy. Believe me, it makes for much better operational planning and execution if the family are fully onboard with us."

"I can see that," said Jazz, nodding.

They were silent for a moment before Trench spoke again.

"He has a point, though."

"About leaks from the investigation?" asked Jazz.

"Well, yeah, that too unfortunately," said Trench.

"That's your cock on the block, skipper" said Jazz, using the nickname she used when she jokingly passed responsibility onto Trench, as the senior detective. "That much was crystal clear. I'll bet he really does have a hotline to the brass. If not higher. All those government contracts for his company? He probably has ministers' numbers on speed dial."

"No doubt," said Trench grimly. "But what I mean is, what he was saying to Mrs Osbourne when we walked in. He has a point. The letter could be fake. It could be some scammer just trying to make a few quid by jumping on the back of her disappearance."

"You think? How would they know she was missing though? He dropped it at four o'clock this morning," said Jazz sceptically.

"You said it was on the net yesterday evening. When we were down in Oldbury Woods. Celebs-dot-com or something."

"Oh yeah, celebscene-dot-com. That's true," she conceded. "In fact, didn't mainstream have it by around midnight?"

"Exactly. So the guy sees it, scrawls out the letter, creates the email address and just waits until it's dark. Easily done."

"And he knows which house it is because he's been here before. Hence your request for the list from Krige."

"It's worth checking out," said Trench. "Okay, got to call Pyle."

Trench called Lewis's desk phone but it went to voicemail. He was tempted to leave a short message, but instead decided to try his mobile. Lewis answered on the first ring.

"What's the latest?" he answered.

Trench gave him a brief update on the CCTV footage and the contents of the letter. He decided not to mention any suspicions about who the kidnapper could be or his request for the list of visitors from Krige. He didn't want Lewis making an off the cuff decision that may hamper their activity or send them off in some other direction. He felt it would be better to discuss the options in the next briefing, when they could have a detailed discussion before making decisions.

They agreed to meet at the station incident room within the hour. Lewis alluded to 'others' wanting to get involved, but didn't elaborate. Trench had a feeling he knew who that would be. When they got back to the station they learned that Lewis had left earlier to go New Scotland Yard. This only served to reinforce Trench's suspicion.

# Ten

Trench went to his desk and Jazz went to drop the ransom letter to the Lab. Trench left his mobile phone on his desk while he went to the bathroom. When he came back he didn't log in to his computer, instead heading straight to the last office on the right-hand side at the end of the CID squad room. This was where the Vanessa Osbourne incident room had been set up.

He walked into the room and found that there was no-one else there. This immediately annoyed him. He would have expected to see at least a couple of people researching her background or making calls to potential witnesses. He started to leave the room to find out where everyone was, but then thought better of it. He wanted to look around to see what they had so far.

The window blinds in the room were pulled shut, as they usually were. Despite being four floors up, there was always the lingering suspicion that the press, or other prying eyes, would find ways of peering in through windows. Daylight was deemed an acceptable sacrifice to ensure greater secrecy. Or perhaps more importantly, to avoid any potentially embarrassing leaks. But it made for an oppressive feel inside the small room, which the old style, long fluorescent tube lighting only made worse.

The walls were painted in the typical institutional green favoured by most public buildings, from hospitals and asylums to jails and police stations. There was a long rectangular table in the centre of the room with seating for a dozen or so people. A couple of computers sat on the table, but neither were turned on. Whiteboards lined the walls on either side of the table, and a flipchart stood at the front of the room.

On one of the whiteboards someone had stuck a picture of Vanessa Osbourne at the top, and drawn a few lines down from it. One led to a list entitled 'Boyfriend.' Under this was Sheldon's name, followed by a question mark and the letters TBI, 'to be interviewed'. Trench picked up a red marker and rubbed out TBI. He wrote 'Interviewed' with today's date, adding 'Not likely involved.' Fuck Lewis's insistence that they bring him in immediately. He would argue the point during the meeting if needs be.

Another line down from the photo of Vanessa led to 'Last known movements.' There were a few bullets saying the last known contact with the parents was Tuesday afternoon, and that she had attended the gala dinner on Tuesday night.

Beside this someone had written 'Attendance confirmed?' Underneath that was a notation indicating that Vanessa's mother had gone to her flat late Wednesday morning and found no trace of her. The call to police to report Vanessa as a missing person, made by Mrs Osbourne, was logged at 11:31.

The only other line pointed to the words 'Ransom note received,' with today's date. There was already a printed photo of the letter, which Trench assumed Jazz had just added, before delivering the letter to the Lab.

Trench reread the few short entries summarising her last known movements, and could feel the anger rising inside him. He would have expected to see reference to a comprehensive list of witness statements and CCTV footage, indicating precisely where she was last seen and by whom. Also details of her last few phone conversations. Even where her car was. The fact that none of this information was referenced left him in little doubt. This work had probably not yet been done. He blew out his cheeks, both in exasperation and as an attempt to stem the rising anger.

He took a step back and surveyed the whiteboard in full. He felt chastened by the relatively meek amount of information displayed. If this was an accurate reflection of where they were at, then they badly needed to inject more urgency. He was well aware of the less than encouraging outcomes from previous famous cases of people being kidnapped for ransom. He knew that roughly half of those kidnapped were killed by their captors. And that the captors always went ahead with ransom demands anyway, often successfully extracting millions from their victims' families, despite the fact they had already killed their victims. The thought did not improve his mood.

He stared at the picture of the ransom note. He knew that this would be given priority, and knew that this was the right approach. But he was conscious that this shouldn't be their only avenue of investigation. He felt they needed to do much more background on Vanessa Osbourne. Who was she? Who were her friends? Her enemies? And if she was seeing someone else, as her boyfriend had suggested, then who was it? That felt like the most important question to answer.

"And what were her last known fucking movements?" he said out loud as he turned away from the board, anger boiling over.

He checked his watch, increasingly agitated that the incident room was still empty. But he knew he had to wait for Lewis before gathering people for the update briefing. He decided instead to find Barton to check how he was getting on with searching the databases. He went back into the squad room and looked around, but then realised he didn't know what Barton looked like. There was a smattering of officers of various rank seated throughout the office.

He was about to walk over to where the constables mostly sat, but then reconsidered. If the person he asked to point out Barton turned out to be Barton himself, then the junior officer would probably be embarrassed. It wouldn't bother Trench, but it might piss Barton off. Given that Trench was developing a favourable view of him, he decided against it.

Instead he went over to Detective Sergeant Mark Thomson, who was in charge of assigning duties to most of the constables.

"Thomson," he said bending slightly and lowering his voice. "Need a favour."

Thomson appeared in the mood to chat. He immediately pushed his chair out from his desk and leaned back, raising a foot and resting it on his knee.

"Trench, long time no speak. What's up?"

Trench motioned with his head over to where the constables sat.

"Which one is Barton?"

"I'll show you," said Thomson, starting to get up out of his chair.

"No, don't show me. Just tell me."

"It's no problem, I'll introduce you—"

"Just fucking tell me, will you. I don't want an introduction."

It sounded more forceful than he had intended given his mood, though he had managed to kept his voice down.

Thomson looked at him for a second, as if about to protest. Instead he just tutted, settling for a look that made it clear he thought Trench was an asshole. He nodded toward the constables' seating area.

"Brown hair, spotty face. Red jacket on the back of his chair," he drawled as he sat back down.

He then stared at his screen with much more intent than he had when Trench had first come over.

Trench walked over confidently, but as he approached he wondered if Thomson had stitched him up because he had pissed him off. Still walking toward the seat with the red jacket on it, but far enough that he could change direction if he needed to, he slowed slightly and called out loudly.

"Barton, good morning."

Sure enough the guy with the red jacket turned in his seat.

"Morning, guv. How's it going?"

He wasn't spotty, but had a few freckles. CID could be as mercilessly juvenile as anywhere when it came to blagging colleagues. Probably much more so. It acted as a kind of defence mechanism. You had to have thick skin to survive. If you couldn't take a bit of ribbing from colleagues you had no chance out on the street. Scum smelled weakness. Sniffed it out and used it as a weapon against you.

Barton stood, but Trench motioned for him to stay seated.

"How're you getting on with the databases?"

"I'm just fine tuning the search parameters," replied Barton as he sat down. "I got a bit delayed after the morning briefing."

Trench could see he had the criminal records database open on his screen. The familiar grey screen was one of about fifty thousand access terminals to the police database throughout the UK. It looked like Barton had been making notes on a jotter open beside him. Barton picked up the jotter and referred to it as he spoke.

"But I'm pretty much ready to go now," Barton continued. "I'll make sure not to exclude too much information at this stage, like you said on the phone. I'll come over to you when I have the data."

"Right, sounds good," said Trench. "Can you show me the parameters you're going to use."

He leaned down to have a look at the jotter but couldn't really understand the scribbles Barton had made on it. He was about to ask Barton what it meant, but noticed the look on the constable's face. Trench suddenly had visions of how he himself felt when someone like Lewis tried to micro-manage him.

"You know what, forget it. You've got this, I can see that. Park it for a minute though. We need to get to the incident room for a briefing."

Barton got up and they walked back to the incident room. Jazz was already there. As they sat down, she confirmed she'd delivered the ransom letter to the Lab. A few minutes later, Lewis came into the room, followed by Commander Leroy

Campbell, confirming Trench's earlier suspicions. Lewis sat down beside Trench, leaving the head of the table free.

Campbell stood looking around the room. He kept his face passive, but Trench presumed Campbell was as surprised as he was at the apparent lack of urgency in the investigation. Campbell turned to fully face the whiteboard with the case details on it. The harsh white fluorescent lights glared brightly off the top of his shaven brown skull. Without turning around, Campbell spoke in his ultra-deep, slow drawl. Trench sometimes wondered if he deliberately nurtured the strong Barbadian accent as a kind of fuck you to anyone who still had a problem with his advancement, whatever improvements the McPherson Report had tried to implement.

"Trench, I understand you're in charge. What's the situation?"

He waited for Trench to start speaking before turning around.

"Vanessa Osbourne hasn't been seen since she attended a dinner in central London on Tuesday night. When she failed to show up for an appointment with her Mum on Wednesday morning, her Mum went to her flat because she couldn't get her on the phone. She let herself in, but found no sign of Vanessa. She believes her bed hadn't been slept in. Her Mum then called it in.

"At around half three this morning, a guy on a bicycle and dressed in blacked out gear dropped a ransom note into the letterbox of the parents' house. It's a demand for two million quid. The note gave an email address that the parents should contact to get further instructions.

"We have the guy on camera, but his face is completely covered. The clip has audio though. He says something to himself just before he puts it in the letter box. We can't make out what he says because it's a bit muffled, but we'll get the Lab working on enhancing it. They're also working on the note to see if there's any trace DNA or fingerprints. That's where we're at."

He deliberately kept it high level. He knew from previous experience that Campbell would not want opinion or conjecture unless he asked for it. But all he had asked for was a summary of the situation.

Campbell said nothing and remained standing. After a few seconds Lewis sat back in his seat and turned his head slightly to look at Trench. He hadn't worked with Campbell for long. Trench could tell he was beginning to feel awkward by the silence. But Trench knew from experience this was just how Campbell operated.

He would take as long as he wanted before responding. Trench had never been able to figure out if this was just because he was thinking through what he was going to say, or because he was waiting to see if anyone else felt awkward enough to fill the silence first.

After another few seconds, Lewis turned back to look at Campbell, clearly expecting him to respond to Trench's summary. When he didn't, Lewis cleared his throat, about to say something. Only then did Campbell respond.

"Do you know for sure she attended the dinner?"

Trench realised he didn't know the answer to this. He glanced around, only belatedly realising that Higgins, who had previously been leading the investigation, was not in the room. Instead he turned to Barton and raised his eyebrows. He hoped Barton had been involved from the start.

Barton looked a little taken aback, but then gathered himself.

"Yes sir, I believe that's been confirmed," he said.

He looked like he was about to say something further but thought better of it. He was catching on fast. Trench noted another plus in his favour.

"Believe?" said Campbell.

"The previous investigation lead will have covered that," said Trench stepping in. "And we're just double checking that, but Higgins couldn't make this meeting."

Campbell looked at Trench for a second, then pulled out the chair to sit down. Trench was sure he saw a flicker of smugness as he did so.

"I can confirm it," he said. "I've spoken to some people who were there. She was there until at least midnight. Confirmed."

There it was. He was now formally involving himself in the investigation. Trench had dealt with him enough in the past to know the signal. He wouldn't taint himself by contributing to any plan, but he'd sure as hell be there to front any successful conclusion.

This didn't bother Trench. He wasn't interested in any glory or praise. He'd even welcome Campbell's involvement. It would make things easier if he could use the Commander's name to add some pressure internally. He realised at that moment that he'd also prefer the more hands-off approach of Campbell to the Lewis' recent nit-picking. He looked at Campbell for a moment to see if he wanted to say anything else, but true to form Campbell just looked back at him expectantly.

"Good, thanks," he said. "We're aiming to get statements from some people who attended the dinner to see if we can get a handle on her frame of mind, whether she appeared herself or not—"

"My understanding is that she seemed to be having a great time," said Campbell. "She gave a short speech, danced at some point. Seems she even tried to get the Prime Minister herself onto the dance floor."

No-one said anything for a moment, each probably trying hard not to envisage that particular sight.

"Right, thanks," replied Trench.

The implications began dawning on him as he spoke. It wasn't as if the case was going to need any more high-profile attention, but there could be absolutely no doubt about that now. He began to feel his anger rising again, this time with himself. He hadn't thought clearly enough to realise that a gala dinner for the next generation of Tory leaders would include the current crop – which would include the Prime Minister herself.

Everything about this investigation would be subject to maximum scrutiny. Both internally by the police hierarchy and sooner or later by the media. Ultimately that meant politicians were likely to be sleazing all over it too. Sniffing around for a head to roll, depending on whatever hysterical tabloid headline seemed to have best whipped up the baying crowd that day.

It had become impossible to tell who started this most vicious of circles. The cravenly fickle politicians, shamelessly selling their souls for votes, or the bloodthirsty editors prepared to hack into the phones of dead schoolgirls for a boost in their daily circulation numbers. The fact she may have gone missing after an event attended by the Prime Minister would have them salivating all the more.

Which in turn meant police command would be on high alert. Every decision, every action, would be scrutinised and second guessed by various links along the chain of command. Trench wasn't worried about his own decisions coming under scrutiny. He was confident in his own investigative ability. Any mistakes or errors he made would be for the right reasons.

But he *was* worried about the potential for decision making to be slowed down by senior people meddling. And also about having to waste countless hours completing reports and in meetings to update hordes of people. Lots of cooks were suddenly crowding around the broth.

"She hasn't made contact with either her parents or her boyfriend since then," he said, pushing the thoughts from his mind. "Her boyfriend wasn't at the dinner. He's alibied up as being out in public on the other side of town – in Shoreditch having a few pints – until around midnight."

He didn't look directly at Lewis as he said this because he didn't want to revisit their earlier exchange on the subject. But he did want to make the point that Sheldon was a low priority in the investigation. He turned to Barton.

"Barton, when we're done here can you ask Higgins for the witness statements from the people who attended the dinner. And have him arrange the CCTV footage from that night so we can review it at our next briefing this afternoon. We need a much better understanding of her last known movements. We can assume there's no footage of the actual abduction or he'd have told us that, but we need to know where the last confirmed sighting was. If we're lucky maybe we can identify anyone suspicious in the area around the same time."

Barton nodded. Trench turned to Jazz. He reached into his pocket and took out the datastick.

"And can you work with Linguistics to identify the voice, or even language from this footage."

He handed her the datastick.

"Okay, our immediate priority now is to respond to the ransom note," he continued. "We need to send an email to the kidnapper and we expect he'll reply with details of how he wants the drop to go. We're writing as if we're Vanessa's parents. We have their permission to do so. The key thing is to confirm our willingness to pay. We need to make that absolutely clear to try to minimise the chances of him harming her. Then we'll ask for the instructions. I reckon we leave it at that, keep it brief and simple."

He was thinking of the relatively crude nature of the ransom note. He didn't want to leave any room for confusion in their response. Even more so given his suspicions that the kidnapper was not a native English speaker. Jazz responded first.

"Agreed. What about asking for proof—"

"Hang on, wait a minute," said Lewis, leaning forward and raising one hand in the air. "Shouldn't we be involving the NCA at this point. The AKEU was created especially for cases like this."

The room fell into a stunned silence.

Lewis had directed the question at Trench, but he then turned to look at Campbell. Which suited Trench because he had no intention of responding. It was up to Campbell, as the most senior officer present, to make jurisdictional calls on the investigation. Trench was also reeling in surprise. He couldn't believe what Lewis had just said.

He had pronounced AKEU as '*ah-cue*,' and was referring to the National Crime Agency's specialist Anti Kidnap and Extortion Unit. This had been created to provide, in theory, tactical support to law enforcement agencies to ensure the safe release of hostages and deal with attempts at blackmail or extortion. However, much like the entire NCA itself, in practice things worked very differently.

The NCA had been set up in 2013, yet another totalitarian contrivance of the then-Home Secretary. It was designed to serve nationwide as a parallel police force, but with one key difference to the existing independent constabularies of the UK – its operations and focus could be instructed directly by the Home Secretary.

The obvious suspicion this prompted amongst senior police commanders was hardly helped by the brazen announcement in Parliament by the Home Secretary that the NCA was going to take over the investigation of all 'serious crime' in the country, leaving the existing police force to focus on what was inevitably interpreted as petty crime. Trench could recall the incredulous reaction across the force. Many were incensed, but others just laughed. They knew it was doomed from the start.

And sure enough this breathtakingly sinister intent was undone by the familiar incompetence in translating corrupt ambition into practical planning. A chronic lack of funding created problems for the NCA from the start. Resources as basic as computers and IT systems were regarded as not fit for purpose, suffering black outs and not working for days.

Trench had known former colleagues who joined the agency. They told how this contributed to a collapse in staff morale, already low due to the minister's constant meddling in decision-making. Morale was further damaged by a series of high-profile failures in cases handled by the NCA. These included the agency having to pay £3m to a convict from whom they were trying to seize assets, and failing to act on information about a known paedophile, a hospital consultant later sentenced to

22 years in prison for the offences he committed against patients. This culminated in the early resignation of the agency's first director general, along with nearly half his fellow board members.

The calamitous establishment of the agency inevitably fuelled jurisdictional issues with other police forces right from the start. In addition to the relatively tame territorial and pride issues, were the genuine concerns about the over-eagerness of extremist politicians to control such a fundamental instrument of a free society. These fears were borne out when the powers of the NCA's director general were later enhanced to include the authority to direct the chief officers of other police forces. Which, given the NCA could in turn be directed by the Home Secretary, was a bridge too far for many.

Police commanders therefore retained a healthy wariness of the NCA. Some forces – including the Met – had explicitly pushed back against the agency's encroaching remit. And the suspicions of commanders inevitably filtered down throughout the rank and file. Trench knew that they were hardly allayed by a succession of increasingly extremist Home Secretaries, each more sinister and seemingly venal than the last in the eyes of many of his colleagues. This even included a minister previously fired from office for unauthorised collusion with a foreign government. Or to put it another way, as many observers noted, treason. Trench almost shook his head at the thought, but managed to stop himself.

But he couldn't believe that Lewis had shown such naivety to volunteer to bring the NCA into a Met investigation. And in front of Campbell too. It was a stark reminder that Lewis was still an outsider in the Met. Even the AKEU, which had initially been set up to help UK forces, later had to be restyled as an advisor to international bodies on kidnap and ransom cases instead. UK Police didn't want to be involved with them. There were similar feelings for the rest of the NCA amongst regular police.

Trench recalled the first time he and some colleagues had seen the new agency's logo, when a NCA investigator showed them his warrant card, expecting to impress. It inexplicably included a cartoonish giant panther, claws out, leaping over a silver globe. They had laughed out loud.

But no-one laughed now. No-one said a word for what seemed like a long moment. Lewis turned back to Trench, but Trench stayed looking at Campbell. This was a question he could deal with. Campbell, as always, gave no indication he was going to answer, continuing to study a spot over Trench's shoulder with a furrowed brow, perhaps waiting for Trench to respond. But Trench had played the waiting game with Campbell before. Eventually Campbell lowered his gaze to look at the desk, before glancing up at Lewis.

"I'm sure the agency can provide some worthwhile advice, Chief Superintendent," Campbell said evenly, after what must have been twenty seconds of silence, "So by all means let's tap into that resource, if necessary. But time is of the essence here. We have to make some decisions that cannot wait. We'll proceed here and keep momentum in the investigation moving. If we wish to draw in additional outside resource, then we will. I'll leave the details up to the individuals involved."

By referring to the NCA as 'outside' resource capable only of providing 'advice', Trench thought it was a pretty firm rebuke, but subtle enough to spare Lewis's immediate blushes. He glanced at Lewis, about to continue, but the look on Lewis's face still showed some confusion. He didn't appear entirely ready to let it go. Trench feared it would get really embarrassing if he argued the point.

But after a moment Lewis just sat back in his seat with a slight nod of his head. Trench tried to remember what they had been talking about, but it took him a second.

"So, do we ask for proof of life?" asked Jazz, reminding him.

"No, not yet. We'll keep it simple. When we get the instructions we can go back and ask for that. We don't want to create any confusion or hint of non-compliance in this first communication."

He looked around the table and everyone nodded. They then debated what address should be used to send their response, finally settling on 'Doctor_and _Mrs_Osbourne.' They would set this up with Hotmail. It was the same email service the kidnapper was using and so would reduce the time it would take to be received. Also, police already had a well-established working relationship with Microsoft, the host of this mail service. They would leverage this as needed.

There was one area that Trench was only too happy to hand over at this stage. He didn't want to appear too keen though, so aimed to delicately tee it up so someone else would take responsibility for it, certain who that would be.

"There's one last thing we should discuss. We need to have a PR strategy. Most news channels have it. There's even a few papps outside the Osbournes' house. Doctor Osbourne is calling in his media contacts to keep if off the wires for now, but that won't hold forever. We need to make sure there's one formal line that we're all sticking to when it breaks. We can then brief the Press Office and refer all enquiries to them."

The Press Office was the correct place to route all enquiries, but doing so would limit the scope for anyone else from the investigation to seduce the media limelight. By dangling it out there like this, Trench was inviting someone else to insert themselves into this process. He was not disappointed.

"DCS Lewis," said Campbell, turning to Lewis, "Why don't you lead on briefing the Press Office. The investigating team will need to focus their energy on finding Vanessa."

"Of course, makes sense, sir," said Lewis.

Lewis then waited a brief moment to see if Campbell had anything else to add. When he didn't, Lewis continued.

"No comment for the moment, anyway. We can update—"

"No, they won't buy that," interrupted Campbell, "Let's say we're aware there have been reports and are looking into them appropriately. That'll act as a holder at least. We can then hold a formal update briefing whenever this ransom situation is resolved. But don't progress that before we've had a chance to get together again."

He said the last sentence while looking squarely at Lewis. It therefore wasn't clear whether he meant those in current attendance should get together again, or just himself and Lewis. But Trench figured he knew how that would go. He was more than satisfied with this outcome.

"Okay, we're done," he said. "Let's meet back here this afternoon for a progress report."

"One final thing," said Campbell. "I appreciate she has only been missing for a couple of days, and there may have been some doubt about whether she had just taken off voluntarily. Which presumably explains why we've made such little progress and why there are so few people here this morning. But it's time to start taking this seriously. This ransom demand changes things. Any doubt about why she's missing is gone. I want every available resource assigned to this case immediately. Finding Vanessa Osbourne is top priority now, understood?"

Campbell hadn't looked directly at Lewis but assigning people to a case was squarely his responsibility. Everyone in the room nodded. Campbell then stood up and headed for the door.

“Trench, my number hasn’t changed,” he said without turning around as he left the room.

The rest of them remained seated for a moment. Trench looked at Lewis to see if he wanted to add anything. Instead Lewis stood up, gave a slight nod and then left the room. Trench shared a quick glance with Jazz, but didn’t want to say anything in front of Barton.

Instead he turned to Barton.

“Barton, I want you to stay focused on the database search. I’m going to get more bodies in here from now on, we all heard the Commander. But we need those search results. That’s your priority for now.”

He planned to use Campbell’s name to get other officers assigned to the case, so could spare Barton for the moment.

“And on second thought, forget about speaking to Higgins. I’ll take care of that.”

He would find Higgins himself and instruct him either to handover whatever he had from the dinner guests, or to drop everything and get on with interviewing them. All three of them then left the incident room, with Jazz heading off to bring the datastick to the Linguistics experts.

# Eleven

When Trench got back to his desk he emailed their draft wording of the response to the ransom note to the Cyber Crime Unit. He knew they could use specialist software to attach tracers to the metadata of the email they sent. In addition to generating a read receipt, much more valuable was that this would allow police to trace the IP address to the specific computer accessing the email.

It was possible the kidnapper had software to counter such measures. But judging by the level of sophistication he had shown so far, Trench felt there was a good chance he did not. Immediately after sending the email, he strode down to the Cyber Crime Unit to ensure they gave it maximum priority.

It only took him about fifteen minutes to clarify the situation to the Unit. He knew the senior officer in charge, who assigned a specialist technical support officer called Willard to the task. Trench sat with her for a few minutes as she registered the Hotmail account and prepared the email. After some discussion they used the subject "Response to ransom letter" and hit send. He then hurried back to CID to look for Higgins.

As he passed his own desk he noticed the background light on his phone was on. As he got closer he realised it was vibrating. He reached for it but it stopped before he could pick it up. He saw he had two missed calls. He checked the numbers. One was business, one was either business or pleasure. Or possibly both. He felt a quick pang of guilt looking at the second number, but pushed the thought to one side. He decided to try to find Higgins first and respond to the calls afterwards.

He found Higgins at his desk, where he seemed to spend an awful lot of time for a detective sergeant. His desk was at the far end of the room, beside a window. His seat faced the other way, so he had his back to Trench as he approached. Normally windows were reserved for more senior officers but somehow Higgins had one. Trench's seat was at the end of the aisle furthest from the window. He knew some people cared about such things, but it didn't interest him. It was just a desk, and he didn't spend much time there anyway.

"Higgins," Trench said to his back as he approached.

Higgins was slumped down in his seat, looking at his screen. When he got closer, Trench could see his shoes were off. Higgins turned slightly in his seat. He was quite tall but stout, so it took some manoeuvring as he turned to face Trench, trying to sit up slightly straighter.

"Trench," he said casually, turning back to his screen.

"I need the list of attendees from the Leadership 2030 dinner, key witness statements and copies of all CCTV footage. In fact, just send me the key highlights of the CCTV, from your own review."

Higgins began turning in his seat again, trying to sit up.

"My review of what?"

"Is this the list?" Trench said, picking up a manilla folder that was sitting on his desk.

He opened the folder, noticing a rap sheet alongside a photo of a kid who could be no older than mid-teens.

"What? No, give me that," said Higgins, grabbing for the file as he got to his feet.

He hadn't pushed the chair out far enough, so was standing bent at the knees. Trench moved the file further out of his reach.

"Where's the list? And the CCTV footage?"

"The list isn't complete, alright. And they're still going through the CCTV footage. I'm not on the case anymore, remember? Lewis said you're taking over, so it's on you."

He finally managed to step free of the chair and grabbed the file. He seemed to feel exposed, and tried stepping into his shoes. They had laces, so he had to sit down again to tie them up.

"So what have you done on it? In the *days* since you've been in charge?"

"We took a statement from the parents. And Walker is up there full tim—

"Listen Higgins, stop fucking around. The daughter of one of the wealthiest families in the country is missing. And until now, you've been responsible for finding her. Don't tell me you've been sitting here that whole time. That's not what you've been doing, right Higgins?"

"No, I..."

"Get the list now, okay. Prioritise who on there she knows, who she spent time with on the night. And complete the review of all available CCTV footage from the dinner. Then summarise that to only include footage she's in. Then do the same for the surrounding streets, showing what time, how and with who she left. And if she stopped for a fucking kebab, did she have garlic or chilli sauce on it? Send all of that to me. Do it today, Higgins."

"What about Barton?"

"Today, Higgins. And let me give you a hint. On the list of people she spent time with you'll find the Prime Minister. She fucking danced with her. I know because Commander Campbell told me. He led the briefing on the case this morning. He'll be leading the briefing on it this afternoon. You'll be attending that to provide your update. You can turn up and say you spent forty-eight hours building a case on some juvie fucking shoplifter if you like, but I wouldn't recommend it."

"That's not…I'm not doing that. We didn't even know if she was missing or not. It's been, what, a couple of days?"

Trench walked away, back toward his own desk. When he reached it he sat down and took a moment to let the anger burn off. Or at least some of it. After a moment he picked up his phone to return the calls he'd missed. Krige was the first missed call, so he called him back first. After exchanging brief greetings Krige sounded upbeat.

"Got some good news for you, if you haven't figured this out already," he said. "We've identified the word from the CCTV footage."

Krige then paused, letting it hang there. He had Trench's full attention now. But Trench didn't want to admit police hadn't got that far yet. He couldn't say for sure why. Admitting any form of police shortcomings to outsiders always just felt instinctively wrong. They could bitch and moan amongst themselves internally, but there was an unspoken rule that almost every officer observed. Everything was kept inhouse.

"Right. What do you guys think it is?" said Trench evenly.

"It's Polish," Krige stated enthusiastically, clearly pleased they had figured it out. "Means 'shit', like 'oh shit'. The word is 'gówno'. It's pronounced 'guv-no.' One of our analysts is Polish. She got it straight away."

Trench immediately knew it made sense. The guy dropped the letter, said 'shit' to himself and picked it back up. It also tallied with his earlier suspicion that the ransom note was written by a non-native English speaker.

Trench felt his heart beat pick up, the familiar rush when a piece of the puzzle came more clearly into focus.

"Good. Yeah, it makes sense, doesn't it," he said noncommittally.

No harm if Krige interpreted it that Trench was just hearing him out rather than learning new information.

"Absolutely, mate," replied Krige.

"Have you sent the list of visitors I asked for?"

"Yes mate, sent it after we spoke earlier. Should be in your inbox."

"Okay, thanks, been busy. I'll check that now."

He paused to think whether there was anything else he would need from Krige.

"We might need to come back to you to get further details for some of the guys on there," he said after a moment.

"Ja, anyone Polish, right?" Krige returned with a chuckle. "No problem, mate. We're having a look ourselves too."

This put Trench on alert. He wasn't comfortable with the thought of Krige's team effectively running a parallel investigation. But as he considered it, he realised there wasn't much he could do about it. He understood that if Krige's team got there first, it would be priceless PR for their business. It was a huge incentive.

"Listen, Krige, be careful how you tread with that, okay," he warned.

"Ja, I understand."

"I hope you do. You don't want to be playing around with this."

"Ja, I understand, but...," he paused for a moment, then became more serious himself. "Whether it's true or not, some people are going to think this happened on our watch. That makes it our fault. Reputation is everything in our line of work. We don't advertise on telly, mate, you know. All our business comes from referrals. That means conversations amongst people when we're not in the room. And it doesn't matter that we don't have a detail on Vanessa. When the people that matter ask 'who was doing security for the Osbournes?' The answer they'll get is Imperium Security. We've got to do what we can to get ahead of that, you know what I mean?"

"I know what you mean. And I get that you're going to look into it. That's fair game. I'd do the same if I was in your shoes. But it cuts both ways. If you trace the guy and hunt him down and something goes wrong…if this doesn't turn out the way we all hope it does, and you're associated with that, there's probably no coming back from that, right?"

Krige was silent for a moment. When he spoke again it was without much of his previous enthusiasm.

"Ja, I understand what you're saying. I get that. And look, we're not going to go all Leroy Jenkins on it, I promise you that. But like you said, put yourself in my shoes. I'm not going to bullshit you that we're just going to sit here twiddling our thumbs, you get me?"

Trench did get what he was saying. If the tables were turned and he were in Krige's position, he knew he would be doing everything possible to pursue every lead to find Vanessa. If he then learned of this information, a full riot squad couldn't stop him chasing it down.

"I do," he said. "I'll make a deal with you. You do whatever you need to do. Follow wherever your work leads you. If it leads you to a particular suspect, and you have enough evidence to firmly believe he may be the guy, then you do not engage him. You call me immediately with whatever you've got and I'll bring in the cavalry.

"In exchange, I'll make sure Imperium is front and centre of every bit of media coverage this case gets – and there'll be lots of that. I'll make the Osbourne's fully aware of how integral you've been to the efforts to get their daughter back. And I'll happily endorse Imperium or provide references to whoever you want me to in future."

He was silent for a moment to let Krige think about it. When Krige didn't respond after a few seconds he continued.

"Look, this is the best outcome for you, Krige. What's the alternative? Your crew storms the kidnapper's base, rescues Vanessa and captures the kidnapper? This is the real world, it doesn't work like that. Check the case history of kidnap for ransom. And even if you tried but failed, something goes wrong…it's just not worth thinking about. The downside is a whole lot deeper than the upside."

"Ja, I understand. I agree to your deal." He paused for a second, sounding sombre when he continued. "But there's also the fact we *know* Vanessa. Some of my guys are pretty close to her. We're hurting, man, you know what I mean."

"Yeah, I hear you. But that's all the more reason to step off if things start getting hot. Believe me, the last place in the world you want to be is making a life-or-death decision with a head full of burning rage. That never ends well. For anyone."

Krige didn't say anything for a long moment. Trench was glad he was taking the time to let it sink in. He had no doubt that if Krige pursued his investigation, he could potentially end up facing some split-second, life changing decisions – either his own or someone else's. He took it as a good sign that he was giving it some serious consideration.

"Let's stay in touch, okay," he said after a while. "On any significant developments or leads. That goes both ways. I'll keep you posted as much as I reasonably can."

"Ja, okay, mate. Thanks. And good luck – to us both."

When he hung up, Trench immediately accessed his email. The email from Krige had arrived over an hour ago. When he opened the attachment he could see it was a download from the system Krige had shown them at Blenheim.

There were one hundred and fifty-three names on the list. At first glance, less than half seemed to be English names. At least thirty or forty looked Eastern European. He highlighted these then emailed Jazz a copy. He included a couple of sentences explaining that he'd take the first half of the list, which turned out to be eighteen names, while Jazz could take the second eighteen.

They would check each name against police or DVLA databases to get their address. They would then visit each, starting with those who had a criminal record. Trench planned to use Campbell's name to enlist as many constables as possible to help with the visits. He intended to go over to DS Thomson again to relay this as an order as soon as they were done.

Just then, Jazz returned to her seat.

"I spoke with Krige," he said, "I've just sent you the list of visitors to Blenheim. Even better, the guy from the camera—"

He was cut short by the sound of his phone vibrating. He looked at the screen and realised he had forgotten to return the second call he had missed that morning. She was calling again. He thought for a brief moment and then decided to answer it.

But he didn't want to take the call in the middle of the squad room. He got to his feet and started walking as he answered.

"Back in a sec," he said to Jazz before hitting the answer button on the phone.

"Hey, was just about to call you back," he said as he answered.

"Yeah, sure Trench. And you're just coming out of the florist, right?" said Nadia Swanson.

He headed toward the privacy booths but they were both occupied. Instead, he exited the squad room.

"Hang on a sec," he said, bounding down the steps.

"Of course! What's another few seconds after all this time…"

On ground floor he left the station and stepped onto Agar street. He took a right and headed for the Strand. Much greater privacy given how busy it would be. He started wandering slowly along the Strand as he spoke.

"Hi, sorry about that. How've you been?" he asked.

He'd been expecting the call. Actually, he had intended to call her himself, but hadn't quite gotten around to it, for indeterminable reasons.

He'd met Swanson for dinner a couple of weeks before. She'd asked him a few times and he'd finally agreed. She'd picked the place – Hakkasan, the first Chinese restaurant in Britain to receive a Michelin star. It was a cut above the typical restaurant that a reporter and a cop would meet.

He'd had a really enjoyable time. She was great company. Witty and smart, she also had a good understanding of the nature of police work. What it did to those involved. The murky depths of humanity they were obliged to trawl. Even did a bit of trawling herself, as the crime correspondent for London's leading newspaper.

She had also looked stunning in a shoulderless black dress, which stopped little more than halfway down her thighs. With her dark hair pulled back tightly from her face and tied up high in a pony tail, and her lips shining a much darker shade of red than he had seen on her before, they'd spent almost no time talking shop.

After dinner they'd gone to the chic Experimental Cocktail Club in nearby Soho. Trench could remember thinking that he was having as good a time as he could recall on a date. But then thinking he wasn't even sure if it was a date or not. And then she had kissed him. And he had kissed her back. And for that moment his mind was completely free of any thoughts at all. Afterwards they'd smiled, then laughed and carried on having a good time.

Soon though, Trench began to feel the usual doubts. He couldn't say exactly why, but it didn't feel right. She was a reporter, and police needed to be careful interacting with reporters. Especially following the Levenson inquiry into phone hacking and journalists' bribing of police. She was also younger than him. Plus maybe he wasn't ready, it could get complicated…

Shortly afterwards he had rather abruptly excused himself and said he had to get home, citing an early start the next morning. She looked at first a little shocked, then disappointed. Then as he walked her to the Tube she seemed annoyed. From him suddenly saying he had to go when they were seemingly having a great time, to then departing at the Tube was probably no more than fifteen minutes. After having had such a good time for the previous few hours, it was understandable she would be pissed off.

He could understand it when he thought about it later. When he had realised he had over thought the whole thing, as he seemed to have gotten into the habit of doing. It wasn't as if they were about to get married.

But that was a couple of weeks ago, and he'd never gotten around to calling her.

"No problem, no need to be sorry," she said playfully. "Or at least, not for making me wait on the phone for a couple of seconds…"

"Uh, yeah, I've—"

"Anyway, the reason I'm calling is that I've been chatting with the grapevine. Everyone knows VanOz is missing," she said, Trench now realising this was a business call, "But I'm hearing that you've found a body, down in Kent. That's not something everyone knows. Yet."

"Right," said Trench, thinking.

It was always going to get out, and he knew trying to control the press was like trying to catch smoke with a net. He was rapidly considering implications of these facts getting out, on either case. He couldn't immediately think of any specific reason to try to stop it. But his police instincts were always wary of how the press would spin the facts.

"Any comment, on or off the record?"

"Nadia, that's not a story. Not the same story anyway. It wouldn't be right to draw any conclusions."

He was trying to be as blunt as he could without declaring that it wasn't Vanessa Osbourne's body. He couldn't do that in case the press identified the body before the police did, and the victims' family ended up finding out about it that way. That was the worst-case scenario when it came to finding dead bodies.

"Really? She goes missing and then police find a murdered woman in the woods? Quite the coincidence…"

Trench stiffened. How did she know it was a woman? And murdered? He stopped walking.

"What do you mean?" was all he managed.

"I mean it's a pretty big coincidence, wouldn't you say? Have you formally identified the murdered woman? Are you absolutely certain it's not Osbourne?"

Trench felt foolish. Of course she would have other sources. But it caught him off guard that she may have other sources so close to his own squad. And so close to this early-stage investigation that she knew so much already. Then he started thinking maybe she took other people out to dinner too. Maybe it was just part of the gig. It began to cloud his thinking, and then he started getting angry. Not that she would do that. That was entirely fair game, given her role. But angry that he had felt bad, and for thinking that maybe it was something that it obviously wasn't.

"No, it isn't. I mean, yes, it's a pretty big coincidence. A young woman has gone missing – may be gone missing," he corrected himself, "People are saying she might be missing, and then some time after that police may have found a body in a different county. Hardly the biggest coincidence ever."

"Really, Trench? You'd tell me if they were connected, right? I mean, it sure *seems* like a major coincidence…" she sounded a little like she was teasing now.

"Look," he asserted, "You want a coincidence? Write about Violet Jessop. She got a job working for White Star Line, okay. She started on the Olympic, but it crashed into another boat, so she had to go and work on their other ship. And that fucker sank too, hit an ice-berg out in the North Atlantic. You've probably heard the story. She survived though. So again, they sent her to work on yet another ship, the Britannic. And guess what happened to that? Yep, you got it. It sank. Mined by a German U-Boat. And Violet? Died of old age in the nineteen seventies. She was on all three of White Star Line's sunken ships and survived them all. You want to write about a coincidence, you won't get better than that."

"Ehm, ohhhkaaay…," she stammered

"I've got to get back, there's a lot going on."

"Yes, you sure seem busy. Well, maybe give me a call if there's any developments. Or if, you know, you want to…"

"Okay, bye."

He hung up.

He stood there for a moment, gathering his thoughts. He wondered whether the tension in the day had gotten to him and made him overreact. But he didn't feel tense. And he did feel foolish for thinking the dinner might have been something more than—

Someone abruptly put their hand on his shoulder. He gave a start and made a grab for the hand, but then realised he was blocking the door of a Pret-a-Manger. It broke his train of thought so he began walking back toward the station, deciding not to think about the call.

He hurried back into the station and ran up to the CID room. Jazz was still at her desk. He could see she had the list open on her screen.

"The press knows about the body in Kent," he said as he sat down. "They're already linking it to Vanessa Osbourne."

"Not sure it matters, does it?" she didn't look up from her screen. "It's not her, so they can say whatever they want. We can't control it anyway."

Trench turned back to his screen. She was right. The press would run with whatever version of the story they felt would sell the most papers or generate the most clicks. As far as Trench could tell, half the press barely even bothered to pretend they checked facts anymore anyway. They were too busy trying to compete for the public's attention with the faceless keyboard warriors using two hundred and eighty characters to decree on world affairs.

That was probably harsh on Nadia Swanson, he knew, given her reputation for earnest reporting on the London crime scene. But either way, the pressure from greater public awareness of the story was always going to be inevitable.

"Anyway," said Jazz. "You know that one Nadia Swanson? She has a cousin working in the mortuary, I believe. She's bound to hear we've picked up a body. I expect she'll be fishing pretty soon. Though I'm betting she calls you rather than me."

Trench just looked at her.

"Jesus," he muttered.

"Don't say you haven't noticed, Trench," goaded Jazz. "Even you couldn't miss her signals. All the subtlety of a scud missile, that one."

Trench groaned to himself and turned back to his screen. He knew he had probably just ruined any chance of recovering from the last chance he had ruined with Nadia. He didn't want to think about it.

He suddenly remembered that he hadn't told Jazz about the kidnapper being Polish. He was just about to when her phone rang. He thought it could be Linguistics, so he spoke before she picked it up.

"He's Polish."

"What?" she looked at him confusedly as she picked up the phone.

"The kidnapper," he said leaning in toward her, "Polish."

"Hello," Jazz answered. "That was quick," she said into the phone.

Then she turned to look suspiciously at Trench while the person on the phone continued talking. Trench turned back to his own screen.

"I see, thanks a lot. Shit? Yeah, makes sense. Okay, thanks."

She hung up the phone and was about to confront Trench, but his own phone rang. He looked at the caller ID while picking it up.

"Willard," he said, "You got something?"

He listened for a couple of seconds, then stood up as he hung up the phone. He turned to Jazz.

"Speak of the devil."

# Twelve

"What've we got?" asked Trench as they arrived at Willard's desk.

Willard turned her monitor slightly and they both leaned in to read the response.

"That's it?" said Jazz.

The email said: *Confirm the money is possible to deliver tonight? Then you will get more instructions.*

"He's not looking for a pen pal anyway," said Willard.

She flipped into a different programme before they could ask the question.

"And here's the trace. The IP number is showing up at this address. It's Stroud Green Road. That's Finsbury Park area."

"Does it give the exact address?" he asked.

"Yep," replied Willard. She pointed at her screen. "There. Number Two-hundred and seventeen."

"What is it? Can you check," he asked urgently, hoping it was a private residence.

He knew the area. Stroud Green Road was a mix of residential properties and retail outlets like shops and cafes.

"It's showing as Ali Rafiq and Sons Limited. Doesn't say what exactly the business is," said Willard.

"Let's go," he said to Jazz.

They ran out to the car, flipping the blues and twos before they'd cleared the station gates. They immediately got snagged in traffic around the tourist hotspot of Leicester Square. The thin roads and crowded footpaths meant they just had to accept making whatever progress they could until they cleared the area.

As they drove, Jazz put a call in to the station to request a CSI team meet them at the location. She then called DS Thomson and ordered him to also send a constable to meet them. Before she hung up, Trench remembered Krige's list. He hadn't had the chance to tell Thomson to get some of the constables working on it. He told

Jazz to tell Thomson they would be emailing him the list, and to have all of the names checked out. When Jazz had done so she hung up and immediately accessed her email inbox on her phone to forward the list to Thomson.

Trench banged the steering wheel.

"Shit," he said. "We should've responded to the email. Call Willard, tell her to respond. Just say that yes, we can confirm we will have the money tonight and please send the instructions. It might keep the guy there, if he hasn't already left."

"Can we have the money tonight?" said Jazz.

"Don't know, but we can back track later," said Trench. "It's worth it if it'll keep him there until we get there."

Jazz called Willard and dictated the response but then asked Willard to hold for a second. She turned to Trench.

"What about proof of life? Are we asking for that now? We decided not to, right?"

"No, we can do that after we get the instructions. Right now we just need to keep him there."

"Got it," said Willard, without Jazz having to relay. She held on the line, and a few seconds later said, "Okay, I'm hitting send in three, two, one….Sent."

Jazz killed the call.

A few minutes later they turned onto Stroud Green Road. It was jammed with people. They scanned the buildings for numbers. Like most streets in London, only every fourth or fifth property displayed the number. They eventually clocked it and Trench turned right.

People criss-crossed the road at various places, seemingly oblivious to traffic. Only when their car, blue lights flashing and siren wailing, was right upon them did people turn around. There was no surprise on the faces, no concern. There wasn't even interest. The most common reaction seemed to be annoyance that people had to make way.

Trench kept both eyes on the road but was trying to glance around to see street numbers. Jazz was leaning half out the window doing the same.

"One seventy-nine," she said, pointing to the left. Then, "One ninety-five, slow down."

Trench slowed down.

"What was the name again? Ali something?" she said looking at each of the properties.

"Ali Rafiq and Sons," said Trench. "Could be any of these."

None of the shops gave a hint that they might be registered under the name Ali. None of them had numbers either.

The next number they saw was two hundred twenty-five.

"Shit," they said in unison.

Trench immediately jerked the car to the side of the road. It would be quicker to get out than to turn around. Jazz jumped out before the car had fully stopped. She ran back toward the shops. After parking up on the path, Trench jumped out and ran to catch up with her.

The first shop they passed was a dry cleaner. Barely slowing her run, Jazz pointed to the name written across the front window and ran inside. The name was written in an off-white colour, against a yellow background. Trench realised her mistake. It was called '*All Right All White!*' but at running pace it was easy to read the 'All' as 'Ali'.

"Not that one," he yelled to Jazz before the door closed.

She looked around questioningly but came back out. She half pointed at the name, glancing at it before realising her mistake.

"Bloody hell," she exclaimed as she followed Trench.

There was a residence next to the dry cleaner, then a few shops. The first was a café. It was small, with a full windowed front. They stopped running for a second and looked in through the window. The only people they could see inside were two young mothers with prams and an old woman, staring back at them.

"No," called Jazz, and kept moving.

The next was a typical corner store, with numerous flashing neon signs, saying "Phone unlock" and "Off Licence – Best Prices!" Trench saw that the next shop was a hairdresser, clearly for women judging by the interior. But as he ran past the door to the corner store he spotted a small handwritten sign in the window saying 'INTERNET.'

"Here!" he shouted, stopping dead and turning toward the entrance.

Jazz nearly ran into the back of him. He pointed at the sign as he ran inside.

An elderly man was perched on a stool behind the counter. He jolted as they burst in, spinning around to take in their surroundings. The tiny shop was crammed. Two aisles were packed full of canned food, bread and other staples. Fridges ran the full length of the back wall, plastered with brightly coloured signs declaring cut price beer.

The man stood up and hollered.

"What you want?"

"Police," said Trench, striding toward him. "Where is the internet?"

He scanned around as he spoke. He spotted a small doorway halfway down the shop. He could see stairs inside the doorway. Trench pointed and they rushed toward it. They bounded up the stairs, emerging into a room laid out like hundreds of other internet cafes throughout the capital. Each workspace had a computer screen, keyboard and mouse. Two of the units were occupied. Both the occupiers looked up as they clambered into the room.

Trench immediately felt a pang of disappointment. Neither struck him as the person they were looking for. One was a teenage girl no older than fifteen. She wore a thick jacket with a fluffy hood. Trench could see what he took to be a school uniform underneath it. She had a shocked look on her face, which quickly morphed into guilt. She tried looking back at her screen, but couldn't help glancing back at them expectantly.

The man sitting at the other unit was so large he had trouble turning his head to look at the new arrivals. He wore a scruffy red baseball cap pulled low on his head. His woollen jumper looked more like a threadbare carpet from a 1970's pub. It had a hole in it big enough to let a flabby, pasty elbow hang loose. He could have been any age from twenty to fifty.

Trench turned to Jazz, who looked similarly disappointed.

"Can you check these out," said Trench as he moved back to the stairs. "I'll go see if they have CCTV."

He glanced around at the ceiling of the room as he spoke but didn't see any cameras. He clambered back down the stairs. The old man was at the bottom of the stairs.

"We are police," said Trench calmly, to dispel any lingering doubts the man had. "Do you have any security cameras here?"

"Security?" said the man, looking confused. "Internet? You want internet, no?"

"No, we don't want internet. Do you have any security cameras in this shop?"

He pointed at the ceiling as he spoke, looking around inquisitively. The man followed his line of sight but only grew more confused. The man held up a finger to Trench and went over to a phone beside the till. After a conversation that lasted no more than five seconds in a language Trench couldn't place, he turned back and gave a quick nod.

"You wait please."

Trench could hear Jazz speaking to the fat man upstairs. She was using a soothing tone, giving good cop a go. He could just about hear some indecipherable grunts from the man in response.

After a minute or two, a young Asian man came hurriedly into the shop. Trench assumed he was the shop owner's son.

"Y'alright, mate? How can I help?" said the young man in a thick London accent.

"Thank you. We're Met Police. We believe a person of interest has been using your internet café. Do you have CCTV covering your shop? It's extremely urgent."

"Nah, sorry we don't. We used to but they broke."

"Have you or your father been here all day?"

"My Dad's been here since we opened. I've not been in today yet."

"Someone was in here within the last hour. They sent an email from one of your computers. Can you ask your Dad if he remembers who has been here so far today."

The man was already talking to his son, who now spoke over him in an angry tone. After a brief exchange, he turned back to Trench.

"He says a few people were in earlier. Mostly schoolgirls, init. They usually come in before school. Sometimes they stay all day."

"Who else?"

The son spoke again with his Dad. This time the exchange was slightly longer.

"Mostly schoolgirls," he repeated, "Only a few others. Older guys. He said one might still be here."

"What did they look like? Not including the man who's up there now," said Trench.

He wasn't sure what he was expecting their suspect to look like, but hoped he'd know if he heard it. There was another exchange between father and son, this time longer. The son began waving his hands, the man making exaggerated facial expressions of trying to recall. Eventually the son turned back to Trench.

"The only others he can remember was a guy in a postman's uniform and another guy in builder's clothes. Dirty jeans and boots."

"The builder. Did he speak with him?"

The son replied after another quick exchange with his father.

"Not really. He paid for an hour and bought cigarettes."

"Can you describe him? Age, hair colour, any accent if he could tell."

The man appeared strained as he spoke with his son. They both kept looking at Trench as they spoke. A few minutes later the son turned back to Trench.

"He's not able to say his age. I asked if he was older or younger than you and he said he'd guess younger. Shorter too, and much lighter hair colour, though definitely not blond. He paid for an hour but only stayed a few minutes. That was about an hour ago."

Both the description and the timelines fit.

"One last thing, did he speak with an accent?"

"Sorry, yeah I did ask him that. My Dad's not sure, but thinks he was Eastern European. He didn't say much but just from experience, init. He bought rollies, not regular cigarettes. That's common for them."

It wasn't much to go on but it was the best they had. Trench thanked them both and then said they'd have to close the internet café for the rest of the day at least. He turned to go back up to Jazz but the son called out after him.

"Police, one more thing. He thinks he was on a bike. He thinks he locked his bike to the tree outside. When he was leaving he shouted something. My Dad looked up and he thinks he was shouting at a dog who was pissing on the tree. He went over to the bike after."

"Okay, thanks again. Some of our colleagues are on the way. Just make sure no-one else goes upstairs again. That includes both of you."

He started heading back upstairs, but had to stop and step out of the way as the teenage girl came barrelling down the steps. She kept her head down as she practically ran out of the shop, pulling her hood up as she stepped outside.

Trench could hear that Jazz's good cop routine hadn't lasted long. As he stepped back into the room he could see that the fat man had barely moved. Jazz turned to Trench and rolled her eyes. She shook her head to indicate she didn't think he was involved. Just a pain in the ass.

"Says he only just got here. He hasn't seen anyone else. Says he thought he was alone in here until we got here and he noticed the other girl. She didn't see anyone else either."

She then turned back to the man.

"Final warning. Thirty seconds, or you're spending the night in jail."

The man grumbled something unintelligible under his breath, but he started to move. Trench relayed his conversation with the shop owner and his son to Jazz. He then glanced around the room. It looked like it hadn't been cleaned for months. It would be painstaking for CSI but Trench still wanted to try for prints. He figured the kidnapper was less likely to have used gloves here, if it turned out he had been cautious with the ransom note itself. It was at least a back-up in case the Lab got nothing from the note.

"Let's check with the other shops around here to see if any of them have CCTV," he said. "You take this side of the street, I'll start across the road."

Trench checked all the premises that could have had a view of the shop with no luck. He spotted one camera facing prominently onto the street, covering the door to a private residence. But when he knocked on the door the owner said it was for deterrent only. It had stopped working years ago. After ten minutes, he met Jazz back outside the internet store.

"Anything?" he said.

"Nada. The few places that have cameras say they're either not working or only cover inside."

"Shit. Same on that side. He's got to be on some cameras round here."

He looked up and down the street again, checking whether he'd missed any cameras. As he did so, he spotted the CSI vehicle. He walked out into the road and began waving his arms at them. When they pulled up, Trench lead them inside and briefed them on the situation. They looked less than impressed when they saw the state of the room. They even tried to suggest it was useless, given the huge number of fingerprints they were likely get and the time it would take. But Trench insisted they stop moaning and get on with it.

The row didn't help his souring mood. The energy he'd felt on the dash to the shop had turned to frustration, anger not far off. They'd missed the kidnapper. And not by a little. He was long gone by the time they'd gotten there.

As the CSI team began their work in a quiet huff, Trench and Jazz waited outside the shop for the constable to arrive. It started raining. At first a light drizzle, but soon the heavens opened. They stepped back inside the shop to shelter. The old man didn't look happy that they were blocking the door, but their facial expressions dissuaded him from saying so. They stood mostly in silence while they waited.

Trench was mulling their next move. It was possible the kidnapper would return, but if he had half a brain then he wouldn't use the same internet café for the next communication. Even if this one was close to where he lived, there would be another few dozen within easy cycling distance. But they had to stake it out anyway. The constable's afternoon was not likely to be an exciting one.

Trench felt deflated. He knew it had been a long shot the kidnapper would still be at the internet shop when they found it, but he was still frustrated they had missed him. They were only going to get a limited number of chances to catch him, he knew. And if he had hung around the area, and was even right now watching them, then he'd know they could trace his emails.

That thought prompted him to step out of the shop, into the rain, and just glare up and down the street. It was a futile effort – there were hundreds of people milling about – but he couldn't contain the instinct. He hated just standing there, doing nothing. Waiting. He always hated waiting.

A few minutes later he saw a squad car emerge onto the street from the same way they had come. It paused for a moment, then sped towards them, jamming on the brakes as the constable spotted them on the side of the road. The young officer jumped out and ran over to them expectantly. Only when he saw their calm demeanour did he twig his arrival was not as urgent as he seemed to think. His look turned quizzical.

"What's the story?" he asked breathlessly.

"What's your name, son?"

"Peters," replied the constable.

"Right, Peters. This shop here," Trench pointed at the shop. "Anyone comes in here looking to use the internet café upstairs, you get their details and send them away. Except if it's an Eastern European male, possibly in builder's clothes. If it's him, hold him here and give me a call."

Trench handed him his card. Peters took it, realisation dawning that his afternoon was not going to be thrilling. He glanced over Trench's shoulder at the shop.

"And move your car," Trench said. "Park it somewhere out of sight. We don't want to scare him off if he comes back."

Peters started looking around. There was nowhere nearby to move the car so it would be out of sight. He'd probably have to go back around the corner, at the nearest. He looked back at Trench.

"You're our man here until further notice," said Trench, walking back toward their own car.

"Just wait?" Peters asked after him.

"Ninety per cent of police work is waiting, Constable. Surely you've figured that out by now."

"What do I do if he runs for it?" asked Peters exasperated.

Trench stopped and turned.

"You fucking chase him, Peters. You run after the bad guy. That's the other ten per cent."

# Thirteen

"Now what?" asked Jazz.

"We check out her flat. It's not too far from here," said Trench, starting the ignition.

"Right. I'll call Willard and tell her to call us immediately if she receives another email from him."

Trench flipped the lights and sirens, determined to get there as soon as possible despite the now heavy downpour. When she finished the call, Jazz turned the radio on to check whether the story was being given greater prominence on the news stations. There was no mention of it as she flicked between stations. It wasn't main news yet. She also checked her phone.

"Still the same story," she said. "Just 'rumoured to be missing'. No word about a ransom demand anywhere I can see."

"They'll have it soon enough," said Trench grimly.

They followed Camden Road and made it to the neighbourhood in a little under ten minutes. Trench killed the lights and siren as they turned off Camden Road. These were mostly residential streets and he didn't want to cause a commotion or draw unwanted attention. Especially from any paparazzi skulking around, hoping to find a sleazy nugget to pawn off to some unscrupulous editor, despite Doctor Osbourne's attempts to lobby his media contacts.

As they neared the address Trench realised they were close to the home of another young London woman who had been constantly ravaged by the gutter press, the tragic Amy Winehouse. He tried to dispel thoughts of a tragic, premature end to a young woman in her prime as he pulled up to the kerb.

Scoping around, Trench could just make out the silhouettes of two figures sitting in a parked car about twenty yards away, on the opposite side of the road.

"More papps," he said, jerking his head in their direction. "Let's get inside quickly."

He fished the keys Doctor Osbourne had given him out of his pocket. They both slipped on latex gloves, got out of the car and walked swiftly up the concrete steps to the front door. When they got there they realised that the whole building was a single three-storey house, not flats. As they stepped inside Trench called out a loud 'Hello, Police!' He wasn't expecting an answer, but he always called out when entering someone's home unannounced. You never knew who could be inside, friend or foe.

There was no response. They stepped into a long entrance hall and shut the door. They first checked a door to their left, which opened into a large, stately-looking sitting room.

"What age is she again?" he said.

"Maybe her granny helped with the decorating," said Jazz.

"Slightly different décor to the usual post-Uni unemployed digs, alright," replied Trench. "The furniture looks like it's barely out of the showroom."

He turned and walked over to large bay windows and looked out at the street below. From the raised vantage point, he could see all the way into the small green across the road. Which meant someone across the road or in the green could see into this room, if they were using the right lens.

"Probably is little more than a showroom," he said, turning back and heading toward the door, intent on exploring what was more likely to be the real living quarters.

They found a much more relaxed looking living room at the back to the house. Lustrous furniture was matched by huge bright paintings and artworks on most walls.

"Think that's a Damien Hirst," said Jazz pointing at one. "Probably an original."

"A what?" said Trench distractedly, scanning the room.

Jazz knew it would be wasted effort to explain so didn't respond.

"That's where she does her Instagram videos," she said instead, walking toward a huge-screened Apple iMac set up in front of another large, brightly coloured painting, which she then studied. "And this is a Keith Haring."

When Trench glanced over he thought the unremarkable painting simply showed match-stick men dancing. He went over to a silver ice bucket in a stand. It had an open bottle of champagne sitting in what was now just water.

Trench picked up the bottle.

"Quarter full," he said.

"Warm up drinks before heading off to the gala dinner," replied Jazz.

"My kind of woman if she can down three quarters of a bottle of champagne before dinner," he said, looking around for used glasses.

He didn't see any. He spotted a small coffee table placed near the middle one of the sofas in the room.

"Funny place for a coffee table," he said, crouching down to examine the top of the table.

Compared to the other furniture in the room, it was well-worn, with numerous scratches and a couple of glass ring stains on it. But he didn't find what he was looking for.

"You don't think a bottle of champagne was enough of an aperitif?" asked Jazz, realising what he was looking for.

"You never know," he said, standing up. "But there's nothing on there."

"Sheldon did say she's a party girl, but he didn't mention she's a baker," said Jazz, before adding, "Though he's hardly going to just volunteer that to police, I suppose."

"We need to clarify that with him."

"Maybe she wanted to keep on partying after the dinner," ventured Jazz. "Went off to find her dealer. Then he decided he could make more from her than just a few grams of coke."

"Possible. If that's what's happened then we're going to get sucked down the usual rabbit hole of liars and skivers. Her friends won't know whether to give us names or try to protect them."

"Especially when they're all early twenties and just out of Uni," groaned Jazz.

They walked back to the stairs in the hall and decided to check downstairs first. The stairs opened into a large open plan kitchen-diner, that ran the whole length of the property.

"Three people had champagne," said Trench from the sink.

As well as three used champagne flutes, there was also a small silver tray, about the size of a paperback novel. It had ornate handles on either side and its surface was perfectly smooth. He carefully picked it up by the handles using both hands. He held it up to the daylight coming in from the window in front of the sink.

"Maybe she is a baker after all," he said as he tilted the tray either way, holding it right in front of his eyes.

"Traces on it?" said Jazz, walking over.

Trench handed her the tray to look for herself.

"I don't think so. Looks like it's been rinsed, same as the glasses," he nodded with his head into the sink. "But it's the only other dish that's been used."

"We can find out for sure when we identify who else was here for pre-dinner drinks," said Jazz.

"That's a priority for the briefing this afternoon. I'm assigning a team to find out who was here. As soon as we know, we sweat them hard until we get the name of anyone she could be buying off."

On the first floor they found a bathroom and a guest bedroom. Another door toward the front of the house was ajar. When they pushed it, it wouldn't open completely. Something was blocking it, but it opened enough for them to squeeze inside. The room was messy compared to the rest of the house. They could see that what was blocking the door was one of two clothes racks that ran the width of the room. Both were full of brightly coloured dresses, skirts, tops, trousers, jackets and coats. The floor in front of both racks was piled with shoes, many still in boxes.

"Sheeee-it," mumbled Jazz. "Well-jel right now, I admit it."

She walked over to the clothes rack on the opposite wall and flicked through some of the outfits.

"Hmm, she's about my size too. This stuff would look much better on me, don't you think?" she said as she bent down and opened a shoe box that said Kurt Geiger on it.

"Not sure," replied Trench, "Looks like young women's clothes to me."

"Fuck you," she crowed, standing back up. "Most of these things still have the labels on," she added, as she looked around the room.

Trench moved over to the corner by the window, where an old-style, dark mahogany bureau caught his attention. He opened it and found a series of compartments and a couple of miniature drawers. Most compartments were full with assorted jewellery. There were also some hair bobbins and scrunchies tossed in the drawers.

He opened two miniature drawers using just a thumb and forefinger on each because the knobs were so small. The one on the left contained Vanessa Osbourne's passport, driver's license and a few student IDs. A couple of the student IDs were lying with the photo facing upwards. He picked them up for a closer look.

The first one he looked at was from her first year in university. She looked glamorous, made-up. Her hair was done differently, looking more golden than brown. Her lips were pursed in what might have been a pout, as most women seemed to do nowadays, for reasons that were lost on most men. But it was only a half-pout, because it looked like she was about to burst out laughing. There were pronounced smile lines around her eyes. No doubt joking around with some unseen friend as they got their pictures taken during their first days at Uni.

All in all, he thought as he studied the photo, she looked full of life. Like any teenager about to start university. Her face showed an excitement, an eagerness to embark on what people tell freshmen are the greatest years of their lives. She'd probably gotten a make-over especially for the occasion. She showed more character and personality than in any photo he'd seen of her so far. Certainly more than the one pinned to a whiteboard in Charing Cross Police Station, stark against the blunt details of what might have been her last hours alive.

He flicked to the next card, which was from her final year. Although there was less excitement in her face and she wore less make up, she looked just as contented. No pout, just a simple smile. Her eyes were warm and the impression was of someone happy in her own skin. Confidence oozed from her face. The freshman excitement was replaced by the final-year student's accomplished self-assuredness. Those few short years could bestow a wealth of education on the receptive learner, only some fraction of which was academic.

He flipped through the photo pages in each of the other documents, his mind wandering to consider just how much a person grows up during these particular years. In Vanessa's case, as one of the wealthiest heiresses in the country, how much growing up would she need to do to navigate the various challenges and temptations before her? She had options, certainly more than most. Doctor

Osbourne had said as much. He was willing to either give her a job at his company or to have a quiet word with a well-connected contact. And Trench imagined his contacts would be very well connected indeed.

But instead it sounded like she was being tempted into the celebrity lifestyle. A culture with an insatiable appetite for creating a continuous stream of stars and public icons, mostly so they could chew them up and spit them out a short time later. Where being the child of a wealthy family was enough to secure a contract so that you got paid just to turn up at high-society events. Where your birthright meant you were your own brand before you even knew it.

But other people knew it. Faceless promoters and slippery agents with a skill in nothing more than self-proclaimed gumption would seek you out. Promise to make you popular, relevant, feted even. You just had to sign here, so that they got their slice.

How real a world is it for her? Who can you rely on? Who do you tell your secrets to? And what kind of enemies can you make? As he flicked through the photos he felt a pang that they were still struggling to find out who she really is. If she was drifting away from her boyfriend of three years, then who was she drifting towards?

The time warp shown in the pictures jarred with Trench. From schoolgirl, to student, to young woman, to Met police searching your home for evidence to explain your disappearance. He flashed back to the look in Mrs Osbourne's eyes earlier that morning. He felt his jaw clenching. She was still so young, still just a child. He felt a wave of urgent determination. He would stop at nothing to find her.

"She's handsome," said Jazz, who had come over and was now peering over his shoulder. "Not sure I'd call her pretty. Doesn't quite fit."

The comment snapped Trench out of his train of thought. He nodded. It was the right word, though he knew it would be impossible to try to articulate what made some women pretty and some handsome.

"I'm heading upstairs, her bedroom's got to be up there. You coming?" she asked.

Trench began putting the documents and ID cards back into the drawer and glanced at the other drawer he had opened. He could see it contained paperwork, judging by the credit card statement on top.

"No, go ahead," he replied without looking up. "I'll finish looking through here. Be up in a sec."

As Jazz left, he reached in and took out all the paperwork in the small drawer. The monthly credit card statements ran into five figures and were paid off in full by direct debit each month. The next half dozen documents related to sponsorship of various charities. They included Cancer Research, numerous children's charities, Battersea Dogs & Cats Home and a few other animal welfare groups. The donation amounts were substantial. Vanessa Osbourne was as generous to charity as she was prolific with retailers.

The next letter in the stack was from Foxton's estate agents. It was addressed to Vanessa, but before he read any further he was distracted by the fact the letter was stapled in the top left corner. He immediately flipped the page.

The document to which the letter was stapled was a tenancy agreement. Trench scanned the first page. The landlord was named as Noble Realms Properties Limited. The tenant was given as Vanessa Osbourne. This immediately struck Trench as odd. He had assumed that Vanessa, or the Osbourne family at least, owned the house. He flipped back to the letter and read it.

It was generic, simply stating they were enclosing Vanessa's copy of the tenancy agreement. Trench flipped back to the agreement, looking for the address it related to. On page two he saw that the rent was £3,000 per calendar month. Further down the page he found the address: Flat 4, 14 Lewisham Street, SW1.

Trench felt a burst of adrenaline.

He couldn't picture the precise street but knew by the postcode it would be in either Westminster or the West End. He rapidly flipped through the pages of the agreement, looking for the date. He found the signatures on the final page. The agreement had been signed during the second week of September. Which meant Vanessa had taken out a twelve-month tenancy agreement on a flat in central London – about as central as you could get – just two months ago.

His mind began to race as he considered what this could mean. He started playing possible scenarios through his head, trying to find a reasonable explanation for why she would be renting a second flat. And why no-one had told them about it. Surely if they had known about it, her parents would have gone straight there when they were looking for her. It didn't make sense. Her parents clearly didn't know about it.

Sheldon had also made no mention of it. Trench replayed the interview with Sheldon in his head. They hadn't asked him directly if she had a second flat. But as he recalled the interview, he felt there had been enough opportunity for Sheldon to have mentioned it. Surely he would have suggested it as somewhere she may be hiding out or somewhere they should check. But he hadn't. He didn't know either.

His heartbeat picked up. She'd been keeping it secret from both her parents and her boyfriend. Unlocking secrets was key to cracking cases. Trench felt energised. If there was anything about her lifestyle, any secrets that contributed to her disappearance, he felt sure they were getting closer to discovering what they were.

# Fourteen

"Find any keys in here?" quizzed Trench as he entered the bedroom. "House keys."

"Keys? No, why?" answered Jazz.

"She's renting another place," he said, holding up the tenancy agreement. "A flat, in central London."

"Really?" she asked, surprised. "Why would she do that?"

"Exactly. It's in the West End, or maybe Westminster. Three grand a month rent. She signed a twelve-month agreement in September."

"They never mentioned that. None of them."

"They don't know about it. Neither the parents nor Sheldon. They would've mentioned it."

"You think she's…" Jazz trailed off.

"Let's not get our hopes up," said Trench. "But we need to go there right now to check it out."

He glanced around the humongous bedroom. Despite its size, the décor managed to make it seem snug and cosy. There were numerous cabinets and chests of drawers. Jazz appeared to be working her way through them.

"Can you look for the key in here. I'm going to call Osbourne. I need to update him about the email exchange anyway, but I'll find out whether he knows anything about the flat or has a key. Discreetly. I'm not going to tell him about it if he doesn't already know. Don't want him charging down there first."

Jazz nodded, but then looked a little less sure.

"Makes sense. Though the key might be with her main set of keys, which she probably has with her."

"Agreed, but there must be a spare. Have a look anyway."

She'd been going through one of the bedside tables but closed it and began walking over to an ornate wooden chest of drawers.

"Nothing in there. Magazines, condoms, lip balm. It's more likely to be in there," she said.

As she walked across the room her phone started ringing. She took it out of her pocket and looked at the screen.

"Lewis?" she said quizzically, looking at Trench.

She raised her eyebrows, as if to say, why's he calling me?

"Chief," she said by way of greeting.

Trench waited a moment before taking out his own phone to call Doctor Osbourne. He too was curious why Lewis was calling Jazz. It was normal protocol for the commanding officer to call the senior detective if it related to a case they were working on.

"Yeah, that's right sir, we missed him," Jazz was saying, "He'd left as soon as he sent the email, as far as we can tell."

She looked over and her eyes met Trench's. She again raised her eyebrows.

"They don't have cameras. It's basically one of those corner stores with a few computers upsta—"

Jazz stopped talking and Trench assumed it was because Lewis had interrupted her.

"At her house, Vanessa's house," said Jazz. "Okay, yes. See you then."

She killed the call and looked at Trench.

"Sounded like he just wanted an update," she said, confused. "Why's he calling me?"

Trench opted to bite his tongue. He could think of only one reason. To make a point. He wasn't happy that Trench wasn't providing him with frequent updates, so he was calling Jazz instead. It was the only explanation he could think of.

He decided not to dwell on it. As he took out his phone to call Doctor Osbourne, it rang in his hand. He looked at the screen. Lewis. He stepped toward the door of the bedroom.

"The key," he said to Jazz as he stepped out of the bedroom.

"Chief," he said as he answered the phone.

"I heard the email trace was a bust," said Lewis without any introduction.

Trench thought describing it as a bust was an adversarial way to start the call. It had been a long shot that the kidnapper would sit in an internet café waiting around for further correspondence. That was obvious. Trench didn't like the insinuation, nor the tone. Because it was delivered as a statement rather than a question, he decided not to reply.

"Trench?" said Lewis after a couple of seconds.

"Chief," Trench said again.

"He got away, yes?"

Lewis clearly knew this. He seemed to know it before he called Jazz, and he certainly knew it afterwards. Why was he asking questions he already knew the answer to?

"Right," was all he said.

"Why didn't you call it in? Why didn't you update me, Trench?"

Trenched breathed out a long, slow breath. Really?

"It was about twenty minutes ago, Chief. And it's not a development. We didn't have him then and we don't have him now," he was trying to use a matter-of-fact tone, without any exasperation or sign of annoyance. "We've got another briefing in a couple of hours. I'm using that time to progress the investigation and will provide a full update on everything during the briefing. In the meantime, we've got to keep moving. We've got a lot to cover—"

"I have asked you repeatedly to keep me posted. And you keep not doing it. I need to know what's going on, damnit," said Lewis, his voice rising at the end.

Trench had rarely heard him raise his voice since his appointment. He had also spoken slowly, emphasising each word. Like he was admonishing a child. Trench tried to think of a reasonable explanation as to why he could be angry. Surely not because Trench wasn't calling him every few minutes with an update. It seemed too petty. But he couldn't think of any other reason. Perhaps the pressure of the case was getting to him.

Before Trench could respond, Lewis seemed to take his silence as opposition.

"Trench, I've been an investigator for over ten years. Perhaps not as long as you, but I'm the Chief Super now, and that's the way it is. I am in charge, whether you like it or not. And it's not going to work with you running around doing whatever you like without tellin—"

"Chief, listen, that's not what's happening—" Trench felt like he had to interrupt, but he didn't get very far.

"No, you listen," countered Lewis. "I have asked you – ordered you – to keep me posted at every step, but clearly I cannot count on you to do that. You're making my job harder. How am I supposed to keep command updated if I don't know what's going on?"

"That's what the briefings are for, Chief."

He tried not to sound too confrontational because he wanted to get Lewis off the phone so he could check out the flat Vanessa had just started renting.

"The briefings, right. Well, you just make sure you're back here for the next briefing," said Lewis, a triumphant note in his voice.

"Sure, Chief," said Trench, relieved the conversation was nearing an end. "I'll give a full report then and we can agree next steps."

"That's right. See you later then," said Lewis, hanging up.

Trench just looked at his phone and shook his head. What the fuck was all that about? He knew Lewis was getting a reputation as a control freak, but this seemed way over the top. He pushed the thought aside, thinking he could deal with it later. It had tempered some of the buzz he had felt on discovering the flat, but as he put his phone away he felt the energy returning. He walked back into the bedroom. Jazz was looking through the top drawer.

"Anything?" he asked.

"Not yet, there's a tonne of junk in here," she said.

"I'm going to call Osbourne," replied Trench, stepping back out of the room.

He scrolled through his contacts and hit call. Doctor Osbourne answered almost immediately.

"Detective," he said, "What have you found?"

Trench hadn't expected him to recognise the number. He assumed Osbourne must have saved his number in his own phone too.

"I'm calling to update you on a couple of developments, Doctor Osbourne. We haven't found Vanessa yet," he added quickly, as he knew this would be the information he most wanted to hear, "But we've made contact with the kidnapper."

"You have? When are you meeting him?"

He sounded a little flatter than Trench would have expected. Perhaps he'd been holding out hope they would find her immediately.

"We sent an email to the address on the ransom note when we got back to the station this morning. We attached a tracer to the email, which allows us to locate the computer that opens it. The email was opened shortly after we sent it. It turned out to be at an internet café near Finsbury Park."

"Finsbury Park? That's just down the road from here."

"Yes, it's not far. We immediately went to the address but he was gone. Looks like he opened the mail, typed his response then left immediately. They've no CCTV, but we got a decent description of him. It's consistent with the security camera footage from your house of the man who put the note in your letterbox."

"I see. What did he say in the response to your email?"

"It was short. Just a request that we confirm the ransom money could be available immediately."

"I take it you responded in the affirmative," said Doctor Osbourne.

"Yes. And we've attached the tracers to our response again. I assume he'll use a different café, but we're discreetly staking out the last one just in case," he felt he should manage Osbourne's expectations. "He's got lots of options though. There's still hundreds of internet cafes in London. We'll need to get lucky if we're to get him at one of them. But as soon as the tracer sends the alert we'll be all over the location."

"Just make sure you get him, Detective, the son of a bitch," emotion crept into his voice for the first time during the conversation.

Trench thought it sounded more like anger than anything else.

"We'll do everything we can," said Trench, keen to move on to the main purpose of his call. "We're also continuing to investigate Vanessa's routines. We're trying to find where she may have encountered her kidnapper, other places she frequents or hangs out. We're getting details of the places where she socialised from her friends.

But is there anywhere else you can think of where she spends time, any place of work, uh, I mean study, or second homes?"

"Yes, but we've checked them," Doctor Osbourne responded straight away.

It was not the answer Trench had been expecting.

"You've checked them?" he repeated.

"What I mean is, we have a couple of holiday homes. In the Lake District and down on the coast. The alarms have not been triggered and there's been nothing on the CCTV cameras at either house in the days since...since Tuesday evening."

"Okay, but no-one's been to either house in person?"

"No, not in person," said Doctor Osbourne, then after a brief pause added, "Indeed you're certainly welcome to check them. I can have someone from security meet you there to provide you with access. Would you like me to arrange for that?"

Trench thought about this. The properties were well outside London and would take hours to get to. It made no sense for him to check them out himself, especially given the enhanced security arrangements Doctor Osbourne had described. But he thought they should be checked out nonetheless.

"Yes, thank you. We'll have local police check out each one. Is it the same security company you use at Blenheim?"

"Yes, it is."

"Okay, I'll contact them directly to arrange."

"That's fine."

"And those two holiday homes are the only other properties you're aware of?"

"Aware of? What are you getting at, Detective?" replied Osbourne, suspicion creeping into this voice. "Those two holiday homes are the only other properties we own, beyond Blenheim and the children's homes."

Trenched winced at his own clumsy wording. He silently admonished himself for the carelessness. He knew Osbourne was sharper than most. He reminded himself again to keep on his toes when he was talking to him. But before he answered, Doctor Osbourne spoke to clarify his own answer.

"To be precise, the only properties in the UK, that is," he said.

Trench briefly considered whether this was relevant, but discounted it. He felt it unlikely Vanessa had gone abroad, not least because he'd just found her passport.

He was satisfied that Doctor Osbourne did not know about the flat in SW1.

"Thank you, then we'll arrange to check those out as soon as possible," he said, relieved Doctor Osbourne seemed to have dropped his suspicious tone.

He badly wanted to get off the phone now, to go check out the flat.

"I'll call again when we next correspond with the kidnapper," he said.

"Yes, do. And Detective, make sure you do everything you can to get the treacherous son of a bitch," said Doctor Osbourne, spitting out the phrase this time.

His turn of phrase made Trench flash back to the conversation between Doctor Osbourne and his wife when they'd walked into the kitchen earlier that morning to collect the ransom letter.

"We will," was all Trench said.

"I hope you do, Detective. And I have the money here ready to go. I presume someone will come by and pick it up at some stage."

This surprised Trench. He didn't know how long it would take to gather two million pounds in cash, but he'd assumed it would take more than a few hours. He wondered whether Osbourne kept a large amount of cash in a safe at his home.

"Do you have somewhere safe you can keep it for the time being?" he asked. "We'll send someone out to collect it when we get the instructions from the kidnapper."

Trench knew the police would not want to be responsible for the money for any longer than they needed to be. The longer they had it, the greater the chance that some or all of it would go missing. The Met would not want the liability on their hands for any longer than necessary. Nor the temptation.

"I can keep it here for the moment then," replied Doctor Osbourne, almost as if he'd expected the reply.

Trench wondered if he knew the reason. He was clearly a shrewd businessman. Coupled with his extensive commercial experience with politics and the state, he suspected he probably did.

"Good. We'll speak again later today," said Trench, signing off.

Doctor Osbourne said goodbye and Trench hung up. He stood in the landing for a moment, subconsciously staring at his phone. Not just shrewd, he thought. Cool headed too. It was a lot easier dealing with the families of missing person's when they had as much composure as Doctor Osbourne. It was often the case that family members became completely overwhelmed, debilitated even, as Mrs Osbourne appeared to be.

Doctor Osbourne on the other hand was taking all the right actions, checking with security, getting the money ready, letting police take care of the correspondence with the kidnapper without interfering. It certainly helped their investigation. It also reinforced his earlier impression that Doctor Osbourne was a fighter. Rather than losing his head, he was stoically taking care of what needed to be done.

He walked back into the bedroom. Jazz was on her knees in front of the chest of drawers. She had finished going through the other drawers and was now rummaging through the bottom one, the largest. As far as Trench could tell this was the underwear drawer. All kinds of women's lingerie and underwear were piled on the floor beside Jazz.

"I take it you haven't found it."

"Not yet," she replied, but after a couple of seconds she added, "Unless..."

Trench watched as she reached down and pulled out a small box. It looked like a small jewellery box, or one of those old-fashioned music boxes that had a miniature ballerina twirling while music played when the lid was lifted. But the only sound when Jazz opened the box was her own voice.

"Disco," she said.

She reached in and lifted out a small bag of white powder. She held it up for Trench to see.

"Jesus Jazz, I was getting excited. Thought it was the key. I'm going to call Foxton's, see if I can persuade them to meet us there without a warrant."

He turned to leave the room to make another call.

"Hold your horse there, cowboy," she said, rising to her feet still holding the box. "Looks like this box is where she keeps her secret stuff."

Trench turned back to see her reach into the box again. She smiled her smug told-you-so smile and pulled out a key on a keyring. It was a plastic keyring with a white space to write the address on. There was also another plastic attachment on the keyring.

"Now you're talking," said Trench, walking back into the room.

Jazz handed him the key and he checked the key ring. The address section was blank. But as he turned it over in his hand his excitement returned. The key looked like a normal latch key. The other plastic attachment was clearly a fob, like that used to open security gates.

"This has to be it."

# Fifteen

They jumped into the car. Trench turned on the ignition, checked his mirrors, then took off at speed. Within a couple of minutes they were out of the residential area and back onto Camden Road. He flipped the sirens and lights.

"Why do you think she has a flat?" asked Jazz, her voice hopeful.

"Anyone's guess," said Trench, not wanting to allow hope to build.

"She could be there, Trench."

"We'll soon find out. But let's just stick to what we know."

"I know. But it'd be a better outcome. Anything could happen with a ransom exchange."

"But unless we find her first, that's all we've got," said Trench. "At the briefing we need to plan for all the options for that. And you're right. All of them are risky."

"You mean grab the guy or try to follow him?"

"Not quite," said Trench. "The first option is to simply hand over the money and let him walk away, then wait for him to release her. But there's no guarantee he'll keep his side of the bargain. We may never hear from him again."

"Jesus," said Jazz.

"Exactly. I definitely won't go for that, but it's not our decision to make. Not just ours, anyway. The Osbournes'll have a firm say. But from what we know of Osbourne so far, I reckon he'd feel the same way. He's a fighter. Can't say the same about Mrs Osbourne though. We might have to rely on Osbourne to persuade her."

"She'll just want to do whatever the kidnaper says."

"Agreed. Can't blame her either. She'll go for whatever poses the least risk of harm to Vanessa. Thing is, that's probably not the least risky option."

"So what do you think," asked Jazz. "We grab the guy when he tries to pick it up?"

"It's tempting," admitted Trench. "And there'll be loud voices pushing for it. Especially the SO guys, based on my experience working with them."

The natural instinct of any police officer was to capture a suspect when you got the chance. You could work on them from there. He knew most cops would back their own interrogation techniques and ability to break the suspect down. Especially the Specialist Operations Units.

But he also knew the reality was that most cops were wrong. Most suspects didn't crack. The odds were stacked in a suspect's favour and most of them knew it. You couldn't compel them to talk. And you couldn't beat it out of them anymore, even if most of them deserved it. If they grabbed the kidnapper and he denied any knowledge or refused to talk, then they faced the unspeakable torment of 'what if,' as they scrambled around trying to find her before she starved to death or died alone chained up in the dark in some dungeon.

Trench unconsciously gave a shake of his head as he drove. It was barely better than the first option. Arguably worse, if they failed to pin anything on the suspect and ended up having to cut him loose.

"But I'm going to argue against," he said. "We should go through with the exchange and follow him afterwards. I know it's risky, no matter how much planning we do. But none of the options are good, and that's the least bad."

He preferred it for two reasons. The first was that he judged it had the best chance of a successful outcome.

The second was that it meant they would be proactively doing something to take control of the situation, rather than leaving the initiative with the kidnapper. The only thing they would be relying on the kidnapper to do was to follow through on the criminal greed that had put them all in this position: to turn up for the drop. Police could plan and execute an operation to deploy their full might into tracking him after that. Despite the risks, this sat much more easily with Trench.

"What if Osbourne is right?" said Jazz. "What if the guy setting up the ransom is just running a scam?"

As they turned onto Hampstead road and raced south, he considered the possibility.

"We can't rule it out," he said after a minute. "Which just reinforces that the first option is a non-runner. Which means we're left with grabbing him or following him from the drop."

"What if…" Jazz started, but then trailed off.

"Go on."

"What if the whole thing is a sham? What if Vanessa disappeared by herself? And the ransom is just a coincidence? Just some guy acting on the news story. Or could she even be involved with the ransom demand? Maybe she wants more money than whatever allowance she's getting from her parents?"

"I don't see it," said Trench. "She already gets plenty from them. We've just seen the lifestyle she leads. How much more could she want?"

"That's an open question," countered Jazz.

"Okay, true."

"And it may not be about money. There's a million reasons she could want to take time out from her family."

Trench had no response to that. As he thought about it, he knew she was right. And if it turned out that she was holed up in the secret flat for some reason, Trench realised they couldn't compel her to contact her family if she didn't want to. And he had no intention of forcing her to. He would simply relay the hurt and upset her parents were feeling and leave it up to her to decide whether to contact them. It would then be just another family dispute, like a million others that played out every day.

He knew Osbourne would be forceful in his demands to know where his daughter was. But Trench would have no problem being equally forceful in telling him it was no longer police business and then walking away. It would be by far the least bad outcome from the whole sorry affair. He realised then that he was truly hoping she was in the flat, safe and well.

"We'll soon find out," he murmured.

As they made their way back through central London, past Leicester Square and within shouting distance of Charing Cross Police Station, he put such thoughts out of his head. He was getting ahead of himself. He had no idea who or what was in the flat and he knew it would be a mistake to get carried away.

They passed Trafalgar Square and continued at speed down Whitehall. They passed Downing Street, its heavily fortified gates manned by a group of armed police who very publicly toted their deadly-looking sub machine guns, just in case any mischievous eyes were watching. Trench noted it was mostly tourists at the gates, rather than protesters. Maybe things were changing for the better.

The current Prime Minister was much less loathed than her predecessor. He had eventually been hounded out of office when even his closest cronies could no longer pretend they were oblivious to his insidious lies and personal treacheries. They had turned self-serving blind eyes to his ditching his latest wife and children for yet another mistress, herself pregnant by then. They had stood by him as he plundered the nation's goodwill while lying incessantly, often brazenly contradicting his own words from just a day before.

But then he had gotten yet another mistress pregnant shortly after the birth of his latest child. By then no-one knew how many children he had already denied – probably not even himself, as political insiders whispered only half in jest. And this time it was a young staffer, about the same age as Vanessa Osbourne. True to form, he had lied about even knowing her when the story broke. The conmen and lackies he had appointed to Cabinet initially backed him. It was only when his official mistress created one of the most dramatic scenes that famous address had ever seen that even his most toady flunkeys were shamed into accepting his position was untenable.

Trench shook his head as he recalled his pathetic, dumbstruck face as the soiled nappy thumped into his shoulder and exploded all over his head. For an infinite second, both the then-Prime Minister and the world's media that had gathered outside Number 10 for a routine press conference were frozen into the most stunned of silences. The original mistress' shrieks broke the spell, and then all hell broke loose.

That train of thought led Trench to consider the current Prime Minister, the prophetically named Sarah Powers. She seemed to have ridden a wave of sympathy all the way to Number 10. The portrait of a widow whose army captain husband had been killed in Iraq seemed to feature in every paper and news show during the leadership contest.

Trench paid little attention to politics these days, mistrusting all sides equally. Whereas in the eight or nine months since her instalment as PM, Powers had not done anything particularly controversial or blatantly corrupt, Trench just assumed she was either better at hiding it or it was only a matter of time.

As he recalled that she'd attended the same dinner as Vanessa on Tuesday night, he wondered if she was aware yet that Vanessa was missing. He wondered whether she would care. Or whether she would make some kind of a political show of caring. Most of all, he wondered just how much pressure she would feel obliged to put on the Met once the media ran the whole story.

Jazz had been having similar thoughts.

"I know she's not the slipperiest PM we've had recently," she said, jerking her thumb towards Downing Street, "But we can probably expect her to at least enquire with the Commander as soon as the press start reporting she was at the same dinner."

"Yeah well, that's what he's there for. Above our pay grade."

"Seriously though," Jazz continued, "They might even start asking her direct questions about it. She'll want to know what's going on, even if it's just to look like she's in charge."

"I know. But you heard Campbell earlier. He wants to run with the PR. Or at least," Trench corrected himself, "He wants Lewis and himself to look after it. That includes managing communications with any outsiders, as far as I'm concerned."

Jazz didn't answer immediately, but her brow furrowed. After a moment she turned to Trench and spoke again.

"You know, it could be viewed as an opportunity."

Trench looked over at her sceptically but said nothing.

"If she starts getting involved, it's going to be the most high-profile case since…I don't know. Years, anyway," she said.

"And?"

"And we could use that."

Trench made a wry smile, but there was no joy in it. He knew where this was going.

"It's how people get ahead, Trench. Raise your profile with the senior people, build your reputation. I mean, if this ended with us meeting the Prime Minister or her saying we did a great job or something…well, it can't hurt anyway."

"I'd rather meet a gang of pissed up Millwall fans in a dark alley with nothing on me but a plastic fork, than spend one minute with any of those shysters," said Trench.

"Well what's your plan, then? You'll end up being DCI forever."

He turned to look at his partner, but paused before he responded. He didn't want to sound cynical or come across as patronising to her natural instincts to want to advance. He was conscious that he was more experienced than she was. And to his mind, experience pretty much equated to cynicism. Persistently witnessing the very worst that humans did to each other made that inevitable. Though at least there was some redemption in that part of the job. You could contribute something towards making things right by solving cases. By locking away the worst offenders, from whom society needed to be protected.

But there was also the internal politicking, the bureaucracy, the stifling red tape and the often-contradictory meddling from political overlords with dubious intentions. The increasing feeling that the longer you were around, the less trust you had in your own back yard. The growing sense that no-one had your back. The only redemption here was in keeping your back to the wall and trying to see them coming. So you could duck.

"What does getting ahead look like?" he said evenly. "Administrative command? A desk job? *Management?"* He tried not to flinch saying the last word. "It's just a trap, Jazz."

"A trap?"

"To sucker you into thinking like them. To start believing that the stats are the answer. You'll plod along producing whatever numbers they tell you to, that make them look like they know what they're doing," he sighed. "You end up spending your life filling out forms, writing reports and ticking boxes…. Administration hell, in other words. Losing sight of what the whole point is. You're so far from making a difference you may as well give up."

He glanced over at her again. She didn't respond and had turned to look out the passenger window. For a second he wondered if he'd said too much. But she had brought it up. He wasn't going to sugar coat it. He turned back to driving. They were only a couple of minutes from the flat. He pictured the streets in the area where the flat was. He knew there was little on-street parking, so they would most likely have to pull up onto the path and leave the blue lights on.

"I understand what you're saying," Jazz said after a moment. "But I hope I never end up being such a cynical old fart."

Trench smiled.

"If you're doing it right, that's inevitable. Just focus for now on not becoming a cynical *young* fart. Too much road ahead of you for that. I'm just letting you know so it doesn't sneak up on you."

Jazz clasped her hands together under her chin, palms and fingers pressed together, and gave an exaggerated bow of her head.

"Thank you, sensei," she quipped.

They reached Parliament street, slowing down because of the heavy protective infrastructure that had been placed around the Houses of Parliament following the spate of terrorist attacks in the recent years. Concrete jersey blocks, legato blocks and assorted other concrete barriers were scattered all around the area. Trench slowed to walking speed as they crossed the junction onto Parliament Square, knowing this area was thriving with tourists all year round. They were now in the very heart of Westminster.

# Sixteen

A couple of minutes later they passed by the colossal church that took up an entire city block on Storey's Gate. Trench recalled that in the lane that ran behind it lay Conservative Campaign Headquarters. He also knew that the next street was Old Queen Street. He knew it because on the corner of that street, just a crack of the whip from Tory HQ, was the headquarters of the National Crime Agency.

But he was confused for a moment. Google maps was telling them they had arrived at their destination, which was Lewisham Street, but it didn't fit with his knowledge of the area.

Then he saw it. A thin, pedestrianised street immediately to their left. He'd nearly missed it because it was obscured by the canopy of a pub on the corner. He hit the brakes. He was tempted to pull onto Lewisham Street, it looked wide enough. But then he noticed two steel bollards standing in the middle of the entrance to the street. He clearly wasn't the first driver to have the thought.

The area in front of the entrance to Lewisham Street was sectioned off for docking stations for public hire bicycles. Most of the docking stations were empty, meaning there was just about enough space to pull the car in so it was not blocking traffic. He left the blue lights on and they both jumped out.

"What number are we looking for?" asked Jazz as they jostled past the barriers and into Lewisham Street.

"Fourteen."

As he looked at the buildings searching for numbers, he realised they were mostly the backs of buildings, whose entrances must have been on the adjacent street. Most of them didn't even have doorways.

About halfway down they spotted some doors to their right. There were no numbers on the first few doors they saw.

"Look for a fob panel," said Trench, eye-balling the area around the first couple of doors. He didn't see one.

Jazz had walked on to check the next door down. She immediately shouted back to Trench.

"This one has a panel. Could be for a fob."

Trench raced over. He grabbed the keys out of his pocket and held the fob up against the grey panel on the wall beside the door. They could see a metal staircase inside because part of the front of the building was made of glass. He held the fob to the panel and a little light at the top immediately flashed green. They heard the tell-tale low thud of a magnetic door-lock being released. Trench pushed the door open without resistance. They exchanged eager glances and stepped inside.

They were in a very small entrance hall with a door to their right, another door in front of them and the staircase to their left. Knowing they were looking for flat number four, Trench immediately began climbing the stairs. There was another door on a small landing on the first floor but they kept going. The stairs ended on the second floor. A single door stood in front of them. Trench tried the key in the lock. It fit. He knocked heavily on the door. No answer.

He waited a few seconds, then knocked again as he turned the key and pushed the door open.

"Met Police!" he called out as they stepped inside. "Vanessa, it's Met Police. Please respond if you're here. Vanessa Osbourne, this is Met Police."

No response. He found a light switch just inside the door and flipped it on. The entrance hall was narrow and quite dim from limited natural light. A couple of yards inside the flat was an arched doorway without a door. It was a small kitchen/dining area.

After a quick scan they kept going. Two more doors were to the left and one straight ahead. All were closed. The first one they reached was a bathroom. They moved swiftly to the next one. Trench knew if they were going to find anything, it was in either of the doors in front of them. But any hope that Vanessa was hiding out here was fading fast. He had a growing feeling of disappointment, tinged with dread. He wasn't feeling any signs of life the further they went into the flat.

He put his hand on the doorknob, turning to face Jazz. She also looked tense. Figuring it might be a bedroom, he instinctively gave another knock before opening it.

"Vanessa, Police!" he called out, then opened it.

It was a bedroom. But there was no-one in it. The bed was made and everything in the room was clean and tidy. A large vase on a dressing table was filled with bouquets of flowers. Most of them looked dead. There was a huge mirror on the wall above the dresser. As Trench looked at the bedclothes and the snug décor he was reminded of the bedroom they had just come from. Whatever her reason for renting this place, he thought, she wasn't sub-letting it. This was Vanessa's room.

Without a word, they both turned and left the room, moving toward the last door. It was straight in front of them at the end of the hall. Trench grabbed the handle and pushed the door open.

It was a bright, well-appointed living room. Part of the ceiling was in a conservatory style, letting in lots of natural light. They could immediately see there was no one here. Trench's sense of disappointment intensified as he walked into the middle of the room.

For a moment he stood there in the middle of the room looking around. The furniture was bright and comfortable looking. A couple of throws over the sofa and armchairs added to the homely feel, as did a large, gleaming white shag rug on which he stood. Further adding to the personal touch was numerous vases around the room, all filled with bright flowers. Or at least, what used to be bright flowers, judging by the petals now scattered and fading underneath the vases.

"Shit," was all Trench managed to say.

Jazz gave a resigned nod and walked over to a cabinet by the door. Trench leaned down and opened the drawer of a coffee table in the middle of the room.

"Some bills here," said Jazz. "They're in her name."

"Just magazines and junk in here," replied Trench.

He looked up and noticed another small coffee table in the corner by the sofa. There was an ice-bucket and two empty champagne glasses beside it. He walked over and saw the bucket was empty and dry, as were the glasses. Ready for use, as opposed to having been recently used, he thought.

"You start in the bedroom, I'll check the kitchen," he said.

He walked back to the kitchen. The mostly white décor was brightened up by a large modern art style canvas painting. It seemed to show two bodies entwined, their faces obscured, as they twisted endlessly around each other. Trench went straight to the fridge. There was a small amount of food in packaging from Ottolenghi or Whole Foods. A large packet of strawberries, some chocolate bars and three bottles of unopened champagne. It was the same brand they'd found at

Vanessa's house. He checked the date on the strawberries and noted the best before date was a couple of days ago.

He opened a few of the cupboards and found some breakfast cereal, unopened bread, rice crackers and various other snack foods. There was an assortment of different flavoured teabag packets on the counter beside a kettle. Breakfast, Earl Grey, Turmeric with Orange and Star Anise.

"Who drinks this shit?" he muttered to himself.

He left the kitchen and headed back to the bedroom.

"Love nest," said Jazz as he walked in. "That's what this place is."

He looked over and saw she held a couple of sex toys in her hand. They had obviously been in one of the bedside tables. She continued to take them out as she spoke. Soon she had more than she could hold in one hand and so put them on the bed.

Trench walked over to the other bedside table and found a couple more. He put them on the bed and kept looking through the drawer. Other than a couple of packets of wipes, it was empty. He looked over at Jazz. She had a bemused look on her face, counting the total number of the toys they had found.

"Quite a collection," she said. "And you reckon Sheldon doesn't know about this place?"

"He would've mentioned it."

"I guess this confirms his suspicions, then. She's seeing someone else. Or maybe more than one."

"You sure," Trench questioned, glancing down at the bed.

"Oh, come on, Trench," she scoffed. "They're not just for solo artists."

Trench raised his eyebrows but didn't say anything.

"Prude," Jazz mocked, walking over to the dressing table.

She opened both drawers as Trench walked over. Both were filled with lingerie. Jazz pulled out a garment from the top of the pile. It turned out to be an all-in-one body suit. She held it up against herself and looked down at it.

"Kinky," she chirped.

It was only then that Trench noticed the crotch was missing. Jazz put it down and pulled out another item. It was a fishnet body suit. She put it back in the drawer and closed it. She opened the drawer below, which contained a few t-shirts and some silk pyjamas. The last drawer contained a few pairs of fluffy socks and some sweatpants and tops.

"She knows how to show him a good time, got to give her that," said Jazz straightening up.

"So you don't think—"

"No, I don't. Prude," Jazz repeated.

"What?" protested Trench, "I wasn't finished."

"I know what you're thinking," said Jazz, still a hint of mocking in her tone. "And you're wrong. She's not on the game. Just because she's got some kit doesn't mean she's a prostitute. Come on, Trench, get with the real world."

"Uhm," was all he replied with.

"Think about it," she continued. "If she was, there'd be boxes of cock-socks all over this place."

"Cock so—"

"You know, weanie-beanies? Poon balloons? Pickle mittens?"

"Right," nodded Trench, understanding. "Fair point."

He looked around the room but didn't see anywhere else obvious to check.

"I'm going to look in the bathroom again," he said, walking toward the bedroom door.

In the bathroom he peered into the bath, which doubled as a stand-in shower. The area around the bath was cluttered with assorted oils and body wash products. There were also a few ornate candleholders on the edge of the bath, the Jo Malone candles more than halfway burned down.

He opened the cabinet behind the mirror. It was stuffed with various creams and lotions, and numerous bottles of women's fragrances. As he walked back towards the bedroom he realised Jazz was right. There was nothing sleazy or industrial about this place. It wasn't an impersonal sex factory, where countless men would visit to spend the facts of their lives like small change on strangers, in the immortal words of Tom Waits. It may not have been Vanessa's primary home, but it clearly was somewhere private and homely to her.

Her love nest, Trench agreed.

"Has she been here since Tuesday, that's what we need to figure out," he said out loud, walking back into the bedroom.

Jazz was putting the toys back inside the bedside tables. He already knew what he thought was the right answer to the question. The out-of-date strawberries, dying flowers, the ready-to-use champagne flutes and ice bucket.

"It's more likely she intended to come here, probably even right after the dinner. But never made it," he said, answering his own question.

"There's bound to be CCTV all over this area," said Jazz. "You can't walk five yards around here without being clocked by a bunch of cameras. Every second building is a government agency or foreign embassy. I'll get Thomson to put one of the constables on it."

Trench nodded. They could check the CCTV, but he did not believe they would find her on it. Not for Tuesday evening, anyway. This reminded him that he had to chase Higgins again, to get any CCTV footage of her from the night of the dinner. He glanced at his watch.

"Let's get back to the station," he said. "We need to get back for the briefing. And I probably need to bounce someone's head off a desk."

They walked out of the bedroom, Jazz flicking off the switch as they left. Trench opened the door to the flat, but then paused. The rain had intensified. It hammered down onto the glass panels covering the stairwell, the metallic echo bouncing off the stairs, making it even louder. They had to raise their voices as they made their way down the stairs.

"When you're talking to Thomson, just make sure it's not Barton," said Trench.

"Right, he still working the databases?"

"Yes, though he should be done by now. I'll check in with him when we get back. But he's good. I've got other plans for him."

"Campbell did say we could pull in all available resource on this. I'll make the point to Thomson."

"And get them to involve CFIT from the start. That's what they're there for."

He pronounced it *see-fit*, which stood for Central Forensic Image Team. It was the Met's team of 'super recognisers' – trained specialists with an exceptional ability to recognise faces. The small unit of about half a dozen people was considered amongst the best in the world at this craft, even being seconded to other countries' police forces on occasion.

But despite the countless billions spent on the estimated half a million CCTV cameras in London, CFIT was rarely used by Met police in solving crimes. CCTV images were used in only around two per cent of criminal cases in London. This was mainly because police officers simply lacked training or the equipment needed to access and use London's vast spider's web of cameras. Many were also unaware of the procedure for tapping into the CFIT skillset.

But Trench had used CFIT before and knew how effective they were. A former partner had even transferred to the unit, and often impressed upon him the advantages of using the resource as extensively as possible.

"And whoever it is, have them go back a couple of weeks, not just to Tuesday night," he said as they reached the bottom of the stairs.

"You think her mystery man might be on there?" said Jazz. "Maybe they got caught on camera coming back here some time."

"Let's hope so."

It took them a second to find the door release button on the ground floor. They eventually found it and bolted back to the car. Running made no difference though. By the time they got to the car they were both completely soaked through. It was cold, hard rain, that felt more like buckets of iced water than raindrops.

"Bloody hell!" exclaimed Jazz as she jumped in and stamped her feet, "Fucking freezing!"

There was barely an ounce of fat on her well-toned body so she often felt the cold, but rarely complained about it. She preferred to discreetly wear multiple warm layers under her suit, rather than be seen to be complaining. She reached over and started fiddling with the car's heat controls. She pulled her suit jacket tighter around her, before realising that it was soaked and was probably only making her colder. She eventually took it off and hung it on the back of her head rest. She huddled in closer to the heaters.

"So what have we got?" she said after a moment, her teeth still chattering. "She's definitely seeing someone else, that's obvious. But what does it tell us? You think the guy suddenly kidnapped her?"

"Possible. But I don't see it. She's had the flat for a couple of months. Unless she's a really terrible judge of character, it doesn't fit. Surely she'd have sensed something wasn't right with him. But we need to find him. He's going to know things about her, her routines, where she goes, who she spends time with. Maybe he even knows what's happened to her. That flat looks like she was expecting to go there on Tuesday, probably after the dinner. We can assume he was supposed to be there as well. What happened? What changed, and why? If we knew that, we'd at least know more than we do right now. And where to start looking."

"What if they had a fight? Secret lover gets jealous because she won't make it public. Wouldn't be the first time. They have a row, he hurts her. Maybe the whole kidnap thing is a smokescreen. Just a diversion to get us focused somewhere else."

"Also possible. But why bother with the kidnap charade? It'd be easier to just disappear. To distance yourself from her and the crime. Carrying out a sham kidnapping only draws more heat. We could've got him at the internet café earlier if we'd been quicker or if there were cameras there. It just seems to increase the risk of being caught."

The grim thought occurred to him of other cases in the past where kidnappers have gone ahead with ransom demands even after killing their victim. It was the worst-case scenario, but he knew they couldn't dismiss it.

"Unless he plans to use the money to disappear," he said solemnly.

"I'm going to call Willard again," said Jazz, reaching around to get the phone out of her jacket.

"We're nearly there, Jazz. And she would've called if he made contact again," said Trench in a resigned tone.

He knew they had to keep focused on making progress and to avoid the temptation to do things just to make themselves feel like they were being productive. Time was key. They could easily lose time with furious activity that really amounted to nothing more than running around in circles.

"Why there?" he said.

"What?"

"Why is she renting a flat there? I know money is no object, but for that price she could get a much nicer flat somewhere else. And in a much more discreet location too, if she's trying to keep it a secret. Why rent a pokey one bed in the heart of Westminster?"

He realised then what his own hunch was, just as Jazz arrived at the same thought.

"Tory HQ?" she said. "Maybe that's why she's gotten more involved with them again recently. That's what Sheldon said, right. That she became more involved again in the past few months?"

Trench nodded.

"We should look into it. Which leads us back to the dinner. Higgins better have done his homework by now. Either way, let's go through the guest list and narrow it down to potential candidates, based on who she spent time with or sat with at the dinner."

But then he thought of a potential problem with the line of thinking.

"What are the odds any of them are Polish though?" he said.

"Hmm," Jazz snorted, "Not likely. Not exactly the most welcoming of gangs when it comes to foreigners."

"Worth a look," was all Trench said, not wanting to let the political climate interfere with their investigation.

# Seventeen

Once inside the station they went straight back to their desks. Trench had just sat down and was opening his emails to check whether there was anything from either Thomson or Higgins when he noticed the door to Lewis's office opening. His office was further down the CID room to the right. Trench could see the door from his desk without having to turn his head.

He watched as Callow emerged from the office, the habitual self-satisfied smirk etched onto his face. He stole a quick glance in Trench's direction but then diverted his eyes. Lewis followed out behind him. He then also looked over in Trench's direction.

"Trench, you got a minute?" Lewis called out.

"Coming," replied Trench.

He glanced at the screen but the inbox still hadn't loaded. He got up and took a step in the direction of Lewis's office. He then realised he didn't know how long he'd be in there for, so went back and picked up his water bottle and took it with him.

After calling to Trench, Lewis had stood outside his office, staring around the squad room. It was a habit everyone in CID had noticed about the new Chief. Whenever he was waiting for someone, or when he arrived in the morning and also just before he left in the evening, he'd stand outside his office just staring around the room for a few minutes.

Nobody had figured out why and nobody was going to ask him. People assumed it was just a quirky habit, or that he was taking stock of department resources or activity. But someone had come up with the nickname Private Pyle as a result, after the character in the movie Full Metal Jacket with the famously maniacal stare. It had stuck.

Lewis moved aside so Trench could enter his office then followed him in, closing the door behind him. It was a small office, with only enough room for his desk and a small round table in front of it. Trench pulled out one of three seats at the table, but then decided he'd prefer to stand. He hoped not to be in there long.

Lewis walked in behind his desk. He'd recently ordered one of those flexi-desks, that could be raised so that he could stand instead of sitting down while he worked.

It was currently in the lowered position. Come to think of it, Trench wasn't sure he'd ever seen it in the raised position.

There were no personal effects on the desk, no pictures or any other signs of the Detective Chief Superintendent's personal life. Just a few files, neatly stacked. The only other thing on the desk besides his computer was a desk organiser, with holders for pens, pencils, paperclips and a separate section for post-it notes. Trench noticed for the first time that the different coloured pens were all stored together in separate slots.

After initially pulling out his chair to sit down, Lewis noticed Trench was still standing and remained standing himself. He didn't say anything for a moment, instead glancing out through the window into the squad room, as if looking for someone. The blinds were partially open, but it wasn't obvious to Trench what he was looking at.

After another few moments of silence, Trench could feel his impatience growing. He didn't want to waste time, especially as the next update briefing was in a few minutes anyway. But he knew he couldn't just tell Lewis to hurry up.

"What can I do for you, Chief," he said instead.

"So the email trace was a bust," said Lewis.

Trench could hear tension in his voice. It was only then Trench recalled the strained conversation they'd had while he was at Vanessa's house. He had completely put it out of his mind. He realised that Lewis must still have a queen bee in his bonnet. He recalled how he didn't like Lewis's tone then, and he didn't much like it now either.

Trench briefly considered asking Lewis directly if he had some kind of problem with him. But he decided against it. Given they were in the middle of an intense, time-sensitive case, now was not the time for a straightener. They could go for a pint when the case was over to clear things up. Actually maybe a coffee, he thought. No-one ever stays for two coffees, no matter how good it tastes.

He therefore responded in an even tone, not wanting to sound confrontational, but not defensive either.

"We're expecting another email from the kidnapper with instructions for a drop. He already asked for confirmation that the money would be available today, so presumably that'll arrive any minute. I've put the SO Unit on standby. They're ready to go as soon as I say the wor—"

"Ah, here she is," interrupted Lewis, eyes on the window of his office again.

Trench clocked the outline of a person walking past the window but couldn't see who it was. There was a knock on the door before it opened without Lewis having to say anything. Trench turned as the person entered the room.

He almost did a double take when he saw who it was. With some struggle, he managed to kept his reaction in check. He felt his jaw clench. Trench turned back to Lewis and found that he was already glaring at him. Trench couldn't quite tell if his expression was defiance, or just that of an insecure man trying to look like he was in charge.

Investigator Lisa Harding stepped into the room and closed the door. She too then glared at Trench, looking unsure as to what reception to expect. For a moment she didn't say anything, as if waiting for Trench's reaction. Trench just looked at her without saying anything.

He turned back to Lewis.

"Are you fucking serious?" he said, unable to hide his dismay.

Lewis tensed, as did Harding.

"I don't appreciate your tone, Detective," said Lewis stiffly. "And don't use that language in my office. The right protocol here is to involve the NCA and that's what we're going to do. It was agreed in the briefing this morning. You were there."

He paused, as if to give Trench a chance to reply. But Trench didn't reply. He didn't know where to start. That was not what had gone down in the briefing, not by a long shot. Either Lewis was blatantly twisting it or he had somehow missed it. At that moment, Trench couldn't tell which was the case. He also couldn't decide which was worse.

When he didn't respond, Lewis continued speaking.

"I believe you know Investigator Harding?" he said formally, making an elaborate gesture at her in an effort to make Trench acknowledge her.

Trench turned to Harding, trying to gather his thoughts. He had nothing against her personally. She'd seemed harmless enough from the limited interaction Trench had had with her previously, during her brief stint in CID. But as well as being NCA now, she was also a fucking useless cop. That much he did know from her CID days.

As she stood there, he tried to recall if he'd told her this directly. He couldn't be sure, but had vague recollections of being asked about her for a peer review process and resolving to be honest enough to tell her directly rather than through some anonymous feedback charade. Better to get rid of the dead weight sooner rather than later, for everyone's sake.

Either way, here she was. Trench fought back the temptation to share his feedback there and then. He realised that her ineptitude wasn't the biggest problem if Lewis had invited the NCA in. A politically toxic situation was about to get further mired in a jurisdictional pissing contest.

"Hardy," he nodded to her.

"Hello Trench," she replied, seeming to loosen up slightly.

She then turned to Lewis, all business.

"Good to see you, Investigator," said Lewis, his voice still a little tight. "Why don't you bring us up to date from your end, following our phone conversation earlier."

"Sure, Chief Lewis," she said. "First, thanks again for bringing this to our attention. Since your call, we've already kicked into action and are giving this case top priority. Our specialist AKEU Unit are all over it. I understand there's a briefing shortly. We propose using that opportunity for all uh, interested parties, from our respective teams to smash our heads together. We'll sweat all the facts pertinent to the case. With enough blue sky thinking we can then formulate the go-get strategy. My partner is on his way to join us here. The rest of our team will dial in from base."

"Jesus," Trench mumbled, trying hard not to roll his eyes.

Lewis rounded on him.

"Do you have a problem, Detective?" he demanded.

"No problem," Trench replied, but then couldn't help adding, "But if they all speak like that *at base* then I suggest we bring a translator to the briefing."

"It seems to me that you do have a problem," barked Lewis. "You're attitude stinks. And I don't just mean right now. You are flying far, far too close to the sun for my liking. Do you understand me?"

Trench felt his temper flaring. Not just that Lewis's juvenile rebuke had fuelled his growing frustration that Lewis was too petty a man to be dealing with the gravity of the job he was now doing. He was also seeing control of the investigation slipping away. And with it would go effectiveness, because inevitably different people in each outfit would be vying for the same responsibility. Given the considerable suspicion on both sides, when any disagreement occurred it would become tribal, hindering anyone taking any action at all. From previous experience, Trench knew this ran the risk that ultimately no-one would take responsibility.

This was exacerbated by the fact that at least part of the priority of each outfit would be to position themselves to either claim the positive PR from a successful outcome, or to pin the blame on the other side if it all went south. It only added to the suspicion and mistrust. Trench was getting more angry the more he thought about it. The fact that Lewis, his own Chief, didn't get this was only making it worse.

In an effort to count to ten, he unscrewed the lid of his water bottle and took a long drink. By the end of that he had decided that he would not argue with Lewis. Instead he would lay it out for him, making it crystal fucking clear.

Knowing what Commander Campbell's view would be of involving the NCA, he reasoned he was also doing Lewis a favour. One that he probably didn't deserve.

"Listen Chief, we don't have much time here, so I'm going to be blunt," he said. "You're making a mistake. These people, I'm sure they're all fine officers. But they don't bring anything to the party that we don't already have. We've got more practical experience, our tactical guys are better qualified and we've been doing it for a damn sight longer than anyone over there. The only thing they've got that we don't is a fancy fucking name. That, and the grubby mitts of whichever crank happens to squatting in the Home Office right now.

"We're just going to waste more time in these double-speak circle jerks convincing ourselves that we're doing everything people would expect us to do. But what we won't be doing, is taking decisive action quick enough to get us any closer to finding Vanessa."

Lewis glowered at Trench for a few seconds before responding.

"You just don't get it, do you," Lewis retorted, thrusting his finger at Trench. "I was warned about you. You think it's all about you. That you run the whole show. You don't need to check in with anyone or get anyone else's opinion. You can just go out there, do whatever you want and solve everything by yourself. Well, not on my watch. You may not like it but that's not how I will run this squad. We're going to get input and advice from across the force, and we'll be better for it. And I've got news for yo—"

Trench had had enough. He could see Lewis was beyond reason and clearly not willing to listen. Fuck it, Trench wasn't going to listen any further either. He could see what Lewis was describing and it was anathema to everything he believed about running an investigation.

"Investigation by committee, is that what you want?" he snapped back. "Involve a hundred other people so no-one really knows who's accountable for what. Everyone has an opinion but no-one puts their cock on the block. You're hiding! You're hiding in the crowd. Afraid to make a bloody decision, in case it goes tits up. You're damn right I don't like it. At least I'll make a decision. That's the job. If it's wrong then I'll have to live with that, but at least we'll make some fucking progress. That's the whole point. Investigate the circumstances then make a bloody decision. You should try it sometime."

When he stopped speaking he realised he had been jerking his finger at Lewis too. He lowered his hand. Lewis had been glaring at him the whole time but now lowered his gaze, shaking his head.

"You're off the case," he muttered.

"What?"

"I've already decided. Jazz can attend the briefing. Not that there's much to report," he snarled. "You've got nothing but a busted trace. Whatever decisions it is that you're so proud of have gotten us precisely nowhere."

Trench just looked at him. He was going to respond with the fact that he'd been working the case for less than twenty-four hours, but he could see that there was no point in arguing further.

"This is bullshit," was all he could manage.

"You're on the body in Oldbury Woods. You're the SIO on that, so give it your full focus."

"This is bullshit," Trench repeated, louder this time. "This isn't about me, it's about finding Vanessa—"

"You've gotten nowhere! And you've made it clear you're not willing to work with the team on this. I need people in the team who will all be pulling together. If you won't do that, then believe me, I will bring in people who will. And I've spoken with DCS Harris in Kent. You were first on the scene in Oldbury Woods so he's happy we run with it."

Trench just stared at him. He could feel himself fuming. He skimmed his options and realised it would be useless to continue the conversation. Lewis had already spoken with Kent Police. This wasn't spur of the moment. He must have decided this before Trench even walked into the room. Trench shifted his gaze to the floor and shook his head again.

Lewis must have taken this as further insubordination. He screwed his face into a caustic squint, his mouth tightening as he delivered a parting shot.

"There's a decision for you," he sneered.

Trench gave one final shake of the head and headed for the door. Harding skipped away from her position by the door, letting him pass.

"Fucking fool," Trench declared, without looking around as he reached the door.

# Eighteen

He let the door swing closed behind him. It was loud, but wasn't quite a slam. One or two heads turned, but they were probably looking for a distraction anyway. Trench marched back towards his desk. He stopped by the water cooler to refill his bottle, then went back and pulled out his chair. He had seen Jazz's head pop up when the door closed and knew she had watched him as he walked back.

"I'm guessing that wasn't a promotion?" she said with a grimace.

Trench sat down and let out a long sigh. He leant forward and put his head in his hands, running his fingers through his thick black hair. After a moment he sat upright and leaned back in his chair.

"He fucking sandbagged me," he said, turning to Jazz.

"What do you mean? Who was that woman who went in there?"

Trench was shaking his head.

"He set me up, and I walked straight into it."

The only annoyance he felt now was with himself. Lewis was just a second-rate stooge. A patsy who was too far out of his depth. He could see that now. He was going to surround himself with as many people as he could so that he could share the burden of responsibility. The signs had been there. He hadn't given it enough attention.

He knew now that he should have handled the meeting differently. He should have just paid lip service to whatever pantomime Lewis was cooking up and then gone on with this investigation anyway. What did it matter if it was the NCA, Lewis or anyone else that was bitching about not being the loop if they couldn't keep up?

Yes, there was certain to be a territorial battle when it came to providing tactical support for the ransom exchange. But he could have let others deal with that. Get Campbell involved if he had to.

Campbell. As he thought about him, Trench was certain that he did not know of Lewis's decision to bring in the NCA. He was also certain that Campbell would be seething about it when he found out. The Met was always the loudest voice amongst the existing police constabularies to push back against the NCA's creeping agenda. Campbell's ambitions for advancement within the Met would ensure that he would be unequivocal in his resistance to the NCA being involved in such a high profile Met case.

Which meant it was even more odd that Lewis would call them in.

"Set you up how Trench, what are you talking about?" Jazz insisted, sounding frustrated that he wasn't explaining himself.

"I'm off the case," he said, turning to face her. "I'm off the Vanessa Osbourne case."

"*What?!*"

She lowered her voice.

"What the fuck are you talking about? Why?"

"It doesn't matter why. And he's brought in the NCA. I told him that was a bad idea. I spelled it out for him. But he wasn't listening. I'm pretty sure he'd already decided I was off the case before I walked in the room. He was spoiling for a fight the minute I walked in."

"Jesus Christ," said Jazz shaking her head.

Then after a moment of silence, she said, "Am I off it?"

"No," said Trench.

But having had a few minutes to think about it, he figured he might be able to guess more of what was going on.

"At least, not for now. You're giving the update at the briefing in a few minutes. But Lewis talked about bringing in people who are better team players or something. More agreeable people."

"I don't like the sound of that," said Jazz, rolling her eyes.

"Yeah. And someone's been filling his head full of shit. He said something about knowing about my reputation or being warned I'm a rogue detective or something. Off doing my own thing, looking for glory and cutting others out. Some bullshit like that."

"Campbell?" she asked without thinking about it, but didn't sound convinced herself. "Would he say that about you? Why would he…."

Trench shook his head but she had just figured it out for herself.

"Oh, for fuck's sake," she said, looking over in the direction of Callow's desk. "Obviously he's crawling up Lewis's arse the whole time, but why would he want you off the case?"

"He wants on it himself. Higher profile case, greater visibility. You said it yourself, with all the attention it's going to get, it'll be good for advancement. An opportunity, I believe you called it."

"Jesus," groaned Jazz. "Do I think like that piece of shit? I might need to lie down."

"He must've been pushing at an open door. Lewis is not that much of a dupe. He's not going to just do whatever that meat head tells him." He thought for a moment then shrugged. "I guess he really does want hourly updates. Shit, I don't know."

Trench didn't want to talk about it anymore. He was just getting more annoyed. He raised his hands in a surrender motion and turned to face his computer. Jazz could read him well enough and knew to let it rest for now. As Trench turned to his computer, a thought suddenly occurred to him.

Callow was a slippery motherfucker, but he wasn't stupid. He would know that Campbell would be strongly against bringing in the NCA. If Lewis had already discussed with Callow about replacing Trench on the case, then he had probably told him about his intention to bring in the NCA as well. He would have had to, to make sure Callow would agree to work with them without a problem. Which meant that Callow had offered little or no advice against doing so. He had simply let Lewis march right into Campbell's crosshairs.

The more Trench thought about it, the more he felt it fit. He knew Callow's duplicity could make Judas Iscariot look like an altar boy. He'd witnessed it often enough. But this was cut-throat, even for him. He was handing Lewis the pen with which to sign his own CID death certificate.

The reason seemed obvious enough to Trench. He simply wanted Lewis out of the way. The opportunity had presented itself to get rid of Lewis and Callow had just helped to put the wheels in motion. Trench would bet his life that Callow would be first to apply for the position once Lewis was given the bullet. Trench didn't fancy Callow's chances of getting the role, but Callow himself probably did. Sociopaths weren't known to be lacking in self-belief. And if he didn't get it this time, he'd just wait for the next opportunity.

Trench mulled it for another few minutes, but couldn't see it any other way. He was sure he was right. He wondered whether he should somehow warn Lewis, but immediately dismissed the idea. Fuck him, he figured. I just tried that. If he was dumb enough to put himself in that position then CID was better off without him.

His thoughts turned to what it meant for the case. For Vanessa. He had to put that first. His immediate thought was that if Callow was leading the case, his foremost consideration would, as always, be himself. If there was a successful outcome, he would claim it. If there wasn't, he would blame Lewis. He was certain that was the way Callow would approach it. Vanessa's welfare would feature somewhere much further down his list of priorities.

After mulling it for a few minutes, Trench reached a definitive conclusion.

He had to continue to do whatever he could to ensure a positive outcome for the case. Primarily, that would mean continuing to work as closely with Jazz as possible. But he suspected she would probably be off the case soon too. So that left him with only one real option for the moment.

He stood up and looked over to where Callow sat. Trench could just see the top of his head. He took out his phone and copied Doctor Osbourne's phone number onto a piece of paper he tore off a notepad.

"What are you going to do?" asked Jazz, realising where he was looking.

She sounded worried.

"All this bollocks doesn't matter. We still need to find Vanessa. That's the only thing that matters. You're still on the case. Keep me looped in and I'll give you as much help as I can."

"Of course. I was going to do that anyway. But I may get kicked too, you know…partner. As soon as the next briefing is done, I'd say."

"I know," said Trench, still standing. "So I'm going to speak with the new SIO. I'll let him know I'm here to provide whatever help he wants with the case. If I make it clear we just want to help, then at least we can offer him pointers later. Whether he wants them or not."

"Good on you," Jazz nodded.

But as he stepped away from his desk, she crossed the index fingers of both hands, thrusting them at him and making a burning noise.

Trench walked over towards Callow's desk. Callow had his back to him and was busy reading something, so didn't see him coming. As Trench was just a yard away he seemed to sense his presence. Callow began turning in his seat, and seeing it was Trench, stood out of his chair. He nodded at Trench and then raised his eyebrows, as if to say "What's up?"

"Lewis told me you're taking over on Vanessa Osbourne," he gambled, glancing at what Callow had been reading.

He could have guessed what it would be, so added, "We're pretty sure she's not gone fishing, but glad to see you're covering all the angles."

Callow had been flicking through a yachting magazine, as he always seemed to be. He now lowered it onto his desk behind him without looking, maintaining eye contact with Trench. Trench had never been able to envisage him as a sailor, skipping around the deck, winching in sails. But he knew Callow had a boat somewhere, or at least use of a boat, and spent a lot of his free time there. He often wondered if he actually just went on some kind of booze cruise, with other people crewing the boat. That fit much better.

"He told you that?" responded Callow, a hint of surprise in his voice. "Yeah well, probably makes sense for you to be on the body at Oldbury, since you're the SIO and all. We can run with the Osbourne case, considering you've barely got started anyway."

His knowledge of Trench's reassignment and insinuation about Trench's progress in the Osbourne case was all the confirmation Trench needed. He had been right.

"You think just like a Chief, Callow," said Trench deadpan.

It took all the composure he had to keep the conversation constructive. Callow just looked at him. Before he could respond, Trench continued.

"To help you hit the ground running, I want to give you a quick brief on what we've found. It should help focus your investigation."

"Uhm, well I'm sure that's very kind of you, Chambers," replied Callow, still looking a little suspicious, but rapidly reverting to type as the habitual smirk began to form on his face.

He was virtually the only person across the entire police force who called Trench by his last name rather than his nickname. A fact that gave Trench a lot of satisfaction.

"But surely not even you would try to take credit for 'finding' a ransom note that was posted in their letterbox?"

Callow briefly turned to Burgess, who sat in the desk opposite his as he said it, the smirk more pronounced.

"Looks like she was seeing someone else," Trench went on, ignoring the comment. "Someone other than her boyfriend, Mathew Sheldon. She's been renting a flat in Westminster. Stone's throw from Tory HQ. My guess is that she was expecting to go back there on Tuesday night after the dinner. Most likely with this other guy, based on what we found at the flat. We don't know if that's got anything to do with the kidnapping. Even if not, finding him would at least give some insight into Vanessa's life that we don't currently know. Here's the keys to the flat. I presume you'll want to check it out for yourself."

Trench handed him the keys and told him the address. Callow didn't say anything. He appeared to be paying attention now, but Trench noticed he wasn't taking any notes and didn't make any attempt at asking any of the obvious questions about who the guy might be or why she was renting the flat. Trench moved on to the next point.

"The ransom note arrived overnight. The guy who dropped it in is Polish. I don't know if you've seen the note, but it gave an email address at which to contact him. We sent a mail with tracers earlier, then hit the internet café from where the reply was sent—"

"Which was a bust," interjected Callow.

"—we didn't get the bloke but he had replied to our email, requesting confirmation the ransom money would be available immediately," Trench went on, ignoring him, "and nothing else. We sent a second mail asking for instructions for the exchange. We're expecting a reply any time."

"We already know all this," said Callow impatiently. "The ransom note is clearly from Johnny Foreigner given how it's written, but aren't you being a bit presumptuous in saying he's Polish? Or did you just mean foreign?"

The fact he had seen the note bothered Trench more than it should have. Lewis had obviously fully debriefed with Callow already about the case. He briefly wondered at what point it had been decided to cut him out. It certainly hadn't taken Lewis very long to do so.

"No, I mean Polish. Which is only a small part of foreign as it turns out, but it does help us narrow it down," he said, swiftly moving on before Callow reacted to the sarcasm. "So we got a list of all the people who've visited the house over the past couple of years, in case he's someone who's been there before, possibly done some work for the family or something. There's a few dozen Polish sounding names on the list. Thomson's team are running checks on them all right now. It's a long shot, but might give us a route to the guy before the drop."

He paused there, to let Callow digest the information and ask any questions. Callow still hadn't taken any notes, which was bothering Trench. After a moment Callow nodded superficially, barely managing to look like he was processing the information.

"Right," said Callow blithely. "I'll take all that into consideration. You're free to get on with your investigation now, into that dolly bird in the woods. You don't need to waste any more time on this. The only thing I need from you is the number for old man Osbourne. We need to make sure he has the ransom money ready asap. I don't doubt he's good for it, but it'll probably take some time to get that much cash together. Better put a rocket under him. Don't want to delay the whole thing any longer than necessary. Drop the number over to me soon as you can."

"He's already got the cash ready," said Trench, reaching into this pocket to find Doctor Osbourne's number. "He confirmed that a couple of hours ago."

"That's good," said Callow, looking pleasantly surprised. "Good for him, that should save some time. Guess it's just chump change to a guy like that."

He chuckled at that, turning briefly to Burgess again.

"Have you made arrangements yet to pick it up from him?" asked Callow.

"He's going to hang on to if for the moment," said Trench.

He then realised Callow may not twig why, so added further explanation.

"Makes sense. He's obviously got it secured there and we don't want it hanging around here any longer than necessary."

"Right, yeah. We'll get it when we need it," Callow replied with a slight nod. "Anything else?"

"Willard in Cyber Crimes is monitoring the email address we used. Jazz can give you the details in the briefing."

Trench handed over the piece of paper with Doctor Osbourne's number. Callow took it and put it straight into his pocket.

"Last thing I need is to know what the PR schedule is. Is there a press conference I need to prepare for?"

"No," replied Trench. He kept any hint of satisfaction out of his face when he added, "Campbell is looking after that."

"Right."

They both stood there for another half second, but nothing else occurred to Trench.

"Good luck," he said. "If you need anything else from me, if I can help in any way, let me know."

Callow half nodded and turned back to his desk, indicating he was done talking. Trench stood there for another second, his mind reluctant to simply hand it over and walk away. That was against every instinct he had. He felt another pang of anger that he was off the case. He knew Callow had at least participated in the decision to make that happen. But the brunt of his anger was at Lewis for now. And at himself, for letting it happen. He turned and waked away.

"What a total cluster fuck," he mumbled to himself, as he approached his desk. As he thought of Lewis again, he couldn't help but say out loud, "Asshole."

"Uh, Trench?"

He turned around. Barton was walking up behind him, looking a little uncertain.

He must have thought Trench was talking about him. He held up some paperwork in his hand.

"I have the results from the database search. Uh, sorry if it took longer than you expected. Is now a good time to look at this?"

"Hey Barton," he said, welcoming the distraction. "You're timing couldn't be better. What've you got?"

"Okay, so I started with known sex offenders within a twenty mile radius of where the body was dumped."

"Hang on," said Trench, "Let's grab a room."

He scanned around for a vacant meeting room. The one next to Lewis's office was free but he didn't want to use that one. He wasn't ready to face Lewis and wanted to avoid bumping into him if he came out of the office. Instead he started walking back down the squad room, looking at the meeting rooms lining the opposite side. Barton followed behind but Trench could see him out of the corner of his eye pointing over toward the one beside Lewis's office.

"That one's fre—"

"Here we are," said Trench, spotting a free office at the back of the room.

"Have you got a copy of the results for me?"

He held his hand out as he walked. Barton handed him a copy and told him he had also emailed a copy. Trench studied it as he walked. He skimmed each of the seven pages, trying to interpret the data. He could see names, addresses, date of inclusion on the sex offender's register and length of jail sentence. Though not every entry on the list showed an entry for jail sentence.

"This looks good," he said. "Can you give me a quick summary."

"Right," said Barton, hurrying to catch up to Trench's pace. "So I started looking at known sex offenders within a twenty mile radius of where the body was found. That is, people listed on the sex offenders' register. That produced a lot of results though. Like, more than seven thousand."

"Yeah, that would include most of London, right?" Trench said as they reached the room.

He stood inside, letting Barton pass him and then closed the door. Barton pulled out a seat and sat down but Trench remained standing. He was still too fired up to sit.

"Exactly. So I went back and started the other way round. I've sorted the list so that the known offenders who live nearest the site where the body was found are at the top of the list. As you go down the list, the names are living further away. I also cut the radius down to ten miles."

"Have you looked into any of them? As in, why they're on the register."

He had glanced at the list while Barton was talking. He noted some of the names at the top of the list lived within a couple of miles from where the body was found. But he knew there was a wide range of reasons someone could end up on the sex offenders' register. It varied from a relatively minor offense, like slapping a stranger on the ass in a nightclub as a joke that went very wrong, all the way to the brutal rape of a child. He was thinking that they would need to prioritise their search on those that had committed more serious offences.

"Yes, that's why I included the details of their sentence. That shows how serious their offence is."

Trench looked at the list again.

"Okay, so taking this guy at the top. Actually, the top two. No, make that three. Two of the three who live closest to the site didn't do jail time? So they either got a caution or did community service. And the other did three months? Am I reading this right?"

"Yeah, that's right."

Trench thought for a moment. He knew there was no way of precisely predicting the evolution of a sex offender's crimes, their progression from mildly sexually deviant into the evil beast capable of doing what they had found in Oldbury Woods. But he felt it made more sense to prioritise the more serious offenders. He felt it unlikely that someone would have made the leap from inappropriate touching or peeping tom to full-fledged abduction, torture and murder.

As he flicked through the list, he realised that what they should be prioritising was not convicts, but actual crimes. He still felt it possible the killer would have a criminal record for some form of sexual deviancy. But they also needed to establish a pattern of any recent similar crimes, solved or not, or possible development crimes – ones that may not be on the same scale, but bore similarities.

"Okay, good work putting this together, Barton. I presume you've downloaded this, so we can sort it whatever way we want?" He continued as Barton nodded. "Next, we need to broaden the search to include similar or development crimes. We want to be able to plot on a map, anywhere that similar offences have been committed."

Barton continued to nod so Trench carried on.

"And rather than length of sentence, try to get the details of the crime. Prioritise the victim. We're looking for women, particularly prostitutes, where there's been signs of torture. And forensic awareness. And you'll need to include unsolved cases too. Rather than focus on just the offender, start again and search based on the victim and the crime itself. For the cases where we know who the offender was, mark that down. It'll save us a lot of time if we start with them. But there'll be other crimes on there that no-one's been done for yet. We need those too. Got it?"

"Yeah, I see what you mean."

"Good. And widen the search area. Include all of the South East. Include murders or attempted murders, particularly where sadism or torture was involved."

"Okay, I'll get onto that. It might take a while though, that's a pretty wide net. And uh, can I ask you something, Trench?"

"Shoot. Actually hang on," said Trench, as another thought struck him about how to set up the search. He knew that nearly ninety per cent of sex attacks were committed by someone known to the victim. He thought they could fine tune their search by limiting it to stranger-attacks. That felt much more likely in this case, given the way the victim was found in Oldbury Woods. It wasn't certain, but it would dramatically limit the number of hits. If it didn't work, they could rerun the search.

"Limit it to stranger-attacks as well," he continued. "Exclude everything where the attacker is a family member, boyfriend etcetera."

Barton made a note and nodded his head.

"Sorry, you were going to ask me something," said Trench.

"Yeah, I was just…You think this guy has Vanessa Osbourne?"

Trench paused before answering. From the look on Barton's face he assumed he was asking because he was horrified at the notion of Vanessa being victim to the savage they were searching for. Trench decided not to inform him that he was no longer on the case. He wanted to keep Barton on the Oldbury Woods case. There were plenty of other constables on the Vanessa Osbourne case and he could do with the help. However he decided not to say that explicitly, in case either Barton wanted to stay on the Osbourne case or Lewis got wind of the instruction and overturned it.

"Let's hope not," was all he said. "There's a briefing now, but I want you to skip that. Stay on this. Let me know as soon as you've got the updated results."

Barton nodded and said nothing, despite a mildly quizzical look crossing his face.

Trench had another thought.

"And email me a copy as soon as you're done. I may not be at my desk. I'll call you if I need to discuss."

"Okay, will do," replied Barton.

Trench left the room and trudged back to his desk. Jazz was not at her desk. Glancing at his watch, he assumed she was at the briefing. He was still simmering after the altercation with Lewis, but knew he had to let it go. He tried to console himself by thinking that at least he could give the body in Oldbury Woods his full attention now.

While he waited for the new search results, he decided to make a start on the current search results Barton had just given him. He would go through the background case files of each, looking for similar circumstances to the body at Oldbury Woods and cutting it down to a much shorter list of potential suspects, at which to take a closer look.

But he didn't intend to hang around the station to do this. It would be much harder to focus here, with all the shit still floating around. Everyone was in the briefing for the moment, but they would be out soon enough. Instead, he intended to download the background case files to his laptop and review them at home.

It was Friday. He decided he was going to pick Milo up early and then review the case files after Milo had gone to bed. The thought of picking Milo up immediately started putting him in better form. It was tinged with a slight doubt, as always. He knew he would have to first negotiate the earlier pick up with Vivian, Milo's Mum. And that was rarely straight forward. But either way, he would be seeing him soon. He smiled to himself as the thought of his son, and how there would be absolutely no chance of anything invading his mind with Milo's unrelenting questioning and messing around.

He opened the mail from Barton and clicked on the attachment. He recognised it as the same list he had just reviewed. He created a new folder on his desktop called "Oldbury Woods" and saved a copy of the list. He then opened that copy and had another look at it. He sorted it by length of prison sentence. This meant the first few names on the list consisted of people who had been sentenced to much longer prison terms, the highest being nineteen years.

He recognised the name for that one so checked date of offence, and groaned. It was four years ago. Which meant the guy was almost certainly still in prison. He scanned the next few and saw that they would also still be in prison. He realised then that most of those convicted of either murder or manslaughter would likely still be in prison, serving long sentences. For the next twenty minutes he went through the rest of the list deleting those names who were still in prison.

When he got to the section where the sentences did not involve prison time, he paused. He initially considered just excluding all of these names, which was about a third of the list, because their crimes would be relatively minor. But he knew that despite sentencing guidelines, the actual sentence handed down to people convicted of the same crime varied dramatically depending on external factors. Some of those factors were reasonable, such as a person's criminal record. But others were not reasonable. They were just the random variables that gave the so-called justice system an element of lottery.

One such factor was geography. Sentencing patterns for the same crime varied widely across the forty-three different regional police jurisdictions. Some regions consistently delivered much tougher sentences than others, while some were consistently much more lenient.

Another factor was the type of court. Trench knew that wily criminal defence lawyers manoeuvred to get their clients' cases heard in Crown Courts, where a judge presided, rather than in a Magistrates Court. Magistrates were essentially well-intentioned volunteers, selected from amongst the upstanding citizens of the local community. Unpaid for their work, they were often drawn from outside the legal profession. They therefore tended to be much more shocked by the brutal reality of society's dark side, and so meted out harsher punishments. Judges had seen it all before. A good defence lawyer could knock a sizeable chunk off his client's sentence by playing the system.

Knowing this, and wanting to cast a wider net to begin with, he left the names of the people who received a sentence that did not involve prison time on the list. As he worked through the list he recognised another handful of the names. It made him realise just how grim a task he was facing, sifting through the case files of the most depraved criminals out there.

# Nineteen

Fifteen minutes later, Trench was on his bike, weaving his way through traffic on New Camberwell Road. His laptop was in his bag, strapped to the saddle behind him. It had stopped raining but the streets were still soaked from the earlier downpours.

Before leaving the station he had considered phoning Vivian to arrange the early pick up. But he couldn't face potentially having another shitty conversation. He sent a text instead, while sitting on his bike, ready to go. He had then put the phone on silent so that he would not hear the message notification through the Bluetooth connection to his helmet. He wanted to at least enjoy the music on his ride home. It was a well-worn tactic. It was also a note-to-self. You know you're having a bad day when the commute is the best part of it.

He followed that thought by noting that the day was about to get much better. Even if Vivian didn't agree to an early pick up, he would review more of the case files and then see Milo later. When he arrived home, only after he had gone inside and changed his clothes did he check his phone. No new messages. He felt relaxed enough after the ride home to call Vivian instead of sending another text. It was answered on the first ring.

"Let me guess, you're not picking him up tonight," Vivian sighed as she answered.

"No, I am. Did you get my text?"

After a short pause she said, "No, no text. Are you sure it was me you sent it to?"

Trench felt a flash of irritation at the potentially incendiary comment. Vivian's persistent accusations that he was cheating had been one of the main reasons irreparable cracks had appeared in their relationship. He never had been and there had never been any legitimate reason to suspect him. But countless arguments had started by comments like this one. He supressed the irritation and ignored the comment.

"I want to pick Milo up from school today. I'm back home now and well, I missed him last night. I'm hoping to surprise him by picking him up from school. He'd love that."

Another pause, then, "Everything alright? Not like you to finish early?"

"Everything's fine. I'm just about to get into the car now and go to the school. Hopefully it frees up your afternoon too. We'll call you later to say good night."

He knew he was pressing, but he didn't want to spend any more time on the call than he had to. There was another pause before she replied.

"Okay, fine. Make sure you tell him I said it was okay. And do call me later."

"Okay. Bye."

He pulled on a warm hoodie and got his car keys from his bedroom. With the green light to pick Milo up, his heavy mood from earlier all but disappeared.

His car was parked out the front of the house, rather than in the back lane where his bike shed was. It was a beat up old 4x4. He wasn't much of a petrol head. Besides, he could barely afford having both and prioritised the quality of his bike over the car.

He was way too early, but much preferred to get there and wait rather than risk being late. He parked and walked to the school gates. As he got closer, he could see there was already a handful of other parents at the gate. He knew some of the faces but not their names. And although he would recognise some faces, he could never remember whose child was theirs. He decided to hang back.

He spent the next few minutes mulling both cases. He knew he should let the Vanessa Osbourne case go, but he couldn't do that completely. He was tempted to call Jazz to find out what had happened at the briefing but decided against it. If they had heard from the kidnapper again, Jazz would have called. If not, then the only thing they could have discussed was various what-if scenarios and assigning roles for the now myriad people involved in the investigation. He didn't want to hear about that.

He turned his attention to the body in Oldbury Woods. He tried to tally what little information they had to go on so far. Painfully little, he knew. It would be a difficult investigation. With the postmortem not producing much by way of evidence, he felt he had to give primary focus to finding out the woman's identity. If he was right that she was a prostitute, then maybe they could at least narrow the search to a specific location. A place where she was known to regularly hook. Once they had that, he would call in CFIT to analyse all footage from the area over the past couple of weeks.

He would also speak with other hookers who worked the same area. In his experience, women who worked the same patch tended to look out for each other.

Although in theory they were competing for the same sordid business, there were always more than enough customers to go round. The greater danger was from the customers themselves. So the women usually swapped stories about which johns to avoid, what car they drove, which ones liked funny stuff or were into the rough trade.

If he was lucky, someone might even know who the victim had last been seen with. Failing that, they might know of customers who had particularly sadistic or violent tendencies. Trench was convinced that this was not the one and only time the killer had tried to fulfil his fantasy. Just his most thorough, he thought grimly.

And he had indeed been thorough. The vast majority of sex worker murders involved killers that psychologists would call disorganised. There was rarely any premeditation. Where there was, it was for the killing itself rather than the cover-up afterwards. They left a chaotic, messy scene behind, awash with forensic evidence. This made it easier to identify and catch the killer.

This killer was different. He was forensically aware, methodical in his clean-up of the body. The level of premeditation was substantial. Not just with the clean-up, but in commission of the crime itself. Wharton had said she had been kept alive for an extended period, being repeatedly choked out and then woken up. If the process had lasted many hours, days even, then the killer had to have some place where he knew he would not be disturbed.

Trench's thoughts were interrupted by a loud, persistent bell. School was out. Almost immediately, the universal chorus of young children's excited chatter filled the air. He walked closer to the school gates, looking up at the school, which was on a slight hill at the top of a path leading down to the school gates. Milo's class was not amongst the first to make their way down the hill, but Trench spotted his teacher after a few minutes.

He then saw Milo, his unmistakable black hair bouncing along as he held hands with a young classmate. He seemed to be chatting animatedly with the girl. Trench smiled inwardly as he saw his son's unkempt hair, the unruly tuft of jet-black hair at the very top of his head sticking straight up, as it always did.

As the teacher leading the class arrived at the gate, she glanced around, clocking the parents of each child in her class, then motioning the child forward. Trench instinctively tried to make himself taller, so that she would spot him before Milo did. But Milo was quicker off the mark.

"Daddeeeeeeee," he screamed out excitedly, and immediately charged in Trench's direction, completely oblivious to his teacher's warnings to slow down and be careful. He raced toward Trench, the improbably large bookbag on his back bouncing way over his head with each step. Trench beamed as he watched the delight on his son's face. He was growing up fast and Trench was always conscious of the need to treasure such moments.

Still a few feet away, Milo launched himself into the air. Trench caught him under each arm, bracing himself for the increasing weight as his son grew. But he wasn't so big yet. Trench gathered him without much effort and lifted him up into a hug. Milo hugged him back as hard as he could. In those few seconds, Trench completely forgot about anything else in his world.

"Why are you here, Daddy? I didn't think you were going to pick me up?" said Milo excitedly as he released his grip.

"I left work early to pick you up. I wanted to surprise you."

"You definitely did, and I *love* surprises," hollered Milo, hugging him again. When he stopped he had a thoughtful look on his face. "I mean, I love happy surprises. I don't like bad surprises though."

"You never have bad surprises, Milo. Only good ones."

He put Milo down and held his hand as they started walking towards the car.

"How was school today?"

"Same," said Milo immediately.

He had the reply on automatic, used to the same question every time Trench picked him up.

"Learn anything interesting?" asked Trench.

"No," replied Milo without thinking about it.

Trench was well used to the exchange. He knew he would never get a considered answer to the direct question. Instead, he would turn the conversation toward certain topics and Milo would spontaneously take over, subconsciously demonstrating whatever he had recently learned.

When they got back home, Milo went straight into his bedroom to change out of his school uniform without having to be told. Trench went into the kitchen and began making dinner. When Milo came into the kitchen, his T-shirt was inside out and his shorts were back to front. Trench didn't bother telling him. If he was comfortable, it didn't matter.

When Trench put a full plate of pesto-pasta and grilled chicken with broccoli down in front of Milo, he yelped.

"Ugh! I *hate* broccoli," he cried, aghast.

"What? You love broccoli," said Trench in amusement. "Since when?"

"No I don't. I *HATE* broccoli. I've always hated it," Milo protested. "*Everyone* hates broccoli. Will hates it, Martha hates it, Billy hates it, Jonnie hates it. Actually only Jonnie F. I don't know if Jonnie R hates it, because I didn't ask him. But he probably does. *Everyone* hates broccoli."

Trench just shrugged. He was getting used to the dramatic changes in preferences since Milo had started school. It was an acute demonstration of peer power. He told Milo to ignore it, but Milo remained staring aghast at the plate. Eventually Trench scraped the broccoli onto this own plate and Milo dived into his dinner.

When they were finished, Trench washed up while Milo belted out the songs they were learning for the upcoming school nativity play. He couldn't hold a note. But he could sure carry his voice. Finished in the kitchen, they went into the living room and played snap. As always, Milo treated it like the World Cup final, doing laps of the room when he won and huffing intensely when he didn't.

Trench was sure to never simply let him win. Even though schools had banned the concept of competition, of winning and losing, from all forms of sport and activities, Trench didn't believe that was right. It was a tough world. Kids needed to learn how to lose, how to win, and how to conduct yourself irrespective of the outcome. He was still working on the latter with Milo.

At bedtime, Trench lay down beside Milo and told him the same story he had told a hundred times before. Milo laughed raucously in all the same places, but still found a new question or two to ask during the story. When the story was done, he immediately turned around onto his stomach and instructed Trench to scratch his back. Trench duly obliged, knowing that it wouldn't last long. Milo was snoring his head off almost immediately.

Trench watched his son for another few minutes, enjoying the peacefulness and utter relaxation he was able to achieve almost as soon as his head hit the pillow. For what must have been the thousandth time, he hoped his son would always retain such an ability to sleep so solidly. He stopped short of considering at what stage life began to intrude on a person's sleep.

# Twenty

When Trench got up and left Milo's room, his mind immediately turned to the night's work ahead. He retrieved his laptop and notebook from his bag and brought them into the small desk in the living room. As he waited for his laptop to boot up, he checked his phone for messages or missed calls. There were none. He again wondered why he had not heard from Jazz about the arrangements for the ransom drop, and again concluded it meant they had not heard back from the kidnapper yet. He resolved that if he had not heard anything by mid-morning tomorrow, he would call Jazz.

He first checked his emails but didn't see anything he thought was worth opening. Barton had obviously not completed the revised search, focusing on crimes and the victims, rather than ex-cons on the sex-offenders register. It bothered him a bit that he did not have what he considered to be a more useful analysis of similar crimes, but he ignored the thought and opened the list of known sex offenders that he had saved on his hard drive before leaving the station.

Starting at the top, he went through the list and isolated those whose crimes included either murder or manslaughter. Having earlier excluded those who were still in jail, this left only half a dozen names. Working through them, he saw that three were aged over sixty-five. Bearing in mind the location and circumstances in which the victim was found, he decided to exclude them. Not many geriatrics living off prison food for decades would be fit enough to carry the body through the woods and then rig it up in the manner they had found it. They were looking for a younger man.

As he started looking into the first of the remaining three names, he immediately felt it could fit. The man had served seventeen years for the rape and stabbing to death of a prostitute in Croydon, South London. His release date was four years before. Trench calculated that his current age was early fifties. Possible. He then checked for any other convictions, but there were none since his release. Maybe the experience of getting caught had made him more careful. But then his eyes caught a short note further down the page of the man's file. Deceased. It was dated a couple of years ago, and gave the cause of death as 'unexplained; London Coroner.'

This prompted him to check the files for the remaining two names. He found that one of the other men was also now deceased. The other did not have such a notation on the file, but his address was in Scotland. Noting that he was also sixty-three years old, Trench decided to delete his name.

He worked swiftly through the rest of the list and was able to whittle it down to just over a single page. A depressing number of entries related to paedophiles. That didn't fit the profile he was looking for so he deleted all of those. He then went back to the top of the list and began taking a more detailed look at the crimes for which each person had been sentenced.

The first entry on the amended list related to an assault against a male prostitute. He therefore went down the rest of the list, scanning the files and deleting all entries where the victim was male. When he had finished, he could see that the most common victims amongst the remaining entries were prostitutes.

He read through the details of the crime now at the top of the list. It concerned a man, previously a regular john, who had taken to picking up working girls from the streets near the City of London and bringing them back to cheap hotels nearby. Instead of paying them for sex, he battered them, robbed them of whatever meagre pickings they had, raped them, then left the hotel.

In a frenzied two-week period, the man had attacked nine prostitutes. The fact he had previously been a regular customer meant most of his victims had trusted him and did not feel threatened until he started beating them. It also meant he was easily identified, and police were waiting for him when he went to pick up his tenth victim. The arresting officers had found two large knives in his car. The man had started using a knife during his most recent crimes, with both the eighth and ninth victims requiring stitches for wounds inflicted during the attack.

The presence of a knife particularly piqued Trench's attention. He immediately felt the man fit the profile. He read more about his circumstances. In court, the man's lawyer had presented mitigation along the lines of having recently lost his job, been kicked out of the home he had shared with his wife and 'having sought to self-medicate through alcohol and recreational drugs.' He had spiralled out of control rapidly and started attacking the women.

It was a sorry story that Trench was all too familiar with. Almost every criminal court case involving unprovoked violence seemed to centre around alcohol and/or drug use. A huge number also featured a recent row with a partner or spouse. He noted the man, Steven Fuller, had been released from prison two years ago, having served six and half years of a ten-year sentence.

The latest address he had for the man was in East London, which was certainly within striking distance of Oldbury Woods. When he searched the DVLA's database, he saw that the man's Driver's License had been cancelled around the same time as his offences. He checked back through the details of arrest and learned the man was three times the legal drink-drive limit at the time of his arrest. Trench surmised that he had not regained his license after his release from prison.

Although this suggested it was unlikely he now owned a car, Trench knew that many of the worst offenders paid little attention to driving bans, or the need for a license or insurance. He highlighted Fuller's name on the list, meaning he intended to interview the man. Once he had identified all those to be interviewed, he would prioritise them and begin the process of visiting them at their homes, unannounced, starting Monday morning. He moved on to the next entry on the list.

Over the next two hours, Trench drew up a not-so-short list of forty-seven names. The vast majority of these had multiple convictions in addition to the sexual assault, mainly for offences such as GBH, shoplifting or drunk and disorderly. Nearly every person with multiple convictions also had convictions for motoring offences: drink-driving, driving without insurance or without a license. For their sexual crimes, the majority had been violent toward prostitutes, either robbing or raping them, often both. In a dozen cases, the perpetrator had attacked both prostitutes and non-prostitutes.

Trench paused and let out a deep breath. Any of the people on the list could be the man he was looking for. Or none of them could be. After considering for a moment, he then went back through the forty-seven names, highlighting the ones where a weapon had been used. It turned out to be the vast majority of cases. He then focused on instances where the weapon was a knife, or some other cutting implement. But this did not reduce the number materially. Most used knives. Like every other criminal in London.

Again, he paused to think about how best to prioritise. He considered what had driven the killer. Assuming the body in Oldbury Woods was the pinnacle of the killer's fantasy, what other features should he be looking for in their known criminal history?

Abduction, he thought immediately. Cases where the killer had taken the victim to a secluded or secure location and had spent a lengthy amount of time carrying out his attack. Any signs of torture or violence during, rather than before or after, the sexual assault would also warrant further investigation.

Nearly thirty of the names on the list had included abduction or withholding the victim from leaving the scene after the attack. Working through those, he isolated eighteen cases where the main purpose of the crime seemed to be sexual. The others looked to be at least partially motivated by either robbery or incidental violence. That is, the cold, empty, carnal transaction appeared to be standard. It was only afterwards the perpetrator became violent, either demanding a return of his money or reacting to some perceived slight or antagonism. Trench believed these did not fit. He was looking for a man for whom violence during sex was the dominant paraphilia. The particular perversion that drove his sadistic crimes.

He highlighted these eighteen names and started going through each case file in detail. As he studied them, he made notes about each case in his notebook. It took nearly ninety minutes to go through all the cases. He focused on the specific elements of the crime: the victim, location, length of time it took to commit the crime and the nature of any torture or violence.

As a result of the process, he was only able to remove a couple of names. When he was done, he carefully reviewed his handwritten notes on the remaining sixteen cases. He considered each one in turn, making a final call on whether or not they fit the profile of the killer. For each one, he was satisfied that they could be the man he was looking for.

He had known before he started that he had to keep an open mind, and looking at this final shortlist of sixteen men, he was reminded as to why. They came from all walks of life, all socio-economic backgrounds, professions and levels of education. Trench had never worked in the specialist sex crimes unit. But he had enough experience to know why his colleagues considered it the great leveller in the pantheon of crimes against the person. The devil could indeed be wearing Prada, or a hard hat or in one case, a tennis coach's whites.

Trench got up from the desk to refill his water bottle. He glanced at the clock in the kitchen and was surprised to see he'd been at his desk for well over three hours. But he was pleased with the work. It gave him a good starting point. The next thing he intended to do was put together the timetable, prioritising which ones to see on Monday and working out how long it would take to visit them all. After he had filled his water bottle, he decided he'd prefer a beer instead. He got a cold bottle from the fridge and brought it back into his desk. He sat down and took a long slug from it. Good decision.

As he focused again on the screen he noticed the icon in bottom corner indicating he had new mail. For a second he debated whether to check it. He didn't want to break his stride. Or ruin his mood. After a moment, he decided to have a glance and flipped into his inbox, even though he doubted it could be anything that would improve his mood. He was wrong.

"Barton…good man," he said out loud, pleasantly surprised.

It was the new search results. There was a short covering email saying the attachment included details of all the most violent sex attacks from Greater London and the surrounding police jurisdictions. Trench opened the attachment and was initially surprised that it comprised only two pages, before remembering that it was limited to stranger-attacks.

He then checked the format to figure out how the results were being displayed. For each reported attack, the data downloaded from the database included the category the police used to record the attack, the date, the police jurisdiction, victim profile, a summary of the details of the crime as entered by the SIO and whether either the attacker had been caught or there was a firm suspect. Trench saved a copy to his laptop and then sorted the list by category of attack.

The first thing that struck him was that there were five homicides on the list. For each, he checked the victim profile and saw three had been prostitutes. The attacks were spread out, with one each in London, Thames Valley and Sussex. He started with the London one, but then noticed the attack was two years ago and the attacker had been caught and jailed. He moved onto the Thames Valley one. It was marked open-unsolved. He read the details.

The body of twenty-four year old Sharon Brimms had been found floating in the River Kennet near Reading, on a Monday morning in mid-October. A known sex-worker, she had not been reported missing before her body was found. It was therefore not known how long she had been missing. The latest confirmed sighting was the previous Thursday. That afternoon, she had left the flat of a friend with whom she occasionally stayed. The friend wasn't sure when she was expected back so hadn't reported her missing.

She had multiple prior arrests for solicitation and drug possession, mostly heroine and crack cocaine. Her address was given as NFA, 'no fixed abode.' Reading between the lines, this explained to Trench why the friend didn't know when to expect her back or why she had not been reported missing. The friend was probably a fellow junkie with whom Brimms stayed from time to time, before disappearing to who knows where. Of much greater interest was the description of the circumstances in which the body was found. The description contained only a few lines, but it was enough to make Trench sit bolt upright in his seat.

Naked, her hands and feet were bound with cable ties. There were 'multiple lacerations' to her upper body. Rape was noted as 'probable'. Cause of death was given as 'ligature strangulation (hyoid fracture)', not drowning. Trench knew the hyoid bone was the small U-shaped bone in the neck that was found to be fractured in around one third of strangulation cases. Police used it as a solid tell of the cause of death.

The part of the river where the body was found was surrounded by fields, although it was not known where the body had entered the river. No usable DNA had been recovered. The word 'river' was in brackets after this.

Trench reread it a couple of times. The similarities were unmistakable. The cable ties, the lack of DNA – whether this was due to the river or something the killer had done prior to dumping her in the river. The fact she was naked and presumed raped. But most of all, the lacerations. If they were prominent enough to be mentioned as part of the summary that meant they were not mere scratches or scrapes.

Trench felt a rush of adrenaline. He immediately regretted not being able to access the full case file to see the pictures. He instinctively checked the time, but knew it was too late to call Thames Valley CID. He would call first thing in the morning. He flipped back to his inbox and started typing a reply to Barton, asking him to send the full case details. He left it unsent, deciding he would send it after he had gone through the whole list.

But he also wanted to talk to the SIO from Thames Valley directly. He may know things about the case that would not be in the files. Gut feelings, impressions from any interviews they had with potential suspects or any other conjecture or guess work that had not made it into the official files.

He thought for a moment if there was anything else he could do right now to get more information. He opened Google and searched the name Sharon Brimms, adding words like 'murder', 'homicide' and 'prostitute' to narrow the results. Nothing relevant came up. He tried a few times alternating the words, adding 'Reading' and 'Thames Valley Police', but still got nothing.

He wasn't surprised. The press chose only a handful of homicides a year to cover in detail, from the many hundreds of available options. The harsh reality was that they picked the ones most likely to generate the clicks and circulation they needed to get paid. The pitiful death of a transient hooker with no permanent home or friends did not come close to fitting the bill. Not even for the local papers.

He was impatient to get more details but decided to move on. He could wait until tomorrow. The disappointment of not being able to get more details was more than offset by the high of finding a case that was potentially linked. He went back to the search results and looked at the next entry, the case in Sussex. He scanned the information to see if it was worth looking into in more detail. It took only a couple of seconds.

"Son of a bitch…"

There was less information than for the previous entry, but he could see immediately that it fit. The body of a 32-year-old prostitute had been found in the River Ouse near the south coast. It was just off a dirt track used to access a remote quarry, surrounded for miles by open fields. The body was naked and the short description contained the words 'evidence of restraints used', but didn't give more details.

It did however say the body 'may have multiple premortem lacerations', and the cause of death was noted as 'probable strangulation – not drowning'. The case was marked as open-unsolved and there were no suspects.

Trench felt his pulse rate quicken. He read the date. April. He reread the summary again. He assumed that the vagueness about the lacerations was most likely caused by the body being in the water. He knew from experience that immersing a body in water could significantly hinder the ability of the pathologist to be precise about the nature of wounds on the body.

But the cause of death was not drowning, they were precise about that. And restraints were used. Which meant she did not end up in the water by herself.

He sat back in his chair and blew out his cheeks. Including the body in Oldbury Woods, that made three sex-workers killed in similar circumstances in six months. Although in different jurisdictions, the distance between the three sites was barely a few hours by car. That was not a normal rate of homicide, even for sex-workers.

That was a pattern.

He opened Google. This time when he entered the name of the victim, Amber Kendall, with the same search words, he did get a hit. The *Crawley Observer* carried a short story from mid-April. It stated that the body of local woman Kendall had been found 'in suspicious circumstances.' It described her as a 'socialite and sometime escort.' She had been assumed missing for a couple of weeks. There was a photo, but it was so blurry all Trench could make out was that she had light brown hair.

He reached for his beer and raised it to his lips, but found it was empty. He got up to get another from the fridge. He took the moment to make sure he wasn't getting ahead of himself. But he felt sure he wasn't. There were occasional spikes in crimes, even homicides, due to exogenous factors like particularly good weather or dire economic times. But he knew neither could explain the pattern he was looking at.

Three prostitutes being killed separately in such a short timeframe was not beyond the realms of possibility. But such strong similarities in the circumstance of their murders was beyond coincidence. He could feel it. He knew he had found something. He grabbed a beer from the fridge and went straight back to his desk.

He wanted to check whether there were any other attacks that may fit the pattern. He first looked at the other two murders, of non-prostitutes. He ruled out the first, because it was an elderly woman who had been sexually assaulted and killed in her own home. Although strangled, the house had also been burgled and the assault itself did not appear to be the sole motivation of the killer. It did not fit the pattern.

He also felt the last murder, in which a young woman had been sexually assaulted, battered and left for dead in a wooded area just south of Salisbury, did not fit the pattern. It seemed too chaotic, not least because the assault had taken place in the area where the body was found.

Finished examining the murders, he then carefully checked through all the other attacks listed in the search results. He was checking to see if any others bore the same hallmarks, even though none had involved murdering the victim. A handful struck him as possible initially. But when he looked into each, he ultimately determined that none of the other attacks had a sufficiently similar MO.

Satisfied with having thoroughly gone through the full list of search results, he wrote down a summary of what he had found in his notebook. Three prostitutes, each tortured and strangled. All with knife wounds. All restrained. The bodies all dumped in a way which inhibited the retrieval of DNA evidence, either from being in water or from the body itself being cleaned as with the body in Oldbury Woods.

From what Wharton had said, the body they had found had been subjected to a lengthy assault, possibly for days. The other two appeared to have been missing for days before their bodies were found. He would have to check with the SIO for each case for the estimated time of death. But for the moment it certainly seemed possible that they were alive for some time after their disappearance.

As another thought formed in his head, he instinctively glanced at his notes, even though he didn't need to look again. The first killing had been in April, the second in October and the most recent in November. He knew that serial killers worked in cycles. Each killing would satisfy the urge for a time. But the urge would return. Looking at the dates of the three murders, the interval between them was getting shorter.

He felt a sharp pang of urgency.

He stood up and paced the room. The movement helped clarify his thinking. There were clear similarities between the cases, he felt no doubt about that. But then he considered the glaring difference. The first two victims had simply been discarded when he was finished with them, their bodies just thrown away. But with the most recent victim, he hadn't simply dumped her. He had taken great risk to elaborately display her in the provocative, demeaning pose in which they'd found her. Why?

Trench wondered whether this meant the killer had felt greater anger toward this victim for some reason. Maybe it was more personal to him, and he wanted to degrade her more than the others. Or maybe she had put up more of a fight, causing him to want to punish her further, even after she was dead.

Or did it say more about the killer himself than about the victim? Was he growing into his crimes, going further to indulge a compulsion to more fully carry out whatever fantasy was driving him?

It also suggested an ominous sense of confidence by the killer. It showed a chilling calm, to take the time and effort to string her up like that in a relatively public setting. Either he was confident that he would not be caught in the act, or he didn't fear the consequences of being caught. Either way, Trench figured this made him extremely dangerous.

As he thought about this, he made two decisions. The first was to make another call in the morning, this one to Kevin Johnson, a psychological profiler in the Met's Forensic Psychology Unit. Trench had worked with him before and knew he was better placed to make a judgement on what it could mean.

The second decision was that it didn't matter what the killer's reason was. Not to Trench. That could be argued about or speculated on much later, by people specially trained to interpret such actions when deciding the killer's fate. Trench knew that at that time, he would argue as forcefully as he could that no matter what the reason, this beast should be locked away forever.

But for now, the only thing that mattered was catching this savage. As quickly as possible. He had enough experience to know that if the same man was responsible for killing three women in six months, he wasn't going to just stop. They had to catch him.

He had to catch him.

# Twenty-One

Trench got up early Saturday morning. He wanted to progress as much as he could before Milo woke up. He first sent an email to Kevin Johnson, figuring he would not be in the office this early on a Saturday, if at all, for a phone call.

In the short email he stated bluntly that he had found compelling evidence that the same killer was responsible for at least three sexually motivated murders in the last six months, and he wanted his opinion as soon as possible. He assumed Johnson was as under-resourced and overworked as everyone else on the police force, so wanted to make sure this got his full attention immediately. He therefore included that he believed the killer would strike again in the very near future. He wasn't sure if Johnson worked weekends, but he said he wanted the analysis within twenty-four hours anyway.

He then called Thames Valley police and asked to be put through to their CID after identifying himself. It was answered on the first ring.

"CID, Griffiths."

"Griffiths, this is DCI Trent Chambers from Met CID. How're you doing?"

"Busy, DCI Chambers from the Met. What can you do for me?" responded Griffiths coolly.

The standoffish tone was not a surprise to Trench. Nearly every CID squad in the country was overrun. Most of the time when other constabularies called it was to ask for help with their own cases, adding to CID's workload. But Trench figured he would pleasantly surprise Griffiths on this occasion.

"I hear you. Aren't we all. But I think I can help you, or one of your squad. Who's working the murder of Sharon Brimms?"

"Oh yeah?" said Griffiths, more interested now. "That's DI Mike Ward's case. He's not on duty today. But if you've got something, I'll take it and pass it on to him."

"Right, thanks. Yeah, I can leave a message, but I'll need to speak to Ward too, as soon as he's back on. And I'm also after the case file. I want to go through everything you've got. Can you send me the file now? It would be useful to review it before I speak with Ward."

"Yeah, well, it's not my case, Chambers. Can't you just get the details off the system? And you still haven't told me what you can do for us."

"I can get it off Central, sure," said Trench. "But I want to get anything else the SIO might have, that hasn't made it into the official file. I also want to discuss it in detail, so best to get his version. And what I can do for you, is send you the file of a case I'm working on with the same MO. Almost identical. She was found in West Kent, not a million miles from where you found Brimms. It's not one hundred per cent confirmed yet, but it's very possible it's the same guy who killed Sharon Brimms. I'll send it so Ward can see for himself."

He decided not to mention the other potentially linked case yet. He wanted to review that file in detail, before bringing it up with Ward when they spoke.

"Shit, really?" said Griffiths, now giving it his full attention.

"As I say, it's not a hundred per cent, but yeah. I'm thinking it's the same killer."

"Okay, Chambers. I'll send you over the Brimms file later today, as soon as I get a chance. I'll let Mike know to call you. You can send me what you've got and I'll send it to Mike."

They exchanged emails and hung up. Trench was just about to call Sussex CID when he heard Milo getting out of bed and plodding into Trench's bedroom. He got up from his desk in the living room and quietly followed him in. He watched as Milo, still half asleep, climbed into his bed, lay face down on the pillow and then lifted his left arm up and plonked it down on Trench's pillow. He did the same thing every morning. Sometimes the arm in the face was how Trench woke up.

This time, after a couple of seconds it must have registered to Milo that Trench's face seemed softer than normal. He suddenly pulled his arm back and lifted himself up on both arms, looking over. He stared at the empty pillow for a second, then pulled back the duvet. He started smiling, assuming Trench was hiding down below the duvet. He sat up and pulled it down further, but then spotted Trench in the doorway smiling at him.

"You tricked me," he said, rubbing his eyes.

"No trick," laughed Trench, going over and sitting down on the bed. "I just got up early today, that's all. You hungry?"

"Starving," replied Milo enthusiastically.

Trench picked him up and carried back into his room.

"Good, you get yourself dressed and I'll go make breakfast. It's not raining, but it's a little cold so put on some warm clothes," he said, although he then went to the wardrobe and took out the warm clothes himself, laying them on the bed.

"We'll head to the park for a while after breakie."

They were in the park before nine. The only other people there were other parents with young kids and a couple of dog walkers. They kicked a ball around for a while, before Trench steered them over to the playground area. He had spotted there were other kids of similar age there and wanted Milo to mingle with them. He enjoyed playing just the two of them, but he also knew that kids could create fun between themselves that adults could never replicate. Milo was soon belting around with a couple of other kids, all of them in hysterics.

With Milo's attention fully focused on the game with the other kids, Trench walked over to the railings around the playground. Still watching Milo, he stood out of earshot of any of the benches where other parents may sit down. As he was taking his phone out to call Sussex CID, it rang in his hand.

"Morning, Jazz," he answered.

"No response yet," she said. "What do you think it means?"

"Best guess is he hasn't settled on the details of the drop yet. He knows it's not going to be easy to just pick up the money and walk away."

There was a pause before Jazz continued.

"Do you think he shopped us? At the internet place? Maybe he's freaked we got so close."

"I don't see it," said Trench. "Even if he did, he won't be surprised police are all over this."

"Uhm," said Jazz, but she sounded flat.

"It suits him to wait, Jazz. The family will be going through hell. The longer this goes on, the quicker they'll agree to whatever demands he makes."

"I suppose so."

"It creates tension, too. Between police and the family. The more time passes, the more likely the family are to lose faith in the cops. It's human nature," said Trench.

As another thought occurred to him, he continued.

"If it was me, I'd wait a few weeks then try to contact the family directly. Tell them if cops stay involved, they'll never see her again. Get one of them to sneak off somewhere and do the drop. I'd go for the mother. At this point, she'd drive anywhere and turn up alone with as much cash as she could fit into her car. Come to think of it, we should probably be keeping an eye on the parents. And you know what, even if she's dead, even if he's killed her, he'll still come looking for the ransom. They always do."

Jazz was quiet for a moment before responding.

"Have you ever considered taking up motivational speaking, Trench? You're a natural."

"Just calling it like I see it, Jazz. No point going around with our heads up our ass hoping for rainbows."

"Uhm."

"It doesn't mean we have to sit around and wait for him. What has Thomson done with the names Krige gave us?"

"We started hitting them this morning. We're taking half and the NCA are on the other half. I was on two names, teamed with Barton. He's good, you know. Knew how to posture. And knew when to shut up too. We got both our guys first thing, but nothing cooking. We cleared them both."

"How'd the other teams do?"

"Mixed bag. Most are cleared, some unaccounted for and one guy taken into custody, unrelated. Assaulting a police officer. Apparently, he was pissed out of his mind when the NCA lads got there at six. Didn't take kindly to them turning up. But not all teams have reported back here yet."

"What do you mean unaccounted for?"

"There were a few names on Krige's list that we couldn't get IDs or addresses for. At the briefing yesterday, they made the call to hit the rest of them this morning anyway."

"What about those ones though, what are we doing about them? And how many were there?" pressed Trench.

He was thinking that if someone on the list was now missing or harder to trace, that would put them at the top of his priorities if he was leading the investigation.

"Three. Harding took them. They're trying to chase them down. I know at least one of them is presumed gone home. We got hold of the company he used to work for and that's what they said. He's Bulgarian anyway."

"Let's hope she finds the other two," said Trench, trying to keep the doubt out of his tone.

He wondered what kind of visibility his CID colleagues would have into the NCA's efforts to find them. There was no way he would have handed them over. Particularly given his negative view of Harding's abilities. As he thought about it, he could not comprehend how a lead investigator, or Chief if that's who had decided, could pass over responsibility for the most important leads.

He shook his head, trying to shake the thoughts away. He was tempted to ask if Commander Campbell was aware of the NCA's involvement yet, or how the briefings had gone since the NCA's involvement, but there was no point. Again, he made a concerted effort to let it go. He had news for Jazz anyway.

"Listen, I need you to send me some files," he said, changing the subject. "It's about the Oldbury Woods body. I found something."

"Oh?" said Jazz, perking up.

"A link. Actually, more than one. I found two other cases that match the MO."

"Shit!" said Jazz, now on full alert. "Where? When?"

"One in Reading, the other down near the south coast, Brighton way. Both hookers, both within the last six months. Both dumped in rivers, so no DNA. Both with hands tied. And both covered in knife wounds."

"Bloody hell!"

"Yeah. I haven't seen the full case files for either of them yet, just a summary. So I need you to send me the full files. I spoke with Thames Valley CID this morning, told them a bit about what we'd found. The SIO isn't on today but I'll speak with him asap. I'm going to call Sussex CID today too. But can you send me the files so I can make a start even if these guys don't get around to sending them to me."

Trench gave her the details of both cases. Jazz repeated them, obviously writing them down as she did so.

"Have a look at both files yourself, if you get the time," he said. "We can compare notes."

Jazz repeated the second name, then spoke.

"Yeah, about that...I'll have time alright. I've been dropped from the Osbourne case. Lewis told me after this morning's briefing. He said that once I'd done my names from Krige's list this morning, I'd be reassigned. They have enough resource on the Osbourne taskforce. I'll be drafted back in if and when they need more *resource.*"

Trench realised she was probably tainted by association, as far as Lewis was concerned. She would have divided loyalties, so he probably didn't want her around. It was petty, and showed an insecurity that Trench found contemptuous. But he focused on the plus side. At least she would now be working the case with him.

"Well, we're going to have our hands full if this turns out the way it's looking. There'll be no time for the bullshit," he said. "And in a few days, everyone will find their cool heads again. We'll be able to help find Vanessa."

He didn't really believe what he said about cooler heads prevailing, but he wanted to allay any concerns Jazz had. He knew how a heavy atmosphere in the squad room could badly affect morale. Which in turn had a direct, negative impact on the unit's effectiveness. As Chief, morale was Lewis's responsibility. Yet another reason to believe he was out of his depth.

"Yeah, I hope you're right," said Jazz. "Hey, how about today? Any chance you're free for lunch or something? I wouldn't mind getting out of here. I can review the files beforehand. I know you probably won't get a chance to look at them until later, but I can brief you. Discreetly, of course, not in front of Milo," said Jazz.

Trench was glad to hear the more upbeat tone to her voice, and thought it would be good to build momentum with the case.

"Sure, good idea. Why don't you come to ours. We can discuss while Milo watches TV for a bit. Assuming he gives you a minute's peace, that is."

"How's Milo doing, by the way? Sorry, I should have asked before. Be great to see him again, it's been ages."

"He's good, thanks. You can ask him yourself later. If you can get a word in."

"Aww, so cute. Looking forward to it."

"See you later, whatever time suits."

"I can call Sussex too if you want. I know a few girls down there, they can put me onto whoever the SIO is," said Jazz. "I'll review the file before speaking with them. Unless you want to speak to them yourself?"

Trench thought about it for a second. He'd rather speak to the SIO himself but he knew it made sense, especially if Jazz knew people there.

"No, that's fine. Go ahead," he answered.

He hung up and, without having to make the call to Sussex, went over to a bench near to where Milo and the other kids were playing. They stayed in the playground for nearly an hour, Milo charging around non-stop for almost the whole time. Eventually Milo came over to the bench, cheeks flushed red, looking for a drink of water. Trench gave him the water bottle he had brought in his backpack. Despite initially saying he wasn't hungry, after sitting on the bench for a couple of minutes, Milo declared that he was starving.

They left the park and stopped in a coffee shop for their usual – a black coffee for Trench and a Mochaccino and banana for Milo. They walked home and changed out of their winter wear, both putting on sweats and t-shirts. They played board games for a while, though Milo got up and turned on the TV not long after they sat down. He made no attempt to watch it, and sat with his back to it. He didn't even check which channel it was on.

Trench had noticed before how Milo always asked for either the TV or radio to be on whenever they were at home. He had figured out it was an instinctive move, adding company to the house with just the two of them in it. It pulled a little at his heart every time, but he had learned to accept it. Trench had always imagined he'd have a large brood of kids in a stable, happy home. But fate had had other plans. Now he was just glad to be out of it in one piece. Or not too many pieces, anyway. There had been times during those painful years when he thought he was going to lose everything.

When there was a knock on the door a short while later, Milo immediately jumped up but then paused.

"Who is that?" he asked, excited but with confusion writ large on his face.

Trench hadn't told him they were expecting anyone. He had long ago learned not to tell Milo when someone was expected. If they were unable to come for whatever reason, the disappointment Milo showed when he told him they weren't coming was something he always tried to avoid.

"Not sure, let's go check," he replied, getting up deliberately slowly.

Milo raced ahead to the door. Trench got to the hall just as Milo opened the door.

"Jazzeeee!" he screamed when he opened it.

He leapt at Jazz, who deftly stooped low so she wouldn't have to catch his full weight while standing still. Milo gave her a long, tight hug, then turned his head around.

"Daddy, it's Jazzee!" he called over his shoulder, then grabbed her hand and led her inside.

They both brushed right past Trench and into the living room, Jazz just managing to put her bag down on the way past. Milo insisted Jazz sit down and started taking out pieces from the box so she could join their game. Jazz listened attentively to Milo's instructions, slipping off her coat and tossing it over to Trench. They continued playing for half an hour, mostly adhering to the various elaborate rules Milo added as they played.

Something on the TV caught Trench's attention. The news had come on and the newscaster had definitely said the name Vanessa Osbourne. Jazz heard it too. Trench leaned over and picked up the remote. He turned up the volume.

"*...worried parents have now made an appeal for the safe return of their daughter and are offering a substantial reward for any information leading to her safe return. Our reporter Tim Burrows has more.*"

Doctor Clarence Osbourne appeared on the screen, looking fraught and haggard, sitting behind a table and flanked by a man on each side. Trench recognised neither man. Trench instinctively stood up and took a step towards the TV. The male voiceover explained Doctor Osbourne had just released a statement to the media. Osbourne then started speaking.

"*I am appealing directly to my daughter, to Vanessa. Darling, we love you. Please come home, Vanessa. Your mother is very worried about you. We love you very much. Please, Vanessa, just let us know you are okay,*" he pleaded, staring directly into the camera, his voice quivering at times.

Doctor Osbourne then looked down for a second, visibly taking a deep breathe. When he looked back into the camera, he appeared stronger. His eyebrows tightened, his eyes squinted slightly for focus.

*"If someone is with Vanessa,"* he continued, stern now, *"Let my daughter return home to her family. Let Vanessa come home to where she belongs. We love her very much. Let my daughter come home."*

He then paused for a moment, and when he continued, his delivery was much more solid than before. He slightly raised his chin as he spoke, his jaw seeming to clench. The camera slowly started to zoom in on his face. Soon it was all you could see on the screen.

*"To the man that has taken Vanessa, I tell you this. I am prepared to make you an offer. If Vanessa is returned home within the next twenty-four hours, then you will also get what you want. You have my word on that. Furthermore, I will not look for you. And I will stand down all of the authorities who are now hunting for you. They are hunting for you right now as we speak. This is the only outcome that is good for you.*

*"To everyone else that sees this message, I make an alternate offer. Anyone who provides information that leads to the safe return of Vanessa will receive one million pounds in reward. I, personally, will pay this money to you directly. No taxes, no small print or any other complication. I will pay you one million pounds if you provide substantiated information that results in the safe return of my daughter."*

Doctor Osbourne stared into the camera but didn't say anymore. After a few seconds the shot cut back to the newscaster.

*"A deeply impassioned plea there from billionaire and entrepreneur Doctor Clarence Osbourne for the safe return of his daughter, Vanessa, who has apparently been missing since earlier this week. We can go live now to the Osbourne residence where our reporter Tim Burrows has been watching events unfold. Tim?"*

The shot switched to a man standing outside what Trench recognised as the black gates of Blenheim.

*'Dianne, we are bringing a really sensational development to our viewers live here from the Osbourne family home. Rumours of Vanessa Osbourne's disappearance have grown over the past couple of days, and this announcement from Doctor Osbourne confirms what is really the worst-case scenario for any parent. I think, reading between the lines, we can assume that she has been kidnapped. Doctor Osbourne seemed to be appealing directly to her kidnapper, with that dramatic, almost challenge, to release his daughter immediately. And further adding a reward to any member of the public who –"*

Trench killed it. He stared at the blank TV screen. He was totally dumbstruck. Jazz had turned in her seat to watch. She was also staring at the TV, her mouth wide open. She slowly turned to look at Trench. Neither spoke – could speak – for about a minute.

"What the fucking hell was that," Trench eventually managed, still staring at the screen.

# Twenty-Two

"I don't even…why?" said Trench.

"Who are those people sitting with him?" asked Jazz.

"It can't be NCA. Not even they would…How did this happen?"

Trench stayed standing for another few seconds, but then let out a deep breath and sat down.

"Daddy, it's your turn," said Milo, handing him the dice.

"Okay, thanks son," said Trench before letting the two dice fall out of his hand and roll onto the board. "Can you move me please, Milo."

He immediately stood back up again.

"Sorry Milo, we just need to take a break for a minute, okay. I'm going to turn on a movie for you. We'll finish the game after lunch."

"Okay," said Milo, moving over to sit on the sofa where Trench had been sitting, so he could see the TV.

Trench went to the pre-recorded movies and turned on one he knew Milo liked. He leant down and planted a kiss on the top of his head.

"We'll be back in a few minutes, okay. Just going to the kitchen to make lunch."

"Okay," said Milo again, already distracted by the movie.

Jazz followed him into the kitchen.

"What the hell was that?" Trench repeated. "What the fuck is he doing?"

"NCA wouldn't let him do that, would they?" asked Jazz.

"No. No way. Surely not. Not even they would…"

He trailed off. He felt sure the NCA wouldn't be party to what they had just witnessed. But he wasn't one hundred per cent certain. He realised he didn't know much about the inner workings of their specialist units. And Harding…

"No, I can't believe they would," he said after thinking about it.

Then he remembered something.

"Remember Osbourne said to us the other night that he wanted to offer a reward? And we had to talk him out of it? He talked about offering a million quid for information. He must be doing this by himself."

Jazz nodded.

"But we made it pretty clear that'd create a proper snafu for the investigation. I guess he's not used to taking instruction from people."

"Fucking idiot!" said Trench.

He was getting more worked up the more he replayed it in his mind.

"What the fuck was he thinking? He made it sound like a bloody business deal. And he's threatening the guy? Jesus Christ."

"And now we're going to have every noodle in the country calling up taking a shot at the million quid reward," added Jazz, similarly exasperated. "I'm surprised he didn't give out our number. In fact, who are people going to call? Half the fuckwits will probably dial nine-nine-nine."

Trench knew she was right. The emergency services were certain to experience a surge in calls from people taking a free shot at a million pounds. Free money, and lots of it. Why wouldn't they call? But it was hugely irresponsible of Osbourne. He could understand the man was upset, desperate even. But his ill-considered announcement would put a strain on the entire country's emergency service lines for at least a couple of days.

But as he thought it through, he began to wonder if maybe there was more to it. Osbourne was no fool, he was sure of that.

"Maybe that's what he wants," he said.

"What do you mean?"

"He's a shrewd operator. Maybe he knows exactly what he's doing. Think about it. He's just commandeered the entire emergency services nationwide to focus on looking for his daughter. And he's created an army of searchers. Millions will see this and at least give it some thought. And thousands, maybe tens of thousands, will actually go out and start looking for her, trying for the million quid. He doesn't care if it takes police focus off everything else going on. He only cares about one thing. And now that's all anyone else is going to be able to focus on for the next few days."

"Shit. You think?" said Jazz, but it sounded like a rhetorical question.

It wasn't that much of a stretch and she knew it.

"Yeah, I do," sighed Trench, "After we spoke with him, I thought he might struggle with the fact he'd run into a problem his money couldn't fix. I guess he just couldn't accept that. He's trying to fix it with money anyway."

"But he's not fixing it, Trench. He's probably making it worse! He's probably even put her in greater danger. If this guy gets jumpy he could just walk away. And tie up the loose ends..."

"We know that, but he must not see it like that. You saw his demeanour in there. He was feisty. He's not going to roll over for this guy. It's obviously just not the way he's built. He's fighting back, that's the way he's looking at this. He even said he'd call off police. He can't fucking do that. That's not his decision. Ever. But he's used to being the boss. He thinks he can call the shots, every time. But this time, his bloody pride could cost his daughter her life."

"Bloody hell, the more I think about this, I'm seething," Jazz said, starting to pace the floor. "You know what this is? Male fucking ego. He's made it all about himself. He's turned it into some kind of pissing contest, him against the kidnapper. That's not what this about, Trench. This is about his daughter. His own daughter! He's a fuc—"

She was interrupted by the sound of Trench's phone ringing. He looked at the screen. Nadia Swanson, the reporter. It reminded him of their strained call the day before. He'd been thinking about trying to make amends for that but hadn't gotten around to it. Now was not the time.

"Press," he said, silencing the ringer and putting the phone back down.

"That's another thing," Jazz continued, "The bloody media will have a field day with this. That was box office for them. '*Billionaire father challenges daughter's kidnapper live on TV*'. It's going to be twenty-four seven on every channel."

Trench knew there was little they could do about it now. They were both off the case and whatever Doctor Osbourne had just started was someone else's shitshow to deal with. There was no point in getting themselves worked up about it, though it was difficult not to. He decided to change the subject.

"Yeah well, we can't do anything about it now. We've got our own case. What did you find in the case files—"

He was interrupted by Jazz's phone ringing this time. She picked it up and stared at the screen for a long moment.

"HQ," she said looking at Trench. "I know what this is. Prick. If he thinks I'm just going to be *resource* to answer phones while every sap in the country piles in with claims of a million quid, he can go fuck himself."

After another second, she answered.

"Hello," she said sternly. "Oh, hey, Barton."

She listened for a second before turning and rolling her eyes at Trench. Trench took it as confirmation she was right. He went over to the fridge and took out the food to prepare lunch.

"Right, well I would've been delighted to of course, but our other case just got red hot," Jazz explained into the phone.

After another moment she continued.

"Yeah, I get that, Barton. But there's plenty of bodies to work on that. It means that others – including you – won't be able to do anything on the Oldbury Woods case now. I'm officially off Vanessa Osbourne and on this case and we are going to need at least two bodies on that full time. We'll aim to have it wrapped up as soon as possible and then I'll dive straight onto the phones. Can't wait."

There was a final pause, which Trench assumed was Barton trying to relay just how firm an order Lewis had given him to contact Jazz. But he hadn't been brave enough or bothered enough to do it himself. Barton was now caught in the middle. The pettiness just mounted up.

"I understand, thank you for the message," Jazz said curtly. "You shouldn't be in the middle here, and it's not your problem. But as I said, I'll report onto phone duty when I can. Gotta go."

Jazz hung up and put her phone down.

"You know, he's not going to like that. He seems to want a tight leash on his subordinates," said Trench.

Jazz raised her eyebrows.

"Hmm, advice from the 'managing up' guru himself. I must be in a worse pickle than I thought."

"Touché," said Trench. "Eyes wide open, is all I'm saying. And if you can keep him off your back, better still. It'll make your life easier. Take it from me."

Jazz nodded but didn't reply. She understood he was trying to steer her away from ending up in a similar situation with Lewis to the one he was in. But the look on her face suggested she wasn't in the mood to back down.

"I've put lunch on," said Trench, parking the subject for now. "Let me just check on Milo and then you can brief me on what you found in the files."

When Trench returned to the kitchen, Jazz was sitting down at the kitchen table. There were two documents folders on table in front of the seat opposite her own. She was reading through her notebook.

"There's your copies of both files," she said as Trench sat down. "I've emailed you copies but got hard copies printed off too. I know you prefer those. Let's do this chronologically. I'll start with Amber Kendall because she was found in April."

"Sounds good."

He took out his own notebook. He decided against opening the files yet. They didn't have enough time to go through them in detail. He would study them later after Milo had gone to bed. For now, he was keen just to get the main points from Jazz.

"I went through the file in detail and then called my mate in Sussex. She gave me the name of the SIO, DI Scott Parson. I spoke with him as well. To cut to the chase, I reckon there's a high probability it's our guy. It's not as clear cut as the other one, but there are enough similarities.

"Parson said they weren't sure what they had initially. There was even some debate as to whether she was murdered or not. The body had been in the water for up to a week. And the hands, feet and knees were all badly cut up. Even the face a bit. You'll see that in the photos. And take my word for it, don't look at them on a full stomach.

"They figured out that most of those cuts were postmortem. It's not the first body they've taken out of that river. It's shallow in parts and the hands and feet etcetera can drag along the bottom and through debris. They're assuming she travelled quite a distance in the water. There's hundreds of miles of tributaries and streams flowing into it. Most of them cut through open land or forests. They've not been able to tell where she entered the water. CID wanted to close it as suicide, but Parson wasn't happy. He—"

"Wait, what did the pathologist say about it being suicide? The brass can't just decide that. Especially if the SIO disagrees," interrupted Trench.

"Hang on a sec, I'm coming to that. And none of this is in the file, by the way. Parson told me on the phone. Parson didn't think it was suicide. He'd noticed a cable tie around one wrist. He figured it could've been used to tie both hands and one just worked loose as she tumbled downstream. After I told him what we've got, he's convinced that's what happened now. It must have worked loose just before the body got jammed in tree roots where they eventually found it.

"The brass tried to argue it was just more debris. But he also pointed out that some cuts on her back and backside looked different to the other scrapes and scratches. They were longer, and almost all in straight lines. It was hard to tell given the state of decomp, but he pressed for a postmortem. The brass refused. Didn't want to pay for one, if you can believe that. The budget's tight, and they can cost up to four grand a pop.

"But Parson went to the coroner off his own bat and made the case. The coroner agreed and ordered a forensic postmortem. Get this, the brass dropped their opposition then, because it would come out of the coroner's budget rather than CID's. The fee charged by the forensic pathologist is paid by whoever orders the postmortem."

Both she and Trench shook their head at that. Trench had heard of such cases before. He wondered what it said about society that police chiefs would argue not to investigate a suspicious death because the government wouldn't make enough money available. Too busy stealing it for themselves by fiddling expense claims or awarding bogus grants to their lovers or family members.

"So he backed Parson after the postmortem, I presume? The pathologist," he asked.

"She, actually. But yeah, she declared it suspicious and it went back to CID as a murder investigation."

"Only 'suspicious'? Why not murder?"

"The state of the body. Decomp was slow when it was in the water, but it accelerates when the body is taken out. The argument about whether to have a postmortem took a few days. By the time it was resolved, the body had decomposed so much that she couldn't declare murder for certain. It was harder to distinguish between the knife wounds, the injuries from being in the river and the animals and bugs that had been at her in the water.

"But she was able to tell that she hadn't drowned. With reasonable suspicion around some of the flesh wounds, also trace marks of restraints on the ankles and wrists, and the presence of the cable ties, she concluded 'suspicious'. To be honest, looking at the photos, I wasn't able to see any marks from restraints. Maybe she took Parson's word on that. He saw the body in the water, before the real decomp happened while they were arguing about the postmortem. But putting it all together, I reckon the pathologist did right by the victim calling it suspicious so that it would be investigated."

Trench thought about everything Jazz had said. He agreed with her conclusion but wanted to consider whether they were missing anything or conceding to investigative bias, trying to make the facts fit their theory.

"And Parson thought it was murder all along?"

"Yeah, he did. Sounded like we made his day actually. Seems he's had some tension with the brass for going behind their back on the postmortem, even though they didn't end up paying for it. And they're still giving him grief for adding a murder to their numbers when they don't think it's going to be solved. So he was glad to hear what we had to say. He was pretty fired up by the time we finished talking."

"Well, we're fighting our own Chief. May as well pile into fights with other Chiefs around the country too," said Trench drolly.

He wasn't sure whether to be happy other detectives had similar beefs with their brass or depressed at the state of the force nationwide. Jazz raised her hands in a surrender motion.

"Look, we're just doing our job. Same as Parson, from what it sounds like. If the brass are more worried about—"

"Hey, I know, I get it. It's me, right," said Trench, cutting her off. "Jesus, you really are starting to sound like me. But yeah, at least we're not the only ones. What about suspects? Did Parson have anything?"

"Nada. But he believes he knows how she met her killer. After they ID'd her, which was confirmed by dental records after she was reported missing, they pulled her phone records. She had a couple of different phones, one which she used just for her work as an escort. The last few calls she exchanged were with what turned out to be a burner. They were from a couple of weeks before her body was found. Parson reckons that's how she arranged to meet the guy."

"Did they trace the movement of those phones?" asked Trench, hopeful they may have a workable lead. He meant both her phone and also the one that had called her.

"Yeah, dead end. The signal from both ends on the outskirts of Crawley. Wherever they hooked up, he must've taken her phone and smashed them both up."

"Shit."

It sounded like Parson's investigation had been thorough, but that he had hit a dead end.

"Okay, there's a strong possibility this is our guy. What about the Reading case, Sharon Brimms?" Trench asked, getting up to check on the lunch.

It was nearly done, so he started taking out plates and cutlery while they spoke.

"The file is pretty skinny, the SIO – DI Michael Ward in Reading – obviously isn't a big fan of paperwork. But I think there's no doubt about it. This is him," asserted Jazz. "She was only in the water for about twelve hours when she was found. You'll see the photos. The knife wounds, the cable ties on hands and feet, she was strangled, most likely with a thin cable or wire. It's like looking at the same body, Trench. And there was no confusion from police or the pathologist on this one. Murder."

"Anything in the file about suspects?"

"A few potentials, yeah. They interviewed a bunch of blokes who were seen cruising the red-light district in Reading in the weeks prior. They eliminated most, but not all. They also asked the rest of the working girls in the area. That was her patch, most of the other girls knew her. A couple thought they saw her on the Thursday too. One even gave a description of a van she saw her getting into at some stage on Thursday evening. It's definitely something to ask the SIO about when you speak with him. That was a few weeks ago and the file's not really been updated since then."

"What about time of death?" asked Trench.

"The pathologist said some time on Sunday. They got lucky. The body was found pretty soon after entering the water. Even twelve hours in water can obscure the time of death estimate, but not that much."

"Okay. I'll ask Ward in Thames Valley when I speak with him."

They had been working for nearly half an hour so decided to wrap up. Trench called Milo in to join them and they all ate lunch at the kitchen table. Jazz left shortly after they finished. Later that night, after Milo had gone to bed, Trench went through each of the files in detail. Jazz had provided a good summary of each and he made few additional notes. But when he read through the postmortem report for Amber Kendall, he spotted something that Jazz hadn't mentioned.

In a single sentence in which the pathologist noted the various debris found in the mouth, throat and lungs, Trench noticed a reference to a small number of bright yellow fibres found wedged between her teeth. He recalled that Wharton had found similar fibres on the Oldbury Woods body, also in the mouth.

The pathologist for the Kendall case had understandably not found anything notable about this, given how long the body had been in the water. She categorised it along with all the other debris present. But it stuck out to Trench. It was definitely worth comparing with the fibre they had from the Oldbury Woods body. It could prove to be another vital link between the cases.

He then made a start on the Decision Log for the Oldbury Woods case, the main document kept by the SIO for every murder file. It acted as a live document throughout the investigation and formed the basis for the police's input during any future trial. Trench's approach was always to make the Log as detailed as possible. Given the way this case was turning out, he made sure not to leave anything out.

When he was satisfied with his draft, he checked for any email from Griffiths at Thames Valley. It was there, Griffith having sent it earlier that afternoon. Trench hit reply and attached a copy of the Decision Log and the other documents associated with the Oldbury Woods case.

By then, it wasn't too late but he was tired from the concentration of going through the files and writing up the Decision Log. He put the files into his bag and went to bed.

The next day, after a lazy, winter Sunday during which Milo stayed in his pyjamas until mid-afternoon, they began their wind down ritual after dinner. Milo knew he was going to be dropped back to his Mum's that evening and began to grow quieter.

It was usually the only time Milo ever became petulant or threw tantrums. He didn't do it often, but Trench always gave him a bit more leeway if he started acting up.

The drop off went relatively smoothly. Milo begged Trench to stay a little while, and Trench had no problem relenting. He ended up putting Milo to bed and telling him a story until he fell asleep.

When he got home, Trench reread the Decision Log with the intention of making any edits or updates that occurred to him. But he had done a good job the night before and only made a small number of amendments. He knew he wouldn't sleep if he got into bed because it was too early, so he played his guitar for a while. It was one of only a tiny number of activities that Trench could truly lose himself in. What seemed like a few minutes turned into a couple of hours.

Neither Jazz nor anyone else called during the day, which he took to mean that Vanessa's kidnapper had still not made contact. Later, he flicked on the TV to catch the news to make sure. Vanessa Osbourne's case was the second item. He could tell there was nothing new to report because they started by replaying Doctor Osbourne's statement from the day before.

However, Trench did stop what he was doing for a moment when the newsreader said that even the Prime Minister had spoken about Vanessa. The newsreader made reference to the fact that the Prime Minister knew the young Conservative Party activist. The screen showed footage of the Prime Minister walking towards Downing Street, while a rabble of journalists shouted questions at her about the missing girl.

At one point, the Prime Minister stopped walking and turned to face the cameras. She spoke briefly, saying she added her own hopes and prayers to those of the whole nation, in wishing the best outcome for Vanessa and her family at this difficult time. Trench had to admit she managed to look genuinely downcast as she spoke. Previously he'd only ever seen her speak about banal political matters, like budget cuts or foreign trade.

This time she was making a good show of displaying more humanity and emotion than he had seen from a politician for some time. But when she seemed to wipe a tear from her eye as she turned away from the camera, he rolled his eyes. It reminded him of just how much politics now mimicked Hollywood. The best actors were the ones who rose to the top. The ones best able to adapt to the prevailing mood of the electorate.

He clicked the TV off, silently trying to convince himself that he wasn't a callous cynic. Just a realist. As he headed off to bed he started to wonder if there was any difference these days.

# Twenty-Three

The benefit of the work they'd done at the weekend came into sharp focus first thing Monday morning. DI Mike Ward from Thames Valley CID called Trench just after seven. Trench was already at his desk, finalising the running order for the suspects he intended to visit unannounced over the next couple of days. Ward sounded younger than Trench had expected and had a thick Welsh accent. After brief introductions he got straight down to business. Trench liked his style.

"Griffith said you think you might have a vic from our guy, that about right?"

"That's right. And after having a proper look at your case file, I'm certain of it. We've found another one as well, in Sussex."

"Another victim? A third one?" asked Ward, his interest clearly rising.

"A third one," Trench confirmed. "A hooker, missing for a couple of weeks, then found naked, strangled, tied up with cable ties, slashed with a knife and dumped in a river. That one was in April."

"Shit, sounds similar alright," said Ward. "What about your case?"

"We found her on Thursday, in some woods in Kent. She had cable ties on her hands and feet. Half her face wrapped in duct tape. She'd been tortured, for what looks like a few days. Raped, slashed with a knife all over her back, torso, everywhere. Burnt with cigarettes. He eventually strangled her. With a wire."

After a moment's silence, Ward said, "You find her in water? You said in woods."

"No, she wasn't in water. But she'd been soaked in bleach or chemical cleaner, probably for a couple of days. If the reason he dumped the other bodies in water was to wipe the DNA, this works just as well. Better, even. You guys found Sharon Brimms shortly after she went into the water, right?"

"No more than twelve hours," confirmed Ward. "But that was enough. We didn't get any usable DNA."

"Yeah, but maybe it was a little too close for comfort for the guy. If he knew you got to her so quickly, maybe it freaked him out. The woman in Sussex was in the water for around a week. There was no chance of getting any DNA after that. But twelve hours, you might've been able to get something. He got lucky, but he could've been sweating, waiting for cops to kick his door in. Maybe he wanted to make sure next time, so used the bleach."

"Maybe," said Ward, clearly thinking about it.

"But there's another reason," said Trench. "He didn't just dump her. He displayed her. He strung her up in the forest, in a cuckold position. You'll see the photos in the file I sent to Griffith. It's a public place and would've taken time and effort to do. The body was about a hundred yards from the nearest place he could've parked. And he did it during the night. It would've been a lot easier to dump her in a river."

Trench made it as an open statement, deliberately teeing it up to see if Ward would offer his own theory about why the killer had done this. He wanted to see if he drew the same conclusion. Trench was sure it showed the pattern of a killer evolving his MO, probably becoming more deranged and almost certainly more dangerous. Ward was silent for a long moment, and Trench assumed he was processing the information before drawing a conclusion.

But when he spoke, it was not what Trench was expecting.

"You know, it's funny," said Ward, "You always hear that the real monsters never turn out to be like people imagine. They're not six foot, cross-eyed bogey men with a hunchback. Just scrawny, run-of-the-mill deadbeats. I guess it's true."

It took Trench a moment to follow Ward's train of thought. Then it hit him. He sat bolt upright, an electrical current shooting through him.

"You've got a bead on someone," he said tensely.

"That's right, Detective. We're pretty sure we know who our guy is."

Trench felt the hairs on his neck standing on end.

"What have you got?"

"One of the girls who knew Brimms saw her getting into a car, a van actually, on the night she went missing. All she could tell us was that it's white. The area where the girls work isn't covered by cameras. They're careful about that. So we pulled CCTV from across the entire city for that night and the whole week before. We ran the plates from all white vans and finally came back with a hit. Don't think I've updated the file yet, but we got a bloke with a record that fit. Did a stretch for rape, kidnap, battery. Grabbed a girl off the street and took her out to the middle of nowhere. The bastard kept her there for hours, putting her through the horrors.

He made her wear a bag over her head the whole time. He even wore jonnies. But guess how he got done?"

"DNA," said Trench, putting it together. "Hair or something. Fibres."

"Yep, pubes. Sounds like he's learned the lesson. Bet he shaves now, too."

"Who is the guy?"

"His name's Howard Chapman. We raided his digs on Friday but it looked like he hadn't been there for a while. We've had a couple of lads sitting on it ever since, but he must've done a runner. We found his van burnt out not far from the house."

Howard Chapman.

Trench knew the name but couldn't remember where from. He leaned forward, dropping his head into his free hand. He rubbed his fingers through his hair for a few seconds, then sat bolt upright again.

"The tennis coach," he said.

It was one of the names on the list he had reviewed at the weekend. The details all came back to him now and he recalled the case that Ward had just described. The one for which Chapman had been jailed.

"He only got out late last year, right?" he said, remembering the details.

He started flicking through the pages of his notebook.

"You know the guy?" Ward said, surprised.

"He's on a list of possibles, based on his prior."

He got to the page where he had summarised Chapman's information.

"The address you raided is in High Wycombe?"

"Yeah, that's right. It's a halfway house. He'd been signing on at High Wycombe Station every week but no-one at the house had seen him for over a month by the time we got there. He stopped signing on the same week Brimms went missing. The locals hadn't gotten around to sending someone to check on him."

Trench had been intending to go to the address later that day. He decided immediately that he still would, unless Ward had anything else.

"Any lead on where he could be now?"

"Nothing. Kept himself to himself for the short time he was at the house, then split. Barely anyone there even knew his name. Not that they were the most helpful lot. Scumbags, the lot of 'em."

"Anything from KA's?" asked Trench, more in hope than expectation. Known associates rarely snitched to police.

"He was inside so long we haven't been able to find anyone who knows him, even from before. His parents cut him off after his conviction. We spoke with them on Saturday. Fair to say he won't be welcomed home by them any time soon."

The next obvious question was whether Ward had put an 'Immediate' BOLO out for Chapman, a Be On the Look Out order. But Trench knew he hadn't, because a force-wide Immediate BOLO would have flagged up in his search results. He was about to ask why not, but then stopped himself. It would highlight a shortcoming in Ward's paperwork on the case. Another one. He didn't want to risk damaging their relationship already.

Ward obviously twigged where the conversation was going.

"Our plan was to give it the weekend to see if our boys could nab him, either at the house or his parents. If not, we were going to put out an Immediate BOLO. I have the paperwork here and was just about to sort it, but got your message and figured I'd return your call first. Glad I did now."

Before hanging up, Ward said he would complete the BOLO alert right away and pull his men off the surveillance of Chapman's address. The chances of him returning there were negligible and it now seemed like a waste of already scarce resource. They agreed to talk again later in the day. Trench explained that he would call DI Parson in Sussex, so that he was fully up to date.

When he hung up, Trench was charged. He'd been expecting to spend the day knocking on dingy doors in rundown neighbourhoods that probably wouldn't be answered. But instead he had a rock-solid lead.

He knew he was getting closer to catching the killer.

*

Trench eased off the throttle, slowing right down as he looked around for a street sign confirming he was in the right place. He didn't see one. He'd only seen a couple in the past few minutes. But he could tell he was in the right area. He had Googled the address of the halfway house and then used street view. He was now crawling through the low-rise, brown-brick estate, looking for the right house. He turned onto a street where the houses were slightly bigger than before, and not because of the homemade extensions that some of the houses on the previous street had.

He spotted the house he was looking for. It was end-of-terrace, next to a field that backed onto a railway track. Curtains were drawn across all windows, except the ones that were permanently taped up with newspapers, daylight never welcome in those rooms. The garden was a mess of rubble, haphazard stacks of wooden planks and the stripped carcasses of now indeterminate machinery. The sense of edge-of-civilisation emanating from the house was strong, even if you didn't already know that's exactly what it was.

Trench pulled up to the kerb outside the house and sat for a moment thinking about his approach. He had hoped to speak with at least one of the residents, to hear first-hand anything that could provide some insight into Howard Chapman. He figured he might have a better chance than Ward's full riot squad, who'd turned up in force and probably bashed the door down.

But as he looked at the house now, he knew his chances of getting any cooperation were minimal. If any of the occupants had been teetering on the edge before, when they realised that their life choices meant living in this place was the best they could hope for, it would surely have pushed them over.

This was confirmed when he got off his bike and knocked heavily on the door. He had to bang hard for a full ten minutes before he got any sign of life from inside.

"Fuck off, pigs!" someone shouted from inside.

"We'll fuck off only after we've seen the room," he shouted in the letter box. "We'll keep banging until someone opens up or we knock it down."

After another five minutes of constant banging, Trench heard someone shuffle up to the door and release the latch. He pushed it open to get a full view inside and saw a figure in baggy tracksuit bottoms shuffling back up the stairs. He stepped inside the squalid entrance hall and called after the figure.

"Which room is Howard Chapman's?"

"That one," croaked the figure, seeming to pause at the top of the stairs.

Trench stepped forward to see which way he was pointing. He just clocked the direction the figure pointed in before he was gone. Trench heard a door closing as he went up the stairs and turned in the direction the figure had pointed. He was able to tell which room was Chapman's because of the deep, round gouges beside the now useless handle, where the door had been smashed open. The door itself was ajar, hanging loosely by a single hinge on the doorframe.

Stepping inside the room, Trench thought it was probably smaller than the cell Chapman had spent the previous decade in. It seemed smaller still now the meagre contents of the room were upended and tossed all over the floor. Ward's squad hadn't been concerned about tidying up after themselves. Or maybe that was the way they found it.

Trench poked around at the debris on the floor with his foot. When he lifted up the mattress with his foot and pushed it against the far wall, he saw a pile of old newspapers, empty pot noodle containers and tins of own-brand supermarket soup. This gave him an idea. He pushed around the assorted rubbish on the floor, looking for as many tins of soup as he could find. He turned over each of the tins with his foot, checking that they were all the same brand. They were.

It gave him at least some hope that his trip out to High Wycombe had been worth it.

# Twenty-Four

After clambering back into his suit in the station, Trench bounded up the stairs to get Jazz. When he'd called her earlier to relay his conversation with Ward, she'd agreed he should shoot out to High Wycombe on his bike, rather than wait for her and then take a car. She clearly thought it would be a wasted trip. But now Trench was going up to tell her that they might have a way to get ahead of the BOLO and narrow down the search for Chapman.

Trench walked into the CID squad room and could tell immediately that something was happening. The louder than usual buzz of animated voices rippled with excitement.

"What's up?" he said to Jazz as he got to his desk.

"He sent the drop details," she said, turning around and standing up. "It's tonight."

"Tonight? Where?"

"I'm not sure of the details. Barton literally just told me. The mail must have come in overnight, or else first thing this morning."

"Any idea what the plan is?"

He realised he was still hopeful that maybe they would be drafted in for the operation. He'd assumed that between CID, Specialist Operations and NCA it was unlikely. But now that it was actually happening, he again felt the sharp sting from being excluded. Jazz picked up on the hopeful tone of his voice.

"Don't get your hopes up. They've just called a briefing. I saw Thornton going in," she said, disappointment unmistakable in her voice.

Chief Inspector Dean Thornton was head of the SO Unit responsible for the operation to carry out the ransom drop. If he was attending the briefing it meant they were carefully planning the execution of the operation. Deciding each individual's role, right down to where they would stand and what they would do throughout.

What Jazz didn't need to say was that neither of them had been invited to the briefing. They weren't going to be involved in the operation.

Neither spoke for a moment. Trench knew that being excluded from the ransom operation was always going to be a low point of being kicked from the case. It was tougher to accept being kicked at a time like this. His feelings were mixed, somewhere between disappointment and anger.

But a thought was forming in his head. If the drop was tonight, then he had time to figure out just how much he was going to accept being excluded.

"I know you're gutted. I am too. But look, this is good news for Vanessa," he said, wanting to change the subject. "Let's hope it goes smoothly. But for now, let's go."

Jazz looked at him but didn't move. He could tell she was also feeling the sting of exclusion. Probably more so, given she'd been sitting in the squad room when it all kicked off. But Trench figured the gaining momentum in the Oldbury Woods case would energise her as much as it was him.

"Hey, we'll get more info from Barton after the briefing," he said. "I know it's a pisser to be out at a time like this, but who knows what can happen. Besides, I've got an idea how we can find Howard Chapman. Let's go."

A few minutes later they were speeding toward South London.

"Are you going to tell me where we're going now?" asked Jazz impatiently.

"To the supermarket."

"That's great, Trench," Jazz replied, throwing up her hands.

She knew he was winding her up, but used the opportunity to vent anyway.

"It'll really soften the blow of missing out on the drop if we get a breakfast roll from fucking Sainsbury's."

"Tesco, actually," said Trench, enjoying needling her.

She stared at him for a second, then suddenly pointed out the window as they sped down a street with numerous retail units. Her finger followed where she was pointing, ending up pointing out the back window of the car.

"There goes a Tesco, right there. Second one we've passed since we left the station, Trench. Not to mention the one across the road from the station…"

"This is a special Tesco. And after I introduce you to this guy, you're going to think so too."

'This guy' was Cedric Rollins, security manager at Tesco in Catford. When Trench introduced him to Jazz after they were shown to the security office, Trench could tell she was still impatient to understand what was going on. But Trench hadn't seen Rollins for nearly a year.

Rollins stood up in his office and gave them an exaggerated welcome. He clearly wanted to catch up, and Trench knew he should indulge him for a little while before making his request for the old copper's trick he had used many times in the past.

They chatted mostly about crime and policing levels, as they had done for most of the nearly fifteen years since Trench had first encountered Rollins. Trench had been a constable on the beat in Catford, while Rollins was doing the same job he was doing now. The stories were mostly the same too, though Rollins lamented that now nearly every crime he encountered, from shoplifting to loitering, ended with someone pulling a knife. He said four staff had suffered knife wounds in just the previous six months.

Eventually Trench steered the conversation around to the purpose of their visit.

"Jazz here is too young to remember life before knife crime, ay Jazz?" Trench said.

Jazz was about to respond when Rollins got there first.

"Different world, Detective Jasmine. It's like the whole world jumped through some apocalypse switch a decade ago, and now everything is a fight to death. People been killed for they shoes. They shoes! Our staff here be scared half to death when them drillers come in with they hoods up, trousers hanging off they skinny little asses..." he snorted. "I blame that Great Financial Crisis in two thousand and eight. Ain't nothin' been the same since. People got nothin' to lose now."

Rollins shook his head and looked away into the middle distance for a long moment.

"That's what we're trying to do right now Cedric, take one more dangerous maniac with a knife off the streets," said Trench. "He's done a runner, so we're trying to get a steer on where he is."

"Straight up, Trench," Rollins snapped back to the present and started nodding his head, "Always happy to do our bit to make our streets safer. You reckon—"

"Every little helps...," said Jazz softly, almost songfully.

Trench and Rollins turned to look at her. She looked a little surprised herself that it had come out. After a long moment of silently eyeballing her, Rollins eventually turned back toward his desk.

"You reckon he's on our ticket, Trench?" he asked, sitting down and shaking his mouse to wake up his screen. "Not one of them heretics off with them German imposters, I hope."

"I'm willing to bet he is. His room only had Tesco stuff in it and I didn't see any Lidl or Aldi's near his place. There's a Tesco Superstore within walking distance."

"Okay, name?" asked Rollins, fingers hovering above his keyboard.

"Howard Chapman."

"Location?" said Rollins after a moment, looking at a screen full of 'Howard Chapman' listings.

"High Wycombe."

It took Rollins just a couple of seconds to home in.

"Two," he said pointing at his screen. "You know which one of them two is your man?"

Trench leaned in closer to look at the two entries. The full address for each was showing in a column to the right.

"Gotchya," said Trench. "The first one."

He gave Jazz a sharp, invigorated nod. She'd gradually begun leaning closer to the screen when they'd started the search. Now she stood up straight, looking half-excited, half-confused at Trench.

"What are we looking at?" she asked.

"The only trail most of these guys leave behind," said Trench. "They'll change addresses, skip town, duck signing on, shave their head, whatever...but they never stop collecting their Clubcard points. Works nine times out of ten. And Cedric's got the magic to tell us which shop Chapman' s been using since he stopped using High Wycombe. Including when and where he did his most recent shop."

"Uh huh," agreed Rollins. "Been getting around, your boy. Kilburn, Woking, Richmond, Bromley, Horley. Those are all in just the past month. The Horley one was a few days ago."

"Bromley?" echoed Trench. He knew Bromley was only about fifteen minutes' drive from where they'd found the body in Oldbury Hill. "What date was that?"

"Twenty seventh of October, around nine pm. You want to know what he bought?" asked Rollins.

Trench thought for a moment before replying. That was about a week before they found the body. Wharton had said she'd been kept alive for at least a few days and then soaked in cleaning agent for another couple of days after her death. They could now place their suspect in Bromley about a week before she was found.

That made it a good starting place to try to identify the victim, he reasoned. It wasn't rock solid. But it was a lot more than they had a few minutes ago.

"Cedric, can you print off the details for each of those shops. Time, date and what he bought."

"Sure thing."

He would have asked for the CCTV footage but Trench knew that Rollins couldn't access that from his store in Catford. To get that, they would have to go through Tesco's corporate headquarters, probably with a warrant. Trench figured they could do that later when building a case, after they'd captured Chapman. Rollins hit some keys and they heard a printer chirping into life somewhere in the room. Trench turned to Jazz.

"Twenty seventh of October in Bromley. That timeframe fits."

Jazz nodded, then turned to Rollins. She was on full alert now.

"What about Horley, Cedric. When was that, exactly? Horley's in Surrey, right?"

"Uh huh, it's right beside Gatwick airport. Date was…" he flipped back into the screen showing the search results, "…sixth of November. Last Friday."

"Last Friday," repeated Trench. "So while Ward's crew was kicking in his door in Wycombe, he was casually doing his shopping down in Horley."

Jazz looked at him.

"And the timeline could fit too. Horley isn't far from Oldbury Woods either. It's poss—"

"That ain't the only time he's been in Horley, by the way," interrupted Rollins. "You said to look at just the past month. But looking back before then, he's been using that one in Horley more than the rest. More than High Wycombe even. Look here."

They both leaned it to look at the screen. Rollins was dragging his finger down the screen.

"One, two, three, four.....yep, he been there a tonna times. This is showing the whole year. He's been in that Horley one must be a dozen times, see?"

"Cedric, you're a wizard," said Trench, straightening up. He hadn't quite put a full timeline together, but his mind was racing. "Can you print off all those results too. For the whole year."

"You got it, Trench."

Trench studied the screen, now showing the full year's records. He could see hits from across London and the South East. Chapman was a man on the move. It didn't take much to imagine what he was doing. Prowling. Hunting. Searching for the next woman he would defile and destroy.

But he kept coming back to the same store in Horley. It must mean something to him.

If Chapman was their man, they nearly had him in their cross hairs.

# Twenty-Five

"It was a just regular shop," said Trench, studying the print-out. "Food, booze, smokes, loo roll."

"How many days' worth?" asked Jazz, not taking her eyes off the road.

She hadn't flipped the blues and twos but had her foot down as they raced back to the station.

"Might get a week out of it. And he can probably go to a corner store in the meantime. But we need to be up on this asap."

"Surrey, though…" said Jazz pensively. "We really should be going through Lewis. It's his old turf."

"Yeah."

Jazz was right, but Trench didn't want to go to Lewis. Not yet. His gut told him that Lewis would just get in the way. He was fully occupied with the arrangements for the drop, but he was fussy enough to probably insist on getting involved anyway. That would almost certainly slow them down. And that was before factoring in the current state of their relationship.

Bottom line, he just didn't trust that Lewis would call it right, whatever the reason.

"He's got his hands full. He hasn't got the space to get this running. Let's call Ward when we get back, and Parson. Between the three of us, we can decide who puts the call in to Surrey."

"You mean, which one of them?" said Jazz.

They had better deniability if the call to Surrey for help in setting up surveillance on the supermarket came from either Thames Valley or Sussex CID. It made it much harder for Lewis to grief them about it.

Trench gave a short nod and moved on.

"We need to work out a timetable too, with Ward and Parson, for when each of us sits with Surrey on the surveillance. If I'm reading Ward right, he'll want to be a part of it. Maybe Parson too, based on what you said about him."

"For sure. He'll be all over it."

"Good. But that's why we need a timetable. If we're not careful, there'll be more coppers than shoppers at the place. He could be jumpy, we don't want to scare him off."

Jazz glanced over at Trench, raising her eyebrows.

"Kudos for taking down a serial killer?" she said. "It'll be ten to one, coppers over shoppers."

Trench just nodded again. It didn't matter to him who got the kudos. Just as long as they got him.

The squad room seemed unusually quiet when they got back, in stark contrast to earlier that morning. They assumed it was because everyone was still in the operational planning session. Trench knew the atmosphere in there would be tense, fused with excitement. Precision planning for the deployment of armed response officers (ARO), surveillance analysts and operational specialists always got the squad's juices flowing. It was the tip of the policing spear.

But so was hunting hot on the heels of an active serial killer, who right now was possibly stalking for his next victim. Any disappointment they'd felt earlier about being excluded from the drop was gone. They were both pumped.

They grabbed their laptops and immediately went to one of the privacy booths. They didn't want to be interrupted if the planning session for the drop broke up. They spent the next thirty minutes going through everything they could find on the various police systems about Howard Chapman. Trench started by reviewing the case file for the attack for which Chapman was jailed.

It was a particularly savage attack. Chapman crept up behind his 19-year-old victim as she walked along a quiet rural lane near her home. He slammed a cloth sack down over her head then repeatedly punched her in the face until she submitted. Dragging her back to his van, he then drove a few miles to a disused quarry.

He spent the next six hours brutalising the young woman in unspeakable ways. He tightened the sack around her neck, keeping it in place for the entire duration of the attack. Whereas he did not slash her with a knife, he improvised with weapons from the scene – stones, rocks, branches and other unknown items – to continually beat, whip and otherwise degrade and abuse the victim throughout. The level of violence was extreme. The degree of sadism as bad as almost anything Trench had seen before.

Eventually he had left, driving off and leaving the young woman fighting for her life in the isolated quarry, pitch black in the middle of the night. She was discovered the next morning, having somehow managed to crawl onto a side road, before collapsing into a coma.

As he read the case file, Trench realised that Ward had been incorrect. The victim wasn't a complete stranger. She was a member of the same private tennis club where the then-28-year-old Chapman had been working as a coach. The case file stated that the young woman did not know her attacker. But that did not mean Chapman did not know her. The language used in the case file was typically clinical and circumspect. There was no room for conjecture or speculation. But the charges did not include premeditation. From this, Trench inferred that Chapman must have denied knowing her.

After studying the files for a further few minutes, Trench sat back, deep in thought. Jazz gave him a questioning look.

"What's missing here?" he said, gesturing at his laptop.

"From his file you mean?"

He nodded. Jazz thought for a moment. She looked back at his file, which contained only one conviction. Then it hit her.

"Priors. Or rather, lack of. It's a pretty big ticket for his first conviction."

"Right. No pattern, no build-up of lesser offenses showing developing deviance. Just, boom. Straight in with this absolutely savage attack on the young victim."

"He's careful," agreed Jazz. "And smart."

"Exactly. Right from the start of his descent into sex crimes he's been extremely careful. There had to have been some kind of background offending, but he never got done for anything."

"That's also consistent with our scene. The clean-up, lack of evidence. It definitely feels like the same culprit."

"Agreed," said Trench. "But that's all we've really got. Feelings. No evidence."

"We've got a witness. She said she saw Brimms getting into his van."

"A prostitute, probably also a junkie, claims she might have seen Brimms getting into a white van," said Trench. "A van registered to Chapman was seen on CCTV in the same city at roughly the same time. It probably isn't even enough to bring charges, let alone get a conviction."

"Not great," agreed Jazz.

"If we pick him up now, we've got twenty-four hours to either charge him or release him. Look at the guy's file. Do you fancy our odds of cracking him in interview?"

Jazz thought hard for a moment before responding.

"No comment," she said eventually, shaking her head.

"Exactly. He'll just 'no comment' his way to freedom. Like they all do."

"We need hard evidence."

"Or, better yet, to catch him in the act," ventured Trench

"Put four teams on him round the clock for six months until he strikes again?" said Jazz sceptically. "Good luck finding the budget for that. Or a chief willing to take the risk of leaving him loose to carry on hunting that whole time. Jesus, can you imagine the shitshow if he struck again?"

"True. What about his lair? He's got them for days. There must be somewhere he's taking them. Maybe we could tail him just until he leads us there."

"Still a lot riskier than just grabbing him and getting that out of him in interview," said Jazz, then holding up her hands when she saw Trench about to argue the point. "I'm not saying it's the best option. But I can't see the brass agreeing to anything other than grabbing him the minute we see him."

Trench nodded, not wanting to argue the point. He knew she was right. But it niggled at him and began to sow the seeds of worry in his mind. Hauling Chapman in and then having to release him without charge due to lack of evidence was too nightmarish to even think about.

He went back to the file, looking for some further background on Chapman or his known addresses. But beyond the crime itself, there wasn't much context or background information in the police file.

He flipped into Google and searched for more details of the case. He entered Howard Chapman's name and some details of the crime and hit search. There were lots of hits. He immediately knew this meant there was something unusual about the case. He scanned the headlines from the search page and could instantly tell what it was.

The sensationalist tone of the headlines made it clear that Chapman came from a privileged background. He'd enjoyed a stable upbringing in a wealthy home. His father was a doctor, while his mother stayed at home raising him and his two brothers. He'd grown up in an affluent suburb of Dorking and had been privately educated. One of the articles mentioned a 'chequered' disciplinary record at school, but most chose to highlight the idyllic upbringing. It made for a better story.

Piecing together the snippets from various stories, Trench was able to figure out that Chapman had not gone on to further education. After finishing school, he started working as a groundsman at the local tennis club where the family were all members. He then ended up coaching children at the club during summer holidays.

He had been living with his parents at the time of his arrest, working only a handful of hours per week. One of the articles mentioned that the small club had closed down following Chapman's conviction. Trench could easily imagine how that went, with other members not wanting to face the Chapman family, who themselves had probably struggled to get on with their own lives.

His brow furrowed and Trench bumped his fist gently off the table. Chapman was born into opportunity. He'd started life with the type of advantages most people could only dream of. Yet he'd chosen instead to destroy his victims' lives, and in the process, destroy his own. And his family's, and the countless other friends and family members of his victims.

Trench knew psychologists could probably find an explanation in some form of personality disorder. Indeed, one of the articles contained an interview with a celebrity psychologist, suggesting that evidence Chapman had been rebuffed by many of the young female members of the tennis club that summer had created a festering, rabid hatred of women. But as far as Trench was concerned, it always came down to personal choices. He could never comprehend what caused people with comfortable lives to make the darkest choices. All he knew was that he would do whatever he could to try to balance some right against their terrible wrongs.

He stared at the screen. None of what he read put him off the idea that they needed to get more evidence before they arrested Chapman. On the contrary, it only made him feel more certain they should expand the surveillance operation to increase their chances of doing so. He decided to at least float the idea with the detectives from Thames Valley and Sussex.

"Let's call Ward and Parson and see what—"

He was interrupted by the sudden eruption of loud voices out in the squad room. They could tell from the volume and tone that the planning session for the drop had broken up. They both instinctively turned and looked out through the half-open blinds. Members of the various teams were making their way boisterously back to their desks.

"Let's call them now," said Jazz reaching for the phone, having understood what Trench was going to say and trying to ignore the kerfuffle.

As she grabbed the phone, there was a knock on the door. She glanced up and saw who was at the door.

"Five Burgers," she shot to Trench.

DI Burgess opened the door and stepped inside.

"Hey guys," he said.

Jazz gave a brief nod.

"Uh, I just wanted to let you know the latest. I know you guys are probably still interested in what's going on with Operation Labrador," he said.

They both stared blankly at him. He realised why and explained.

"That's what we're calling it, Labrador. You know, Labrador Retriever? Cause we're getting Vanessa back?"

Again, neither responded. But they both nodded this time, so Burgess continued.

"The ransom drop is tonight, at seven thirty. He's given us a location in Highbury. He gave instructions for the money to be split into separate bags—"

"Wait," interrupted Trench. "Where exactly in Highbury?"

"Hornsey Road."

"The Emirates?" said Trench. "The Arsenal football stadium is on Hornsey Road."

"Yeah, that's right," confirmed Burgess. "The drop is inside the Club Shop. He wants the money packed into Arsenal Club Shop bags and left in specific places inside the shop."

"There's a game, tonight," twigged Trench. "The derby, against Tottenham."

Burgess nodded.

"Looks like's he going to try to use the crowd as cover. There'll be thousands of people milling around. Probably thousands of customers going into the shop. Seems he's going to try to pick it up in the confusion."

Trench and Jazz exchanged a look. Jazz raised her eyebrows as Trench frowned. Neither knew what to make of such brazen arrangements.

"Risky," was all Trench said.

"You said it," said Burgess. "That goes both ways though. He's said he'll be watching for cops and if he sees anyone monitoring the bags he'll just walk away."

"And then what?" asked Jazz, though she knew the answer. They all did.

Burgess looked down before continuing.

"If that happens, he said the only time we'll ever see Vanessa again – if we ever find her – she'll be a corpse."

Everyone was silent for a moment. It was a sobering thought.

"So what's the plan?" said Trench.

"The plan?" said Burgess, scratching his head. "Well, me and Callow are going to pick up the money from Osbourne now. Someone else is gone to the get the bags from the Club Shop. We'll—"

"No, Burgess, we don't need you to tell us how you're going put the fucking fig into the roll. I mean the kidnapper. You going to pick him up, tail him or what?"

"Oh, right. Sorry," he said sheepishly. "Plan A is to follow him. The guys are also checking out if we could put a miniature tracking device into the bags. It depends on what the bags are made of apparently. You know, how noticeable it would be."

Trench's mind began to race, trying to envisage the situation. He didn't like what he was seeing. Something was nagging him.

"There's more than one of them," he said, realisation dawning. "There's got to be. One bloke can't carry out separate bags. It'd be too obvious."

Burgess was nodding again.

"Yeah, Thornton said the same thing. We've built that into the contingency planning. Different teams will be assigned different marks. If they split up, we'll follow them both. Or more, if necessary."

Trench frowned. The more he heard the less he liked. He had faith in his colleagues, particularly the SO Unit. But this had snafu written all over it. A crowded area, thousands of football fans, half of them pissed, multiple bags, an unknown number of kidnappers…

"Jesus," he muttered. "How many teams have you got?"

Burgess raised his hands in a non-confrontational gesture.

"Uh, look, that's kinda why I'm here. We've got this, you know. I know this is probably a little raw for you two, but we've got the full crew on the operation tonight. SO, ARO, surveillance. Pretty much a full house…"

"What's your point, Burgess," Trench said. "You don't want to answer our questions?"

"I'm just saying…Callow told me just to let you know, we've got it covered," Burgess stammered. "You guys are okay to stand down, and uh, not be a part of it tonight."

"So you're here just to let us know we're not required?" said Jazz annoyedly. "Well, thanks. We've figured that out already."

"No, I just…Well, just in case there's any confusion," Burgess managed.

Trench just grunted and turned back to the files. Jazz said nothing and turned back to her own files.

"Okay, well, we'll let you know how it goes of course. Fingers crossed it'll go as planned," said Burgess.

Neither responded as he slipped out of the room.

"Tosser. Rubbing our nose in it. What's that about?" said Jazz. After a moment thinking about it she added, "Or do you think he thinks we'll crash the party?"

"Whatever," was all Trench said, keen to change the subject. "Anyway, forget it. Let's just hope they've got it covered, like he said. We need to call Ward and Parson and get set up on the shop in Horley asap."

They managed to get both Ward and Parson on a conference call, though Parson was on his mobile from his car. After brief introductions, they got straight down to planning for the surveillance. When they discussed the idea of extending the surveillance, both Ward and Parson agreed with the idea, but said it would never get approval given budget constraints. They all reluctantly agreed to kill the idea.

Ward then explained he had a few contacts in Surrey CID and was happy to brief them on the case and lead on setting up the surveillance with them. Both agreed it made sense to set up shifts of sitting with the Surrey squad, rather than having everyone there the whole time.

After a brief discussion, they decided to rotate in six-hour shifts because the shop was open for eighteen hours a day, from six am to midnight. When it came to allocating slots, Trench was happy to appear conciliatory and allow Ward to take the first slot for that evening. Parson took the second slot, from six am the next day, meaning Trench and Jazz would take the following afternoon. Trench was more than happy with that.

It meant he was free for the evening.

# Twenty-Six

Thousands of people milled about the concourse by the Club Shop. With still an hour to go to kick-off, the area was heaving with fans of both teams. Most were males, from teens to middle age, but there were also some families and children. Trench's seat in the café directly across from the Club Shop was only about fifty yards from the entrance. But his line of sight was constantly being obscured by the flowing crowd.

"Team four, clear," crackled a hushed voice in his earpiece.

All teams were in position and were continually reporting from their posts. He'd arrived early, wearing his blacked-out motorbike gear with a cap pulled down low. He'd half expected an observation team to be posted inside the café. But it was the right call not to, he now realised. Can't see a fucking thing.

"Team five, clear."

At least he had the radio. He'd discreetly picked it up before he left the station, under cover of going over to wish CI Thornton and his SO Unit good luck. He planned to stay put in the café until he either spotted something through the occasional gap in the crowd or heard an alert over the radio. Even then, he did not intend to get involved. Assuming everything went according to plan...

"Team six, clear."

He checked his watch again. Just after seven. He took another bite of his sandwich and scanned the café. He caught the eye of one of a group of teenagers at another table. The kid flashed him a defiant glare as he took a long slug from a bottle of vodka they were blatantly passing around. Trench turned away. His earpiece was in the ear furthest from them and he didn't want them to spot it.

He was tense. He'd prefer to avoid being made by any of his colleagues, but could deal with the consequences if that happened. He was more worried about the completely uncontrollable environment the kidnapper had chosen for the drop.

Fans continued to pour into the area. There was a constant stream of people going into the shop. Sporadic chanting broke out as groups of lagered-up fans came marauding through. One youth broke away from a group and got right up into the face of a uniformed bobby. He started doing a drunken jig, his mates cheering on rowdily. The bobby laughed it off for a second. But only a second. He gave the kid an aggressive shove that sent him crashing back into his mates. The copper stepped forward to challenge anyone who had a problem. The young lads bitched and whined but strutted off in the other direction, heads jerking like pigeons.

"Team seven, clear."

The sound of smashing glass made Trench jump. He turned to see it was the bottle that had been doing the rounds on the other table.

"What you lookin' at mate?" snarled the one he'd exchanged glances with earlier. "It's only a fackin' bottle, init. None of your fackin' business, mate."

Trench ignored him and took a bite of his sandwich, trying to stay calm. He checked his watch. A quarter past.

"Team leader. Team eight, report?"

Trench felt his adrenaline spike. He recognised the team leader's voice as CI Thornton. Every other team had reported in cycle. Team eight hadn't. The tiny deviation from the pattern was enough to stoke his heightened senses.

"Team leader. Team eight, report?"

"Yeah, we're here. Uh, team eight here, all good. Clear."

He recognised Callow's voice and rolled his eyes. The adrenaline dissolved. He finished his sandwich and moved in his seat to try to see around the latest swell in the crowd. He scanned the concourse. Shifted his gaze toward the shop entrance. He checked the other direction.

Suddenly his mind registered a hit.

He'd seen something. He wasn't sure what. But it was there. Something had struck a nerve.

He scoured the crowd. What was it? He studied the shop entrance then began moving his gaze, examining the faces, the shapes, looking for any—

"You finished, mate?"

He turned with a start. The café owner was leaning over his table, about to take his plate. He wanted the seat for the next customer. It was match night.

"I'm taking this, yeah. You want somefink else?" he asked.

Trench turned back to the crowd but it took him a moment to regain his focus.

"Yeah, same again," said Trench, staring back at street outside.

"What, another sandwich? You want a proper drink this time? I've got the real stuff under the counter. But you'll have to use a paper cup, you know. Old Bill's everywhere on match day."

Trench wasn't listening. He wanted the man to just fuck off. He took out a twenty-pound note and thrust it at him without looking, hoping it would do the job. The man shuffled away and Trench tried to refocus on the crowd. His eyes darted around the sea of faces, trying to determine what had struck him previously.

There! He spotted a face he recognised. It took him a split second to place him. Tall, broad shoulders, black bomber, a cap pulled tight on his head. Doherty. From the home security detail. What the…

Thoughts raced through his mind as his adrenaline rushed again. Surely not. He would've picked something up from him. Or would he. He watched as Doherty slowly looked around, scanning the crowd. Doherty stopped and stared straight ahead, seeming to focus on something or someone in the crowd. Trench tried to follow his gaze but there were too many people blocking his view.

"Fuck," he murmured.

Trench was putting it together. He thought he knew what was happening. He grabbed his phone out of his pocket and scrolled through the contacts. He was half looking at his phone and half trying to keep watch on Doherty. He found the number he was looking for and hit dial.

He waited as the phone rang out to voicemail. He debated whether to leave a message. The beep sounded.

"Krige, it's DCI Chambers. Are you guys…"

He killed the call. No point leaving a message. He tried ringing again, but again no answer.

"Shit," he cried, desperation gripping him.

"Team one, clear."

He scrolled through the phone again and hit dial on the number. It was answered after two rings.

"Hi Trent. I was thinking if you would call—"

"Ayala, are you with Krige?" he said urgently.

"What? No, I am home. Are you—"

"Ayala, listen to me. Do you know where Krige is tonight? Are you guys following anyone from the list?"

"Tonight, I am home. Krige is working tonight. What is going on?" she said.

"Are they following someone? Did you guys find someone from the list he sent me?" demanded Trench.

A crowd of people swarmed into his line of sight. He lost Doherty. He stepped away from the table. Out of the corner of his eye he saw the café owner waving at him.

"Uh, I don't know if Krige find someone. He mentioned they working somewhere else tonight. Yes, to do with Vanessa, but not at the house. Is it okay? Is everything fine?"

"Shit," exclaimed Trench, killing the call.

"Hey mate, you want this or not?" called the café owner.

"Keep it," Trench shouted as he moved toward the door.

"Team one, we've got movement."

It was almost a whisper. Trench had previously figured out that team one was inside the shop, eyes on the bags. The hushed voice continued.

"She's picked up the bag. Female, late twenties or early thirties, black jacket, dark blue jeans, black woolly hat."

"Team leader. Keep eyes on her, team one," snapped Thornton's response.

"Team one, roger that. She's…shit. She's switched it. She's put, uh, I think a different bag down. Wait, hang on. The kid has picked it up. There's a kid. Boy, about ten, dark tracksuit top, jeans…Shit!..."

"Team leader. Team one, report," barked Thornton, tension creeping into this tone.

Trench was out the door, pulling his cap down low. He stood and tried to spot Doherty again.

"Team one, there's two kids, a boy and a girl," the whisper was rushed and urgent. "They're with the woman I think. They've taken bags alpha and bravo. Looks like they're headed for the changing rooms, stand by. Wait, they're in the clothes aisles. There's another male…no, two males there…stand by."

The few seconds delay was excruciating to Trench. He couldn't see Doherty. It was much louder outside. He was struggling to hear the exchange in his earpiece. He was only catching some of the words.

"Team one, they've all got bags...multiple target subjects, all are carrying bags…do not have eyes on which bag…behind the clothes aisles, some are in the changing rooms…they've been switching the bags…stand by."

"Team two, move inside," ordered Thornton.

"Team two, moving inside."

Trench spotted Doherty. He was moving toward the door of the shop. He made a hand gesture to point toward the door. Trench looked to where he had directed the gesture, trying to spot whoever was supposed to receive it. He scanned the area.

He spotted Krige, also with a cap pulled down tight. He was striding toward the shop, picking up pace. Doherty went inside. Trench noticed another man similarly dressed clipping closely behind Krige.

"Team three. Another potential subject. Black bomber, cap pulled tight, moving into the shop, toward the aisles…"

"Oh Jesus," Trench said out loud.

He backed off and pulled out his phone. He tried Krige but again no answer. He wouldn't make it to him before he reached the shop. And he knew if he got any closer, he'd only add to the confusion. Either they'd recognise him, causing a distraction, or they'd figure him for another potential subject.

"Team eight, here," boomed the voice in his earpiece. "What the fuck is going on?"

"Team leader. Team eight, stand by. Keep off the air," came the terse reply.

"Yeah but who are we supposed to be following? There's obviously a bunch of them. I presume we're ditching Plan A. Give us the description of—"

"Team leader. Team eight, I repeat, stand by. Get the fuck off the air," Thornton practically shouted.

"Team one, they're leaving the shop. The female and two kids. Carrying a total of four ba—. No make that five bags. Black jacket, black woolly hat on the female. Scratch that, she's removing the hat. Blackish-brown hair. About shoulder length."

Silence on the airwaves. Trench realised they were probably trying to decide whether to follow them or pick them up. He rapidly made his own decision. He hurried back to where he'd parked his bike. It was only a few yards from the café. He threw down his cap and unlocked the chain, which was looped through his helmet.

"Team leader. Team one, how many subjects in total?"

"Team one, uh….female and two kids…. four, maybe five other subjects who they could've switched bags with. Stand b—, scrap that. They are headed for the door now. Jeans, track suit top…."

Trench tried to listen to the full description of each of the subjects but the noise from the crowd drowned it out.

"...three, the kids have split up. The female is alone. All three are going in different directions…the girl is…she's met with another group. Shit, more bags."

Trench groaned. The operation was shot to shit. He figured there were eight tactical teams, but didn't know if there were any more that could be deployed to follow suspects if needed. He waited before starting his engine. It would make it even harder to hear.

Suddenly he heard the sound of engines, getting closer. High-pitched whining that he knew was from a moped. He glanced in his mirror and saw that it was actually three mopeds, coming up the street from behind. Not break-neck speed, but too fast for the crowded area.

As they whined past they completely blocked out his earpiece. He hoped SO command had twigged what was about to happen. There could be other mopeds coming in from other directions. At this point he had no idea how many people were in the kidnap gang. But he realised police weren't going to be able to follow them all.

Whatever the plan, he knew he was on his own from here. He would at least follow one of them, if they made it away from the concourse area. But he fully expected the SO teams to move in any second now. He strained to listen out for the three-word signal – the only time police ever used the word in radio communication, to reduce the risk of confusion or premature deployment. He stood up on his bike stirrups to try to watch where the mopeds went. Just as he started the engine he heard the shouted command in his ear.

"Team leader, move in. All teams, *ATTACK ATTACK ATTACK!*"

# Twenty-Seven

Trench manoeuvred his bike to the edge of the bustling crowd, eyes fixed on the three mopeds. Suddenly three men emerged from the crowd, each jumping onto the back of one of the mopeds. The mopeds shot off in different directions, just as Trench spotted another two, maybe three, mopeds zipping into the crowd from another direction.

He ignored everything except the one moped that came back down the street where he was. He let them get about thirty yards ahead then took off after them. He didn't need to hurry. His bike could close the gap in seconds if he hit the throttle. For now he would just follow them. They might lead him to where Vanessa was being held. He knew the operation had fallen apart and some of the gang would be in custody. If they refused to talk, it might be the only chance they had of finding her.

The moped sped north. It turned onto the wider Seven Sisters Road so it could go faster. But this also meant there was slightly more traffic. Trench hoped it helped him to blend. He kept back from them, weaving on the inside of cars, near the footpath. The moped was travelling in the middle of the lanes. He tried to map out where they were headed.

They were still only about a mile from the stadium. Trench realised they were headed in the direction of Finsbury Park. He hung back, knowing he could accelerate to keep up if they turned a corner.

Suddenly, Trench clocked a car speeding out from Iseldon Road to the right, where the two roads merged up ahead. It was going much faster than any other car on the road. Soon it was only a couple of cars' length behind the moped. Trench instinctively hit the throttle. He wanted to get a better look at the car and its driver.

As he picked up speed, he nearly missed that a bus was turning right in front of him. The bus belatedly hit the indicator. Trench jammed on the brakes, lurching to a halt, almost going over the handlebars. He screamed at the driver.

The bus turned as slow as a barge. Trench used his feet to reverse his bike so he could go around it. He knew he was losing valuable seconds. After an excruciating delay, he made enough space and steered around the bus. But just as he did, another bus was turning right just in front of him, pulling out from what he now saw was a bus depot. Cursing loudly, he started rolling his bike backwards again. As he did so, a cyclist came flying up behind Trench from the outside and smashed straight into the bus.

He hadn't seen the second bus until it was too late. The bus driver hit the brakes. Passers-by screamed. Trench flipped the stand on his bike and ran over to the cyclist. He was already picking himself up, looking more embarrassed than injured. But the bus driver had gotten out to assess the damage, either to the bus or the cyclist. The bus was going nowhere.

Trench ran around the other side of the bus to see if he could spot the moped or the car. Just as he did so, he heard the unmistakable sound up ahead of a car crashing into something solid. There were more screams from further up the road, even louder this time.

As Trench came out from behind the bus, he spotted the car a couple of hundred yards up ahead. It was stopped in the middle of the road, at an awkward angle. The area was not well lit. Trench couldn't quite make out the full scene in the evening gloom.

A man jumped out of the car and ran around the front. He was dressed in full black with a beanie hat pulled low. Trench started running and caught sight of the moped in a crumpled heap in front of the car. He unfastened his helmet as he ran. It was bouncing around and obscuring his view. The two riders were sprawled across the asphalt, one all the way over on the opposite footpath. The man from the car ran up to the other rider, who was just getting to his feet.

The man from the car reached the rider and violently thrust his foot into his back, slamming him hard into the road. The rider went down in a heap. The man from the car stepped over him, bent down and scooped up two Arsenal Club Shop bags. He raced back to the car, tossing the bags inside and jumping in.

It all happened in a matter of seconds. Trench was still about fifty yards away. The car's wheels screeched and it sped off. He yelled out to the two riders, who were both getting to their feet. One of them picked up the moped and managed to get the engine running. He took off, pulling up beside the other rider, who jumped on the back. They too then sped off up the road.

Trench shouted after them in sheer, desperate frustration. Stunned onlookers were beginning to snap out of their own shock at what they'd just witnessed. Some started shouting after the moped as well. Trench slowed to a jog and then stopped. He bent over, hands on his thighs, panting and catching his breath. His head was spinning. He couldn't believe what he had just seen. The kidnap gang members had escaped. Though he was sure some of the gang would be picked up back at the stadium.

But what was really blowing his mind was that he was sure he recognised the man from the car.

# Twenty-Eight

It was total chaos at the station. The holding area was full of squad members manhandling civilians in handcuffs. Some were shouting and screaming, while others were being strong-armed towards the holding cells. As he walked in, Trench recognised a couple of them from his stake out of the stake out.

"Bit lively tonight, Sarge," he said to the Custody Sergeant, playing dumb. "Did they change the date of New Year's Eve?"

"Huh, something like that," snorted the Sergeant, looking up from some paperwork. "And this is only the warm-up act."

"Ay?"

"Barely half the crew are back from the Osbourne ransom drop so far," said the Sergeant, gesturing at the detainees. "The rest are en route. Sounds like they're bringing a whole bloody army of suspects back with them. This lot's only part of the total. They're spreading them out at stations throughout the city so they can't collude to get their story straight."

"Thornton back yet?" Trench asked.

"Not that I've seen."

"Right. I'll check the SO desk."

As expected, he found no-one at the SO desk. He left the borrowed radio and went up to the CID squad room. As he walked in, he instinctively glanced over and saw that the door to Lewis's office was closed. The blinds were also closed, which was unusual. But he could see the lights were on in there.

He plonked down heavily at his desk. He'd been playing the images over and over in his head on his ride back to the station. Instead of logging on to his computer, he leaned forward on his elbows, linked his fingers and rested his chin on them. He needed to think this through.

He wasn't one hundred per cent certain he knew who the man in the car was. It was possible he was mistaken. But the more he replayed it, the more confident he felt that he wasn't mistaken.

Which left him wondering what he had actually seen. The man had deliberately rammed the scooter. His view of that was obscured by the bus, but he had questioned a few onlookers and they were all certain it was intentional.

And that only reinforced his perception of what he himself had seen. He replayed the scene in his head again. The man, stepping over the kidnappers and going straight for the bags. For the money. The man must have known what was in the bags. He had made no attempt at cuffing or arresting the kidnappers. He had taken the money and scarpered.

Trench breathed out deeply, considering his options. It didn't happen often, but he was at a total loss about what to do. Confronting him would be useless. He'd deny it aggressively – violently even. Trench didn't fancy his chances if it came down to his word against Trench's. Not in the current climate.

He realised he should probably report it, but was unsure who to report to. He knew it risked looking like he was lashing out after being removed from the case. Worse, it could be taken as opportunism. Kicking him while he was down, after the whole operation had gone to shit.

Still undecided, Trench's thoughts were interrupted by the sound of raised voices from inside Lewis's office. Trench looked over just as the door burst open. Lewis came steaming out, his face like a growling bulldog. When Trench saw Lewis, he immediately realised what he had to do. He had to report what he saw. Irrespective of any politics or other bullshit going on. This went way beyond any of that.

He stood up and took a few steps towards Lewis.

"Chief, I've got to talk to y—"

"Not now, Trench," spat Lewis, without breaking stride.

Harding and two other men Trench didn't recognise followed Lewis out of his office.

"Just one minute, Chief, it's important. I saw something—"

"*Not fucking now!*" yelled Lewis.

This time he did stop. He turned to face Trench, and jabbed his finger into his chest.

"What's the matter with you, huh? Always me fucking me," he railed. "This whole thing is gone to shit, which I have to deal with. But you still think the whole world can stop because you want a word? You are un-fucking-believable, you know that."

Trench stared at him without responding. He realised his timing had been poor. The drop had obviously gone as badly as he suspected and Lewis and his NCA cronies were going to be in a world of hurt. Trench had let his own adrenaline cloud his judgement. He should have left it for tonight.

"Okay, Chief," he relented, backing away.

Lewis made to walk away, but then spun back. He jabbed his finger again.

"And you know what? You're just as much to blame as anyone for this....this fucking shambles."

"Me....?" Trench trailed off, confused.

"Yes, you," snarled Lewis. "You wanted off it as soon as you realised there was no invisible gun you could just pluck out of thin air this time. No, this one might actually go south, and where would that leave your pristine fucking record, ay?"

Trench stood in shocked silence. Thoughts and questions were flooding into his head, too jumbled to respond. After a second, Lewis snorted.

"Yeah, Chambers. I've got your number."

Lewis turned and walked away. His NCA cohorts had stopped at the open CID door waiting for him. Trench looked over and caught Harding's eye but she looked away. They all left. Trench stood there for a few minutes, trying to make sense of the exchange. He understood that Lewis was feeling the heat because the drop had gone pear-shaped. Undoubtedly the pressure had caused him to lash out.

But that didn't explain what he had said. Trench mulled the words he'd used. He knew Lewis had been referring to the Nassor case.

And the insinuation was unmistakable.

# Twenty-Nine

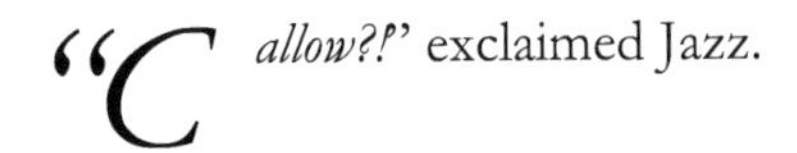

“C*allow?!*” exclaimed Jazz.

Trench nodded.

“Bloody hell,” Jazz continued, shocked. “How sure are you?”

“Sure.”

“Holy fucking shit. What’s he up to? And what are we going to do?”

Trench was glad she said we. He’d barely slept a wink and was feeling frazzled. Having left the station right after his exchange with Lewis, he’d sat in the dark at home brooding over everything that had happened that evening. He eventually went to bed, but after nearly two hours of trying to fool himself that he could sleep, he got up, showered and got dressed.

He texted Jazz to meet early for a coffee before going to the station. He wanted to bring her fully up to speed. They were due to join Surrey CID for the surveillance on Tesco in Horley that afternoon. He was on his second cup when Jazz arrived. He wasn’t sure if the coffee was making things better or worse.

“That I’m less sure about,” he said. “I tried talking to Lewis last night, but my timing was bad. The fallout from the drop was just blowing up in his face. He shut me down.”

“Understandable, I suppose. He’s going to get his balls chewed off if they don’t find her now. I talked to Barton last night. They think some of the gang got away. Which sounds like it’s confirmed, given what you saw. They brought in about a dozen of them last night, but even if some of them crack, surely they’ll have moved her by now.”

“Unless they just cut and run,” Trench said ominously.

“If they do that, let’s hope they don’t stop by wherever they’re holding her first,” said Jazz, trying to sound hopeful. “Their best bet is to get as far away as quick as they can. One of the pricks in custody will crack. They’ve got enough of them in there.”

“True. Although not everyone in custody is in the gang,” sighed Trench.

"You sound certain...?"

"We weren't the only ones watching the gang last night. Krige was there, with at least two of his guys. Doherty, the big guy, and some other guy I didn't recognise. They must have zeroed in on someone from the list he sent us. My guess is they found him and set up a tail. Which led them right into the middle of the drop. The last thing I heard on the radio before I went after the moped was Krige's guys being made as potential marks."

"Oh Jesus," groaned Jazz. "Which means they were definitely lagged in as well."

"I warned Krige. I told him to call me if they had anything. Fucking idiot. He should've done it," said Trench.

"He didn't strike me as the sharpest tool in the shed, but I liked him," said Jazz ruefully. "Maybe they weren't sure yet that the guy they were following was the one."

Trench gave her a sceptical glance.

"Or maybe when Callow went out to Blenheim to take over the case, he told him to call him instead," said Jazz "Anyway, speaking of Callow, what are we going to do? You've got to go to Lewis again."

"Yeah," he said, but didn't sound convinced.

"Trench, you've got to. This is off the fucking charts. You've got to report it. He'd be sacked. Shit, he could be jailed! You can't just sit on it."

"I know, I don't intend to," said Trench. "When I was thinking it through last night, at one point I decided I'd just walk in this morning, slam him up against the wall and slap the cuffs on him. Put some fucking bam in his boozle. But the more I thought about it, I have to be careful here. Bottom line, it's my word against his. And right now, his word is carrying a lot more weight than mine, with Lewis anyway. You know what his last words to me last night were, after he'd had his little tantrum?"

"What?"

"He accused me of planting the gun on the Nassor case," said Trench.

"*Seriously?*" said Jazz, raising her voice again.

"Seriously. He said I'd done it to make myself look good. It's not the first time he's said that to me recently. He's got it into this head that I'm some kind of rogue, bent copper obsessed with my own record or reputation or something."

"Well I guess you were right. Maybe he *was* being weird towards you recently," admitted Jazz, before adding in semi-mock attrition, "Never should've doubted you, partner."

"I'll get over it. But it makes it harder for me to go to him with this. I've got no proof. And he's not going to believe me over Callow. But there's another option."

"What's that?"

"Campbell. I could tell him what I saw. Let him deal with it. Or use it, who knows. He thrives on this shit."

Jazz furrowed her brow, thinking it through. After a moment she started nodding her head.

"I like it," she said. "He'll get why you're going to him instead of Lewis. You've got a beef with Lewis for pulling you from the case so you're going to your old chief – now Lewis's superior – who already involved himself in the case. Yeah, it works."

"I'll call him later," said Trench. "I'm sure he's already figuring out how to play last night. Making sure the NCA are volunteering to take their share of the blame."

He checked his watch.

"Let's head back. We've got a couple of hours before we have to leave to take over the afternoon slot from Parson. I want to call Bromley station after our chat with Cedric yesterday, see if we can match the Oldbury Woods body to anyone reported missing there."

"Okay. I'll find out the latest developments from the drop. See if anyone from the gang is talking yet. Maybe I can vouch for Krige's lot too. Save everyone wasting too much time interviewing them."

"Up to you," replied Trench as they stood up to leave. "Though maybe they deserve some time stewing in the clink for not calling us first."

"How very Trench of you," said Jazz. "What time do you want to head down to Surrey? We need to report to Horley station for eleven forty-five to coordinate the handover from Parson."

"I'll meet you there. I'm going to take my bike. It'll be much quicker for me than coming back into town afterwards."

"Sounds good."

When they got back to the station, Trench went straight to his desk. He glanced over and noticed Lewis's office door was open. Lewis was not at his desk. He looked around the nearly empty squad room and then realised everyone must be in a briefing about the drop.

He checked and saw the door to the Incident Room was closed. He could see bodies in there. For once, he felt relieved he was not involved. The mood would be sour. When the stakes were so high, the blame game brought out the very worst in people.

He went to his desk and called Bromley Police Station. It took only a few minutes to determine that the body did indeed match a recent missing persons report. Savannah Diaz, a thirty-eight year old Spanish national, had been reported missing on Sunday evening. Her flatmate had reported that on the previous weekend, she had gone out on a date from which she had not returned.

Trench spoke with a constable who told him they had determined Diaz was a prostitute who had gone out to meet a john. The report had therefore been assigned a low priority and they had not yet gotten around to doing anything with it. It was a harsh reality, Trench knew, but crimes involving prostitutes were given less priority because they were harder to solve. When Trench explained they had a body they thought could be the missing woman, the constable was only too happy to hand over the report and be done with it.

He emailed Trench a copy of the file as they spoke, which included her Driver's License photo. It was difficult to compare the picture to what he remembered of the body they had found, but the hair colour looked similar. He immediately forwarded the picture to Doctor Wharton. He wrote a single sentence in the email to the pathologist.

*Could this be her?*

Trench asked the constable for the contact number for the flatmate who reported her missing. The flatmate was able to provide a few more details. Diaz had arranged to meet the john in nearby Swanley the previous Friday evening. The flatmate did not have the full address, but she remembered that Diaz had taken a cab because the address was close enough for a cheap fare.

Trench did not tell her they had found a body. Instead, he explained someone from the Met would be around to take her statement officially, and possibly to take DNA samples from Diaz's belongings. The flatmate readily agreed, but then started asking questions about why they would want DNA and whether it was for identification purposes. She was growing more upset the longer the call went on.

As Trench tried to deflect the questions and extricate himself from the call, Jazz came back to her desk. He became aware that Jazz was staring at him expectantly. But he hadn't asked the most important question yet. In between the flatmate's sobs, he asked if Diaz had any birthmarks or tattoos. The flatmate said she had three dots on her left hand and a cross with a loop on the back of her neck.

As the implication of this question landed, she then started screaming, asking why they would want that kind of information. Trench regretted the clumsiness of his approach, but he had to move on. He apologised again and repeated that someone from the Met would be calling to her home.

He hung up the phone, the flatmate's wails ringing in his ears. He stared at the phone for a moment. Dealing with the friends and family was always crushing. But he was glad to put a name to the body. To make a discarded body a real person again. To give her some of her dignity back. That's what he told himself, anyway.

As he gathered himself he realised he was also pleased to have confirmed that the victim was reported missing from London. He could use that later if he needed to.

He was sombre as he turned to Jazz.

"I think we've ID'd the vic. She's a Tom from Bromley. Spanish national, went missing the previous weeken—," he broke off when he noticed the look on her face. "What?"

"Well first, I'm glad we know who she is. At least we can bring some kind of closure to her family," said Jazz. She paused before continuing. "So, I just got the latest from the drop. It gets weirder."

She took a deep breath and blew out her cheeks before continuing.

"Okay, some of this shit is unreal. Callow's being hailed a hero for recovering part of the ransom. Sort of. He turned up at the station late last night with some of the bags. Apparently him and Five Burgers split up to chase different gang members – Burgers backs him up on that. And he's claiming he chased the gang and managed to get them to drop the bags they were carrying."

"He brought them back?" said Trench, surprised. "Okay, that is weird. And technically, I suppose it's true. He did get them to drop it."

"No, that's not the weird part."

Trench frowned at her.

"The bags he brought back – in fact, all of the bags they recovered last night – didn't have any money in them. They recovered a total of more than a dozen bags, because the gang were all carrying bags even before the drop, presumably as decoys. But none of the bags they were carrying had any money in them."

"None of them…?" repeated Trench.

"Nope."

"So they managed to escape with the whole ransom?" Trench asked in disbelief. "How many decoy bags did they have? And how many gang members are there?"

"That's where it gets weird. Thornton's crew are absolutely positive they had eyes on at least two of the bags throughout the whole operation. They're adamant the gang never got close to them. Those two bags are included in the dozen that were recovered."

"What, the ones that didn't have cash in them?"

"Correct," answered Jazz.

"Wait, what are you saying? There was never any cash in those bags?"

"That's exactly what they're saying," confirmed Jazz. "At least not for the entire duration of the operation."

Trench's mind was firing, trying to figure out what it meant.

"What was in those two bags?" he asked.

"Just paper. Small sheets of blank paper, about the size of a bank note. They were tied into bundles and wrapped in brown paper. They found the same thing in three other bags. Including the two Callow recovered."

"What was in the other bags they recovered?"

"Mostly cut up old newspapers and magazines. A couple had some old rags cut up as well."

Trench was silent for a moment, trying to make sense of what he was hearing. He wasn't getting far with it. A sense of foreboding was beginning to crowd his thinking. He knew where this was going but he didn't want to believe it.

"What are they thinking?" he asked.

"They don't know yet. They're still trying to work it through." She grimaced. "I think they're trying to find anything except the inevitable."

"Jesus. Were there any gaps after it was picked up from Osbourne? Any time when it wasn't under observation."

"Officially, no. That's the line right now," she shook her head. "But off the record, there were gaps. We didn't have anyone specifically guarding it once it was back here. It was only here for a few hours after it was picked up from Osbourne, but we're not going to be able to show it was under guard at all times. And it was moved from the car after it was picked up, before being transferred to the Club Shop bags for the drop. And get this, there was a delay of up to an hour between the time it was carried from the car to being loaded into the bags."

"Jesus Christ," groaned Trench. "Where was it?"

"One of the operation rooms downstairs. At least the door was locked," said Jazz, before wincing. "Apparently…"

Trench blew out his cheeks. He ran his hand through his hair and leaned back in his seat. What a monumental cluster fuck.

"This case is cursed," was all he could manage.

"Just wait until Osbourne hears about it. This on top of the drop being a total disaster. It's going to go nuclear."

Trench sat forward, a hopeful thought occurring to him.

"Has any of the gang cracked yet? They giving up her location?"

Jazz shook her head.

"Nothing useful. Most of them are talking, but they're all denying everything. In fact, they're all saying pretty much the same thing. A guy they know asked them to go along last night and carry some bags around, switch them up and then bring them back to his place. This apparent ringleader promised them all a few grand each for an hour's work. One woman even volunteered to bring her kids along if they got a slice too."

"Did we get the address for his place?"

"Thornton's crew hit it last night as soon as they got it," Jazz nodded. "Nothing. Tiny place, apparently. No sign she was there or ever had been. Forensics are taking a look this morning but they're doubtful. But guess what?"

Trench was piecing it together.

"The guy's name was on Krige's list," he said. "The ringleader."

"Yes," said Jazz, surprised he'd got it. "Pavel Kozlowski. He was one of the names we couldn't find when we raided the list at the weekend. But he—"

"He's one of the ones who escaped last night," Trench finished.

"Right, how'd you know?"

"Because you would've said they sweated him all night, rather than just hit the address. And because this fucking case is cursed…"

They were both silent for a moment, digesting the latest information. Trench had so many questions but knew he wouldn't like any of the answers. The whole story was almost too grim to take in. The cold facts were jarring.

Most depressingly, Vanessa was still missing. Now the ransom money was also missing. The apparent ringleader was missing. And now there was a doom-laden black cloud of suspicion brewing over the entire police force.

If one of those facts hit the media, there'd be an outcry. If all of it became known, it would be a scandal beyond anything Trench could immediately recall.

He also knew it would be 'when', not if.

Trench shook his head again but it didn't shake loose any positivity from the news. Nor the growing nagging feeling that he was missing something. Or probably lots of things. All he could think was that if he was in charge of the case, he'd prioritise finding Vanessa. He wasn't sure what he'd do beyond that. But everything else was a distant priority.

"What are they doing about finding Vanessa?" he said.

"Thornton's squad are trying to track down Kozlowski. That's the priority. If it's true that the rest of the gang were just gofers for the drop, that's the only way we're going to find her."

"So they're going to be hitting every address they can shake from the gang. And any hangouts, KA's addresses, places of work, anything. It's all they can do," said Trench.

"Pretty much," agreed Jazz.

"But it's also not exactly a stealth operation," said Trench. "We might be able to keep a lid on last night's operation, just explain it as football hooliganism or something. But there's no way we can keep this out of the press when they start twigging the raids. A day, maybe two. At best."

"We're going to go with drug raids for a while," said Jazz.

"Not for long. The press'll expect results then. Tables full of confiscated gear or weapons," Trench shook his head. "A couple of days if we're lucky."

Trench glanced at the clock on his computer. They needed to start making a move to Surrey.

"Let's go. We can talk it over while we're watching the Tesco," he said.

They walked down to the ground floor together, where Jazz left for an unmarked car and Trench went to change into his motorbike gear. He mulled the latest developments as he did so. He kept replaying the scenes from the previous night, trying to tally them with what he had just learned. The nagging feeling was growing.

His thoughts were interrupted by the sound of his phone ringing. Half dressed, he rummaged through the pile of his clothes and eventually found his phone. He answered it without looking at the screen in case the person hung up.

"Hello?"

"Yes, I think that's her, Trench," said Doctor Wharton solemnly. "Who is she?"

"I thought so, thanks Doc. After I sent it to you her flatmate also confirmed she has the same tattoos. We're sending someone around to get her DNA, but that's probably just for certainty at this stage. It's her."

"Who is she, Trench?" Wharton repeated.

"Her name's Savannah Diaz. Thirty-eight, from Spain. She was working as a prostitute and didn't return from a trick last weekend."

"Jesus, the poor soul. Any leads?" Wharton almost pleaded.

"Actually we do, Doc. I'll give you the drill later, but we're onto someone. Ex-con, not long out after doing a stretch for sexual battery and rape. Savage attack," said Trench, trying to step into his leather bike pants.

"Christ. Why don't they throw away the key on these guys?" spat Wharton.

"Amen to that. I think they will when we get this guy. It looks like Savannah Diaz is not the only one he's killed."

"What? There's more? Where? I don't recall seeing anything similar," asked Wharton.

Trench could tell he was searching his memory as he said it.

"There's a couple more from across the South East," said Trench, shifting the phone to the other ear, still trying and failing to get dressed. "Same MO, same wounds. Look Doc, I'll call you with the details a bit later. I'm on my way out the door to try to get the guy. We've zeroed in on him and are staking the place out. I'm going there right now."

"Of course, go. Get the bastard," said Wharton, before adding after a pause, "I hope you're bringing a Trojan. So you can end this wherever you find him."

Trojan was the shorthand name for the Met's Armed Response Vehicle. Heavily modified BMW's equipped with specialist satellite navigation and communications gear. They also carried a range of firearms and weaponry. The doctor's meaning was clear.

"I hear you, Doc," said Trench as he hung up.

Once changed, he hung his suit back in the cupboard, grabbed his helmet and trotted out the door. As he hurried past the bottom of the stairs he stepped out at exactly the same moment as someone stepped down off the last step, both blindsided. They bumped into each other hard.

"Shit, sorr—" began Trench.

"Fuck's sake! Who—"

Callow.

As they straightened up, their eyes caught as they each realised who they had bumped into. For a second neither said a word. They both just stared. Trench held the stare, searching for anything that could explain the intention behind what he had seen last night. Another second passed. Nothing. All he saw was anger.

He decided to break the ice. He hadn't yet worked through his own thoughts to figure out what those intentions had been.

"Tough gig last night," he said.

"Yeah," said Callow, still just staring.

He then ran his eyes down Trench's bike gear. Trench wondered if it was twigging anything for him from the previous night.

"I hear you're the hero. Bringing back the ransom like that," Trench floated.

Callow half snorted, half sneered. As Trench studied him, he realised Callow's face was racked with rage. His jaw was clenched, his eyes seemed blackened by what looked like fury. Trench decided to try conciliatory to keep him talking.

"Any of the gang talking?"

"I don't know. Ask Thornton. Or Lewis," spat Callow. "I've got to go."

He went to push past Trench.

"I meant what I said, Callow," said Trench as he passed.

Callow stopped and turned around.

"And what's that, Chambers?"

"If there's anything I can do to help, let me know," said Trench, watching him.

"Yeah, right," said Callow, turning to leave again.

"Yeah. That's right," said Trench. "I still want to help find her. Find Vanessa."

Callow grumbled but made to keep walking away.

"Have you emailed them yet?" Trench called after him.

Callow stopped and turned around again, confused and bothered.

"What? Emailed who?" he said, before understanding. "We've got half of them in custody. Some on the run. But uh, yeah I'm sure we're going to email them. We're all over it."

"Pity we couldn't get them all last night."

Callow glared at Trench again, but eventually turned away.

"I've got to go, Chambers. I'm going to see Osbourne."

"Right," said Trench. "You're making quite a habit of that."

Callow didn't respond so Trench said after him.

"Didn't you go there yesterday as well? To pick up the ransom?"

He half turned his head so Trench could see the scowl, but he kept walking away. Trench watched him go.

When he walked out the door a moment later he caught a glimpse of Callow in the passenger seat of an unmarked car, Burgess behind the wheel. The car exited the station's gate and took off at speed. Within a couple of minutes, Trench was also out the gate on his bike, heading for Surrey. He'd chosen an upbeat trance album by Hernan Cattaneo for the ride. He wanted the fast-paced beats to keep his mind moving rapidly. He needed to think everything through.

Callow's dark mood struck Trench as uncharacteristic. He struggled to believe it was genuine concern for Vanessa after the failed operation. It was more likely that he was feeling some heat as the details of that debacle made their way up the chain of command. Callow was SIO now, so couldn't escape blame. Maybe that was why he was being sent out to deliver the update to Doctor Osbourne. The messenger to be shot.

But the nagging feeling would not go away. Trench knew he was missing something. Even if Callow was feeling the heat, Trench knew he could still brazen it out. Especially if he was being lauded for recovering what he believed to be the ransom.

That thought caused Trench to again replay the scene he had witnessed the previous night. Callow kicking the injured kidnapper back down onto the ground. Stepping over him. Grabbing the bags. Getting into the car and driving away.

And then bringing the bags back to the station?

No, this last act didn't fit. The thought fell loose and struck Trench. He realised he now knew what had been niggling at him. Callow hadn't grabbed the bags with the intention of bringing them back to the station. He grabbed them because he thought the ransom was inside. He only brought them back to the station when he discovered it wasn't. His fury was because he didn't get the ransom.

The realisation set Trench's mind racing even faster, the implications firing his thoughts like sparks.

# Thirty

Only Jazz knew that Trench was on a bike. He decided to use this by going straight to Tesco without identifying himself to see if he could spot the surveillance teams, before reporting to Horley Police Station. He figured if he could spot them, then Chapman could if he was being careful.

He was also still feeling charged from the realisations he'd made on the way down. He wasn't ready yet to sit in a car and just wait, probably for hours.

He cruised into the car park. It was less than half full, given it was noon on a Tuesday. He did a wide lap around the section of the car park closest to the main door of the shop. He spotted two vans he believed were part of the surveillance. They appeared empty, but had blacked-out windows in the back. They would not likely be made as surveillance unless someone was particularly paranoid.

He thought one of the men collecting trolleys in the car park could be part of the team, but he wasn't certain. He expected there would be others placed inside the store disguised as Tesco employees, and another sitting with the store's security team monitoring the internal cameras. He was satisfied the operation was being well executed.

He left the car park and headed for the station. Although it was known as Horley Police Station, it was actually based just inside the grounds of Gatwick airport, barely a mile from the Tesco store. As he approached a roundabout, he spotted a petrol station off to the right. Glancing down at the clock on the bike's display screen, he saw he had plenty of time. He decided to fill the tank. A full tank was always a better option.

He hit the throttle to slip through the cars queuing at the roundabout then made the right turn. There was only one other car on the forecourt, so he pulled up at the pump nearest the kiosk. When he turned to the pump he noticed it had a pay-at-pump option. He selected this so he wouldn't have to go into the kiosk. He entered his card pin and began pumping.

He instinctively glanced around at the other car. An elderly woman seemed to be berating the pump and waving her bank card angrily at it. Shouldn't have selected pay-at-pump, thought Trench, casually turning fully in the opposite direction. He had quite enough bullshit on his plate without getting dragged into that developing fiasco. He was grateful the relatively small fuel tank on the bike would be full by the time the woman started screaming for the cavalry.

When he turned away from her, he realised there was another vehicle on the forecourt. A beat-up old blue hatchback van was stationed at the air and water pumps, across the far side of the forecourt. Trench instinctively cast a quizzical eye over it. It was at least ten years old. The two tyres he could see looked worn to the point of being illegal. Or maybe beyond that. There was one large dent and a couple of smaller scratches on the body. The passenger wing mirror was held together by tape.

Trench immediately knew that if he ran the plate, it would come back as having no tax and almost certainly no insurance. Any cop with more than a few months' experience would know. The thought crossed his mind, but he knew he had no time. He had to let it go. Reluctantly. He could see the driver bent down putting air into the front tyre on the far side. He was trying to decide between giving the driver a quick verbal warning or just a long, confrontational stare when the pump clicked in his hand. The tank was full.

Trench lifted the nozzle and topped the fuel right up. He then lifted his head to put the pump back in its cradle. At the same moment the driver of the van stood up.

Trench froze.

A shock of adrenaline pulsed down his spine. Instinct caused him to almost duck behind the pump. He just managed to stay calm and avoid the sudden movement. He quickly cradled the nozzle and took off his helmet to get a better view.

The unkempt hair was dirtier. Some flecks of grey. The hairline had receded. There was more than a few days' stubble. This man looked much older. But Trench had studied the file photos intensively.

He was almost certain the man standing by the blue van was Howard Chapman.

As he watched, the man tossed the air pump back toward its cradle. Trench immediately realised he wouldn't get there in time if the man got back into his car. The distance was too far, even at full sprint. He'd have to follow him on his bike. But then the man turned and started walking towards the kiosk, his back to Trench.

Trench immediately fast-walked towards the van. This kept him on the man's blindside, rather than if he tried to intercept him. He reached the van as the man entered the kiosk. Trench swiftly bent down and peered in the windows of the van.

There was no-one else in there. He didn't see any weapons. The floor was covered in empty food wrappers and other rubbish.

Looking in the back of the van, he saw more rubbish scattered everywhere. He noticed the handle of a hammer or similar tool jutting out from the rubbish. He strained to focus and then figured out what it was. The handle of a tennis racket. There was a second one. He noticed the strings on this one were loose, some missing. Then he spotted a couple of tennis balls amongst the junk. They looked relatively new.

Bright greenish-yellow.

His heart pumped faster. Bright greenish-yellow fibres. Wharton had found them during the postmortem on who he now knew to be Savannah Diaz. They were also mentioned in the postmortem report for Amber Kendall. In both cases the fibres were found inside the mouth. Which had evidence of being gagged with duct tape.

His mind raced. Any doubt that the man was Chapman evaporated. He straightened up and looked at the kiosk. No sign of the man. He had to act fast. He only had seconds to decide what to do.

His immediate urge was to overpower Chapman. Take him from his blindside as he came out of the kiosk. He had no doubt he could subdue him, especially with the element of surprise. Hold him until the others could get there. Tesco was less than half a mile away.

But it suddenly occurred to him he also had an opportunity to sidestep a potential bureaucratic fuss. He grabbed his phone from his pocket and dialled Jazz's number.

"You here?" she answered.

"There's a petrol station by the roundabout halfway between the Horley police station and Tesco. Get here right now," he said in a hurried, hushed tone.

"What? Where are you?"

Trench raised his voice as loudly as he dared. He walked slowly toward the kiosk.

"Right now, Jazz. You need to get here. The petrol station between Horley station and Tesco. It's two minutes from the station," he said. "He's here."

"Who is? Chapman?"

"*Now*, Jazz. Yes, Chapman. I've got him," he said, trying to stay calm. "Come by yourself. Bring the car. *DO IT NOW!*"

He hung up.

He was nearly at the kiosk. He knew what he would do, but glanced around to see if he could improve upon the loose plan he'd formed. Nothing came to mind. He suddenly became aware of the old woman's voice.

"You there! I need help. Hoy, you there!"

In his peripheral vision he could see her ambling towards him. The door to the kiosk opened. Chapman came shuffling out. Just a few yards away now. Trench scanned his hands. Cigarettes, a can of coke, chocolate bar. Nothing threatening.

Chapman looked up, directly at Trench. Their eyes met. Grey eyes, an empty stare. A hint of wariness. But mostly nothing. The cold dead eyes of a mind that felt nothing for anyone.

"You! I'm talking to you there. I need help," screeched the old woman, closer now.

Chapman turned to glance at her, but only for a split second. He blankly turned away. Trench wondered if he'd even registered the woman. They were nearly side by side. Their eyes met again. Trench nodded toward the old woman and smirked, his eyes never leaving Chapman's.

"All yours, mate. Think she needs your help."

Chapman looked at him but didn't even flicker at the joke. He didn't glance toward the woman again as Trench had hoped. He did nothing. As he passed by Trench shoulder-to-shoulder he stared straight ahead. Trench let him go past a single step, then sprung.

He suddenly spun, swinging his right arm around Chapman's neck. He brought his left arm up to the other side of Chapman's head, locking his arms together. His left hand was on the top of Chapman's head, pushing forward. Chokehold. Pushing his neck into Trench's right arm. He squeezed as hard as he could. Chapman's arms flung up, clawing at his grip. Trench squeezed tighter.

Anger mixed with adrenaline. Flashes of the body in the woods. Strung up and cut to pieces. Raped. Brutalised. Crime scene photos of the bodies in the water. Trench felt a surge of rage and jerked his left hand forward, ramming Chapman's head tighter into the grip. Chapman's hands dropped away. Trench bent his knees and started lowering him down. He knew he was nearly out.

As they hit the ground Trench suddenly caught a glimpse of a flash of steel. Arcing towards his head. He jerked his head to the left. The knife hammered down, striking his shoulder, where his head had been a split-second before. He felt no pain but the move had loosened his grip. Chapman was squirming onto his belly, swinging the knife again. Trench let go. Both men on their knees, scrambling to get up. Chapman swung the knife again as he lurched forwards. A practiced shiv fighter.

Trench leaned back out of his range, rolled up onto his feet. He stood upright, bracing himself for another attack. His heart was pounding. He suddenly remembered his leather jacket was armoured. Protection down both arms. He bent his arms at the elbow and raised them. The only defence he had against the knife. Chapman made to swing again. Trench planted his feet, ready to parry.

Chapman jerked forward and Trench's reflexes pushed his arms out to meet the blow. No impact. Chapman spun and bolted back towards the van. The fake gave him a split-second head start. He moved faster than he looked, his primal, fight-for-life prison experience kicking in. Trench hurled after him, his heavy motorbike boots pounding on the concrete.

Chapman was at the car, pulling open the door, squirming to get inside. Trench still a few yards away launched himself. Chapman was half in the door, but not enough. Trench's full weight came crashing into the door. Crushing Chapman's body against the car. He swung the knife again. Trench was in close and jerked his arm up to block. He pressed his body into the door, pinning Chapman half in, half out.

Trench smashed his forehead down into Chapman's face. Burst his nose. The impact caused Chapman to smack the back of his head off the car. Trench reeled his neck back and smashed again. Harder. Burning fury. He brought his right arm up and grabbed Chapman's neck. He held his face steady and smashed a third time. Chapman's legs sagged.

Trench grabbed the knife hand with both hands, violently twisting it and hammering it off the car. He moved a few inches away from the door, easing the pin on Chapman's body. He smashed the knife hand again and again off the car. The door crept open another inch and Trench braced and rammed himself hard into it again. Chapman whelped and buckled. The knife dropped. Trench jumped backwards letting the door open fully. He dragged the battered Chapman out by his arm. Dragged him down flat to the ground and pounced onto his back.

He swept both Chapman's hands behind him and violently jerked them high up his back. He knelt on them, pinning them in place. He grabbed Chapman's hair and pulled his head off the ground. Twisted it to see his face.

"*Motherfucker!*" he was shouting. "*You had enough? They didn't fight back, did they? When you tied them. You piece of fucking shit!*"

Chapman's eyes were closed. Trench couldn't tell if he was out or not. He bounced his head off the concrete once. Then pushed it into the ground. Pinning his whole body tight.

"You brute! Get off him. I saw what you did," the old woman was nearly on him.

She raised her handbag and swung it at Trench. Missed. It felt like slow motion compared to the frenzied battle with Chapman. She gathered herself for another swing.

"Ma'am, get the fuck out of here," Trench yelled. "Police! Police business. Just…"

The adrenaline was subsiding. He was coming back out of it. He trailed off. Braced himself for the pathetic blow when it came. He couldn't let go of Chapman no matter what. That's all he knew. He flinched to take the blow. The sound of the hit mixed with the screech of tyres. A door slammed.

"I'm not afraid. You evil brute! I saw it all," the woman ranted.

"Okay Ma'am, that's enough. Back off," shouted Jazz. "Police! Police!"

Trench turned as Jazz pushed past the woman.

"Cuff him," roared Trench.

Jazz immediately ran back to the car, just a few yards away. She was back in a flash, cuffing Chapman.

"Trench, let his arms go," she said after she cuffed one.

Trench reluctantly raised his knees enough for her to lower his hands. When they were straightened behind his back she cuffed the other one.

"Get him up," she commanded.

Trench eased off him. They took one arm each and yanked him to his feet. Chapman's floppy legs could barely support his own weight. Trench began dragging him by the arm toward the car. Jazz used both hands to drag him by the other arm. Trench pulled the door open. They swung him head first into the car. He landed face down but bounced off onto the floor. Trench grabbed his legs and pushed them in. They were bent back awkwardly, pushing Chapman's face further into the floor. Trench slammed the door.

"Think he knew he was this good at Yoga before now?" said Jazz.

Trench walked around to the passenger door.

"We can straighten him up on the road. Let's get out of here," he said.

As he got to the front of the car, the old woman was standing a few yards away. Still scowling at him.

"And you," said Trench as he got in the car. "Thanks for trying to do the right thing. I hope you never get a walking stick."

# Thirty-One

"He was always going to have a knife," admonished Jazz. "How could you miss that?"

Trench was going to say it was spur of the moment. But thinking about it now, he knew she was right. He just nodded. He didn't want to think about it anymore. The adrenaline was gone and he was feeling the physical impact of the tussle. He wasn't going to let himself start feeling the emotional impact as well.

"You're so fucking lucky you're in your biker gear," Jazz continued.

She looked down at the jacket that Trench held on his knees. He had his finger in the hole on the right shoulder pad. The Teflon armour inside had a deep gash in it. She was right again. It would have been his head if he hadn't caught the shimmer of the blade.

"We need to make some calls," he said.

He turned again and looked down at Chapman, barely ten seconds since the last time.

"Pull over somewhere and I'll straighten him up," said Trench.

Jazz pulled in at the side of the road. The flashing blue lights and siren made sure they were given enough room from passing cars. After they roughly dragged Chapman out and sat him back in, Trench sat in the backseat beside him. Chapman sat with his head slumped forward, but Trench could see his eyes were open.

Trench stared at him. He knew he couldn't ask him questions now. The interview had to be recorded. There had to be a lawyer present. He had to wait. But that was okay. They were bringing him back to Charing Cross. He would get plenty of time.

Jazz had given Trench the number for the man in Surrey CID in charge of the surveillance operation, Detective Chief Superintendent Roland Hunter. Trench had called him and given him a full update. Hunter went from being delighted he'd been caught, to annoyed Trench had cut his team out, to angry they were taking him back to Charing Cross. He ranted that Surrey had jurisdiction over the arrest. Trench countered by telling him that the victim in Oldbury Woods was from Bromley – Met CID's patch. Hunter had fought back, ultimately threatening Trench that he would make a formal complaint to his Detective Chief

Superintendent. Hunter said he'd worked with Lewis before his transfer to the Met and knew him well.

Trench wished him good luck with that and hung up.

He then called Ward and followed that by calling Parson. On both calls, he explained what had happened and said they should be there to interview the suspect about their specific case. They both agreed, with Ward saying he would come to Charing Cross that evening and Parson saying he'd be there first thing in the morning. Neither had any problem with Trench taking Chapman back to Charing Cross, being indifferent to whether the interviews took place in Surrey or London. Both locations were outside their own jurisdiction anyway.

In the back seat, Trench now kept his stare on Chapman. His nose and mouth were caked in blood. The one eye Trench could see was blackened. His ragged clothes were covered in blood. Trench glanced at his hands behind his back. They were covered in scrapes and scratches. Some were fresh but some looked old.

Ward's words echoed in Trench's ears. The worst monsters aren't like what you'd expect. They were scrawny, ragged losers you'd barely glance at in the street. No threat at all. But Trench had seen his primeval side. He'd felt it. Chapman had fought like a caged animal, instantly ferocious and dangerous in equal measure. His first move had been to try to plant a knife into Trench's skull. He had no doubt he was capable of the brutality they had found.

Trench stared. Studied him. Searching for answers he knew he'd never get. What was going on inside the man's head? From his stable, loving background, what had made him become this beast? This ripper. An urchin of death and torture and pain. The more he stared the more certain he became of only one thing. The man should be put down like a rabid dog.

Chapman sniffed his nose.

Trench watched as he slowly raised his head, eyes forwards. He sniffed again. Like a rat, sniffing the air. His head was fully raised. He was staring straight at the back of Jazz's head. He sniffed hard.

"Always wanted to fuck a Paki," he said. "You'll do."

Trench's fist smashed into his face with full force. It caught him flush on the nose and upper lips. His head went crashing into the window and dropped back down. It sagged there. His eyes stayed closed.

Trench glanced over and caught Jazz's eye in the rear-view mirror. She gave a slight shake of the head. Enough. No more. Trench nodded and they lapsed back into silence. It lasted about ten minutes, before Chapman broke the silence.

"You've got…nothing," he panted, head still sagging, eyes closed.

He spoke softly, but calmly. Trench glared at him. He could feel the weight of Jazz's stare and caught her eye in the mirror again. Again she shook her head. They couldn't talk to him now. No matter what he said.

"Nothing," wheezed Chapman.

His head still sagged but Trench could see a smile form on his lips. Chapman turned his head slightly and opened his eyes. He looked at Trench. Dead, vacant eyes. But the mouth was curled into a snarl.

"You can't put me away," Chapman slowly, painfully, chuckled, blood and spittle dripping from his lips. "You got nothing. No evidence. No links. No witnesses. You've got…" he panted again, "…nothing."

His smile remained as his head bobbed back down. Trench glared at him. He looked almost serenely calm.

"We've got you, motherfucker," said Trench.

# Thirty-Two

The cell door swung open and Trench stepped inside.

"Let's go, Basil Fawlty," he said.

Krige jumped up off the hard concrete bed.

"Hey mate. Glad to see you," he said, reaching a hand out to Trench.

Trench ignored it.

"Don't be. You're a fucking moron. I told you to call me."

"I know, I know, we fucked up," said Krige, dropping his hand. "We were only following him. We weren't sure—"

"It's done now. Let's go. Move it," said Trench, pushing Krige toward the door.

"Thanks mate, I mean it. I've been asking for you, but they said I'd have to be interviewed all over again," said Krige as he walked out the door.

"Don't thank me yet. They do need to interview you again, but they're going to do it right now. I need this cell."

"Ah, shit I've already told them everything. We screwed up. But you can vouch for us, right, Trench?" Krige pleaded.

Trench stopped and turned to him.

"I already did. But they can't just let you walk. They're going to go over your story, then cut you loose. Unless you fuck that up too," he said, then resumed leading the way. "And be happy. They were going to let you guys stew for another few days. I got them to speak to you now."

"Okay mate, I get it. And thanks, I appreciate it."

"Alright, Krige. You helped me earlier. I don't forget that."

Trench led him to the interview room. Krige went inside and Trench went back out to the booking area. Chapman was where he'd left him. Sitting on a bench, hands cuffed, head bowed down. He was flanked by two uniforms. Jazz stood nearby. Trench nodded at the uniforms and they each grabbed an arm. Chapman stood, but then planted his feet and refused to move. He raised his head and stared at Trench. His voice was calm, even as his words were incendiary.

"Get me a fucking lawyer, pig."

Trench gave a slight nod of his head, then made eye contact with one of the uniforms and jerked his head toward the cells. The uniforms began dragging Chapman that way. Chapman no longer resisted. He was led away to the cell as Trench and Jazz watched.

"Thanks, Sarge," Trench said, turning to the Custody Sergeant. "Appreciate it."

"Alright, Trench," replied the Sarge. He nodded at them both. "Good job, you two."

They both returned the nod. When they'd called ahead to get Chapman booked, they were told that all cells were still full from the ransom drop operation. They had initially been diverted, but Trench had persuaded the Custody Sergeant to shuffle things around so they could book Chapman at Charing Cross. This also meant bumping Krige and his men up the order for interview.

"I'm going to change," Trench said to Jazz. "See you up there. Why don't you make a start on the interview prep. Get as many questions as you can think of down on paper. We can work out the order after that."

"Right," said Jazz, heading for the stairs.

In the changing room, Trench decided to have a shower too. He had some of Chapman's blood on his head and hands. He could also do with the jolt of a cold shower. He wanted to have a clear head for the prep, as well as for the interview itself. Chapman's words in the car rang ominously in his ears. They had almost nothing. There was a lot riding on the interview.

After showering, he stood for another few minutes under the water at its coldest setting. It blasted away much of the grogginess, but by the time he had dressed he realised he still needed a coffee. As he turned the key in his locker, he heard the changing room door open.

"Trench, a minute," said Commander Campbell.

"Alright, Commander," said Trench.

Campbell walked into the changing room and was checking each of the shower cubicles. There was no one else in the changing room, but Campbell seemed to pause nonetheless.

"What's up, Commander?" said Trench, curious, but also keen to keep moving.

"Not here," said Campbell, and walked out the door.

Trench followed him out, then past the front desk through to the interview rooms. Campbell checked whether the first room was empty then opened the door. He motioned for Trench to go inside first. Campbell followed him in and closed the door. Trench at first remained standing. He wasn't sure how long they would be there. It also didn't feel right to sit on the suspect's side of the table.

"Sit down, Trench," said Campbell, himself taking a seat. On the interviewer's side of the table.

Seeing Trench hesitate, Campbell raised his arms in a conciliatory gesture.

"Sit down, Trench. It's not an interview. We're just talking here because there's nowhere else. Jazz told me you were getting changed, so I came down before you came up. It's better we talk down here."

Trench sat, then looked at Campbell without saying anything. He had no idea where this was going but was instantly on alert. Why was it better they talk down here rather than upstairs?

Campbell stared down at his hands for a moment, as if gathering his thoughts. He then looked at Trench for a long moment before speaking.

"It's been…quite a few days for the squad," he began slowly.

Trench said nothing, kept his face still.

"No, that's not right," Campbell shook his head, before continuing. "I know you're a straight-talker so let's not bullshit each other here. The events of the past few days have been nothing short of a complete fucking disaster. The way things are shaping up, maybe a bigger disaster than we've had for a very, very long time. I understand you were removed from Operation Labrador, but that you're still aware of what's happened?"

He looked at Trench expectantly. Trench made no reply. He still didn't know where this was going but was concerned by Campbell's candour. It wasn't how he normally spoke. Something was happening. Trench wasn't going to speak until he figured out what. And what blame was being levelled at him.

"I'll take that as a yes," Campbell continued. "In which case you'll know just how exposed we are. We haven't found Vanessa Osbourne. And from what I've just learned upstairs, we are no closer to finding her than we were on day one. It's not even clear to me that we have a solid handle on what exactly is being done to find her, given that our investigation has been…*shared* with our colleagues on Old Queen Street."

He practically snarled the word shared, giving Trench his first hint where this might be going.

"We also don't have the kidnapper," Campbell said, before pausing again. When he resumed speaking, the anger was now barely-disguised rage. "And now, we've also somehow managed to lose the fucking ransom money."

Trench considered telling Campbell the working theory he'd come up with on his bike ride down to Surrey. He'd been so consumed with Chapman that he'd put it completely out of his head. He decided not to say anything yet. He still wasn't certain where Campbell was going.

"I understand you've taken a suspect into custody for the murder of the woman in Oldbury Woods," said Campbell. "And that you've linked the man to at least two other murders."

Trench was surprised by the sudden change of tack. He was also surprised that Campbell knew all of this already. Campbell must have picked up on the confusion that crept onto Trench's face.

"I spoke with Jazz just now, who confirmed the details," said Campbell, before adding cryptically, "But I already knew. It was good work, Trench. Great work. How long have you had that case? Less than a week? And you turned the murder of an unidentified body into the capture of a presumed serial killer. It's a very impressive result. But you know what I like most of all?"

Campbell raised a slight smile, almost conspiratorial. It put Trench on even higher alert. He was feeling even more wrong-footed with how the conversation was going. He raised his eyebrows by way of answering Campbell's question.

"That you brought him back here, Trench. That was a masterstroke. I have always liked the way you operate, you know that. You're a bloody good detective. That has never been in any doubt. And now bringing this guy back here, and all the positive

PR we can get from that, at this moment. That was highly commendable thinking, Trench. Highly commendable."

Campbell paused, as if waiting for Trench's reaction.

PR had absolutely no bearing whatsoever on Trench's decision to bring Chapman back to Charing Cross. He did it solely because he wanted to conduct the interview himself. But he was smart enough to realise there was merit in having Campbell think he had done it for the good of the squad. Although, he realised, Campbell almost certainly knew Trench better than to think that.

Trench began to think he knew where the conversation was going. It certainly wasn't to simply clap him on the back. But he didn't want to make any assumptions. He would let Campbell spell it out. Trench just nodded.

"We'll make the most of that when the time is right," said Campbell, seeming to move on. "But right now, the most immediate concern is of course finding Vanessa. That is our absolute top priority. Nothing is more important. And therefore, of course, we want our best people on it. That's you, Trench. I want you back leading the investigation. You should never have been taken off it. That was a mistake. I did not know about that until later. And I will deal with that at the appropriate time. But right now, only one thing matters. Finding Vanessa Osbourne."

Trench stared at him. This was not where he had initially expected the conversation to go, but he realised he probably shouldn't be surprised. Lewis's decision to involve the NCA was always going to have repercussions. Given how badly everything had gone, those repercussions were going to come with a razor-sharp edge. It was just a matter of how far and how deep the cuts went.

A blizzard of questions ran through Trench's mind. He tossed them over in his head and figured they could wait. He was back on the case. He felt his energy levels picking up. This was good news.

But he had one condition.

Campbell had never before praised Trench like he had just done. Not in the years when he was the squad's chief. Trench decided to press home the advantage.

"I'll give it everything I've got," he said genuinely. "But I'm still interviewing Chapman."

Campbell looked at Trench like he was an adult demanding to wait up to see Santy Claus.

"That's a waste of time," said Campbell, with a dismissive wave of his hand. "He's just going to no comment his way through the next twenty-four hours. You know this."

"Maybe. But I want first crack at him," said Trench firmly. "I'm leading the interview on our case. And we invite the SIOs from the cases in Thames Valley and Sussex too. They can lead on their cases when the time comes. We get the headlines, but we owe them that."

Campbell looked at him for a moment, his savvy eyes scrutinising Trench. He had always been a good reader of people, and he was this time. He soon nodded to himself.

"You don't want anyone from our squad leading the interview," he said. "Okay, I get that. You have first crack. But after that I am putting someone else on Chapman and you are on Operation Labrador. And I will tell you this. If you don't trust your colleagues enough to let them handle an interview, then you are lost, Trench. You cannot continue like that."

"It's not that," Trench protested, but it sounded weak even to himself. "Or not all of them, anyway."

Trench considered whether now was the right time to tell him what he believed he had seen Callow do. But he hadn't yet managed to think it through fully. He wasn't comfortable with how it fit with the other things he had come up with on the bike ride to Surrey. He decided instead to share some of the other realisations he'd had, as well as to plant some seeds.

"I'll get started again immediately on the Vanessa Osbourne case after the interview. And I've been thinking about it. Going through what happened. Do you know who couriered the money from Osbourne's house back to the station?"

"The lead investigators, Callow and Burgess. But," he held up his hands as if to halt Trench's line of reasoning, "They were accompanied by an armed unit. They tailed them the whole time. Literally right behind them. I already checked this. And I don't need you casting insinuations, okay. I know you have history with some of the lads in the squad. Or one of them anyway. Just focus on finding Vanessa."

"I'm not saying that. What I'm saying is, did they eyeball the cash? Did anyone here? Or was it already sealed when Osbourne gave it to them?"

A look of shocked realisation flashed across Campbell's face. His political instincts immediately concealed his reaction and tempered his reply. But Trench had seen it.

"What are you saying, Trench? Remember who you're talking about," he said, but Trench could tell he was intrigued.

"I'm saying, how sure are we that we ever had two million pounds in cash in the station?"

"Jesus," said Campbell, staring off into the distance.

Trench wasn't sure if it was the realisation that Osbourne might have given them a dummy ransom, or the vexing truth that they may never be able to prove it.

Or if it was the implications it made about Doctor Osbourne.

"Find out, Trench. Immediately," said Campbell urgently. "And do it discreetly. Do not breathe a word of this to anyone. I do not want even a hint of this to get outside this room. If we're seen to be trying to shift suspicion onto Osbourne for this, it will make matters infinitely worse. That man has a deep reach. He's got connections up to the very top. And I don't mean the police force."

"There's more important angles here," said Trench, staring hard at Campbell, demanding he consider more than the political implications. "It's not just about money. Why would Osbourne do that?"

There was a long pause before Campbell spoke.

"Follow where the investigation leads you. But be careful. Be very fucking careful. I do not believe for one second that Osbourne is…" he broke off for a moment, searching for the words, "…is somehow involved in his daughter's disappearance. The thought is inconceivable, whatever may or may not have happened with the money. Tread very, very carefully when you ask him about it."

Trench was used to how Campbell communicated. The message was clear. Trench was to somehow find out if Doctor Osbourne had given them a dummy ransom. But if that prompted Doctor Osbourne to accuse police of blaming him and they couldn't prove it, that would be on Trench's head alone.

"There's more," said Trench.

Campbell looked less than keen to hear any more. Trench continued unabated.

"Since the very start, he was reluctant to pay the ransom. He had a blazing row with his wife when the ransom note arrived. He knew," said Trench, replaying the scene in his head. "He knew all along it was a sham. He only relented when his wife lost it. She was screaming at him, to pay anything to get their daughter back. Only after she'd completely broken down did he agree."

"What are you saying?"

"I don't know yet. But something's been off about this from the start. He didn't want to pay the ransom. Then he managed to get his hands on two million quid in the space of a couple of hours. I don't know how banks work for billionaires, but can you just withdraw that much cash in a couple of hours? Then he pulled that stunt on TV, offering the reward. The more I've thought about it, I just can't believe that was real. At first, I thought it was just him fighting back. That his mind was so warped with worry that he was seeing the whole thing as some kind of business deal that he could barter his way out of.

"But it doesn't fit. He's got the whole fucking country out looking for his daughter. But the only person he'd really want to make contact with would have run a million miles when he turned the heat up like that. Either he knew the ransom demand was fake from the start or…"

"Or what?" pressed Campbell.

"Or he knew there was no point negotiating with him."

There was an uneasy silence in the small interview room. Trench had reached these conclusions on the ride to Surrey but he hadn't yet had the opportunity to say them out loud. Even now, he was being less candid than he felt. He was wary of how Campbell would receive his only half thought-out theories. But as he spoke, he felt more conviction that he was on the right track. He decided to continue before Campbell shut him down.

"Even before that, there's been signs," Trench continued. "I asked him if he had checked their other houses. If maybe she was staying at one of them. He answered immediately that they'd checked them. But they hadn't. They'd looked at their CCTV and alarm systems. That might be enough if you're checking to see if you left the fucking washing machine on or the fridge door open. But not for your missing daughter."

"People react differently under extreme situations, you know that," protested Campbell. "And you don't get more extreme than your daughter being kidnapped. He's done some things that I wouldn't do, certainly. But you sound like your imagination is running riot."

"Maybe. I haven't had time to think it all through. But if you add in the fact he gave us a dummy ransom, they start to add up."

"We don't know that yet," said Campbell.

"No, we don't, but it's the most likely scenario."

"That's overstating it. It's a possibility is all," disagreed Campbell.

"For now, yes. But we can check it out. Ordinarily, I'd suggest you tap up some agreeable magistrate to get a warrant for his bank records – I'm sure you have a few of them on hand. We could see if he even withdrew the cash—"

"Hold up man, what—", interrupted Campbell.

"Relax," said Trench, raising his arms in a calming gesture. "I'm not suggesting we do it. This isn't ordinary. The man probably has dozens of bank accounts. We wouldn't even know where to start. But we can easily check with Callow. I presume he's back from Osbourne's so we can ask him if he or anyone else actually eyeballed the money after Osbourne gave it to them."

"Callow's upstairs, I saw him just now. And he won't be going anywhere near Osbourne. I pulled them all off the case last night when I heard about that shitshow up at the Emirates," Campbell said tersely, anger flashing again. "That includes the NCA. I shut them all down. It's your case and you report to me directly."

"Not to DCS Lewis?" said Trench.

He couldn't resist fishing to find out just how bad things were for those previously running the case. Campbell eyed him up, knowing exactly what Trench was doing.

"I said to me. Don't involve yourself in things that do not concern you," he said sternly.

"Right."

"Are we done?" asked Campbell.

Trench considered whether to continue the discussion about Doctor Osbourne. Having floated his theories out loud he was confident they weren't wild. They were supported by evidence, though maybe not enough. They were still in the realm of gut feelings, rather than provable facts. But he was glad he had marked Campbell's card that this was the way the investigation may go.

“For now,” he said. “I’ll go find out the latest on where we are with finding Vanessa. Are you okay if I schedule a briefing for right now to get up to speed?”

“Yes, go ahead. I don’t need to be there. I’ve just spent the morning doing that.”

“Okay, I’ll make a call on who does what. Then I’ll kick off the interview with Chapman. Either he’ll crack or he won’t. I can turn him over to the other SIO’s and get fully onto Operation Labrador.”

“Call me later this afternoon with an update,” said Campbell, standing up.

Trench agreed and Campbell left the room. Trench sat there for another moment mulling their conversation. He felt the buzz of energy from being reappointed to lead the case. It was quickly followed by a strong sense of urgency to find Vanessa Osbourne. His first port of call would be DCI Thornton, to find out if they’d found the ringleader.

But the person he most wanted to talk to was Doctor Clarence Osbourne.

# Thirty-Three

Trench was in charge of Operation Labrador now. When he exited the interview room instead of turning right toward the stairs up to the squad room, he went left. He checked each of the other interview rooms until he found the one he was looking for. He knocked on the door and opened it. There were two interviewers inside, Detective Inspector Dave Finch and Constable Andy Turner, both CID. Trench knew both were on the Operation Labrador taskforce. They turned around in surprise as Trench stuck his head in the door. So did Krige.

"A quick word," he said to the interviewers, jerking his head.

"Change of plan lads," he said when they'd stepped outside and closed the door. "We're cutting him loose. And the other guys from Imperium Security. I need a word with him first. You guys go back upstairs and get the rest of the taskforce ready for a briefing in ten minutes."

Finch and Turner shared a confused glance before Finch responded.

"Can't do that, Trench," said Finch. "This guy's all over the place. He's talking in circles, contradicting himself, some of –"

"Look, we're cutting him loose, Finch," said Trench, holding up his hand to stop any protests. "He's not the sharpest tool in the shed, but he's not involved."

"Uh, Trench, are you…why are you making this decision?" Finch asked.

"Because I'm leading the investigation," said Trench. "Again. Put it down to recent developments. Let the squad know and I'll join you in the briefing room in ten."

"Okay. That's good," replied Finch genuinely. "Better you than Callow. Or Private Pyle."

Trench nodded his thanks and opened the door to the interview room as Finch and Turner headed back upstairs.

"Sounds like you're about as good at telling stories as you are at making phone calls," he said to Krige as he entered.

"What's that mate?" asked Krige.

"Good news. I'm cutting you loose. I've pulled some strings. You and your guys are free to go."

"Thanks Trench," said Krige, standing up. "Thanks a lot. And sorry again."

"But I need you to do something for me."

"Sure mate, what do you need?"

"I need to know the exact timings of all people coming and going from Blenheim over the past two weeks. Can you go through the security camera footage and send me that information."

"Yeah sure, I can get one of the team do that," said Krige. "Can I ask why. What are—"

"No, you can't, Krige" said Trench cutting him off. "We have to go back over everything that's happened in the past couple of weeks. We need everyone's movements during that time. That includes your team, the family, Vanessa, even you Krige. Everyone."

He hoped he was obscuring his real reason for asking for the information by implying that Krige was still in the frame. He didn't want to tip his hand about his developing suspicions. Especially given how Krige had blown it last time. It seemed to work.

"Me? You don't still think I'm involved in this, do you? Or any of my team?"

"No. But we've got to follow procedure to clear everyone. Better we do it this way than keeping you here for days doing repeated interviews, you get me? We can rule your crew out by knowing where you were and when, where the family was and when, and any visitors. Send me that as soon as possible so we can completely close the book on you."

"Okay, I understand mate. I can send that for the staff and visitors. For the family, there's probably some kind of client confidentiality, I'll need to –"

"That's not going to work," Trench said, shaking his head. "We need all movements in and out of the house. Of everyone. No exceptions. The alternative is you and your team stay here while the investigators figure out exactly what they need from you. You're looking at a couple of days at least."

"Shit, man. Okay, okay. I'll send it to you asap. But it's got to be highly confidential. You can't let it get out that I've sent you that, okay," relented Krige.

"Done. Let's go."

It turned out that three of Krige's colleagues were also being held. It took another fifteen minutes to complete the process of having them released and signed out. They each appeared both tired and embarrassed after their experience. They thanked Trench and left together. Trench immediately went back up to the squad room. As soon as he walked in the door, Jazz turned in her seat and put out her hands in a 'what the hell is going on' gesture.

"Let's go, I'll fill you in after this briefing," said Trench as he got to her desk.

"Briefing? I'm doing the prep for the Chapman interview," she said. "Did Campbell find you? What's going on, Trench? He called me in to Lewis's office when I got here. I'm pretty sure he had just torn Lewis a new one."

"Roger that. We're back on the case. Labrador. I called a briefing for right now so we can get up to speed. We'll do that, then we can finish the interview prep."

"What? Are you serious? Are we still interviewing Chapman?"

"Yep, I'll fill you in on everything right after this briefing. We'll find out exactly where we are with Labrador and make sure everyone knows what they should be doing. Then we'll interview Chapman. Ward is coming here later as well. After we've both had a go at him, we'll make a call on next steps with that. Let's go."

The incident room was packed, with some people having to stand. They had left one seat free at the head of the table. Trench motioned for Jazz to take that and he stood at the front of the room. He glanced around at the faces. Some were looking at him, many were looking down at notepads. The ultimate consequence of the previous night's failure was that they hadn't found Vanessa. Morale was low. Trench hoped he could re-energise the investigation.

"Afternoon all," he started loudly. "The purpose of this briefing is to review where we are right now and decide next steps. Vanessa is still out there somewhere. We're going to find her. For the avoidance of doubt, I'm leading Operation Labrador now. NCA is out, so I mean we in this room are going to find her. If anyone has any ideas or suggestions, then shout. Time is not on our side here. First up, has Thornton's team found the ringleader, Kozlowski, yet?"

He glanced around the faces in the room and spotted a SO officer called Jones. He pointed at him, directing the question to him.

"No, not yet," said Jones. "But within the last half hour we've discovered where he stayed last night after he fled from the drop. An old girlfriend's place in Harrow. He left early this morning in her car. She said she didn't know where he was going, but from things she let slip we're guessing Stanstead airport. We've an immediate BOLO out on her vehicle and we're checking all flights out of Stanstead and all London and regional airports. No matter where he's headed, we'll have him within the hour."

"Okay, good," said Trench. "What about the rest of the gang. Have any of them given us anything on where she might be?"

"Nothing," replied DI Glenda Watson. "They haven't budged from their initial story. They're all still saying the same thing. They only went along to exchange some bags on the promise of a few grand. At this stage, it's looking safe to assume most, possibly all, of them know little if anything about the kidnap."

"Have we emailed the ransomer again since the drop?" Trench asked.

Silence.

"Let's do that now," said Trench. "Barton, you take that. Go down to Willard in Cyber Crimes and work with her to send a mail to try to resume contact. It's unlikely we'll get a response but we have to try. And don't forget, we're writing as her parents. Tell them we'll do whatever it takes to rearrange. No more police, double the money. Whatever. Tell them we, the parents, didn't know police were monitoring the drop. And keep it short and simple. English is not their first language."

He paused for a moment then tried to look at every face in the room as he spoke. He needed them to forget about last night and go full throttle again.

"But look, everyone, we also need to accept the possibility that the whole ransom angle was a sham. Kozlowski, the guy who wrote the note and presumably the ringleader, may not have anything to do with Vanessa's disappearance. We know he did some work on the house previously, so he knew where they lived. He could've gotten wind of Vanessa's disappearance and just tried his luck. The news was out on the internet before he sent the note. We'll continue to chase it down fully – sounds like we'll have him soon – but we've got to look at other angles.

"So, where are we on her last known movements? And have we ID'd her boyfriend yet? Not Sheldon, the secret one."

No-one responded, but a few heads shook around the room. They hadn't ID'd the second boyfriend yet. Trench was disappointed. He still felt this was key. He realised the taskforce had probably put all their focus on the drop when the ransomer had sent the details. But they now needed to move on from that. And he needed to get up to speed on what they had.

"What about bank account activity? Or social media posts? Hits from her mobile phone? Anything?"

"No activity on her bank account or social media," answered someone from the bank. "We're still monitoring both, but nothing since last Tuesday."

"And her phone last pinged on Tuesday night in the Park Lane area," added another officer. "Still nothing since."

Trench nodded. It was what he expected.

"Higgins, I haven't seen the CCTV yet. What have we got?"

"She was there all night, pretty much until the end of the event. We have her arriving with a few friends, then numerous times in the corridor outside the main ballroom during the night, mainly back and forth to the Ladies. Then she left alone at about two thirty and we have her walking out of the hotel. There were no available cabs outside the hotel so she walked out onto the street, presumably to get a cab. That's when we lost her."

"We lost her?" said Trench, dismayed. "What does that mean?"

"Uh, we only have the hotel's cameras. And some from businesses in that area, but they're mostly focused on their own premises. We're trying to get others. The council has no street cameras around there. It's like twenty-sixteen all over again. They keep turning the cameras off to save money. Coverage is patchy. I guess they decided the area around Park Lane doesn't need cameras. It's not exactly a crime hot spot."

Trench couldn't believe his ears. Ranking all cities in the world by the number of security cameras, the only one in the top ten outside of China was London. The average Londoner was captured over three hundred times a day by security cameras. And yet Trench knew what Higgins referred to.

Westminster City Council had a history of turning off their security cameras. Budget cuts meant councils were almost broke, so in 2016 Westminster took the decision to shut them all down to save nearly £3m a year. Although they reversed the decision a few years later, they occasionally pulled the plug on some or all of the cameras when the finances got tight. They just didn't make it public these days, given the huge media backlash when they first announced their plans in 2016.

The news was devastating. Trench immediately understood why the mood in the room was so downbeat. The situation was getting more hopeless the more he heard. Park Lane was one of the city's busiest thoroughfares. There was a dozen side streets she may have gone down looking for a cab. She could even have walked to the nearby, even busier, thoroughfare of Piccadilly. Given the number of cars in the area, it would be virtually impossible to identify the right vehicle.

Trench suddenly thought of another possibility.

"Or maybe she was going to wait somewhere nearby and then meet the guy. So they could go back to her flat together. Did you check for anyone leaving shortly after her, alone and walking out of the hotel grounds as well?"

"Uh, not specifically," said Higgins, "But we've got all the footage of people leaving. We can review it and check for any blokes leaving alone shortly after her. Sure."

"Do it. And shortly before her, of course," said Trench. "Also, Regent's Park is only a couple of hundred yards away. Her flat is right on the other side of that. It practically backs onto the park. Maybe they decided to walk if they couldn't get a cab. Check every business on the route and get every bit of footage you can."

"Okay," said Higgins.

He said it in a less than enthusiastic tone. Almost as if it was hassle. Trench felt a rush of anger and had to check himself. He didn't want to blow a fuse, especially not given the already gloomy mood. He breathed in deep before speaking.

"Liven up there, Higgins. This is urgent. Get on it as soon as we break."

"I understand that, Trench. I'm not saying… What I mean is, it's going to take time, is all. We're all still drowning in these fucking zombie calls from people claiming they've seen her."

"What are you talking about?" said Trench, but even as he said it he twigged what he meant. "Osbourne's reward, you mean. Those calls are being diverted to the taskforce?"

Lots of heads around the room nodded, some vigorously.

"Yeah, the Emergency Services got totally swamped," said Higgins, "So they set up a dedicated line. All our phones are on the loop."

"You're all taking calls?" asked Trench glancing around the room, trying not to let his face betray his thoughts.

There was a chorus of grumbled yeses and more nods.

"Right. That ends now. First thing I do after this meeting is get that line redirected. I'll speak with Thomson and we'll rotate no more than two constables to that line at a time," he said, then glanced around at some of the constables in the room. "One hour each, then we change. We'll review that in the next twenty-four hours to see if there's any point in keeping the line open."

Trench thought he could see relief on some of the faces. It sounded like it would free up more people. He also wanted to make sure they got to the CCTV urgently. It felt like their best hope.

"Higgins, if you haven't already done it, call CFIT in. They'll know how to get and review the footage much more quickly. That's what they're there for."

Higgins nodded. Trench moved on hastily.

"Who spoke with her friends? Particularly the ones at the pre-drinks at her house?" he asked the room.

A WPC named Debbie Gates put up her hand.

"Debs, what've you got. Did they know of her plans for after the dinner?"

"No, Trench, they're claiming they don't. One of them had her suspicions. Chanel Frampton, who seems to have been good friends with her at Uni too. She said Vanessa was in great form. They all said that. But Frampton said she was sure Vanessa was leaving to meet her man, as she put it. They were all pretty tipsy, even had a few lines of coke. But she remembered Vanessa saying something to her about intending to slip away later. She said something like 'don't wait up' or 'got better things to do tonight' than go off with the rest of the girls to a club after."

"But no clue who she may have been going to meet?"

"She said no and I believe her. She would've told us, she's pretty devastated. All her friends are."

"Okay, thanks. What about who she spoke to during the night? Do we know if she spent more time with anyone specific?"

Trench hadn't directed the question at anyone, so WPC Gates answered again.

"They all said no to that too. Sounds like she knew half the people in the room. She made a short speech and was even over at the top table for a while. That's all the senior party bods. Then she was just floating around most of the night. Her friends mentioned a few of their ex-Uni blokes trying it on with her, but she brushed them off. We spoke to them too. We accounted for nearly all of them after the dinner. They're all clear so far."

The mention of the party bods reminded Trench how close her flat was to Conservative Party Headquarters. He couldn't shake the feeling this wasn't a coincidence. Especially given she'd gone missing after a Party event. Her legitimate boyfriend, Sheldon, had said she'd only recently re-engaged with that crowd. And she'd only just started renting the flat, the lovenest, within the past couple of months. A fact she kept secret from her family and her boyfriend. All of which struck Trench as pointing to a relationship with someone who would have been at the event.

But he'd just learned that she left the event alone. She walked out into the November night by herself and disappeared without a trace. He was now less sure it mattered whether she was seeing someone else or who that person was. She could have encountered anyone.

Fake mini-cab drivers preying on night-time partygoers was rife in London. There were even high-profile cases of legitimate black cab drivers drugging and raping women who got into their cabs. What would they do if they got the dose wrong and ended up with a dead body on their hands? She could have been taken in a planned kidnapping by someone who'd been targeting and following her. Or it could have been a random event, a chance encounter. Anything. At this point, they could no longer even discount the theory that she had disappeared voluntarily.

And then there was the dummy ransom to factor in. Voicing his suspicions to Campbell had only made Trench more certain that Doctor Osbourne had questions to answer. But he knew he could not air those suspicions to the whole squad. The thin blue line had holes in it. Holes that leaked. They could not let even a hint of suspicion about Doctor Osbourne's activities leak to the press. Under any circumstances. Trench decided he would take care of that angle of the investigation himself.

He glanced around the room, looking to see if Barker, the Family Liaison Officer, or PC Walker were in the room. He didn't see either of them. He wanted to make sure he spoke with both of them before he approached Doctor Osbourne. It might provide useful background.

"Are Barker and Walker still posted at the Osbourne house?"

"Yes, Walker's still there for sure. I presume Barker is as well," said Higgins, before half mumbling under his breath, "Poor bastard. I hope old man Osbourne didn't take a run at him after Private Pyle delivered the status report this morning. Via phone, of course…"

There was a couple of wry chuckles. Black humour was stock in trade in CID, even at the darkest hour. It was a survival mechanism. Laugh, or you might cry. Bitching about the brass worked just as well. Whatever it took to deflect the grim reality from damaging you.

But something he said struck Trench.

"What do you mean? Lewis updated Osbourne about the operation?"

"Campbell ordered him to, is what I heard. Guess he wanted him to face the music himself. It's almost as if the Commander was teaching him a lesson for inviting his new best mates from Old Queen Street round for a sleepover without asking Big Poppa for permission," said Higgins, to a few more chuckles.

"When?"

"When what?"

"When was that order? When did Lewis make that call?" pressed Trench.

"First thing, I think. Campbell had him in here at the crack of dawn. He wanted to be fully debriefed. Then he ordered Lewis to update Osbourne himself. But he rang instead of going there in person," said Higgins, rolling his eyes.

But that wasn't what bothered Trench. Another question now lodged in his mind but it wasn't for discussion here. It was another thing he'd have to consider after the briefing.

With all the new information, he was getting restless. He wanted to end the briefing so he could get on with solving the puzzles that kept popping up. But they weren't quite done. There was one more area he wanted to know about before assigning activities to the members of the taskforce.

"Who's been leading PR and press briefings? It would be good to keep continuity there if possible, to avoid awkward questions from the media," he asked the room.

"The Press Office," said DI Finch. "All we've done the past few days is issue a couple of press releases. Osbourne's reward offer on Saturday made it difficult for us to say anything without blatantly calling him out for that. I don't think anyone was brave enough to stand in front of the press and take questions. It would show how much we're opposed to it. And then when the details for the drop arrived, they didn't want to take questions and end up saying something that rattled the kidnapper."

"We're going to have to rethink that now," said Trench. "The press aren't going to let us away with that for much longer. We need to try to get ahead of it after last night. I'll speak with Campbell. He can place some stories with trusted reporters. It might buy us some time."

Trench was out of patience. He had to get out of the room and get back out chasing down the leads and answering the questions that were bubbling up in his head. Before ending the briefing, he reconfirmed everyone's responsibilities. The main priority was CCTV. He instructed the majority of people to assist Higgins with that.

The second priority was identifying the second boyfriend. If they couldn't get it from CCTV then they had to get it from somewhere else. He assigned a team responsibility to do so. He split the rest of the taskforce into smaller groups, focused on continuing to question the gang members, the apprehension and questioning of the ringleader and taking witness statements from everyone else who attended the dinner.

Soon everyone filed out, leaving Trench and Jazz alone in the room.

"So what happened with Campbell, Trench? My head is spinning here. Which case are we working?" asked Jazz.

"Right now, both."

Trench brought her up to date on his conversation with Campbell. It was also the first opportunity to explain his theory about the dummy ransom to Jazz. She was initially shocked at the suggestion and pushed back on the theory. They spent a few minutes going back over all their interactions with Doctor Osbourne, looking at them through the lens of this theory. Trench used the same examples he'd given Campbell about Doctor Osbourne's possibly dubious behaviour.

They soon concluded they could not discount the theory.

"Jesus. It really is possible, isn't it?" said Jazz. "But why? Why would he do that?"

"Only one way to find out."

"This doesn't feel like a case of just asking, Trench," she said. "Either he knew the ransom demand was fake or he's so fucking tight he wouldn't pay two million quid to get his own daughter back. Who does he think he is, John Paul Getty?"

She was referring to the infamous case in 1973 when billionaire oil tycoon John Paul Getty refused to pay a ransom when his teenage grandson was kidnapped by the Italian mafia.

"Which is worse?" was all Trench said.

He had already considered these devil's alternatives. But he'd stopped thinking about it because he couldn't answer that question. He didn't know which was worse. All he knew was that thinking about these possibilities clouded his mind with dark, debilitating, accusatory thoughts.

He couldn't let such emotions creep into his judgement. It was a known hazard of missing persons cases, occasionally causing egregious missteps by police. Instead, he resolved to focus everything he had on finding out what had happened to Vanessa. The why would have to wait.

Jazz seemed to be having similar thoughts. She didn't respond to his question, the look on her face suggesting she too was sickened by the possible answers.

"But you're right," continued Trench. "It isn't a case of just asking him. If it was a dummy ransom, he'll have prepared some logical reason for that in case we checked it before the drop. Instead we can ask him about his other activities. Get him talking and see how his story stacks up."

"Okay, sounds good," said Jazz. "I know what my first question is. 'Dear Doctor Osbourne, had you been smoking crack when you came up with your plan for your press conference?'"

"Fair question," Trench agreed wryly. "Might tip our hand a little, though. Let's start out by just getting him talking. The more he says, the more ammo we have to use on him later if he starts contradicting himself. We haven't spoken with him for a few days, so we go there to update him and get him talking."

"Great, we get to be the first ones he sees since last night's clusterfuck," sighed Jazz.

"Not quite. That's another thing that's bothering me, after what Higgins just said. Campbell told me this morning that he pulled everyone off the case last night.

NCA, Lewis, Callow, all of them. And you heard Higgins. Lewis was on the phone to update Osbourne this morning, first thing."

"Right. But all he had to do was hang up. Chickenshit. We're going to be there in person to take the brunt. Unless he's taken it out on poor Barker and Walker."

"But that's not the point, Jazz. When I bumped into Callow this morning, he said he was going to see Osbourne. It was just as I was leaving for Surrey. It must have been hours after Lewis had already spoken with Osbourne."

"Uhm. Maybe he didn't know Lewis had already spoken with him?"

"Campbell told me he pulled them all from the case last night. Sounded like he got them all together for a bollocking too. He made it sound like they were all there."

"Okay, so he's known since last night he was off the case. He probably knew Lewis spoke with Osbourne this morning too. But he told you he was going to see Osbourne?" said Jazz. "Stop the press. He lied to you. He could've been going anywhere."

"True, but why lie? Why tell me anything? I didn't ask him where he was going. He was distracted, angry. It just kind of slipped out."

"Does it matter? He doesn't owe you an explanation for his movements. In fact, you're probably the last person he's going to tell where he's going. He probably said the first thing that came into this head. You said it yourself, he was distracted. If he was angry about being pulled from the case, he'd probably guess Campbell would put you back on it. And then he bumps right into you. Maybe that's why he was so angry."

"Maybe," said Trench.

"Although knowing him he's probably gone off to the boozer for the rest of the day. Says the first thing that pops into his head to get away from you, then hits the bar."

"If so, let's hope he ends up with the mother of all hangovers. Has to sleep it off for a few days."

"We live in hope," Jazz agreed, before changing the subject. "So what about Chapman? I've made a start on the questions. Do you want to have a look at those and then we can add any others?"

"Good. Let's do it," said Trench, heading for the door.

"How do you want to play the interview?" asked Jazz.

Trench thought about it, and immediately got the feeling that he hadn't given it anywhere near enough thought yet. It even took an effort to turn his mind back to Chapman. He realised just how difficult it was going to be to try to juggle the two cases.

He was feeling charged after the Operation Labrador briefing. After giving it his full attention, ideas were already formulating about how best they should proceed. He knew he was subconsciously mapping out how the investigation should be managed from here. He felt an urgent need to keep up the momentum.

But he had to turn his mind back to Chapman now. The interview was critical. They had almost nothing. Unless they could crack him or somehow get him to slip up, he would walk in twenty-four hours. He'd be free to roam the streets. Having looked into his eyes, Trench knew he couldn't let that happen. Evil smouldered in there. A stone-cold killer. One who was evolving. He wasn't going to stop. He would go on ripping up and destroying innocent women. Only now he knew they were on to him.

They had one shot at stopping him. Trench felt a wave of weariness wash over him as the weight of both cases loomed large on his conscience. But he knew he couldn't rest now. Right now, he needed to be at his very best.

# Thirty-Four

DI Ward from Thames Valley CID still hadn't arrived at Charing Cross station by the time they finished their preparation for the interview with Chapman. Trench used the time to update the Decision Log. He included all details leading up to the surveillance operation at Tesco and the capture of Chapman.

He covered the capture in a couple of sentences, stating only that Chapman had resisted but had been overpowered. He then provided a brief summary of their preparation and intended questions for the interview. He noted that Chapman had requested a lawyer, who had duly been appointed and had already spent time consulting with his client. The Custody Sergeant had called earlier to inform Trench of this.

Ward still hadn't arrived by the time he was done. Trench was getting impatient, so called Ward to find out where he was. Ward said he'd be there in ten minutes, so they went down to the control room next to the interview rooms to wait for him. It meant they could watch Chapman on the video monitor while they waited.

They stood in silence, staring at the monitor. Trench wanted to observe his demeanour. He looked for signs of nervousness, anger, emotion. Anything they could use to gain an edge. They usually did their final interview prep after observing the suspect on the monitor for at least a few minutes. It sometimes gave them a steer on how to approach the suspect. Should they try good cop, bad cop. Go hard or try to cajole. Play on a suspect's fears or stoke his anger and hope he slipped up.

Not this time.

Chapman sat in the corner behind the table, arms crossed, head slightly bowed and resting against the wall. His eyes were closed. He could have been sitting in a public library dozing off after lunch. During the time they watched, not a single word had been exchanged between Chapman and his appointed lawyer, who sat in the seat beside him, occasionally making a note on a pad in front of him.

"He's not going to talk," said Trench, still looking at the monitor.

He knew the signs. They both did. Career criminals and ex-cons almost never talked. Having been through it all many times before they knew how to hide within the rules. Most of them knew the rules as well as police did. Knew that the rules favoured the suspect. Everything about Chapman, from the cleanliness of the crime scenes, to his ferocious resistance to being captured, to his brief utterings in the car about them having no evidence made it clear he'd been around the block enough times. He wasn't going to talk.

But they had prepared for that.

"We knew that," said Jazz. "We stick to the plan."

Chapman had given a single tell so far and they planned to use it against him. Trench had been a little uneasy suggesting it to Jazz, but she'd jumped on the idea. They both knew they needed whatever advantage they could get. It was a long shot, but it was the best they could come up with.

"You sure you're okay with this?" asked Trench again.

"I told you, don't worry about me," said Jazz. "I'm more worried about you. If you go punching his head off again, then the whole thing is fucked."

Trench was about to reply when there was a knock on the door. It was opened by the Custody Sergeant, who announced Ward had arrived. He stepped aside and showed Ward into the room. A second man stepped in behind him.

DI Ward looked even younger than Trench had thought he sounded on the phone. But he stood well over six-foot tall and had a rugby player's build. He was dressed smartly in a suit and tie. Smart, rather than sharp. He held out his hand before introducing himself in his thick Welsh lilt.

"DI Ward," he said in a serious but cordial tone. "Call me Mike. This is DS John Duncan."

After introductions were out of the way, Trench recapped everything that had happened since he'd encountered Chapman at the petrol station. Ward asked a few good questions throughout, and again praised their efforts in capturing Chapman. Ward then pointed at the monitor.

"He's looking pretty relaxed," he said. "And he's smaller than his file photos. Hard to believe he's capable of doing what was done to those women."

"He's capable alright. He fought like a dipso at closing time when we took him down. He nearly scalped me, I got lucky," said Trench. "But he's an ex-con. And he's been careful. He's thinking he can no comment his way out of here."

"Yeah, we figured that," said Ward. "But we've still got to put all the questions to him, right. Got to do this one by the book. The case is thin enough, we don't want to make it worse by messing up procedures. CPS would roast us."

Even when a suspect gives a no comment interview, if the case is expected to go to trial police still have to put all relevant questions to the suspect. When the accused finally gives their version of events during the trial, the Crown Prosecution Service try to discredit them by claiming that the accused failed to provide an explanation when given the opportunity during the police interview. The hope is that the jury will infer that the accused is now lying in the trial, having made up their story in the time since the police interview.

"Are we expecting a prepared statement?" Ward then asked.

Most suspects giving a no comment interview start by reading out a statement their lawyer has helped them prepare just prior to the interview. This is usually a very brief, vague version of events designed to either deny involvement or mitigate the most damaging evidence against them.

"We don't know yet," said Jazz. "They haven't even looked at each other in the ten minutes we've been watching. But they've had at least an hour to prepare so it's possible."

"Okay, what's the running order here?" asked Ward. "I'm thinking we go first. Take the cases chronologically, you know?"

"No, we're going to kick off," said Trench. "The Diaz case will be the most recent one in his memory. It's also the one where he took the most risk with the body. He doesn't know how we got to him, so he'll be wondering if he made some kind of mistake with it. We'll try to create doubt in his mind. If he's going to crack at all, that's our best shot."

"Hmm," said Ward. "Although the strongest evidence against him relates to our case, Sharon Brimms. That's where his van was spotted, which put him in the frame in the first place."

Ward said it diplomatically, rather than confrontationally. He had a point, but Trench was not going to be moved.

"There's another reason," he said. "The only way he's going to budge is if we can unsettle him. We need to shake him out of his comfort zone, any way we can. He's been calm as a grave since we grabbed him. Not a peep. I beat seven bells out of him when I was taking him down. No whinging, no squealing about police brutality.

I damn near knocked his head off in the car and he barely flinched. He's ready for the strong arm of the law. He thinks he can bat it all away."

"So what are you thinking?" asked Ward, curious.

"The only reaction we've got from him was in the car. He said something to Jazz. Said what he wanted to do to her. His face screwed up and he was grunting or sniffing or something. It was feral. He was like an animal. It's got to come from the same place that's caused him to do what he did to those women. His problem is women. If we're going to get to him, that's what we need to exploit."

Both Ward and Duncan subconsciously turned to Jazz. Ward was nodding, understanding their thinking. But he wasn't clear on the plan yet.

"Okay. What are you going to do?" he asked.

"Trench is going to take the formalities," explained Jazz, "And I'm going to take him through the crimes. Slowly, explicitly through every detail of the sexual element of the crimes. I'll be as feminine as I can be. I'll make it sound like I'm interested, and try to keep judgement or accusation out of my tone. As much as I can, anyway. So basically, from where he's sitting, I'm a pretty girl talking him through his most extreme sexual fantasies. Maybe we can get him flustered. He thinks it's going to be a cold, routine police interview. Maybe if we heat it up for him it'll put him off balance. We can hit him with direct questions when he's most hot and bothered and see if his reaction tells us anything."

Ward was silent for a moment as he considered the tactic. He frowned but gave a slight nod as he spoke.

"I see what you mean. It's uh, unconventional. Don't think I've heard of that approach before. Especially not with someone accused of crimes like these," he said.

"It's worth a try," said Jazz. "We can mix it up if it's not working, but that's plan A."

"Are you okay with that?" Ward asked Jazz. "Most people would struggle to sit in a room with the sick bastard, let alone talk with him like that."

"You mean most women, right?" said Jazz.

Ward eventually nodded slowly.

"Yeah, I guess I do," he said after appearing to genuinely think about it. "He's a monster. Most men would too. No offence meant."

"None taken," said Jazz, taking off her suit jacket. "Right, shall we do this."

# Thirty-Five

The dead, grey eyes flickered open as they walked into the room. Trench couldn't stop himself from staring into them, still searching for any sign that the mind behind them could be reached. He didn't find one.

Although the eyes opened, the body didn't move. The arms stayed folded, the head stayed bowed, leaning against the wall. Trench dropped his notepad forcefully onto the table. The eyes blinked slowly. But the dull, marble gaze didn't flinch.

Trench sat in the seat opposite the lawyer, and watched the eyes as they watched Jazz sit down in the seat opposite. Watched them as they dropped a little lower as Jazz bent forward to pull her seat in closer to the table. Trench thought he saw them flicker before she straightened back up. He half expected the tongue to flip out and lick its own unblinking eyeball.

He nodded at the lawyer.

"Ready?" he asked.

"Ready," the lawyer responded.

Trench looked at Chapman.

"You ready?"

Chapman blinked and momentarily shifted his gaze from Jazz to Trench. When he spoke it was in a nonchalant, bored tone.

"Fuck you, pig."

His gaze reverted.

Trench stated the date and time for the record, then introduced himself and Jazz.

"We're investigating the abduction and murder of Savannah Diaz. This is the formal interview of Howard Chapman, in the company of his lawyer…," he nodded at the lawyer again.

"James Croft-Hill. Beagle, Barnes and Partners," said the lawyer.

Trench turned to Chapman.

"State your name and address for the record."

Chapman said nothing, keeping his eyes forward. Croft-Hill spoke instead.

"Detective, I'm going to read out a prepared statement from my client. That will include his name, which you can then take as confirmed for the record. His address shall be recorded currently as no fixed abode. My client—"

"Cool your jets there, hotshot," interrupted Trench, turning back to Chapman. "State your name and address for the record."

After a few moments, Chapman flickered his eyes back to Trench. The hint of a smirk appeared on his lips before turning into an exaggerated yawn. The cold stare then returned to straight ahead. The reaction hinted that Chapman was confident he could doze his way through a hardnosed interview. Or Trench hoped it did, anyway.

"Detective, now is an appropriate time for me to read my client's statement, as I have already indicated," said Croft-Hill tersely. "Please desist from futile attempts at forcing my client to respond to police questions. The statement will make clear how my client, under advice from me, will be proceeding with this interview. Now, if you'll refrain from interrupting, here's the statement.

"I, Howard Leonard Chapman, do categorically refute and reject all accusations that I had anything whatsoever to do with the matters under investigation here. I have never met nor heard of Savannah Diaz. I have no knowledge about her disappearance nor alleged murder. There is no evidence to support the allegations of my involvement. I consider my detention in relation to these matters to be wholly inappropriate and a matter of victimisation and bias by police. I demand to be released from police custody immediately. I shall be making no further comment for the duration of my custody."

Croft-Hill placed the statement down on the table, spinning it around and pushing it toward Trench. Trench ignored it. Instead, he picked up his notebook and the printout of the questions he was going to put to Chapman. Croft-Hill cleared his throat, indicating he wasn't finished yet.

"Detectives, might I add," Croft-Hill went on, "I have reviewed the scant evidence provided when I arrived, and I must say it seems like a stretch even to have my client detained at all. When do you intend to provide me with full disclosure of all evidence so that I might prepare a proper rebuttal of these accusations?"

Technically, Chapman had not been arrested yet. Police were under no obligation to disclose all evidence or reasons for their suspicions at such an early stage. It was common practice instead to drip feed evidence to defence lawyers. Trench had instructed the Custody Sergeant to give Chapman's lawyer nothing when he arrived.

"When we're ready," said Trench, keeping his eyes on Chapman. "For now, we're just asking questions. I get that he's too afraid to answer them, but we're still asking. And when we're done, our colleagues from other police forces are going to ask him some more. Then we'll decide what charges he'll face. You'll get all of the evidence against him when we decide to give it to you."

Chapman continued to stare straight ahead, but his feigned boredom seemed to be taking a little more effort now. The mention of other police forces and potential evidence had definitely gotten his attention. The eyes still stared blankly but they were slightly wider now, more alert.

Trench glanced down at the list of questions they had prepared. Reading the mood in the room he decided to skip the first ones that only served to set the scene. He believed he had gotten a reaction, however small, from Chapman. Starting with procedural questions could lose momentum. It could allow Chapman to regain his full composure. He decided instead to go straight for him.

"Why were you in Bromley the Tuesday before last, twenty-seventh of October?"

Chapman stared straight ahead when he responded.

"No comment."

"We can prove you were there, at precisely nine fourteen pm. What were you doing there?"

In giving the precise time, Trench was hoping it suggested they had hard evidence. In truth, it was simply the time that someone had used Chapman's Tesco Club Card in the Bromley store. It would be batted away easily by a defence lawyer.

But Chapman didn't know that. Trench was sure Chapman's brow creased slightly as he answered.

"No comment."

"Where did you get the phone number for Savannah Diaz?"

"No comment."

"We'll find your number on her phone records, don't worry about that. And we'll be searching your phone records too. How're you going to explain that?"

This time Trench saw a definite smirk cross Chapman face. He adjusted his posture slightly as he spoke, lifting his head off the wall and turning his eyes to Trench.

"No comment," he said, with more confidence than before.

Trench realised he had misstepped. Chapman had probably used a burner. They wouldn't be able to trace it. He tried to change tack so Chapman couldn't get comfortable.

"When did you last use your van? The one you burnt out last week, not that piece of shit you were in today."

"No comm—"

Croft-Hill interrupted.

"Detective, I hardly think that's appropriate language. And you're accusing my client of vehicular arson now too? When are you going to provide me with evidence?" he whined in a high-pitched tone, showily indignant.

Trench got the feeling Croft-Hill had been waiting for any opportunity to interject. He hadn't heard his own voice for nearly five minutes. He was bubbling like uncorked champagne.

"I'm asking the questions," barked Trench. "You can peddle your bog-standard jailhouse advice to him all you want but stop pestering me with the same question. I've already answered that. Are you deliberately trying to obstruct this process?"

"What? That is absurd," spouted Croft-Hill, looking as if Trench had pissed in his tea. "I'm merely defending my clients' rights. And as for the obscene language you're—"

"Murder, counsellor," said Trench forcefully. He watched Chapman as he said the rest. "We're talking about murder. Torture, rape and murder. The obscenity hasn't started yet. Buckle up."

Croft-Hill said nothing, instead starting to furiously make notes in his notepad. Chapman had straightened up slightly more during the brief exchange. Trench hoped Chapman picked up that they would not be deferring to every objection the lawyer ventured. He also hoped they had at least a few minutes of silence from Croft-Hill. He turned and nodded at Jazz. She leaned in and put her arms on the table, speaking softly.

"Howard, when we found Savannah, she was completely nude. She had been stripped naked. What can you tell us about that?"

Chapman's eyes flipped back to Jazz. Her soft, almost seductive tone right after the gruff exchange seemed to confuse him for a second, before he remembered to respond.

"No comment."

Jazz nodded as if understanding.

"We believe things were done to her when she was held captive. Can you tell us about that?"

"No comment."

"What kind of underwear was she wearing?"

"No comment."

"Was she wearing a thong? Crotchless panties? What colour where they?"

A brief pause before he responded. His eyes squinted slightly.

"No comment."

"Did she take them off, or did you take them off? Or maybe you cut them off?"

"No comment."

"Was she shaved?"

"Wh—. No comment."

"Was her pussy shaved, Howard?" asked Jazz slowly, rolling the words around her mouth.

Croft-Hill's head shot up from his notepad. Trench immediately turned and fixed him an aggressive stare. Croft-Hill stared back but didn't say anything.

"No comment," managed Chapman after a long pause, but confusion definitely rippled across his face for a moment.

"Do you like to hog-tie girls during sex, Howard?"

"Uh, no comment."

"Do you like to take them from behind, when they're tied up in front of you?" asked Jazz suggestively.

"No comment."

"Like this," said Jazz, pushing her chair back from the table.

Trench watched as Jazz pushed her chair aside and knelt down on the floor. This hadn't been part of the preparation. She faced toward the wall, away from Chapman. Trench turned to watch his reaction. Chapman leaned in closer, putting his elbows on the table.

She definitely had his attention now. Even Croft-Hill seemed stupefied, leaning in further across the table. Jazz put her arms back above her behind, and held the wrists together as if bound. Her blouse rode up and revealed the skin on her back. The top of her underwear was visible too, poking out above her trousers.

She leaned her head to the side when she asked her next question.

"Like this, Howard. Is this how you like your girls during sex?"

Chapman leered for a long moment, his eyes wide open. He opened his mouth a couple of times but didn't say anything. His breathing had clearly gotten heavier. Trench watched his eyes creep over Jazz. He had to contain himself from grabbing Chapman and bouncing his head off the wall. It was difficult.

After a moment Jazz brought her hands back down in front of her and turned just slightly so her eyes met Chapman's.

"Like this, Howard? Do you like your girls like this, when they're naked? When you're having sex with them?"

Chapman stared at Jazz's behind. Trench was getting deeply uncomfortable. This was much further than he'd intended. He could feel his blood beginning to boil. He stared at Chapman. He was completely transfixed. No doubt his blood was rushing too. Now was the time to strike.

"Why Horley?" bawled Trench. "What's in Horley?"

Chapman snapped out of wherever his mind had been with an angry snarl.

"Nothing," he barked back. Too defensive. "It's not—. There's nothing there."

Croft-Hill snapped out of it too. He straightened up as he spoke.

"Mr Chapman," he blurted. "My advice remains to make no comment."

"No fucking comment," said Chapman, pushing back into this chair. "No comment."

"And detectives, I must strongly protest," whimpered Croft-Hill. "This is highly…unorthodox…"

Trench waved a dismissive hand without looking at the lawyer. They had broken no rules in re-enacting the scene. Unorthodox, it was. But it had been effective.

Chapman folded his arms aggressively across his chest again. A look of defiance on his face. This time it was Trench's turn to smirk.

"That was a little too firm, *Howard,"* he said. "Bit of a giveaway. That's where you take them, right? To Horley."

"Fuck you. No comment," he grunted through gritted teeth.

"That's why you keep going back there," said Trench antagonistically. "That's right, we know you've been going to Horley frequently since you got out. We've got dates, times. You've spent more time there than at that palace in High Wycombe you're supposed to be staying. Why don't you just give us the address? You know we're going to find it soon enough."

"No comment."

Chapman was back to staring straight ahead. He spoke quietly, answering almost before Trench had finished speaking. The only difference from before was that he had a slight frown rather than the completely blank expression. But his reflex no comment answer was back in place. Trench figured they had probably gotten all they would get from him.

He decided to push on with a few more questions about the murder, before returning to the initial scene-setting questions for the record. He could use these questions to turn the screw on Chapman by giving him something to think about when the interview was done. To allude to how they were building the case against him, and hint at how much they knew. Maybe it would create an opening for Ward's interview next. Or they could let him stew in it overnight and see if it changed his position. Trench doubted it, but it wouldn't do any harm.

"Why'd you leave her in the woods? Why not in water again?"

"No comment."

"Why did you tie her up like that when she was already dead?"

"No comment."

"Why take the risk? It's a popular spot. And the woods don't destroy evidence like the water does. Well, sometimes does."

"No comment."

The baiting wasn't working. Chapman was muttering his no comment response even before Trench had finished asking the question. Trench was trying to insinuate that they had found evidence in the woods or elsewhere, but Chapman was no longer listening. He was blanking everything out. He might as well have had his fingers jammed in his ears.

Trench decided to wrap up. He spent the next fifteen minutes reading through the list of skipped questions, with Chapman continuing to mutter no comment halfway through the question. When he was done, Trench again stated the time and date for the recording, then said they were taking a break in the interview. He and Jazz got up and left the room.

# Thirty-Six

"You okay?" he said to Jazz as soon as the door was closed.

"Yeah, I'm okay," Jazz sighed. "But I need to soak in a long, hot bath. For a week."

She abruptly shivered as if to make the point.

"You did great in there," said Trench. "That was way beyond what I was thinking."

"Me too," said Jazz. "It just kind of came to me. He looked like he wasn't going to budge so I figured I'd go as far as I could. Seemed like it worked though. What'd you reckon?"

"Definitely," agreed Trench. "You got him. His reaction was a clear tell. He didn't want us to go there. It confirms Horley is important to him. It's got to be where he's taking them."

"Trouble is, where? It could be a million places."

"True. But there's got to be a way to narrow it down. Let's debrief with Ward and Duncan."

They walked the short distance back to the control room. Ward and Duncan immediately came over to congratulate Jazz. Ward appeared genuinely concerned when asking if she was okay. Jazz assured him she was fine.

"That was probably the most effective interview I've ever seen against a suspect who, I'll be honest, I never thought would crack," said Ward sincerely.

"Thanks," said Jazz. "But he hardly cracked. He's not exactly spilling his guts in there."

"Well, you know what I mean," said Ward. "He gave us something. It's more than I thought we'd get. He didn't like being asked about Horley. Not one bit. Everything's pointing to that being where he's taking them."

"Yeah, but where?" said Jazz.

"We've got to dig into his background, find any connection," said Ward. "KA's, previous addresses, anything we can find."

"I'm going to speak with his parents too," said Trench. "See if they know of any connections he had there."

"Go for it," Ward nodded. "But they won't thank you for reminding them about him."

"Did we get anything from the van he was driving? Anyone run the plates yet even?" asked Jazz.

"Yeah, I spoke with Surrey Police a little earlier," said Ward. "Forensics are all over it. The plates were fake, but they ID'd the van. It was stolen in Woking a couple of weeks ago. It's a dead end."

"Any chance he's come onto their radar down there in the year since he's been out?" asked Trench hopefully. "If they picked him up for something maybe they got an address."

"No, never," said Duncan. "We checked everything with them when we went down for the stake out. They've got nothing on him."

"We'll press him on it now," said Ward. "It clearly rattled him so we'll keep pushing it. Wouldn't bank on it though. He looked like he'd shut down by the time you guys left."

"I make you right on that, but we've got to try," said Trench. "Call us when you get out, let us know how it goes."

"You're not staying?" asked Ward.

"No, we've got to go. Back to Horley."

"Horley?" said Jazz, matching the quizzical look Ward and Duncan gave Trench.

"My bike is still down there. I left it sitting on the forecourt of that petrol station. I can't just leave it there."

"You said 'we' are going to Horley," said Jazz sceptically.

"We can discuss the case on the way down," said Trench. "I'll grab the file. Maybe we missed some connection to Horley in there."

"An hour sitting in traffic," said Jazz. "Not quite the hot bath I had in mind."

They wished Ward and Duncan good luck and left.

Ten minutes later they were crossing Westminster Bridge heading south. Jazz was at the wheel, while Trench studied the Chapman file, looking for any connection to Horley they might have missed. Rain hammered down loudly on the roof of the car. Inch deep rivers ran along both sides of the road. Visibility was down to a hundred yards as evening stole into the afternoon. They had the radio on low, in case Vanessa Osbourne's name was mentioned on any news bulletins.

"I thought we were going to see Doctor Osbourne," said Jazz.

"We are," said Trench, picking up his phone and scrolling through the emails. He didn't find the one he was looking for.

"But not yet. We'll go there when we get back, either way."

"Either way what, Trench?" asked Jazz, confused.

"Whether Krige's sent the movements of everyone in that house or not. I want to know as much as we can before we confront Osbourne. He's been acting strange but it'd be better to prove he's been holding back on us rather than just asking him. Catch him in one lie and we can use that. I'll chase Krige now—"

His phone rang just as he spoke. He glanced at the screen.

"Shit, forgot to update him," he muttered before answering. "Commander, we're just out of the interview now."

"The interview, right. Get anything?" asked Campbell in an unlikely tone.

"Maybe. But he isn't signing a confession any time soon."

"No," said Campbell, unsurprised. "Someone else can take that over now. Like we agreed."

Trench reluctantly nodded. They had agreed it, and he knew it was the right call. He had to give priority to finding Vanessa.

Ward was impressive, he thought to himself. He could provide continuity on the Chapman case and bring the replacement from Met CID up to speed. Trench realised he should have mentioned this to Ward at the station. Ward could have met and debriefed the replacement in person before leaving Charing Cross.

Trench hadn't spoken so Campbell pressed on. When he did so, Trench thought he detected a slight tension in his voice.

"I'll make that happen right away. And what about Operation Labrador? I told you to keep me updated."

Trench spent a few minutes updating Campbell on the briefing earlier. The information was not new to Campbell, other than the various duties Trench had assigned to the taskforce. Campbell cut in before he had finished.

"When did you speak with Osbourne?" he demanded.

"I haven't spoken with him yet. I was in the interview. I want to speak with him in person, I'm not just going to phone him."

"You haven't?" Campbell sounded surprised.

"Not yet, no. But I intend to go there tonight. I have something else brewing that I'd like to get confirmed first, but it's not a show-stopper."

"Hmm," said Campbell.

There was a long pause before he spoke again.

"What about the ringleader. Have we got him yet?"

"Not yet, but it won't be long."

"Sooner would be better," said Campbell. "We need to bring better news to tomorrow's briefing. With the Prime Minister."

"The fuc— What?" said Trench.

"She called me directly earlier. She said she wants to meet with the lead investigator. That's you, Trench. I'll be there too, of course, but it's just the two of us. I told you there was interest in this case. Admittedly, I didn't see this coming, but maybe we should have. She knows Osbourne. She's dealt with him in the past, when she was Minister of Defence. Hell, he probably knows half the government. I warned you, the man has a very deep reach."

Trench didn't say anything. He was trying to figure out what it could mean, but wasn't getting anywhere with the thought. Campbell spoke again after a few moments of silence.

"But you're saying you haven't spoken with him yet. I think we can expect to get our arse kicked for the shambles at the drop then. Get on to Thornton. Make sure we get the ringleader. At least that'll be some progress to report."

"Why do I need to be there?" asked Trench, suddenly annoyed.

There was a brief pause before Campbell responded, firmly.

"Because she asked for you to be there, Trench. Asked, as in ordered. Don't start your bullshit. You're SIO, you provide the update. What do you not understand about that?"

All his earlier concerns about the case getting mired in political pettifoggery came roaring back. It reignited the smouldering anger at the prospect of wasting countless precious hours in meaningless political pantomimes that would get them nowhere. He started counting to ten, but didn't make it to two.

"This is bullshit!" he exclaimed. "We're fighting the clock here. I can't be taking hours out of the day for this. Just tell her I'm working the case, trying to find Vanessa. Surely she can understand that. Bring Lewis along if she wants someone's balls to chew on."

"Calm down, man," said Campbell, raising his voice. "It'll be fifteen minutes at the very most. She's no fool, she doesn't want to impede the investigation. She knows the man. She's met Vanessa, even. She was there at the dinner. We'll go there, give her the update and be out inside twenty minutes. Grow up, Trench. This is the real world."

Trench said nothing. He knew it was pointless to argue but that didn't make his anger subside.

"I'll call you tomorrow as soon as I know the time," said Campbell. "Just make sure we have the ringleader."

He hung up. Trench turned to Jazz.

"What a load of bollocks."

"I'd normally say at least you get to meet the PM," she said. "But I know you'd rather just borrow my plastic fork and go meet some Millwall fans..."

Trench held up a finger, then reached over and turned up the volume on the radio.

*"…and four days since her father, billionaire Doctor Clarence Osbourne, made the dramatic appeal for information about his missing daughter. We understand there have been hundreds of reported sightings, but that none have been verified and police are no closer to finding her.*

*While police chiefs remain tight-lipped about efforts to find Vanessa, a source from inside police headquarters, who spoke to our reporters on the condition of anonymity, said that a major operation to identify the kidnapper and rescue Vanessa appears to have failed. Details of the operation have not been made public, but unconfirmed reports suggest it's related to a series of raids on properties across London late last night and early this morning. Witnesses at various locations say armed police carried out the raids—"*

Trench switched it off.

"We should be getting ahead of this," he said. "We'd be better off announcing we responded to a ransom demand and drip-feeding updates rather than waiting for some bastard to leak it. We're on the back foot now, looking like we're trying to hide something."

"We are trying to hide something," said Jazz.

"Yeah well, that's always easier if you give them something," said Trench. "We get a few hours out of each new piece of information we give them. If we don't give them anything, they just start speculating and we start springing leaks."

"You should have said that to Campbell just now," said Jazz.

"True," said Trench. "I thought he would've taken care of it already. I'll ask him later. I also should have told Ward someone else from CID would be taking this over now. I'll call him now. He can pick up the message when he gets out of the interview."

As he unlocked his phone to dial, he remembered there was something else he had said he would take care of. He started leafing through the Chapman file. He eventually found the number he was looking for. He noted it was a landline number.

"What are you doing?" asked Jazz.

"I said I'd call Chapman's parents to see if they're aware of any connection with Horley. I'll do that before we clock off with Ward," he replied, dialling the number.

The call rang for a while before a male voice answered.

"Hello?"

"Good afternoon, this is DCI Trent Chambers from London Metropolitan Police. Is that Henry Chapman?"

"Yes it is, what can I do for you?" said Chapman Senior, before adding in a weary tone. "Is this about Howard?"

"Yes it is," confirmed Trench. "We'd just like to ask you a few questions."

"We haven't seen that boy for over ten years, Detective. I keep telling your people that," Chapman sounded exasperated. "He's not part of this family and we don't know anything about him anymore."

"I understand that, sir. I just need—"

"Your people were here just last week asking questions. What more do you want from us?" said Chapman. "When will it end?"

Trench could hear the anguish in his voice and immediately felt sorry for the man. He was an unwitting and innocent victim in all of this too. The whole Chapman family was. But Trench had to ask his questions. He silently hoped that putting Chapman away for the rest of his life would bring some closure to the man and his family.

"Hopefully soon, Mr Chapman. We're working on it," he said, hoping Chapman picked up on the implicit message. "For now, I just need to know of any connections you're aware of that Howard may have had to Horley."

"As I keep telling you people, we have had no contact with him since before he went to prison, more than a decade ago," said Chapman, sounding tired rather than angry.

"I understand that, but he hasn't been out that long," said Trench. "Is there any connection from before he went to prison? Any friends there or places he used to stay?"

"We didn't know much about his life, Detective, even back then," said Chapman. "He had a bedroom here. That's where he stayed most of the time, but he stayed away often enough too. We never knew where. He didn't have any friends that we knew of. He had always been a loner, I suppose. Sorry, I can't help you. These are painful memories."

"Can you think of any reason why he'd be in that area?" pressed Trench, knowing he was losing him. He tried giving it one last go before Chapman hung up. "Were you ever aware of him being there, for any reason?"

"Sorry Detective, no," said Chapman. "The only place we knew for sure he went was the Club, and that's only because I got him a job there. What a terrible mistake that was..."

"The tennis club?" said Trench, suddenly remembering something he had read about it. "It closed down after the uh, incident, right?"

"Yes," replied Chapman, sounding like he was trying not to recall the memories.

"Where was that?"

"It was on Horse Hill Road, between Dorking and..., well not that far from Horley now that you mention it. About a mile or so outside the town centre, as the crow flies. It was handy for where we live, only about fifteen minutes away. They're country roads so there's never much traffic."

Trench and Jazz stared at each other. A buzz of excitement filled the car.

"Do you have the exact address?"

"That's it," said Chapman. "Green Lawns Tennis Club, Horse Hill Road, Surrey. I can't recall the postcode, but it's not a long road. They may have built more houses on it since then, but it's a country road. The entrance to the Club was about halfway along."

"Okay, thank you. We appreciate your help," said Trench.

He couldn't wait to get off the call now. He felt the car jolt forward as Jazz put her foot down.

"I have a question for you, Detective," said Chapman.

"What's that?"

"Is this about that missing girl? The Osbourne girl?" he asked painfully.

Trench realised it was a natural assumption. He moved to dispel the poor man's concerns. Although he knew he was only delaying his misery. There was plenty more coming down the line.

"No sir, it's not," he said.

He then realised he should give the man at least some kind of warning of what was to come for him.

"Not that girl, anyway."

# Thirty-Seven

There were no streetlights on Horse Hill Road. Heavy rain pelted the windscreen almost faster than the wipers could swash it away. Tall trees either side of the road blocked out any residual daylight from the late afternoon. It felt pitch black. They could barely see twenty yards in front of them. They were both craned forward in their seats, looking for the entrance. They were doing less than twenty miles per hour.

"Slow down," said Trench, spotting a driveway entrance on the left.

They crawled up to the driveway. It was a house. Not what they were looking for. They had passed a handful of houses and a couple of businesses so far, all of which had long, private driveways. They had to slow down and check out each one.

Jazz sped up slightly. They had been on the road for a few minutes but had no idea if they were halfway along yet. Soon the trees thinned out and they passed entrances for a few small businesses.

"There," said Trench, pointing at another driveway, barely visible through overgrown bushes and shrubs.

Jazz slowed and pulled up at the driveway. They could see the outline of tarmac, mostly hidden under weeds and moss. It turned behind some trees after about ten yards, obscuring their view any further.

"Could be," said Jazz.

Trench nodded and pointed down the driveway indicating they should proceed.

She reversed slightly then pulled the car onto the driveway. They followed it around the turn. As soon as they made the turn Trench realised this had to be it. A run down, one-storey building was set back from an overgrown parking area. The building had once been painted white, but the paint now looked grubby and was peeling off in large patches. Many of the windows at the front of the building were smashed.

Jazz pulled up much closer to the building, letting the headlights illuminate it through the dark and blustering rain. They could see glass double doors to the main entrance, held closed by a padlocked chain, looped through the handles.

"Keep the lights on the door," said Trench as he opened his door. "Let's go."

He stepped out of the car and immediately was thoroughly drenched by the rain. He trotted around to the boot and retrieved a couple of torches, two pairs of latex gloves and a bolt cutter. Jazz got out of the car and they both dashed over to the main door. There was a porch over the door but it provided little cover. Rain swirled at them from all angles. It flowed off their faces. They had to raise their voices above the sound of howling wind and rain smashing off glass and mud.

"What are you waiting for?" shouted Jazz, as Trench glanced around at the rest of the building.

"This doesn't feel right," Trench yelled back.

"What are you talking about, we have to go in," Jazz shouted. "You want to wait for back up all of a sudden?"

She sounded incredulous. It would be a first.

"It's too open. Not secure enough," he yelled. "Anyone could climb in any of these windows. He couldn't keep someone in there for a week."

"Just cut the fucking chain, Trench. Or else let's get back in the car."

"Hang on a sec," shouted Trench, thrusting one of the torches at Jazz.

He then stepped back and jogged down the length of the building.

"Where are you going?" Jazz yelled after him, but he was soon out of earshot.

Trench got to the end of the building and continued around the side. He followed the side of the building. It was almost pitch black. He switched on the torch. Connected to the rear of the building was a wooden fence, the same height as the building. He tried jumping up to see what was on the other side but it was too high. He shone the torchlight along the fence to see how far back it went. After about ten yards it was joined by a wire fence of the same height.

He dashed down to the wire fence and shone the light inside it. He could just about see the outline of a badly overgrown tennis court. He could see the markings and one of the metal pillars that had previously held the net. It was too dark to see anything beyond that. He aimed the torch toward the building but the wooden fence continued at a perpendicular angle to where it intersected with the wire fence. He couldn't see the back of the building.

He ran back toward the front of the building and nearly banged into Jazz, who had come round to follow him.

"What the fuck, Trench?" she roared.

"Forget it, let's go back to the main door."

They ran back to the main entrance, both stepping in huge puddles that were unavoidable in the uneven surface.

"Hold this," said Trench, handing her his torch.

She shone both lights on the lock as Trench lifted the bolt cutter up to it. The chain was too thick for the bolt cutter to get any purchase. He tried the padlock itself. The jaws of the bolt cutter just about fit around it. He tried to hold steady, then clenched the arms of the bolt cutter as tightly as he could.

The jaws slipped off the lock. It was too slippery in the downpour, making it harder to get any purchase. Trench stepped closer to the lock and stood up on his toes, hoping the downward pressure would hold the jaws in place. He squeezed the arms of the bolt cutter again. It wouldn't budge. He squeezed as hard as he could, letting out a grunt as his arms burned with the effort. It still wouldn't budge. He let out a roar and gave it one last squeeze with every bit of energy and strength he had. Snap!

The lock fell away but Trench slammed forward as his momentum from the downward force carried him into the door. His head hit the door and instantly slid down. He lost his balance and his trajectory kept him tumbling forward. His face smashed into the door handle. His lip burst open. His nose banged into it full force.

"Fuck!" he exclaimed, dropping to his knees.

His hands went to his face. He could see blood flowing through them onto the ground. It looked worse because of the rain. He wiped it away. He grabbed the door handle to drag himself back to his feet. Jazz picked up the bolt cutter as Trench pulled the loose chain off the handles. He flung it to one side and yanked open the door.

They stepped inside. The beams from the car helped the torches illuminate the inner porch area. Jazz turned to look at Trench, his face bloodied and lip already swollen. His suit and shirt were also covered in blood.

"Always a man for the grand entrance," she said.

Trench glared at her.

"Thanks partner."

He grabbed his torch back. They slipped on their latex gloves then both shone the beams further inside the building. There was another set of glass double doors right in front of them. Beyond that, they could make out a reception area. There was a desk with more glass double doors to its immediate right, a waiting area to the left. Corridors went off in each direction. There was an open archway in behind the desk.

Trench pushed open the glass door and paced into the reception area. Jazz followed. They stood for a moment, shining the beams all around. The light from the car barely made it into this area. They shone the torch beams down the corridor in each direction.

"Which way?" said Jazz.

Trench thought for a moment.

"Changing rooms," he answered, shifting the beam to the walls, looking for a sign.

He found it. Changing rooms were to the left.

"Let's go."

They walked slowly, shining the beams around the area as they went. The changing rooms were dead ahead. The first door was the Ladies. Trench put his hand on the door and pushed it open.

"Police!" he yelled. "Anyone here? Police!"

Nothing.

There was another door immediately in front of the first. He pushed it open, calling out again, louder. Still nothing.

They stepped into a typical old-fashioned sports changing room. Wooden benches against the walls and in the middle of the room. Hangers along the wall behind them. Lockers covered one wall. Rain hammered hard on the glazed windows. Two of them were smashed, the rain pelting through. It bounced heavily off the concrete floor, spraying splashes up into the room. Large puddles covered most of the floor.

The room was empty.

There was an archway to the left. The shower area. They went slowly toward it. Trench suddenly spotted movement. To their right. Down low. He spun with his torch in his left hand, instinctively raising the bolt cutter with his right. Jazz's beam followed.

A huge black rat scurried under the bench along the wall. It squeaked as the light hit it. They both instinctively stepped to the left, giving it a wide berth. It scurried toward the open door and snuck out through the gap.

In silence, they stepped slowly toward the shower area. There were individual cubicles. The first two were toilets, both doors hanging open. The ones further inside were showers. Some still had the shower curtain in place. Trench nodded to the right, indicating Jazz should check those ones while he checked the ones to the left. They progressed slowly, scanning each cubicle, pushing aside the occasional curtain. Trench reached the end of his row. Nothing.

He turned just as Jazz reached the end of her row. A shower curtain covered the final cubicle. He shone his light there as Jazz reached it. She glanced at Trench as her hand grabbed the curtain. They both nodded. Jazz yanked back the curtain. Nothing.

"Men's," said Trench, heading back to the door.

As they left the room they focused their beams on the floor this time, scouring under the benches for any more vermin. The Men's changing room was a further few steps down the corridor. When they reached it Trench again put his hand on the door and again called out.

"Police! Anyone here?"

Nothing.

They hastened through the door and then the second door. Similar layout. Wooden benches. Hooks along the walls. Lockers. Nearly all the windows were smashed in here. The floor was one huge puddle, rain rampaging around the room.

"There's no-one here," said Trench, shaking his head. "It's too open."

As he spoke he strode over to the shower area. There were no cubicles, just an open plan shower area. As they scanned their torches inside, another few rats hissed and squawked at them. But they were the only things in there.

"It'll be a storage area or an office or something," said Trench. "Somewhere with a lock. More secure."

They left the changing room. The corridor ended a few feet after the door to the Men's. There was a fire escape door at the end of the corridor. It looked to be locked. They turned and headed back down the corridor toward the reception area. The corridor to the right had three doors. Two were at the front of the building.

Both doors were open, one hanging off its hinges. They scanned the rooms. They both looked like offices. More smashed windows, soaked floors.

The third door was on other side of the corridor, meaning it opened further into the building. The door was closed. Trench tried the handle. Locked. Trench banged on the door and called out again. Nothing.

They glanced at each other, stepping away from the door. Trench lined himself up square to the door. In one swift movement he raised his foot and slammed into the door. He aimed for just below the handle. The flimsy door split on impact and burst open. They both rushed forward and shone their lights inside. It was definitely a storage room, filled with dirty old boxes piled on shelves and scattered across the floor. But other than that, it was empty.

"Shit," said Jazz, leading the way back to reception.

Next they tried the glass doors beside reception. They shone their lights inside. They could see it was a large room. Violent shadows leapt around the room. There were lots of windows or maybe skylights in there. The doors were unlocked. They pushed them open and stepped inside. The sound of rain crashing on glass was much louder in here, but the floor was dry.

Tables and chairs were scattered around the room. Sofas and softer seats lined the walls. They stepped further into the room and saw a small kitchen/bar area to the right. Trench paced over to it but found nothing. There was another small storage room beside it. Its door was flat on the floor in front of it. Whatever contents had been there had long since been looted.

"Here!" called Jazz.

Trench spun around and hurried over to the far side of the room. Jazz was standing beside the far wall, her light shining onto one of the sofas.

"Someone's been here," she said excitedly.

Trench shone his light too. He could see that another sofa had been moved and was pushed up against the one that lined the wall. It created an enclosed area, the seat of the two sofas joined together. A huge pile of sleeping bags and duvets was bundled there. It was someone's bed.

"This is where he's been sleeping," said Jazz.

"Someone sure has," said Trench.

He hunkered down and shone his light under the sofas. There was a couple of cardboard boxes underneath. He leant forward and pulled the first one out. There was food in there. Bread, crisps, tins of tuna, cereal, milk. He lifted out the milk and checked the Use By date. It was today.

"It matches," he said, standing up and turning to Jazz. "The receipts Cedric gave us. A lot of this stuff was on the most recent one."

"This is it," said Jazz.

His heartbeat picked up.

"But where did he keep them?"

They both spun around. They had checked the whole room. It was too open, too unsecured. They shone the torches around the room again. They focused on the far wall. It was mostly made of glass. Full length windows. They hurried over to it. They scanned their torches until they found the doors. There was a fire extinguisher pushed up against one of the doors. Trench rolled it out of the way and the door rattled. He tried the handle. It was unlocked.

He yanked it open. They both stepped outside into the gusting rain. They were on a large, open patio area which eventually led away to the tennis courts. Trench started quickly toward the courts. They were enclosed by the wire fence he had seen earlier.

"Look for an outhouse or shed," he shouted, the rain howling over them.

They could only see half of the first court in the torchlight, the rest lost to the night and the squall. They ran further onto the court, beams dead ahead. They were halfway down the other side of the court when they spotted it.

"There!" yelled Jazz.

A small concrete building sat off behind the end of the court. It was almost engulfed in the encroaching undergrowth and bushes. They ran toward it. As they got closer they could make out a heavy wooden door. Soon they saw the heavy bolt lock on the door. A glistening steel padlock hanging from it. Brand new. When he saw that Trench had no doubt. They had found it.

# Thirty-Eight

What an hour before had been a dark, desolate ruin was now an orgy of light. Dazzling white forensic floodlights, bobbing yellow torch beams, a sea of flashing blue lights and a barrage of xenon headlights from a dozen vehicles. A swarm of white plastic forensic suits milled about the property. If Surrey Police had missed out on the capture of Chapman, they weren't going to miss the taming of his lair. DCS Hunter had commanded his troops out in force.

To his credit, he had also dropped any sign of hostility despite the frosty phone call with Trench following Chapman's capture. When Trench called him to report what they'd found he'd immediately kicked into full operational mode. Uniforms had arrived within minutes to secure the scene. They cordoned off both the clubhouse and the outhouse, and blocked the driveway with their vehicles. They cleared everyone else arriving at the scene before allowing them access.

Forensics Units began arriving shortly afterwards. Among them was Danny Kenner and his team. Trench was glad to see him. Not only because of their good working relationship, but also because he had been at the scene of Savannah Diaz's body. Trench figured he could get an unofficial report from Kenner before having to wait for official channels. He would trust Kenner's analysis as to whether the two scenes were linked.

Trench had briefed each of the Forensics Units on arrival, explaining what they would find in each building. Each one asked what they had touched and where they had been. He answered truthfully, that they had searched the clubhouse thoroughly but had only given the shed a cursory examination from the doorway without stepping inside.

It had been enough.

Pulling open the door had unleashed a pungent chemical murk that washed over them. It was strong, but not strong enough to mask the stench of death. They had both instinctively raised their free hand to cover their nose and mouth. Instead of stepping inside they scanned their torch beams around the interior. Neither spoke, neither moved for more than a minute. They wordlessly scanned their beams, their police instincts trying to process what they were seeing. Their human instincts trying not to. They were peering into a vision of hell.

Knives hung from nails in the walls. A couple of dozen knives, all shapes and sizes. Nearly all the blades stained red. A filthy mattress lay in the middle of the room, flattened and worn, splattered crimson patches all over. A heavy steel chain lay across the mattress, one end bolted to the concrete floor. The other end fixed to a thick leather dog collar.

The floor was awash with tell-tale detritus. Cable ties strewn amongst shreds of clothes. Crumpled underwear. Food wrappers. Condom wrappers. Duct tape. Used condoms. Cigarette butts. Empty beer cans. Whiskey bottles. Their beams illuminated more dark red stains on the concrete floor itself. Amongst the harrowing signs of torture, the seemingly innocuous sight of some tennis balls. A couple of tennis rackets with their strings gone. Innocuous, except they now knew what they had been used for. A couple of the balls still had duct tape clinging to them. The racket strings lay in coils on the mattress. The cause of the chafing around the dead women's necks.

In the corner to the right was a huge plastic barrel. It was easily big enough to fit a human body. It was heavily stained by drip marks down all sides, even though it was not full to the brim. Not without a body inside, anyway. Dozens of empty plastic containers were strewn around the barrel. They could see the labels on some. Ammonia, Phthalates, Triclosan. Chlorine.

Whatever fear the women had felt when they realised they'd been abducted must have become apocalyptic when this door opened. There could be no mistaking what this place was. And they had each been here for days. The mattress already stained from the victim before. The knives already stained.

Trench and Jazz had already seen the gruesome fate of the women who'd been here. Slain, cut to shreds, hogtied to a tree in a lonely rural forest or floating face down for miles through filthy rivers. But seeing this place now, understanding the horror of their final hours and days, was almost overwhelming.

"Let's call it in," Trench croaked, making no attempt to go inside.

They didn't need to. They could see all the proof they needed from the doorway.

*

In between briefing each of the arriving Forensics Units, they retreated to the car to shelter from the torrential rain and freezing wind. Jazz insisted they turn the engine on so the heaters could function and Trench didn't argue. They were both completely soaked through. The heaters did little to dry their clothes but at least provided some superficial warmth.

While they waited, DI Glenda Watson from the Operation Labrador taskforce called to say Thornton's SO unit had captured Pavel Kozlowski, the ringleader of the ransom gang. An Automatic Number Plate Recognition camera had picked up the car he was driving on the M11 and they had made the arrest on the slip road at Stanstead airport. Trench instructed Watson to lead the interview. She had led many of the interviews with other gang members so was well placed to compare their version with the story the ringleader gave. Although he would have attended the interview if he was available, he did not consider it worth delaying until he was able to get back to the station.

Trench then called to say good night to Milo. He was already in bed, but Vivian held the phone up to his ear so Trench could say good night and hear Milo say it back to him. Hearing his voice was like an anchor to reality in the sea of insanity the old tennis club had now become.

"Where the hell is Hunter?" Trench griped for the umpteenth time after he hung up.

They did not want to leave the scene without briefing him in person. They'd been ready to leave for a while but had decided to wait for him.

"They said he'd be here any minute," said Jazz again, having already asked the uniforms twice.

"They've been saying that for half an hour."

Just as he said it, they spotted the headlights of a car turn onto the driveway of the disused tennis club. They watched as one of the uniforms got out of his car to approach the vehicle, but then turn and run back to his own car. He reversed it out of the way, having recognised the incoming car or its driver. As the car pulled into the parking area they could see Hunter behind the wheel.

"At last," said Trench, as they both opened their doors.

The fresh blast of frigid rain and wind sent another chill through their already freezing bodies. They dashed over to Hunter's car. Before he was fully out of his car, they both opened the back doors and jumped in.

"Let's talk in here," shouted Trench over the storm as he got inside.

Hunter sat back down into his seat and closed the door. He turned in his seat.

"Looks like this is the payload," said Hunter. "Montgomery's been briefing me on what we've got here. There can be no doubt."

Montgomery was the lead forensic officer from Surrey Police. He had introduced himself as such when he'd arrived earlier.

"How'd you know it was here?" asked Hunter, before adding quickly, "Though we would have put it together eventually."

Trench ignored the seemingly petty attempt at saving face, instead acknowledging the likelihood. He then told Hunter about the phone call with Chapman's father and gave him a summary of their actions when they arrived.

"I presume you've told Ward?" said Hunter.

"Yeah, we called him earlier," said Trench. "Right after we called you. He was already on his way back to Thames Valley. He said they'd come here in the morning to see it for themselves."

"I understand another team from Met CID will be coming down as well," said Hunter. "The ones leading the case now. Lewis told me that technically you're both no longer on this case?"

Jazz shot a quick glance at Trench but he ignored it. He wasn't surprised that Hunter had spoken with Lewis, nor that Campbell had obviously already issued the command that the Chapman case be reassigned. Campbell had made it clear he wanted their full focus on Operation Labrador as soon as the interview with Chapman was done.

"I'm sure they'll be down first thing," he simply said.

"Ay, if not before," said Hunter. "Well, I guess you guys will be heading off soon. Good work today. I can't say I like all your methods, but we've got the right result. That's all that matters."

Trench and Jazz both nodded sincerely. They said goodbye and ran back to their own car. Jazz started the engine and turned the car. She eased past the many cars that had arrived after them and headed down the drive. Just as she did so, another car pulled into the driveway coming from the opposite direction. A grey Ford Mondeo. They couldn't make out the occupants behind the glare of the Mondeo's headlights, but they knew who it was.

"Seriously?" exclaimed Jazz. "They're our replacement again?!"

"S'ppose they're at a loose end after being canned from Labrador."

Neither car moved for a moment, but then Jazz turned slightly to the left. She pulled in as close to the overgrown trees as she could, trying to make enough space for both cars to pass. Eventually the Mondeo did the same. They inched along and were soon side by side. Jazz put her window down slightly. Burgess did the same in the driver's seat of the Mondeo.

"Just happen to be nearby again?" yelled Jazz above the storm.

"Lewis told us to work this one now," Burgess called out. "We just got here."

"No shit. Knock yourselves out," responded Jazz.

"Will do," replied Burgess, beginning to put his window up. "Pity we didn't know about this place when we interviewed Chapman."

Trench leaned forward in his seat and shouted over to Burgess.

"You spoke to him?"

But Burgess had already begun moving. Their car rolled forward and out of earshot. Jazz turned to Trench.

"Was that the royal 'we', or did he mean they actually spoke with Chapman?" she said.

"Fuck knows," shrugged Trench. "Maybe they interviewed him after Ward and Duncan left."

"Yeah, Campbell seemed pretty keen to reassign the case and get us focused on finding Vanessa," agreed Jazz.

Trench nodded.

"Ward said they didn't get a peep out of him," he said. "I doubt Bill and Ben there could do any better. No harm in them trying if it's their case now, I suppose. I'm just surprised they bothered. It's dangerously close to actual police work."

Trench was sanguine about them taking over the case. As far as he was concerned, it looked like they now had enough to put Chapman away forever. That was all that mattered.

They left the club and drove the short distance to the petrol station where Trench had left his bike. On the way he checked his emails but still had not received anything from Krige. Trench called him but it went straight to voicemail. He left a gruff message, demanding Krige send him the information he had asked for or call him immediately to explain what the problem was.

When they got to the petrol station, Trench was relieved to see his bike was still there. Someone had rolled it away from the pump, over to the side of the forecourt. Chapman's van was gone, presumably having been taken in by Forensics. Jazz pulled up beside the bike.

"Still want to talk to Osbourne tonight?" asked Jazz.

Trench mulled it. He checked the time on the car's display. He calculated that it would be after midnight by the time they got to Blenheim. They were freezing cold, soaking wet and dog tired. They didn't have the information from Krige, which he wanted before facing Osbourne. They also hadn't eaten since lunch time. It wasn't a difficult decision to make.

"We're going to need our wits about us when we talk to him," he said. "Sounds like he's already on our case, getting the bloody Prime Minister to give us a bollocking. If we blow it, we might not get another chance. We'll go there first thing tomorrow instead."

"Agreed," said Jazz, shivering as if to make the point. "Better to tackle him with a fresh head in the morning."

They agreed to meet at the station early the next morning. Jazz left in the car and Trench set off on his bike. It was miserable riding weather, some of the worst he could remember. The rain hammered hard onto his helmet, almost completely drowning out the music. He had to wipe his visor every few seconds.

The gusting winds were so strong on the M23 that he had to move to an inner lane and keep his speed down. He was fully focused on the road for nearly the entire hour-long journey. The only exception was the final ten minutes, when his mind wandered to the ongoing debate he'd been having with himself recently. Was it finally time to get heated riding gloves…

Once home, he peeled off his drenched leathers and headed straight for the shower. He set it to piping hot and stood under the blast, his fingers tingling as the circulation returned to them. Maybe another decision that shouldn't be difficult to make.

His mind turned to the day's dramatic events. It felt like weeks ago that he had sat in a coffee shop explaining to Jazz what he had seen after the ransom drop. The day had started out with uncertainty and pessimism. But as he reflected now, he felt content – pleased even – with what they'd achieved.

Chapman was not only behind bars, he was finished. Forever. It was a remarkable result. Trench rarely indulged in self-congratulation, but he allowed himself to acknowledge that they had done good work. Very good work.

It made him feel more positive about the Vanessa Osbourne case. Lots of questions still needed to be answered. Not least the biggest question of them all. But he felt they were beginning to move in the right direction. They knew more of the questions that needed to be answered, even if they didn't have those answers yet. The taskforce was covering a multitude of lines of enquiry. And he would be asking some of the most intriguing questions himself early the next day. It would be his full focus. Yes, he was fine with handing over the Chapman case, even to Callow. It would clear him up to take the full benefit of momentum into the Osbourne case. And to find Vanessa.

# Thirty-Nine

He was falling.

Tumbling at a speed he knew meant he would be damaged when he hit the ground. It was pitch dark. He was calm but he knew he shouldn't be. He had no way of stopping his fall. He tried to twist around. It somehow seemed better to land on all fours than on his back. Even though he knew he'd been falling for far, far too long for it to make a difference.

He wasn't able to turn around. Suddenly he wasn't feeling calm. He was picking up speed, falling faster. He had to turn around! It was getting brighter. He was nearing the bottom, fast. He had to turn around!

But he was out of time.

Trench sat bolt upright in bed. He may have roared out. His heart was thumping. The dream was so real he was clenching the duvet with both hands. His eyes were wide open, but it was too dark to see anything. He swung his legs over and got out of bed. He could feel his heart beat as he switched on the light. He stood for a moment, confused. What the fuck. When was the last time he'd had a nightmare?!

He shook his head and tried to chuckle, as if to shake it off as meaningless. But it was hard to shake the fug. He picked up his phone. 05:14. He sat down on the bed and dialled Danny Kenner's number. It was answered after four rings.

"Tell me you've been to bed, Trench?" said Kenner by way of greeting.

"Sounds like that would make one of us," said Trench, picking up the background noise.

"Yeah, well I hope you had sweet dreams. Because this place is a living nightmare. Literally. Those women lived through unspeakable shit here. And we've only scratched the surface," said Kenner grimly.

"Uh," grunted Trench, his brain still not yet fully alert. It was bothering him that it was taking longer than usual to wake up.

"What have you got?" he eventually managed.

"You saw it, Trench. There's no doubt this is where he kept them, if that's what you're asking. He made no attempt to destroy evidence or cover his tracks. He clearly didn't think we'd find this place. Or else he's so far gone he didn't care. I'll let you guys figure that one out."

"Can we tie him to the bodies?"

"Oh hell, yeah," said Kenner. "We haven't tested anything yet of course, but the whole place is heaving with trace. We've already carted off a truck-load of samples and we're barely a few feet in the door. You can bet the crown jewels we'll be tying him to multiple victims, at least four I'd say. He even left used condoms lying around, if you can believe that. Not only will we be able to say whether a woman was here, we'll be able to say he had sex with them. Yeah, we can tie him to the bodies alright."

Trench was suddenly wide awake.

"Four?" he said, bolting up off the bed. "You said four victims?"

"Best guess. We're a long way from confirming, but that's what I'm thinking at this stage."

"Why?" pressed Trench.

"Couple of reasons. First, it looks like at least four pairs of women's underwear. Not exactly scientific, but we'll know more once we begin testing. You sound surprised. Was that not the number you were expecting?"

"What else? Just the underwear?" said Trench, his mind beginning to race. "Hookers often bring more than one pair with them."

"Yeah, you're right," backtracked Kenner. "Hey, I don't want to mislead you, I spoke out of turn. I'll wait for—"

"No, it's fine Kenner. It's not that. I trust your judgement. I want your opinion. What else makes you think there's four victims?"

"Well apart from the underwear, panties that is, I've seen four bras, all different sizes. That's why I'm thinking four. There's also some jewellery. I'm not sure if he was taking trophies, but I'd guess not. They seem to be loosely piled in different areas, some scattered around. If they were trophies, they weren't very precious to him. But there's at least four different piles. Each is pretty distinct, some obviously cheap, some look expensive. Makes me think he took them off each victim and put them down in a different place to the previous victim. But again, this isn't science, Trench. I probably shouldn't be saying anything yet. I don't want to mislead you."

Trench tried to think if there was anything else he should ask Kenner that might provide a clue as to the number of victims.

"Shoes," he said. "How many pairs of shoes did you find?"

"So far we've found two shoes. That's two different shoes, not a single pair. But there's not that many other items of clothing besides the underwear. There's a few bits, but probably not a single outfit. I'm guessing he might've dumped the clothes and shoes but not the underwear."

Trench couldn't think of anything else to ask.

"I could text you photos of some of the stuff if it would help you ID potential victims," said Kenner. "Although, Callow may have sent them to you already? He was here taking photos earlier."

"No, he –" Trench broke off to quickly check his phone, but saw no messages. "No, he didn't. But don't worry about it, I'll ask him to send me what he's got."

"Okay," said Kenner. "When you're speaking to him, do me a favour. Remind him that the bull in the China shop is not the cool guy in the story. He's not the important guy either. He's the asshole guy. And next time, he's the don't-come-anywhere-fucking-near-my-scene guy."

"Will do," said Trench as he hung up.

He was rattled. The good feeling he'd had going to bed was gone. Four victims, not the three they'd identified. Expensive jewellery. A fleeting thought flashed into his mind. Chapman's father asking if this was about the Osbourne girl. Trench had dismissed it.

He dismissed it again now. It couldn't be. Chapman's victims were all prostitutes, all living transient lifestyles. No-one knew they were missing and no-one looked for them until they were long gone or their bodies discovered. But it took a little longer for him to find the same assuredness with which he had dismissed it before. The nightmare that he was falling came back into his head. Was his subconscious telling him something that his conscious mind had not yet grasped?

He forced the thought out of his mind as he went into the kitchen. He poured some oats into a pot, ran it under the tap and put the pot on the stove as he got into the shower. Quick and cold this time. The porridge was ready by the time he got out and he ate it while quickly changing. He was moving fast to distract himself. He wanted to be thinking about interviewing Doctor Osbourne, not wildly speculating about what Kenner had said.

He picked up his phone and checked his emails. Krige had come through. He'd sent the email at nearly one am. Trench shot him a quick one liner to say thanks. He clicked the attachment but he couldn't read it on his phone. He cursed and made for the front door. He could study it at the station. Just as he grabbed the handle to leave the house, his phone rang. He checked the screen.

"Commander," answered Trench.

"We're on at seven thirty with the PM," said Campbell. "Can you get here asap so we can debrief beforehand?"

"On my way."

"I'll be on the penthouse floor. It'll be quieter there," said Campbell, signing off.

Trench sent a text to Jazz informing her that he'd be later than planned getting to the station. He also asked that she lead the morning briefing in his absence, and that she print off and review the attachment in the email he was about to send. He forwarded Krige's email then left.

He made a quick stop at Charing Cross Police Station to change into a suit. He arrived at New Scotland Yard within thirty minutes of the phone call. After clearing security, he took one of the glass lifts up to the penthouse meeting areas on the sixth floor.

The lift provided a complete overview of each of the five open-plan office floors as it rose through the inside of the building. It was an architectural paradox – complete openness right at the heart of the nation's primary security apparatus. But Trench knew the Met's recently made-over HQ was full of surprises. All the way down to the toilets that were tiled in patterns that matched police vehicles, including the infamous blue and yellow chequerboard. It was a deliberate nod by the designers to the most important tool in the police survival kit – a sense of humour.

He found Campbell sitting in a corner seat by the window directly overlooking the Houses of Parliament. He nodded as Trench approached. Trench clocked the hint of a grin on his face. It might have been smugness. It definitely reminded Trench to keep his wits about him. Campbell on home turf.

As he sat down, he returned the nod and waited. Campbell just looked at him, allowing his customary awkward silence to join the meeting.

"Have you spoken with Callow this morning?" Campbell eventually said, his baritone drawl sounding even deeper bouncing off the oak wood floors.

"No."

"The site you found yesterday. After we spoke about you handing over the Chapman investigation," said Campbell.

He seemed to be waiting for Trench to say something. Trench just raised his eyebrows.

"Are you aware of what he found there?" asked Campbell.

"No," said Trench, figuring it was better to get Campbell's take than to mention what Kenner had told him earlier.

"I instructed DCS Lewis to assign a different team to that case after you interviewed the suspect. As you and I had agreed," said Campbell. "He put Callow and Burgess on it. They went down there last night and made some…disturbing discoveries."

"Jewellery," said Trench, trying to make Campbell get to the point.

"So you do know?" said Campbell, raising his own eyebrows.

"What's this got to do with briefing the Prime Minister about Operation Labrador?" said Trench, ignoring the question. "Sir."

"Do you know Callow sent pictures of some of the items of jewellery to Doctor Osbourne last night?" said Campbell.

This instantly put Trench on maximum alert. Why was Campbell telling him this? There could be only one reason. No words came out as he realised what Campbell was about to tell him.

"Osbourne confirmed it. They belong to Vanessa."

For a split-second Trench was falling again. His mind exploded in possibilities. And doubts. He gripped hard on the arms of the seat. Could it be…

"I don't…when?" was all he could stammer.

"Right away. Last night. So you see, this is very pertinent to our briefing with the PM," said Campbell. "Very pertinent indeed."

"It can't be," said Trench, almost to himself.

"Can't be what?"

"We can't tell her that," blurted Trench. "Because of a couple of pictures? No, this isn't right. We need to check everything out."

"What do you mean? Ask Osbourne to look again?" said Campbell dubiously. "You don't think he would have double checked? Osbourne was sure. One hundred per cent."

"This can't be right," insisted Trench. "It doesn't fit with what we know so far."

"He has her jewellery, Trench. There's also underwear from numerous women, quite possibly from Vanessa. We'll probably find her DNA down there. It's not the outcome any of us hoped for. God bless the poor girl. But it is what it is."

Trench ran both hands through his hair.

"No. This isn't possible..."

Campbell furrowed his brow and sat forward in his seat.

"What's the matter here? Is this pride, Trench, because you didn't find the jewellery? You found the whole site, for God's sake. It better not be because it was Callow that found it."

"No, it's...," Trench trailed off, thinking.

"Because of your dislike for Osbourne? If, and I mean *if*, he sent us a dummy ransom then that is reprehensible. It's not something you or I could ever hope to understand. But don't let your imagination run away with you. Don't let it cloud your judgement."

Trench wasn't listening. He was still trying to process, trying to figure out exactly why the news was so anathema to him. Campbell continued.

"Or is it because you didn't see it? You missed the connection between the cases?"

This time Trench did hear. It was said in an even tone, but to Trench's ears the words sounded heavy with accusation. He wasn't sure if that was coming from Campbell or if it was his own conscience interpreting the words like that. Had he missed it? Had he been blinded to the possibility that Chapman had grabbed Vanessa?

"This isn't right," he repeated, more urgent this time. He leaned forward. "It can't be. He takes prostitutes. Low profile, unknown, out of the way hookers. Not this. Not the highest profile young woman in the whole fucking UK."

"A killer's a killer, Trench. If he had the opportunity are you saying he wouldn't do it? Come on."

"He's stealthy. And careful. That's his whole thing. He's taken women that aren't missed and who no-one looks for. He's smart. He's taken them from different police jurisdictions to slow us down. We didn't even know he existed until a week ago. He was getting away with it, as far as he knew. Why would he suddenly change everything and take someone he knows is going to draw half the cops in the country after him?"

"That may be so. But you're forgetting something. He's also a raving fucking mad man. He's unravelling," Campbell shrugged. "They always do. Even the body you found. That was displayed in a public wooded area, right? He's not careful anymore."

Trench stood up. He had to pace.

"It doesn't fit," he repeated.

"So how do you explain it then?" said Campbell, leaning back in his chair.

Trench didn't respond. He couldn't explain it. It just didn't fit with where his gut had been telling him the case was going. Thoughts were jumping around his head but he didn't want to think out loud. Not with Campbell.

He was aware Campbell was watching him intently. He could feel him ready to challenge any ill-thought-out speculation. He was also becoming increasingly aware that that was all he had. Speculation. Some of Doctor Osbourne's actions had certainly jarred with him. He couldn't square them with how he would have expected the man to act when his daughter was missing. They raised questions, definitely. But this development was suddenly creating doubt in his mind.

Trench stopped pacing.

"I have to go. I have to speak with Osbourne."

"What are you talking about?" dismissed Campbell. "We're leaving in ten minutes to go see the Prime Minister."

"It'll have to wait. Tell her there's been an urgent development. We can brief her later."

"Sit down, man," barked Campbell. "You're not going anywhere. Get a hold of yourself."

"Look, Commander, this is—"

"No! You look," growled Campbell. "It's not up for debate. You can do whatever you have to do when we're done. Now sit down. We're going to agree exactly what we're going to say to her."

Trench stared at him. He realised this wasn't a fight he wanted to have. He had Campbell's backing for now and that was better than having him any other way. He sat back down.

"Fine," he said. "But I still don't think we should mention this to her."

"Why not? It's an important development. Maybe the most important so far. If she's calling us in because Osbourne told her about the ransom fiasco, then we can assume he'll tell her about this. I am not going to have her come back to me asking why I held this from her. That's not going to happen," insisted Campbell.

Hearing him put it like that, Trench realised he would never be able to dissuade Campbell. That was the ultimate worst-case scenario for him, the PM thinking he had withheld information. He decided that the quickest way to get back to the investigation was to just go along with whatever Campbell had already schemed up. He was certain he'd have schemed something up.

"How do you want to play it?" he said.

"We'll just tell her exactly what has happened," said Campbell, a sly look crossing his face. "One of the numerous avenues of investigation we've been pursing has produced this very strong evidence. Osbourne himself has confirmed it. Separately, we of course had to pursue the ransom avenue, despite our misgivings about its validity from the outset. We've now rounded up all members of the scamming ransom gang and they will feel the full force of Her Majesty's justice.

"We decided to let the media run with that line to give us cover for our pursuit of the real primary suspect. This was the avenue to which we assigned our lead detective, who duly cracked the case, inside of a week. Naturally, we're devastated at the grim probability that Vanessa has fallen victim to this madman. She wasn't his first, but she will be his last. He will never see the light of day again."

He looked at Trench expectantly. Trench nodded slowly. If that was how Campbell wanted to spin it, then that was up to him. Trench would simply sit there and nod along. The only hard part would be biting his tongue.

"Fine," said Trench. "I presume you'll do most of the talking. I'll answer any questions she asks me directly, but I'll keep it short. And feel free to jump in any time you want. For example, on every question."

Campbell stared at him for a long moment.

"I'm glad we understand each other then," he said. "Just try not to leave her with the mistaken impression that CID's lead detective is a stubborn, petulant, annoying ass, who won't collaborate with evidence uncovered by colleagues simply because he doesn't like them. I don't want her to think we're prone to operational dysfunction because of juvenile squabbles and tantrums."

"Yeah well, I'm sure she's acutely familiar with the concept," said Trench. "I take it that means you'll be answering any questions about the ransom drop? I was off pursuing our primary line of investigation at the time, after all."

"Yes, I'll handle that. And leave any questions about the missing ransom money to me too. I don't expect her to raise it, there's no reason she should be aware of any anomaly with that. But if she does, I'll take it. And for God's sake, do not mention any of the stuff you said to me yesterday about Osbourne."

Two million pounds that should have been used to save a young woman's life, but instead went missing in the most dubious of circumstances, was now simply an anomaly. Trench wanted to end this conversation. He wanted to be done with the briefing and get back to the investigation. Being so close to the sordid process of devising cover ups and creating spin made his skin crawl.

"Let's just go," he said.

Campbell checked his watch and agreed. They both stood and headed for the lifts.

# Forty

Downing Street was less than ten minutes' walk away. Dawn had not yet broken, leaving the streets in a dull twilight glow. It was dry, but a cutting wind blew in off the Thames. They walked briskly, Campbell with a *Johnston of Elgin* cashmere beanie covering his shorn bonce, his hands tucked deep inside his woollen overcoat.

They discussed the plan for briefing the press once they'd confirmed the latest developments. Trench let Campbell do most of the talking, only advising that they wait until they were absolutely certain before providing any updates to the press. Campbell nodded knowingly. Dealing with the media was his domain.

They broke off as they reached the security booth at the entrance to Downing Street. The young officers at the desk recognised Campbell, so the clearance process was swift.

The door to Number 10 opened just as they got to it. An officious young woman urgently beckoned them inside. She was dressed only in a blouse and skirt. Trench figured her urgency had more to do with the freezing wind now blowing through the open door than anything else. They stepped onto the infamous black and white chequered floor while the woman went over to a screen just inside the door.

"Good morning. Names please."

She then checked their names on the screen before nodding to herself.

"Please follow me," she said, marching swiftly off.

They duly followed and after a few seconds arrived in an ornately decorated drawing room. The orange walls and green, rigid-looking furniture seemed more fussy than functional to Trench, but the giant Persian rug had character.

"Please wait here. The Prime Minister will join you when she can," said the woman curtly.

When she left, both men remained standing. Trench guessed the furniture was designed to ensure guests did. He could appreciate the logic. Guests were less likely to linger if they were standing.

"This is the Terracotta Room," said Campbell in a hushed tone, glancing around. "Its name changes according to whatever colour the incumbent PM decides to decorate it."

"So why isn't it called the green and orange room? Or the Persian room?" said Trench. "Unpalatable connotations?"

Campbell stared at him with a mix of disappointment and rebuke, before turning to continue looking around the room. They stood in silence for only a few more minutes before the door opened again. Trench was surprised when Prime Minister Sarah Powers herself walked in. It was a good start. He'd assumed they'd have a long wait before she would make time to see them. She strode briskly over to them. She was followed by the woman who had greeted them at the door.

"Gentlemen, good morning," she said, firm but not unpleasant. "Leroy, nice to see you again."

"You too, Prime Minister," said Campbell, his smile wider than Trench had realised his face was capable of. "This is Detective Chief Inspector Trent Chambers from Met CID. He's been leading the investigation."

"Detective," she said, giving him a firm handshake and looking him directly in the eye. "Thank you for coming. I won't keep you long. Please, take a seat gentlemen. Would you like something to drink?"

She motioned to the couch behind where they stood, while the woman from reception stepped closer to take their drinks order. As both Campbell and Trench asked for black coffee, Trench noted that Powers pulled over a chair as opposed to sitting on the couch opposite them. The couches were separated by a large coffee table, so sitting in the seat meant she would be much closer to them.

"Usual tea for you Ma'am?" asked the young woman.

"Yes please, Becky, thank you," said Powers.

She then started speaking almost before Becky had turned to leave.

"Gentlemen, thank you for coming," she repeated. "I'd like an update on your investigation into finding Vanessa Osbourne please."

She glanced between Campbell and Trench as she spoke, clearly indifferent to whichever of the two men provided the update. She spoke quickly and had gotten straight to the point. Whilst her manner was forthright, she came across as genuine. There was even a certain warmth. None of the faux smiles, exaggerated conceit or laboured pomposity that characterised virtually every other politician Trench had ever encountered.

"Yes Ma'am, certainly," began Campbell, sitting up straighter in his seat. "The moment we learned she was missing, we set up a taskforce, codenamed Operation Lab—"

"Sorry, Leroy," interrupted Powers, holding up a hand. "I don't need the official report. I just want an update. Do you know where she is, and if not what are you doing to find her?"

As she spoke, she glanced at Trench. It was a subtle signal to communicate that if Campbell was here to provide the formalities, he could get out of the way now and hand over to the person who could talk about the investigation. It was deftly done. Still polite, but unmistakably firm.

"Uh, yes Ma'am, understood," said Campbell, interpreting the signal and realising he had started out on the wrong track. "The ransom demand was a hoax. We've rounded up the whole gang involved and we are positive they never had her. Last night, Trench – sorry, DCI Chambers here – discovered the location where our prime suspect, an ex-con named Howard Chapman, has taken previous women he's abducted. From our overnight search of that premises, we have strong reason to believe that Vanessa Osbourne was among the women he abducted—"

"What reason?" demanded Powers.

She said it with such force that Campbell almost flinched. She leant forward in her seat and clasped her hands together. Trench thought he saw a stricken look sweep across her face.

"What happened to the other women you're referring to?" she pressed, before Campbell had even answered her previous question.

Trench had observed thousands of people in countless conversations, judging their body language and trying to read their reactions. He was suddenly sure of one thing. They weren't here to get a bollocking on behalf of Doctor Osbourne. This was something else.

"Jewellery," said Campbell. "We found some of her jewellery at the scene. It's been confirmed by her father as belonging to her. We're also taking other samples from the location to try to confirm DNA as we speak. But early indications are grim. The rest of the women he's taken are dead. Murdered. We've recovered the bodies of three previous victims. There was torture involved, rape…sorry."

When he saw the Prime Minister's reaction, Campbell broke off, realising he may have gone into too much detail. The Prime Minister's face had frozen and she was staring off into the distance. Her hand slowly went to her face. Campbell looked down at the floor, as if giving her some space.

Trench kept watching her. For a couple of seconds she was miles away, before her eyes caught his.

"I know her…" she said softly. "This is…"

She broke off and lowered her head.

"I'm sorry," said Campbell. "The poor girl. It's a dreadful business."

A second later she raised her head and looked right at Trench, a little more composed now.

"I know her. She's active with the Party," she said, seemingly wanting to explain her reaction. "She pops around to our headquarters quite a bit. So you haven't found her…remains?"

"No," said Trench, deliberately brief, now watching her intently.

"Not yet," said Campbell at the same time.

"How sure are you that this man has taken her?" asked Powers.

She looked at Trench as she spoke but he stayed silent. He let Campbell answer, but held her glassing eyes. He was sending his own signal. This wasn't coming from him.

He was also trying to make sense of what he was seeing and hearing. He could feel his thoughts stirring, searching for order.

"We're sure it's her jewellery," said Campbell. "Or as sure as we can be. We're making every effort to find her bod—, remains, but uh, we're not giving up hope either. The reprobate is refusing to talk to us, but we'll press him as hard as we can."

"What about these other women you mentioned, did you find their bodies at the scene?" asked Powers, as the door to the Terracotta Room opened.

Becky walked in with a tray as Campbell answered.

"No, they were all found in separate places. Two in rivers, one dumped in a forest. Their abductions were months apart."

He broke off as Becky approached the table. The Prime Minister first looked away, then stood as Becky approached the table. Trench was sure her eyes had moistened as she did so. She strode over to the window as Becky put the cups on the table. The Prime Minister stood with her back to them as Becky then left the room.

Trench reached down to pick up his coffee. He glanced at the cups to see which was his. Two had black coffee so he picked one up. He saw that Becky had put the cup of tea nearest to the Prime Minister's seat. The tea bag was still in the cup, its label dangling down the side of the cup. A light slammed on inside his mind. The cogs inside his brain crashed into place. Shocked realisation gave him an almost physical jolt.

"Turmeric with Orange and Star Anise," he said out loud, his spine tingling.

Campbell turned to look at him quizzically.

"You said 'pops around' to your Headquarters," said Trench, louder this time.

The Prime Minister slowly turned from the window. She looked at Trench, tears now streaked down her face. She looked into his eyes. She knew he knew.

"That's why we couldn't find any condoms," said Trench.

Campbell spat a mouthful of coffee over himself. He practically threw his cup on the table as he turned to Trench.

"Jesus Christ, Trench, what the fu—," he exclaimed. "What are you on about?"

He turned to check if the Prime Minister had heard, though it was impossible she had not.

"Sorry Ma'am, I don't know what he's talking about."

But the look on her face made him realise that he was the only one in the room who didn't know what Trench was talking about. He looked back at Trench. Campbell was smart enough to say no more. Instead, he slowly turned back to the Prime Minister. She started walking slowly back to her seat. She had produced a tissue from somewhere and was dabbing her streaming eyes.

She sat down, picking up the tea and wrapping it in both hands. She took a sip, then raised her eyes to meet Trench's.

"Did you know before coming here?" she asked.

"No," said Trench. "We knew there was someone else. Her boyfriend told us that right at the beginning. I figured it was someone associated with the Party. Someone who could 'pop around' to her secret flat from Tory HQ. But I had no idea it was you until right now."

Campbell turned to stare at the Prime Minister.

"Stop looking at me like that, Leroy. I'm human too," she snapped, then turned back to Trench. "So, what are you going to do now?"

"First, I'm going to ask you if you had anything to do with her disappearance," said Trench, trying to remain calm despite the adrenaline now coursing through his veins.

"I understand," nodded Powers. "No, Detective, I did not. But before we go any further, I need to understand how this is going to play out. I appreciate most people, certainly those running our gutter press, do not believe I am entitled to a private life. I disagree. And I wish to keep my relationship with Vanessa private. I am not the scurrilous lech my predecessor was, far from it. But he permeated enough sleaze to sully this office for a generation. I do not wish to perpetuate that image of politics."

Trench looked back at her impassively. Campbell also remained silent, looking at her with a blank expression that was hard to read.

"But more importantly," she said, softer now. "People close to me and close to Vanessa would be hurt if this gets out. We have always sworn that we will do this properly. We will keep it out of the limelight and if we still feel the same way when I leave this office then we will make a proper go of it. Until that time, and despite the circumstances, I am adamant that my relationship with Vanessa remains private."

She held Trench's stare for a moment, then turned to Campbell with the same steady stare. Tears still dripped from her eyes, but there was a steeliness there too. Neither man spoke. Trench could feel that Campbell was even more tense than he was. He was also too savvy, or maybe too stunned, to fill the silence. After a moment, the Prime Minister continued.

"I believe this presents you with a dilemma. If you wish to continue this conversation as a police interview, then I cannot say any more. I will ask you to leave and direct any further attempt to speak with me to my lawyers. If that happens, the likelihood of us ever speaking again is negligible. You would be free to make public your theory that Vanessa and I were involved. But as theories go, I'm sure you'll agree this one will sound quite absurd, even to the most extreme conspiracy theorists out there. Because I can assure you, you won't find a single shred of evidence to back up your outlandish claims.

"And let's not forget, the credibility of police is hardly better than that of politicians nowadays. The best-case scenario is that you make the Met look like a sensationalist cabal trying to score political points in the perennial row over police funding. And for the avoidance of doubt, you would be the first two casualties of such a row. I doubt the Commissioner would hesitate to sacrifice the sources of such preposterous allegations," she turned to Campbell. There was no menace in her tone, it was all delivered matter-of-factly. "As you well know, Leroy, Jodie would be only too happy to be rid of you from her rear-view mirror."

She was referring to the current Police Commissioner of the Met, Jodie Hemmell. Having been in the job only a few years, Hemmell was mostly popular with both the rank and file and the general public – or rather the media, who controlled the perception of a public usually too bombarded with information to bother reading beyond tabloid headlines.

Popular or not, she was still the current occupant of the job Campbell was always rumoured to have his eye on. Although Trench doubted whether rumour was still an accurate description, given it was the Prime Minister making the point. Campbell's face betrayed nothing as Powers continued.

"However, I would rather not go down that route," she said, softening again. "Vanessa means a lot to me. I want to help you. To help her. Therefore, if we can continue this conversation off the record, meaning that nothing we discuss can ever leave this room, then I will provide you with as much information as I can. How do you wish to proceed?"

Campbell gave a slight nod, demonstrating his understanding of the dilemma. He briefly averted his gaze, turning to look toward the window. His brow furrowed in a show of deep concentration.

"We're off the record," announced Trench decisively, causing Campbell to quickly snap his head around. "None of what you tell us here will leave this room. Unless you lie or in some way mislead the investigation. If there's things you cannot tell us for whatever reason, then just say that. We haven't found Vanessa yet. We cannot be certain of her fate until we find her one way or another. Do not mislead us. Time is of the essence."

Powers looked at Trench, clearly a little surprised either by the answer or by the fact Trench had provided it rather than the much more senior Campbell. Campbell himself was also staring at Trench, his brow now frowning rather than furrowed.

"Trench, thank you," he started in a diplomatic tone, "But there are things—"

"You people can work through whatever bullshit you want later," said Trench. "I'll leave here when we're done and you can knock yourselves out. But if there's information that could help us with the investigation then that is the priority."

Trench knew that they would ultimately have agreed to speak off the record anyway. The other option was a non-runner. Campbell was delaying only so he could figure out how best to use the situation to his own political advantage. Powers' thinly veiled threats were just the opening salvos to that negotiation. But Trench was not about to sit through that process. Not when it meant delaying or even compromising the information that Powers provided them.

Campbell glared at him for another long moment, before his face broke into a smile, genuine as a nine-bob note.

"Of course," he said, then turned to Powers. "We all want the same thing here. Trench fancies himself as a bit of a gun slinger when it comes to how he speaks to his superiors. A real maverick." He smiled patronisingly. "But he of course speaks for all of us right now. We are off the record. Anything you can tell us to help with the investigation will not leave this room, Ma'am."

"Thank you, gentlemen," said Powers. "We are all agreed. Now, where do we start?"

"When was the last time you saw her?" said Trench.

"Last Tuesday evening. At the dinner. I'm sure you've watched footage from that event."

"So you didn't see her after the event?"

"No, I did not," Powers shook her head.

"But you had planned to meet at her flat afterwards?" pressed Trench.

Powers delayed slightly before responding. She lowered her head and wiped another tear from her eye. Trench was watching her for any sign of deception. He wasn't seeing any. He was seeing genuine grief.

"That's right," she said softly. "That's where we sometimes met, if not here. I would always call from the car before going to the flat. I had to be sure she was there. But that night she didn't answer. When I tried a few minutes later it went straight to voicemail, like she'd turned it off. I presumed she was in a huff or something, she could be like that sometimes. I drove by the flat. I even stopped the car nearby for a little while and tried her phone a few more times but it went straight to voicemail each time. Eventually I had to let it go.

"And don't get any ideas, Detective. I meant what I said about there being no evidence out there. The very small number of people who know about this would never, ever betray that confidence."

Trench just nodded. But she was correct. He was indeed thinking about who else knew of their relationship. A driver and some security people at the very least.

"How small a number of people?" he said.

"A handful," she said, waving a hand dismissively. "That's not germane to your investigation."

"Unless someone thought she was a national security risk…"

She looked at him for a moment before responding.

"I understand you need to ask your questions, no matter how preposterous they are. And I will give you as much information as I can. As Leroy said, we all want the same thing. But you will have to take it from me that you are barking up the wrong tree with that line of thinking. Which is to say, you would be wasting time. Next question."

"Fair enough," said Trench, though he was far from satisfied. "We can come back to that later if needs be."

"And I thought you said she's been abducted by this murderer?" said Powers.

At this point, Campbell also turned to look at Trench, raising his eyebrows to acknowledge the validity of the question. Trench had to be careful here. Campbell had already provided the Prime Minister with a strong indication that Vanessa had fallen victim to Chapman. Trench did not want to contradict him. Especially considering he had no alternate explanation for the jewellery. But he was still not yet ready to close his mind to alternate theories for what had happened to her.

"Until we find her, we need to keep an open mind," he said, before quickly moving on. "How long have you been seeing her?"

"Since early summer," replied Powers.

"How did your relationship start?"

Powers smiled nostalgically for a split second, before it was gone.

"I suppose you could say she played me. Not my finest hour, admittedly. But, anyway, I called her bluff. She's very charismatic, and charming. She had ample access through her activities with the Party. She was at all the functions at HQ and always seemed to make a beeline for me. And I enjoyed her company. I knew what she was doing of course. But I was flattered. She told me later that she'd heard rumours of a previous fling I'd had and so decided to try it on. And believe me, she has a way of getting what she wants. She can be incredibly single minded."

"What do you mean, you called her bluff?"

"Well, as I say it's not my finest hour. After we'd been together for a little while, she told me that she had originally intended to blackmail me," Powers gave a choked chuckle. "Can you believe that? Oh, the blind ambition of youth. When it came to it, she almost jokingly put it to me, but I simply refused. I laughed it off. And she had changed her mind anyway. It turned out she had fallen quite hard too."

"Blackmail?" said Trench, confused. "Why would she blackmail you? She doesn't need money."

"No, not money," said Powers. "Her father's company is a key supplier to the Ministry of Defence. It's a huge contract and it's coming up for retender in the new year. It'll be a public tender of course, and it's by no means a forgone conclusion that they'll retain the contract. Vanessa's original intention had been to blackmail me into awarding the contract to her father's company again. It was a ludicrous plan for someone so smart. We laughed about it later, but that's why she came on to me in the first place."

Trench was struck by the reference to Clarence Osbourne. He had known he would come up in their discussion, not least because they had mistakenly assumed the

Prime Minister had summoned them at his behest. But this context was unexpected. His mind ticked faster as he thought through what it could mean.

"Was her father involved in this plan to blackmail you?" he asked.

"No, no," Powers said with a laugh that had no humour in it. "He had no idea. I doubt he even knows the contract is under threat. He believes the retender exercise is a formality. Vanessa had figured out it wasn't though. She has worked at Futurnautics from time to time and she learned from other senior leaders of the company that the renewal was going to be tougher than her father believed. She told me she tried speaking to Clarence about it but he didn't pay her any heed. So she decided to do something about it. That's her style. She's quite head strong. Crazy as the plan was, I confess to quite admiring her for trying it."

"Why didn't he believe her, do you think? When we spoke with him, he spoke highly of Vanessa's aptitude for the business."

"Absolutely. She's very bright. But I suspect Clarence doesn't listen to anyone anymore."

"Why would you say that?"

"He was quite brilliant in the field a decade ago, but he has succumbed to hubris in recent times," said Powers. "Perhaps it's inevitable with so much success and wealth. His focus has probably waned, and that doesn't cut it in the industry we're talking about. Innovations are rapid. There are no margins for error or slippage. The money involved is measured in the billions, or hundreds of billions, of pounds."

Campbell, who had remained silent throughout the exchange so far, turned slightly in his seat to watch Trench. He had clearly noticed that Trench was steering the conversation toward Clarence Osbourne. Trench avoided his gaze for a moment, but then caught his eye. Campbell stared hard at him.

Trench knew what he was conveying. He had previously warned Trench not to bring up any of his questions about Doctor Osbourne with the Prime Minister. He was now reminding Trench of that warning.

But Trench was deliberately ignoring the warning. He knew there were very few people that could give him an accurate picture of Doctor Osbourne. He intended to get as much information as he could while she still seemed willing to talk. He was also conscious their time was running out. She would be summoned away to her next engagement at any moment.

"So this contract is worth billions to Futurnautics?" he said.

"I can't get into specifics obviously," said Powers, "But that's a fair assumption."

As she answered there was a gentle knock on the door, and Becky stepped inside the room.

"Excuse me, Ma'am," she said, "They're all seated in the Cabinet Room. They're ready and waiting for you."

Becky left the room again, but the intrusion had broken the momentum of the conversation. The Prime Minster sat back in her seat and absent-mindedly straightened the legs of her suit pants. She wiped her eyes again, but the tears had by now dried up. The transformation from stricken woman concerned about a lover to necessarily cold, clinical Prime Minister was swift.

"I must go," she said, standing up. "Thank you again for coming. I'm not sure I've been of any help to you in the end. Please keep me posted, with whatever you discover. But I'm glad I'm forewarned about your finding Vanessa's jewellery. It would've been a dreadful shock to learn of that on the news. I hope your presumptions are wrong of course, and that she is out there somewhere laughing at all this fuss. That was my first suspicion, that she has simply taken off somewhere for a break. And I shall cling to that until it is confirmed otherwise."

"One last question," said Trench as she turned to go.

She paused and then nodded for him to continue.

"If Vanessa's blackmail attempt hadn't been so uh, well received by you, what would've happened to Futurnautics' retender bid?"

Powers thought about it for a second before responding.

"At best, they would have been disqualified from participating. At worst, people – or Vanessa, at least – would have gone to prison."

# Forty-One

Trench hated walking slowly. Right now he felt like a race horse chomping at the bit. But Campbell never changed his slow, deliberate strut. Trench was walking half a step in front of him, arguing over his shoulder.

"I told you, I didn't know. I had no fucking idea. If I had known, I'd have been pushing to interview her as soon as I found out."

"Okay," said Campbell, finally sounding satisfied. "Well, I'm not often surprised, Trench, I'll give you that. But I damn near shit my pants in there."

Trench said nothing. He was pulsing with energy. He stepped up the pace, hoping Campbell would do likewise. But he just ended up a further few paces in front, so had to slow down again.

"Well done for putting it together," said Campbell, with a still-disbelieving shake of the head. "But I didn't like where you went with it afterwards."

Trench had anticipated the rebuke and decided not to respond. There was nothing Campbell could say that would put him off track now. He desperately wanted time alone to think through the morning's developments, to try to make sense of them. He had not had a moment to himself to fully digest everything. But he was sure of one thing. Regardless of the jewellery, Clarence Osbourne remained stubbornly close to the centre of the case.

"I warned you not to air your questions about Doctor Osbourne with her," Campbell went on. "You came pretty close to turning the whole conversation into a background check on him."

"I didn't bring him up, she did. He was bang in the middle of her explanation about how the whole affair started, you heard her. Vanessa Osbourne was bribing the Prime Minister on behalf of her father's company."

"That is not what I heard," insisted Campbell. "There may have been some half-baked, childish charade at the outset, but it was nothing more than a running joke between two consenting adults. She just told us they even laughed about the notion of blackmail. Osbourne doesn't know about his daughter's antics. And it certainly wasn't anything to do with his company."

"Just because sh—"

"Listen to me, Trench," barked Campbell.

He stopped walking and held up a hand to halt Trench's words.

"I've indulged enough of your concerns about Osbourne," Campbell continued. "You even had me wondering about him after we spoke yesterday. But to carry them on now, even after we can definitively place Vanessa inside that madman's torture chamber, is too much. It crosses the line, and you risk jeopardising the investigation. Let it go. You need to focus all your efforts on finding Vanessa. Most probably that means finding her corpse. That is your priority now. At least it will provide closure, and whatever modicum of solace that can bring to the people that loved her."

"Fine," said Trench, as he started walking again.

"I mean it, Trench," stated Campbell, still standing in the same spot. "Find her. Maybe then you'll think differently about your next conversation with Osbourne."

"Fine," repeated Trench, continuing to walk. He'd had enough. He couldn't wait around any longer. "I have to go. I'll call you later."

"Make sure you do," he heard Campbell call after him.

He quickened his pace, marching faster. It was pointless to continue squabbling with Campbell. Instead, he turned his thoughts to all the new information and how it fit with everything else he'd learned so far. Snippets of conversations he'd had with Doctor Osbourne were jumbling through his mind, mixed with images of Savannah Diaz's body in the darkened woods. Images of Callow stepping over the prostrate kidnapper and grabbing the bags, jumping into the car and speeding off. Of Chapman, sniffing the air in the back of the car after his arrest. Of the inside of his torture chamber, bloodstained knives dangling from the grimy walls, the storm blasting them as they stood in the doorway, peering into hell.

Trench quickened his pace still more. The steady rhythm of steps was jolting his mind, helping to order his thoughts. The chilly breeze heightened his senses. He was back at Vanessa's house, searching through her bureaux and finding drawers full of jewellery. Clothes and shoe boxes everywhere, the full drawer of underwear in her bedroom.

He flashed back to the conversation they'd walked in on between Doctor Osbourne and his wife when the ransom letter had arrived. He knew it was fake. He'd been vociferously arguing with his wife until his face went red. He only conceded when she had screamed at him and stormed out of the room.

And now it turned out that Vanessa's secret lover was none other than Prime Minister Sarah Powers. Campbell wasn't the only one stunned by that. The fact alone was shocking enough, but how it fit with the rest of the mystery left Trench at a complete loss.

He thought again about the circle of people close to Powers who must have known about the affair. He had to admit that he'd been much less repelled by Powers than he'd expected. She was probably the first politician he'd ever come across that he didn't instantly despise. He may even have somewhat warmed to her. But he immediately dismissed her assurances that all those close to her who knew of the affair were beyond suspicion. He would never take anyone's word for who should or should not be considered a suspect in a case.

He started thinking about who would have known about the affair and what their prerogative would be. Did the affair make Vanessa a security risk? Powers had told them about Vanessa's intended plan to bribe her.

Yes, Trench realised. It was certainly not a stretch to consider Vanessa a national security risk. And if that was the case, how would the security services react? How would they counter that risk?

Presumably there were people responsible for evaluating the risk and deciding how to neutralise it. If the Prime Minister was as smitten as she seemed to be, then there must be some protocol which enabled those people to eliminate the risk without the permission of the Prime Minister. He began to think specifically of who amongst the Prime Minister's staff might know about the affair.

The most obvious person was her driver. He couldn't think of any reason a driver would have an issue, but then realised the driver was probably also part of the Prime Minister's security detail. In fact, was it possible the driver was the only person who knew of the affair? Could the Prime Minister travel in a single-car motorcade, late on a November night after a Party event in the Dorchester, given the ostensibly short distance back to Downing Street?

Trench didn't know, but it wouldn't be difficult to find out. He made a mental note to do so, but then became agitated. He began to feel unsure whether he was getting carried away with what he'd learned. He had no doubt Her Majesty's secret service was as capable of nefarious black ops in the name of national security as any other nation. But she was hardly the first Prime Minister to have an affair, as she herself had alluded to. And he wasn't sure how this theory fit with what they already knew about the case.

A thought suddenly struck him. It stopped him in his tracks. What if Doctor Osbourne *did* learn of the affair? Powers had insisted he was not aware, but she had also made it sound like Osbourne was some kind of dithery old fool. That did not fit. All of Trench's instincts had told him that Osbourne was anything but an old fool. That feeling had grown stronger the more Trench had considered his actions. Maybe it was the Prime Minister who was underestimating Doctor Osbourne. She can't have spent much time with him in recent years.

Trench started walking again, even faster now. He was only a few minutes from Charing Cross Station. His thoughts came rapidly. Doctor Osbourne had dealt with the MoD for years. He was privy to clandestine workings of the government's security and defence apparatus. He would understand the implications for his daughter if she had put herself in the position of being considered a national security risk.

And he would act to protect her.

Trench had to speak with Doctor Osbourne. Right now. It could no longer wait. As he reached Trafalgar Square, Trench pulled out his phone and dialled.

"Hey mate," answered Krige. "You get my email?"

"Yes, thanks," said Trench, though he had forgotten about the email. "But for now, I just want to check whether Doctor Osbourne is at home right now? I'm on my way to see him so just want to make sure I haven't missed him."

"Oh, sorry mate, you have missed him," said Krige. "I think he stayed at his office last night."

"His office? At Blenheim?" said Trench, confused.

"No, not at the house. He has an apartment at the company's office in town. He stays there when he's super busy or whatever."

"Okay, thanks," said Trench, hanging up.

He cursed to himself. He decided to call Osbourne directly and arrange to meet him. He'd been putting off calling him because he wanted to gauge his reaction in person to anything that was said. But now he put greater importance on just securing the meeting. There had been too many distractions and delays. All roads were leading to Doctor Osbourne.

Trench felt he now had enough to ask him directly about his suspicious activity, rather than run a play trying to rumble him. He still wanted to do that in person, so decided he would keep it as brief as possible on the phone, just informing Doctor Osbourne that he was on his way and to remain where he was.

He scrolled through his phone, found the number and hit dial. After five rings the phone went to voicemail. Trench was still deciding whether to leave a voicemail when he heard the beep.

"Uh, Doctor Osbourne, good morning," he started, still trying to decide what to say. "It's DCI Chambers from Met Police. It's just after eight AM on Wednesday morning. I'm calling because I want to arrange to meet with you as soon as possible. Please call me as soon as you get this message. I will come to meet you wherever you are. It's urgent. Thank you. My number should be on your screen there from the missed call, if you don't already have it."

He hung up, annoyed that the message had been rambling and that he had messed up the way he had said the time. When he arrived at Charing Cross station a couple of minutes later, he decided not to go inside. He took out his phone and called Jazz.

"The Prime Minister didn't send you to Broadmoor, then?" she answered.

It took Trench a second to realise that she was joking, still working on the assumption that the Prime Minister had summoned them to bollock them for the failed ransom drop. Broadmoor, the UK's highest security psychiatric hospital, was home to some of the nation's most dangerous criminals.

"Not quite," said Trench. "Though that would've been less of a shock. Are you in the station?"

"Ugh, sounds grim. Hope you told her you weren't involved with the drop. Yep, I'm here. We just finished the morning briefing. Not a huge amount to update you on but I'll tell you when I see you. You on your way back?"

"I'm outside, but I'm not coming in. Can you meet me at the Portrait right now? There's a lot I need to update you on."

"On my way," said Jazz. "I've got something to tell you too. I'll be there in five."

Trench hung up and headed back toward Trafalgar Square. He wanted privacy for the discussion they were about to have. He intended to update her on everything he had learned that morning and on what he thought it all meant. It was not a conversation he wanted to have inside the police station.

# Forty-Two

Jazz stared at Trench, her mouth hanging open, her head craned forwards. She had stopped asking questions and was just trying to take it all in. He told her everything, including about Vanessa's affair with the Prime Minister. He reasoned that the figurative four walls of the Terracotta Room extended to include his partner. There could be no secrets on cases they worked together.

She sat stunned, incredulous.

"Say something, Jazz. You look like you've been lobotomised."

She blinked a few times before speaking.

"I don't even know where to start," she said. "It's a lot to take in…"

"Yeah," agreed Trench.

"And there's some things, I really, really don't want to be thinking about," she said, trying to shake the thoughts from her mind. "Her flat, those—"

"Let's not go there," said Trench, not wanting to think about it himself.

He wanted to soundboard the working theory that had begun forming in his head. He had alluded to it while he was updating Jazz, but now he wanted to put it all together and test it. To pull it apart and see if it sounded credible and fit with the facts they now knew.

"Let's just focus on what we've got," he said. "Some things we know for sure, and for others we're going to have to trust our instincts."

"You sound like you've got some ideas?"

"I do," said Trench. "First, I'm convinced that Vanessa wasn't taken by Chapman. It—"

"Shit!" said Jazz. "I forgot to tell you. When I got to the station this morning I checked the tapes from the interview yesterday. I watched Ward's interview with Chapman. Afterwards, I noticed there was another tape there too. I checked it and it was Callow and Burgess interviewing Chapman, some time after Ward."

"So they did speak with him."

"Yeah, but not for long," said Jazz. "And they got a totally different reaction. He just no commented his way through Ward's interview. Literally not a single word other than no comment for the whole thing. Not even a fuck you. But then later they brought him back in. Callow immediately started by saying they were questioning him about the disappearance of Vanessa Osbourne. Chapman watched him for a while. He seemed wary and suspicious. When Callow asked when he had taken her and what he had done with her, Chapman screamed at him. Said something about being framed and police corruption. Plenty of fuck you's after that. His solicitor had to step in. Callow and Burgess left. They were only in there for a few minutes but they definitely got to him."

Trench considered this. He thought about how it fit with the rest of his working theory. He glanced around the room as he gathered his thoughts. They were sitting in the Portrait Restaurant on top of the National Portrait Gallery in Trafalgar Square. Trench always liked the ambiance here when he wanted to think. It was large, with well-spaced tables, and at this hour of the morning was deserted. It was where they came when they wanted to be sure there would be no other police within earshot. You could never be sure with the other coffee shops and cafes near the station.

After a couple of minutes, he decided this didn't change his theory. In fact, it probably supported it. He let out a joyless snort.

"Shit," he said. "You know we're in trouble when the serial murderer is the only one telling the truth."

"You think?" said Jazz grimly.

"Yeah. I think he's telling the truth. Chapman didn't take her. It just doesn't fit with anything else we know about him or his MO."

"Then what about the jewellery? Is Osbourne lying that it's hers?"

"Possibly," said Trench. "But unlikely. It'll be checked and it would be too easy to prove it wasn't hers."

"Right, so it is her jewellery. Which means..."

"Callow planted it," said Trench. "It's the only thing that fits."

"Callow... How does he fit into it?"

"I don't know yet," admitted Trench. "But it's the only thing that makes sense. We know he was at the tennis club last night. When I spoke with Danny Kenner this morning he made a comment about Callow being all over the place, getting in the way, messing the scene. That's obviously when he planted it. Then he took the pictures. Kenner also told me he saw Callow texting right after taking the pictures. He thought he was sending them to me as SIO.

"But he was obviously sending them to Osbourne. It didn't feel right this morning when Campbell told me Osbourne had already ID'd the jewellery. It was too soon for Callow to send Osbourne pictures like that, and too quick for Osbourne to have confirmed. It must have been choreographed."

"What are we saying here, Trench? Callow and Osbourne are working together?"

"It looks that way," said Trench, though not without some doubt in his tone.

"Why?"

"I don't know yet," admitted Trench.

"And how?" said Jazz. "How does Callow even know him?"

"I don't know," said Trench again. "But it's the only thing that fits. Callow's been skulking around since he's been involved. His stunt with the ransom must be a part of it too. That's been bothering me, and I still can't figure it out. When it happened I presumed he was nicking the ransom money. I certainly wouldn't put that past him. But when I heard about the jewellery this morning, it made me think there's more to it. He's more involved, somehow."

"Wait, what does this mean for Vanessa? Where is she?" asked Jazz.

"I don't know that either," said Trench. "But I think I know who does."

"Who?"

"Osbourne," he said. "I keep coming back to him. He knew from the start that the ransom demand was fake. That's why he gave us the bogus ransom money. He knew there was no downside to using fake money, even if the ransomer discovered it was fake. Then he ran that misdirection with his press conference. He made it look like he wanted everyone out looking for her. But all that did was create confusion and clog up Operation Labrador, and the entire emergency services. And now the jewellery. More misdirection. He's at the centre of it all."

Jazz was silent for a moment. After a moment she began to look doubtful.

"And he's buying Callow off for his help?"

Trench nodded.

"That's the only explanation that fits."

"It's quite a conspiracy, Trench," said Jazz.

Trench looked at her. He knew she was right, but he wasn't seeing any other possibility.

"And you still haven't said why," she said. "Why would Osbourne do all this?"

"I get you're sceptical," said Trench. "I am too. But this is what the evidence is telling us. Just keep that in mind. Because the 'why' part is where it starts to get a little stretched…"

"Starts?" said Jazz. "It started looking stretchy from the bit where we point the finger at Osbourne for being responsible his own daughter's disappearance."

"Responsible, maybe. Or maybe he just helped her. I don't know why yet. But based on what we learned this morning, I have a theory—"

"Right, where we begin to get a little stretched," she said, no longer keeping the scepticism out of her voice.

"Just hear me out," said Trench. "If Osbourne somehow learned of Vanessa's affair with the PM, and worse, that she'd tried to bribe the PM, what would he do?"

"Who knows. Go fucking ballistic, probably."

"Okay, but after that."

"I don't know, Trench, what?"

"Don't forget he knows how the government works. He's been doing deals with them for decades. More importantly, he knows how the security services work. His first instincts would be to protect her, Jazz. To get her out of harm's way. That's what parents do. Shit, if Milo ever got himself into something like this, there's nothing I wouldn't do."

"So you're saying he's helped her disappear?" said Jazz.

"And all this other stuff he's been doing, this misdirection, is to further cover for her," confirmed Trench, nodding.

Jazz was silent for a moment as she thought it through. Trench continued speaking.

"When I asked him whether he'd checked his other properties, he said yes immediately—"

"I know, you told me that. But he had only checked their security cameras, which you don't think is enough."

"Yes, but not only that. He also said he'd only checked his properties in the UK. What about other properties overseas?"

"But we found her passport," protested Jazz. "It was in her house."

"I know, but he's a billionaire. He's got his own private jets. I'm sure he could get her out of the country off to some place where they're a little less strict on passport control. I'm sure there's plenty of places where they'd happily accept an envelope full of cash over a passport. Although he could probably get her a passport no problem anyway. We know it's not that hard."

"And then what? He fakes her death?" said Jazz. "Tees it up so everyone thinks she was raped and murdered by a serial sadist? Bit over the top isn't it."

"That's the part I haven't figured out yet," admitted Trench. "Maybe it's just more misdirection. Throw everyone off to give him time to sort everything out with the security services."

They sat in silence for a moment, mulling what they had discussed. Trench liked it up to a point, but he had to admit it was far from watertight.

"There's a lot we don't know," he sighed. "I know it gets a little loose on the why part. But we have enough to ask Osbourne directly what's going on. I'm going to call him again and we'll go see him right now."

He took out his phone and called Doctor Osbourne again. Again, there was no answer. He decided against leaving another message. He looked at his watch. It didn't feel right to him that Osbourne would be away from his phone for such a long time.

"He's avoiding my call."

"Maybe," said Jazz.

"He must be," said Trench.

He put his phone down on the table but then picked it immediately back up.

"But he's not the only one we need to get answers from," he said as he dialled another number.

"Who—," started Jazz, before she twigged. "Callow?"

Trench nodded as the phone made the connection. It was answered after only a few rings.

"Hello?"

"We need to talk," said Trench. "Where are you?"

"About what?" said Callow.

"The investigation. Where are you?"

"I'm down at Chapman's lair. We're leading this case now, I presume you know that?"

"Right. I'm on my way," said Trench.

"Is this about the jewellery?" asked Callow. "I meant to send you some pictures, now you're leading Labrador again. But I got a little excited when I found them last night and sent them directly to old man Osbourne. I presume you've heard. They're hers. She was here."

"We can talk about that when I get there."

"Look uh, Chambers," said Callow, sounding contrite. "I didn't mean to step on toes. I wasn't trying to steal your thunder. I had his number and I saw the jewellery and it just made sense to check, you know. It's still your case, I know that."

Hearing Callow's false contrition, and knowing he was trying to play him, riled Trench.

"Let me ask you something, Callow," he said, unable to bite his tongue. "How many pictures of jewellery did you take?".

"Uh, I don't know, half a dozen maybe. Why?"

"And how many did you send to Osbourne?"

Callow didn't reply. Trench figured that if the move was indeed choreographed, then Callow had probably only sent Osbourne the pictures he knew were of Vanessa's jewellery, and not that of any of the other victims. Which would at least cast suspicion that the identification of Vanessa's jewellery was just going through the motions. Otherwise, surely Callow would have sent pictures of all the jewellery found at the scene.

Callow was probably belatedly thinking the same thing, and also realising that given text messages were time stamped, there was no way to rectify the mistake.

"I sent the ones that fit her style," said Callow after a pause. "And that looked expensive. Anyway, what does it matter? He's positive it's hers, if that's what you're trying to check with Osbourne? I'll send you all the pictures myself, but you just said you're coming down here, right? You should. You can see everything for yourself. You can join the search too. The dogs will be here later as well."

"Yeah, I'll do that," said Trench. "See you later. And then we can talk properly, Callow. About everything."

Trench killed the call.

"Bullshit," he said to Jazz.

He quickly relayed Callow's side of the call to her.

"So now he can tell what style of jewellery a 22-year old woman would wear?" he said. "Plus he seems to know I've been trying to call Osbourne. Osbourne must've called him, which means he knows we're looking for him. Callow stinks, Jazz. He's in it up to his bollocks."

"Well if he is, then you just tipped our hand," she admonished. "You basically told him you have doubts about the jewellery."

"Yeah, I know," said Trench, annoyance with himself growing. "Maybe it doesn't matter. Let's just hit him with both barrels when we get there. I doubt he's got a big enough shovel to dig himself out of the shit heap he's in."

They both stood up to leave.

"You want to go see him before Osbourne?" asked Jazz.

"At least we know where he is," said Trench. "Osbourne could be anywhere. Especially now he knows we're looking for him."

# Forty-Three

Jazz kept her foot on the pedal as they tore through south London, siren wailing. They were travelling much faster than in the storm the previous day. Trench tried Doctor Osbourne's phone again, but again it went unanswered. He was now convinced he was deliberately avoiding him. After ten minutes he gave it another try. He knew it wouldn't be answered, but he wanted to squeeze Osbourne. He imagined him sitting somewhere staring at the phone, pulling at his collar as police persistently hounded him.

"No answer," he said unnecessarily. "But he's going to have to answer our questions sooner or later."

Then he remembered something else.

"Did you print off that attachment I emailed you earlier?"

"In my bag," said Jazz.

Trench reached around and picked up her backpack from behind the driver's seat. He quickly found the printout. It was only a couple of pages of single line entries. Each line showed a date and time, a name, car reg and whether they were entering or leaving Blenheim. Trench quickly scanned down to the date he was looking for. The previous Tuesday evening. The night of the gala dinner. He ran his finger down the entries for that date, narrowing in on the those for late that evening. Then he checked the entries for the small hours of the following morning.

"Shit," he said.

"What?"

"It's not here."

"What, Trench? Explain, will you," said Jazz. "What is that, I only glanced at it? Looked like a travel log but there's no title on it."

"It's Blenheim," he said. "All cars coming and going in the past two weeks."

"Okay. What's not there?"

"Osbourne. I thought maybe he'd left that night—"

He broke off, quickly realising there was another possibility. He studied the printout, this time going backwards through the same day. He found what he was looking for at 0717 that morning. He went forward again, and found the expected corresponding entry late afternoon the next day. He tapped the printout with his finger.

"Knew it," he said.

Jazz quickly turned to look at him before putting her eyes back on the road.

"Tell me."

"Osbourne left home early on Tuesday morning and didn't return until the following day," he said, turning to Jazz. "He wasn't at home at the time Vanessa went missing."

*

Jazz killed the siren but kept the blue lights on as she sped through the rural roads on the approach to Green Lawns Tennis Club. Now more familiar with the area, she made the distance in a fraction of the time it had taken the day before. When they got there she turned onto the club's driveway, but it was so crowded with vehicles she could only make it to the edge of the parking area. There were even more vehicles than the previous day. The majority were from various Forensic Units, though the one parked in front of them was a Dog Support Unit.

Jazz pulled in and they both got out. It was colder here than in the city. A thick white mist rose steadily from the surrounding fields, still soaked from the previous day's downpour. The drab setting was eerily quiet. No birdsong or crickets chirping, nor any sound of wildlife. Just the faint din of distant barking.

"Just a sec," said Jazz, grabbing a thick winter jacket from the backseat. "I'm prepared this time. Bloody freezing down here."

"Just be glad it's stopped raining," said Trench, regretting he hadn't changed out of the suit he'd worn for the meeting with the Prime Minister.

A uniformed officer stepped out of a marked police car and walked over to them. He had a clipboard in one hand and raised the other in a halt sign as he spoke.

"Names and ranks," he said.

Trench responded with both names, and for good measure added he was SIO for the investigation. He didn't say for which investigation and the uniform didn't ask.

As the uniform noted their names on the crime scene log, Trench glanced around at the other vehicles. He didn't immediately see the one he was looking for. They began walking toward the clubhouse. He saw another couple of DSU vehicles but still couldn't see a grey Ford Mondeo anywhere.

"Hang on a sec," he said, turning around.

He walked swiftly back to the uniform, reaching him just as he opened his car door.

"Hey, let me see that log," Trench said.

"Eh?" grunted the officer, turning around.

"The scene log," said Trench, holding out his hand. "Give it to me."

The uniform paused, as if searching for a reason not to hand it over. Apparently failing to find one, he handed it to Trench. Trench ran his eye down the list, looking for the familiar registration. It was near the top, having arrived early that morning. But it wasn't the arrival time that made him react.

"Fucking bastard," he spat.

He thrust the log back into the hands of the uniform and marched back over to where Jazz was standing. She could see the fury on his face.

"What's up?" she said.

"He's gone," seethed Trench through gritted teeth, rummaging for his phone. "Left about half an hour ago. That fuc—"

The clubhouse doors burst open. Two officers dressed in waterproof overalls and heavy boots hurried out. Daniel Kenner was right behind them. They immediately turned and hurried down the side of the building. They hadn't seen Trench and Jazz approach.

"Kenner," Trench called out.

Kenner turned his head, but didn't stop moving until he spotted them. Then he beckoned furiously for them to come over.

"What's going on?" said Trench as they approached.

"Good timing," said Kenner. "One of the DSUs just reported in. He thinks they've found something. Let's go."

A shiver shot down Trench's spine. He glanced at Jazz. She had a similarly confused, apprehensive look on her face. She raised her eyebrows in a questioning manner. The Dog Support Units had search dogs trained in the full range of specialisms, from drugs to explosives, to humans being trafficked inside trucks. Trench knew the dogs currently at the scene were not trained in any of those disciplines, but the question came out anyway.

"What type of dogs?"

"Cadaver," responded Kenner.

"Lead the way," said Trench.

Kenner turned and started after the two DSU officers, who had not stopped. One of them held a radio, and was clearly communicating with their colleague somewhere out in the surrounding fields, getting directions. They were too far in front for Trench to hear what was being said, but the one with the radio occasionally pointed, indicating the direction they should go. He led them out of the tennis club grounds and into the field beyond. Whatever the field was used for during spring, it was now just a mush of mud and nettles.

Trench's foot sank deep with the first step. He could feel the freezing mud squelching inside his shoes. It was soon deep enough to cover his ankle and halfway up his shin. Jazz cursed beside him, being only slightly more appropriately dressed in ankle high boots. The thought occurred that another suit and probably shoes were headed for the dump, but it was only a flicker. He was too angry for the thought to register.

He was furious that Callow had left despite knowing that Trench was coming to speak with him. Trench replayed their phone call in his head, but was convinced there had been no room for doubt. Callow could not have been mistaken. He knew Trench was coming here to speak with him. But he had left anyway. Trench's anger began to give way to something else. Stirring concern.

"I wasn't expecting you here," said Kenner as they walked. "Callow left a while ago to meet you at the station."

"He told you that?" said Trench.

"Yeah. Not as if I asked. I couldn't give a flying fuck where he goes. But he told me to give you a message if I saw you first."

"What message?"

"Said he was gone home to get his jewellery degree, so when he saw you at the station later you could shove it up your ass," said Kenner, followed by a tut. "Hilarious as always."

Both Trench and Jazz stopped walking and stared at Kenner. It caused Kenner to stop walking too.

"What?" said Kenner.

They both stared at him for a long moment. A rush of rage pulsed through Trench. The message was clear. An unambiguous fuck you from Callow. There could be no doubt now. It was no longer a case of figuring out *if* Callow was involved. Now it was a case of finding out exactly what he had done.

"Motherfucker," said Trench, turning to Jazz. "I'm going to...We've got to get him, Jazz."

"What do you want to do?" said Jazz, glancing around.

They were knee deep in mud in the middle of a steaming field. Trench felt an urgent desire to immediately go after Callow. But he was also being pulled to find out what had set the dogs off. He looked back at the clubhouse and then forward at the DSU officers ahead. He knew what they had to do. He didn't want to give Callow too much of a head start, but they couldn't leave without knowing what was ahead. He felt a growing sense of foreboding.

"We check out whatever this is first, then we shift out of here. Let's go."

Both Kenner and Jazz nodded and they started after the DSU officers again. The mud tugged at Trench's shoes. He had to clench his toes tightly to hold them on. At the end of the field, they had to scramble over a waist-high fence made of wood reinforced with wire. This led to an even bigger field, which rose steadily ahead of them. They could just make out the heads of the two DSU officers ahead, obscured by the mist and disappearing down the other side of the hill. They trudged along in silence. The upward slope made the going much more sluggish. Trench's feet were so numb with cold that he had to look down to check if he was still wearing his shoes.

When they reached the top of the hill, they saw where the DSU teams had congregated. They were by a row of bushes about a hundred yards to the right. At first Trench thought the row of bushes looked odd. It seemed to mark the boundary of the field, but zigzagged rather than running in a straight line. Only as they got closer did he realise the bushes ran alongside a stream, which meandered across the land.

Trench focused on the group of about half a dozen DSU officers. He noted four spaniels, all now sitting at heel beside their handlers, their tails wagging wildly. Two of the handlers were petting down on their dogs' heads. The dogs appeared to be straining at the command to heel. One let out an excited bark and leapt forward toward the bank of the stream. The handler yanked its leash and shouted harshly at it to sit.

Trench trudged towards them. He watched the two officers they'd been following arrive on the scene. They exchanged greetings and one of their colleagues pointed. They both stepped forward, peering down into the stream. Just for a second. They turned. One waved animatedly back toward them, as if hurrying their approach.

Trench felt his heartbeat quicken. He tried to hurry. He was wading through glue. He forgot his frozen hands and feet. He managed to speed up. He was slightly ahead of Jazz and Kenner. He moved faster. Exhausted but racked by adrenaline. The ground hardened slightly near the stream. He broke into a laboured jog. Two of the officers were pointing down. Someone said something. He didn't hear. He wanted to see. He clamoured forwards. He grasped one of the officers to steady himself. Pulled himself forward. He reached the bank. Looked down.

His mind exploded. He dropped to his knees. Now there was no sound. No cold. No wet. For a split second, nothing.

Jazz arrived beside him. He turned to look at her. Watched her eyes as she looked down. Saw the hope evaporate as her hand shot to her mouth. It didn't stop her words coming out.

"Oh, Jesus Christ. *No!*"

# Forty-Four

Kenner was last to reach the bank. He peered over at the naked body in the stream below.

"Ah shit," he said. "Another one."

He immediately kicked into operational mode, his training as Crime Scene Manager taking over.

"Okay, everyone, listen up. Firstly, great work by our four-legged comrades, as always. They've earned their chow tonight," he bent down and rubbed the head of the dog nearest to him before continuing. "But I'm going to need everyone to back off now, preferably back the way we just came. Try not to disturb anything else as we go. Does anyone have any tape?"

One of the DSU officers produced a role of crime scene tape from somewhere.

"Good, can you role that out from thirty yards either side of here," said Kenner. "Let's secure as big an area as we can. We can zero it in later, but for now bigger is better."

He turned to Trench and Jazz, who were both still standing at the edge of the bank, staring at the body.

"That goes for you too, I'm afraid," said Kenner. "I'll need to get my team down here to process the scene before you can get any closer. That's probably going to take a while, but I'll let you know as soon as we've got any tatts or birthmarks or anything else that might help with the ID."

Trench looked at him.

"That won't be necessary."

Kenner gave him a quizzical look. Trench clarified for him.

"It's Vanessa Osbourne."

Kenner looked shocked, He turned to look at the body again.

"Oh shit," he said. "Are you sure?"

"Positive," said Trench.

"It's her," added Jazz.

"Oh, man. The poor girl. And her poor family," said Kenner, before adding. "My god, the press are going to go berserk when this gets out."

"Yeah," said Trench. "Listen, Kenner, we need you to keep that strictly confidential for now. That means you don't tell anyone we've ID'd the body. Not even your own team. We cannot let this get out across the wires yet."

"Roger that."

"I mean it, Kenner," reinforced Trench. "Not even your own guys. No-one can know about this. We cannot have the ID being radioed around, not even as a rumour. We've got to manage this."

"I understand Trench, I get it. You want to keep it off the wires," said Kenner nodding.

"And get a tent over her as quickly as possible."

"Of course," replied Kenner, pulling out his phone. "I'm calling my guys back at the clubhouse to get moving on it right now."

"Let me ask you something. First glance, looking at her from here, what are you seeing?" said Trench.

"What do you mean?" said Kenner.

"Look at her neck."

Kenner turned and examined the scene. Vanessa Osbourne's body was about ten feet below the bank on which they were standing. She was lying face up, parallel to the bank of the stream. Her legs were mostly submerged but her torso and upper body protruded out of the water, resting on a mud pile. Her left arm was caught awkwardly under her body, her right arm stretched out above her head. Her hair was matted and stuck to her scalp, exposing her neck. They were standing almost directly above her, which gave Trench an ample view of what he thought he recognised.

"I see what you mean," confirmed Kenner. "But there's also mud patches on her. I can't make a call yet. That could be—"

"I'm not asking for the official word," said Trench. "But help me out. It could be important. That's bruising, in my opinion. She was strangled. Manual rather than ligature."

"I agree," said Jazz. "Mud isn't purple and blue."

After a moment, Kenner responded.

"Okay, unofficial, and at a very, very preliminary stage, I agree. It looks like bruising from here. Whether it's manual or ligature, I'm not prepared to say. The other bodies had both and I'm not ruling out either until we've had a closer look. And anyway, that's up to Wharton to decide."

"The others had chafing, as well as the bruising," said Trench. "From the racket string. I don't see chafing."

"I don't either," relented Kenner. "But I'd like to be ten feet closer before I make that call."

"What about other wounds?" pressed Trench.

Kenner stared again for a long moment, then crouched to his knees. When he was done, he stood up and looked at Trench.

"I'm not seeing anything else obvious," he said.

Trench nodded, then turned to Jazz. She knew where he was going.

"Where's the knife wounds?" she said.

Trench nodded again.

"What about decomp?" he asked Kenner.

"Are you asking for time of death? I can't tell that without—"

"No," Trench interrupted. "I mean how long has she been in water?"

Kenner turned to examine the body again. It was less than a minute when he turned back to them.

"I'll offer an opinion at this stage only with the same caveats. It's not official and is based on the most cursory examination possible. I wouldn't do this for anyone else, but I trust that both of you will treat it appropriately," he spoke in a disapproving tone, then turned and pointed at the body, becoming more consultative. "But look at the skin. Particularly where it meets the water. As you can see, there's very little difference in the condition of the skin whether it's submerged or above the water line. That suggests she has not been in the water long."

Trench had reached the same conclusion, but he wanted to hear Kenner's second opinion. Now that he'd heard it, he pushed for as much precision as possible, despite the cursory level of examination.

"How long? What's the maximum length of time she's been in the water?"

Kenner screwed his face up, looking down at the body again. He nodded to himself then turned back to face them.

"I can't give a maximum timeframe, sorry," he said. "But I will say this. We're talking hours rather than days."

*

"It's not an opinion, Jazz. It's what the evidence is telling us."

"Up to a point," said Jazz. "But there's a big difference between planting evidence and…this."

They'd been discussing it on the long trudge back through the fields. Now in the car, Trench was driving while Jazz sat with her bare feet placed up against the heaters on the dashboard. Her socks and boots were in the footwell, soaking wet and caked in mud. She was leaning forward so she could also hold her hands up to the heaters. It was an awkward posture, but less uncomfortable than sitting with freezing cold feet.

"Maybe. But it's all part of the same play," said Trench. "Chapman didn't put her there. He was sitting in our jail when she went into that water. You heard Kenner. And you saw her. No cuts, no slashes. No chafing. Chapman didn't kill her. He had nothing to do with it. Any doubt about that is gone."

"But Callow?" said Jazz. "Are you saying he killed her?"

Trench didn't answer. He was still working it through in his head. But he felt he had almost put it all together. That came with a growing sense of intense frustration, and guilt with himself for not seeing it sooner.

"Is he involved with the security services, Trench?" pushed Jazz, confused. "How the fuck did that happen?"

Trench banged his hand hard on the steering wheel, frustration at himself boiling over.

"No," he said, staring hard out the windscreen as their surroundings blurred past. "There is no security services. I was wrong about that."

"Then what?"

He let out a long breath before continuing. He felt angry. But most of all he felt foolish. He had badly misjudged the day's events.

"It's not the only thing I was wrong about," he said. "I thought that when Osbourne found out about Vanessa's affair with the PM he'd moved to protect her. Like most parents would." He hit the wheel again. "But he didn't. He moved to protect himself. Protect his business. He killed her, Jazz. I don't know if it was calculated or if it was spur of the moment. We already know they used to argue and we've seen for ourselves what type of a guy he is. But it doesn't matter. He killed her and all his actions since then have been designed to confuse and obstruct the investigation. We weren't wrong about that."

"Jesus," murmured Jazz.

"That's why he knew the ransom was fake."

"But what about Callow? How's he involved?"

"The ransom. What I witnessed was him trying to hijack the ransom. But when he discovered it was fake money, he must've realised that Osbourne knew the ransom demand was a scam and had given us a dummy. When I bumped into him yesterday morning in the station he let slip that he was going to see Osbourne. That was *after* he'd already been dumped off the case. But he wasn't going about the case. He was going to shake him down. He must've figured out that Osbourne had something to hide and gone to put the screw on him.

"If he was wrong, it wouldn't make much difference. We were already fucked. If Osbourne had actually given us real money and we had somehow lost it, on top of then blowing the drop operation, then whatever heat Callow got for trying to turn the screw on him would be lost in the bigger-picture shitstorm the Met would be facing."

"But he wasn't wrong," said Jazz, beginning to see the full picture.

"No, he wasn't. And he offered Osbourne a way out. We had just collared Chapman and Callow saw the opportunity. Whether he had thought through far enough to pin it on Chapman, we don't know. But all he had to say to Osbourne was that he'd make it go away."

"And Osbourne paid him off to do it," finished Jazz.

Trench nodded.

"He got some of her jewellery from her house. I gave him the key when I handed over the case. I'll bet some of the clothes in Chapman's lair are Vanessa's too."

"But dumping her body like that…How could any parent do that?" said Jazz, horrified. "He threatened us with legal action if any tabloids so much as heard what was in her diary. Then he sets it up so she was raped and tortured by a sadistic serial killer, and dumps her naked body in a field in the middle of nowhere? It's almost beyond belief, Trench."

"That's the part I'm not seeing," agreed Trench. "I don't think he signed up for that."

"What do you mean?"

"He's a cold-hearted son of a bitch, that's been obvious from the start. But I can't see him agreeing to allow his daughter to be found like that. Callow must've told him he'd take care of the body. Probably that she'd just disappear. But he knew we wouldn't fully buy that she'd been taken by Chapman without a body. So instead of disposing of her in whatever way he told Osbourne, he went a step further. He dumped her there."

He turned to Jazz.

"Callow might be right, you know," he said.

"Right about what?"

"That we'd believe Chapman was good for this. It was Campbell who told me about the jewellery this morning. He was a damn sight happier with that than he was with my suspicions about Osbourne yesterday. If we find the body at his lair as well, then it's going to be a bitch to convince him Chapman didn't kill her."

"I see what you mean. 'Sorry Chief, it wasn't the serial killer with all the supporting evidence, it was her billionaire Dad with help from a DCI in the Met'," said Jazz. "What are we going to do?"

"We've got to get to Osbourne," said Trench. "Before Callow does."

"You think he's going after him?"

"I don't know. But if I'm right, Osbourne's going to go off the deep end when he hears how we found Vanessa. If he's capable of killing his own daughter, then fuck knows how he'll react to this. Anything is possible."

"So Callow needs to get to him before he finds out."

"Yeah," said Trench. "He might even still need to collect his pay off. Osbourne's shrewd. Maybe he'll only pay once the deed is done."

"Shit, they could be meeting anywhere."

"Try him again," said Trench, fishing his phone from his inside pocket and handing it to Jazz.

She scrolled through the recent calls and hit dial on Osbourne's number. It rang on the hands-free kit but there was no answer. This time Trench decided to leave a message. He couldn't flat out accuse him or say that they'd found Vanessa, given the slim chance that an assistant or someone else picked up the message. But he wanted to be as blunt as he could.

"Doctor Osbourne, it's DCI Chambers again. You need to call me back, urgently. I have a critical update in the search for Vanessa. I appreciate you'll be feeling anxious about our investigation, but it's very important that you call me back. And do not meet with any other police until you and I have spoken. This is extremely important, Doctor Osbourne, for your own safety and security. Do not underestimate what I am saying. Call me back as soon as you get this message."

"Try Callow," he said after she'd hung up.

The call went straight to voicemail, as expected. The phone was most likely switched off.

"What about Burgers?" said Jazz, searching for the number.

"Do it."

"And where does he fit into all of this?" she said as she dialled the number.

Trench didn't answer for a second. He hadn't considered Burgess.

"Not sure," he said, as the call connected. "But let's assume the worst. At the very least, he cannot be trusted."

When Jazz dialled the number, the phone rang but there was no answer.

"Fuck," said Jazz. "Now what?"

"We go find Osbourne, wherever he is," he said, then added, "Try Krige."

Krige answered after one ring, but then confirmed Osbourne had still not come home. Trench told Krige to call him as soon as he came home, or as soon as Krige learned where he was. He appreciated the awkward position Krige was in, being asked to spy on his employer. To overcome Krige's reluctance, he emphasised that Krige still owed him, but if he did this final favour they would be quits. Krige readily agreed and they hung up.

"We'll try his office. Can you search for the address," said Trench.

Within a minute Jazz found the address on Google. She read it out loud.

"That's where we're going," he said.

# Forty-Five

They screeched to a halt outside the address on Upper Belgravia Street. Trench kept the blues and twos on full. He hoped Osbourne would hear the wailing siren and would feel the noose tightening.

The office building was smaller than Trench expected. But then he realised it was probably no more than an administrative office. The main laboratory and manufacturing functions would be in other regions around the country. This headquarters, in one of London's most prestigious quarters, was no more than an ego trip. This was the realm of foreign embassies and five-star hotels. The grounds of Buckingham Palace were literally around the corner. Osbourne could probably see them from his office.

Maybe it would help him adjust to his future of staring at ten-foot walls topped with barbed wire, thought Trench as he clambered out of the car. His trousers were almost entirely covered in mud. There were filthy patches across most of his jacket and even his face, though he no longer noticed. Jazz stepped out gingerly, having cursed like Gordon Ramsey at a sous-chef as she put her freezing socks and boots back on as they drove. By the time they reached the few steps up to the door of the building they were all business.

"He may have told them not to let us in," said Trench.

Jazz nodded, understanding the implicit instruction. This wasn't the time for good cop.

The solid oak door was painted black, with prominent silver bolts in patterns around each panel. It looked more suited to a medieval castle than a modern office. There was an intercom to the left. Jazz hit the buzzer repeatedly. Trench banged on the door with his fist. He wanted there to be no doubt they would be taking full control of the office and everyone in it.

"Hello? What on earth is going on?" came a shrill voice over the intercom.

"Met Police," said Jazz. "Open the door right now."

"I don't thin—"

"Open the fucking door," she hollered. "You've got a camera here, you can see our ID. You've got three seconds to open the door or you'll be done for obstruction."

They both held up their ID, while Trench gave the door another battering. The door buzzed open and they rushed inside. There was another door a few feet in front of them, made of reinforced, inch-thick plastic. It was floor to ceiling, with a fob on one side. They couldn't get beyond it but could see a security guard walking towards them.

The reception desk was to their left. The aging receptionist was dressed as if she was going to a ball at the Waldorf. But as they stepped inside, her expression looked as if she had just slipped and covered her gown in cow shit.

They both pressed their ID's up against the door so the security guard could see them. Trench knocked heavily on the door with an open palm. He wanted to keep the tension high. After a few seconds the security guard was still squinting at the ID, so Trench whipped his away.

"Open this fucking door right now," he commanded.

The security guard looked at him for a second before turning to the receptionist. Trench realised she was probably the one who had to buzz them in.

"And you," he said, pointing directly at her. "You're going to jail. It'll be a week before we've even processed the paperwork. They'd love you in Bronzefield."

Trench didn't know if she'd heard of Bronzefield, the only purpose-built prison for women in Britain, and the largest female prison in Europe. But the point seemed to hit home. A hand shot to her pearl necklace, cow shit threatening to drown her completely. The other hand moved under the desk and they heard a buzzing from the door. Trench pushed it open, the security guard having to step quickly aside to avoid it.

"Thank you," he nodded to them both, before focusing on the receptionist. "Where is Doctor Osbourne's office? We need to see him right now. He's expecting us."

She stammered and struggled to respond, hand moving from necklace to her mouth. Trench turned to the security guard instead.

"You, lead the way. Let's go," he bawled, stepping forward. "Come on!"

He looked around the area for the first time. There was a staircase right in front of them, corridors to either side of it, multiple other doors in the reception area. There was also a couple of lifts. The security guard hadn't moved.

"What are you waiting for, a royal decree? Let's move it," he barked again. "Which way?"

"Uh, sir, wait," stuttered the receptionist. "Doc…Doctor Osbourne isn't here."

"Bullshit," said Trench. "We know he's here. Take us to his office, right now."

"I'm so sorry, sir," she stammered. "He was here, but he left just a little while ago. Truthfully."

"Ah bollocks!" he roared, turning to Jazz. "Let's get out of here."

"Where to?" she said, exasperated.

Trench didn't answer. He wasn't sure where to go next. They marched back to the car and jumped in. Trench was about to start hammering on the wheel again when the high-pitched squeal sounded over the car speakers. He looked at the panel and his pulse spiked in hope.

"Krige," he answered.

"Hey mate," Krige almost whispered. "He's here. He just got back a minute ago."

"You fucking daisy," said Trench, immediately starting the ignition. "We're on our way. Don't tell him we're coming."

He checked over his shoulder then floored the accelerator.

"Ah, just one thing," said Krige, even quieter this time.

"Shoot," said Trench, holding off hitting the siren in case it drowned out Krige's hushed tone. He hit only the lights instead.

"Well look, mate, one of the uh...services we provide to clients, our higher net worth clients, if they want it…This is really sensitive mate, I really shouldn't be telling you this…It's not strictly legal, but there are some bad people that target the wealthy, right? I mean this case is actually a good example—"

"Spit it out, man," said Trench. "What are you saying? He's armed?"

"I think so, mate, ja."

"Why do you think that, Krige? Did you give him a fucking gun or not?"

"Ja, a long time ago. It's something we provide our higher net worth clients if they want it," he said. "We provided one to Osbourne a long time ago. Years ago. I've never seen it since but I know the carrier case. I'm pretty sure I saw him carrying it just now when he came back to the house."

Trench and Jazz exchanged looks. This changed things. Big style. They couldn't just go charging in. There was no telling what Osbourne could do now.

"Did you talk with him?" said Trench. "What kind of mood's he in?"

"No, mate, I didn't. I saw him arrive and watched him on camera getting out of the car. He slammed the door with his foot 'coz he was holding a couple of different cases and he dropped them. That's when I saw it. I didn't speak with him but I could tell he was steaming. Banging the door, slamming the cases around and then he slammed the front door when he came into the house. I reckon it's all just really getting to him now, you know. Vanessa's still missing, he's been staying away, I'm pretty sure him and the missus haven't spoken for a few days. To be honest, I'm worried, mate. I've never seen him like this."

This gave Trench pause. He couldn't tell Krige the true situation, that they strongly suspected he had killed Vanessa. But he also realised that everyone within Osbourne's immediate vicinity was now potentially in danger. If he was unravelling, there was no telling what he could do.

Krige filled the silence before Trench could speak again.

"Maybe I'm overreacting," he said. "And listen, I'd really appreciate it if you don't take what I said any further, you know, about providing the piece. It would ruin our busin—"

"That's not important right now," interrupted Trench. "But it's good to know he has it. You did the right thing telling me. What I need you to do now is to get everyone else out of the house, can you do that?"

"What, everyone? Or just our people?"

"No, everyone," said Trench. "Everyone except Osbourne. And do it without letting him know it's happening. Just tell them it's a staff security drill or something. I don't care how you do it, but try to get them all out."

"Okay, I can try."

"The hard part will be getting Mrs Osbourne out," said Trench, realising just how difficult this would be, without Osbourne himself noticing.

"She's not here," said Krige. "She left a couple of days ago, that's what I'm saying. I think she's at her sister's."

"Okay, that's good. Get your crew and the rest of the staff out. Then you meet us outside. We'll need a key."

"Ja, okay. I can do that. But why Trench, what's going on? …You think he's dangerous?"

"I don't know, Krige. But he might be. He's carrying the gun for a reason. He's probably feeling desperate right now and who knows what he's capable of. Just keep everyone out of his way until we get there. We'll be there in ten minutes."

"Okay, will do. Just get here as quick as you can."

As soon as he hung up Jazz spoke.

"We need to call Barker and Walker. They might still be there."

She had a quick conversation with Barker, telling the Family Liaison Officer that she and PC Walker were to head back to the station immediately for a briefing. When she hung up, Jazz turned to Trench, her face stern.

"We need to get a Trojan out, Trench. God knows what he's going to do."

Trench thought about it for a second. He knew she was right. But he also knew it could severely limit their ability to talk to Osbourne. Trench was certain they now understood what had happened. But they would never truly know until Osbourne told them his version. And they would never be able to prove Callow's complicity without it.

"Call it in," he said. "But we are going there right now. We're not standing by."

Jazz nodded as she reached for her phone. Trench flipped on the siren and floored the accelerator.

# Forty-Six

A Range Rover with blacked-out windows emerged from the gates of Blenheim just as they got there. Ayala was behind the wheel, an elderly looking man in a chef's uniform was in the passenger seat. Ayala pulled up alongside them and put the window down.

"Hey," she said. "I taking the staff to the security drill offsite."

She gestured toward other passengers in the back, though they weren't visible through the tinted windows. Trench was glad to know the staff members were no longer at the house. He had tried Doctor Osbourne's phone again on the way over, but again it went unanswered. He was therefore relying on the latest information he had, from Krige. Osbourne was armed and in a volatile mood. Better these people were out of harm's way. Trench didn't know how much Krige had told Ayala, and didn't want to say much in front of the other staff members. He nodded sombrely to Ayala, then drove through the gates before they closed.

Winter evening had descended, the darkness of the surrounding gardens engulfing the dimly lit driveway. It added an eerie feel Trench hadn't noticed on their previous visits. As they reached the turn in the driveway, another Range Rover made the turn from the opposite direction. Krige was behind the wheel, Doherty in the passenger seat. They pulled up alongside.

"Evening," said Krige. "Here's the key."

He held it out through the window. Trench took it.

"Shit, what happened to you?" said Krige.

The quizzical look on his face prompted Krige to say more.

"You look like you've been playing rugby, mate" he said. "In a mud bath."

"Sort of," was all Trench said.

"Are you armed?" asked Krige, instinctively lowering his voice.

"No," said Trench.

Krige reached down and picked up something up from his lap. When he held it out through the window, Trench saw it was a handgun. Krige was holding it by the muzzle.

"Here," he said. "Just in case."

Trench looked at the gun for a moment before shaking his head.

"Hang on to it," said Trench. "We've got a unit on the way."

"You sure?" said Krige, thrusting the gun toward Trench. "It might help uh, negotiate, if it comes to it. He can be a difficult bastard. It might help you get his attention at least."

"Not worth the paperwork," said Trench. In the back of his mind a thought flickered. He hoped he wouldn't regret the decision later. "And you know, just because you've told me about this extra service you provide to clients doesn't mean it's legit. You might want to start thinking about deniability, depending on what happens here."

Krige retracted the gun quickly, putting it back down somewhere inside the car.

"Okay, mate. Just thought that given it's an emergency and all…"

"Are all your people out now?" said Trench, letting it go for now.

"Yeah, he's the only one there now."

"Do you know where he is in the house?"

"Pretty sure he's in his study. Or at least he was a few minutes ago. Very back of the house, next door to his office. Head through the kitchen and just keep going straight. Second door from the right at the end of the hall."

Trench nodded and put the car back into gear. He was about to go when he remembered a final question.

"Are you able to leave the gate open for the Firearms Unit? They should be here any minute."

"Shit, no mate," said Krige. "I can't keep it open from down there. There's a buzzer on the panel by the front door that opens it. And also one in the security office, on the wall behind the desk. Or we could wait for them down there and open it when they arrived. We're not planning on going far anyway."

Trench didn't like the sound of having them waiting around. Especially not after their stunt at the drop. He had visions of them coming back to the house to try to get involved.

"No, don't wait around. You need to stay well clear of the area. Go back to your base or something. We'll use the buzzer when they arrive."

"Okay. Good luck," said Krige.

Trench nodded and Krige pulled away. Trench drove forward and stopped at the bottom of the staircase leading up to the front door. He turned to Jazz.

"You go to the office and wait for the Trojan. You'll need to open the gates for them. Keep the door closed, locked if you can. I'll go down to the study—"

"What?" said Jazz. "I wait in the office while you go down there alone?"

"It's the only way the Trojan can get in."

"No, Trench," protested Jazz. "He's got a gun! Who knows what he'll do. You heard what Krige said. We need to wait for the Trojan."

Trench shook his head.

"We've got to get him talking. I'm going down. Tell them to follow me down. But quietly. I'll leave the door open so they'll know what's happening. But tell them *do not come in* unless they hear an imminent threat. Charging in like the SAS isn't going to work here."

"Why not? That's exactly what we should be doing. He's armed, desperate and dangerous."

"We've got nothing, Jazz. We need him to talk. The only chance of that is right now. When we take him in, there'll be an army of lawyers between him and us. We'll never hear a word out of his mouth. He could even walk."

"He killed his own fucking daughter, Trench! If you just walk in there and try to arrest him, who's to say he's doesn't try to take you out too?"

"He won't," said Trench, trying to sound more convinced than he felt. "He's not that stupid. There's no way out for him if he does that. Right now, we don't have much of a case against him. We've got guesswork and suspicions. We both know he did it, but it's going to be a bitch to prove it. If he denies everything and Callow denies everything, then we have to somehow convince everyone that they pulled off the most audacious cover up since JFK. I'm not even sure we could convince our own command right now, let alone a court. Hell, it might not even get anywhere near a court given his connections and legal teams."

Jazz didn't say anything but didn't look convinced. Trench took out his phone.

"I'm going to record him, when he thinks it's just me and him. I'm going to try to get him to admit it. It's the only way we're ever going to collar him for this."

Jazz shook her head.

"I don't like this, Trench."

"Neither do I, but it's the best chance we've got of taking him down. The only chance."

Jazz shook her head again but didn't say anything.

"We can't let him walk for this, Jazz. You saw her. He did this. He put her there. We're taking him down."

Trench opened the glove box and took out a pair of handcuffs.

"Let's go."

They got out and took the stairs two steps at a time. Trench used Krige's key to open the door. Once inside he motioned toward the security office. Jazz walked over to it, her face still creased in a deep frown. Trench followed her inside. He then turned on his phone's voice recorder. He stated his name, rank, the date, where they were and what they were doing.

He knew the recording was unlikely to be admissible in any court case. No doubt Osbourne's defence team would find some reason to have it struck out. He was not going to make Osbourne aware that he was recording them, and that alone would likely render it inadmissible. But he intended to use it to pressure Osbourne during the police interviews after his arrest. It could also prove useful to protect Trench if necessary. And to make sure the charges stuck.

Osbourne had power. Trench had no doubt the full force of that power would be directed squarely at him after he made the arrest. Osbourne's lawyers would try to discredit him or claim the arrest was invalid. Osbourne might even try to squirm out from beneath the charges. He would leverage every contact he had, every ounce of sway, to get the charges dropped. Trench knew he couldn't rely on anyone else to protect him, or the investigation. The recording would be his insurance policy.

"I'm going," he said, moving to the door. "Remember, when they get here, tell them not to barge in. And for fuck's sake, don't shoot first."

"We can't tell them that, you know that," said Jazz. "It's their call."

"As things stand, one version of events is that he gave police two million pounds which then went missing," said Trench. "Next thing, we turn up at his house and execute him? I'll let you write the report on that one."

Jazz gave a nervous laugh despite herself. So did Trench. A momentary ease in the growing tension. Trench took the opportunity to leave the room, nodding his goodbye as he did so. Jazz returned the gesture, her frown returning. Trench closed the door behind him and heard the lock click into place.

He turned and made his way slowly down the corridor toward the kitchen. He walked at an even pace, instinctively keeping his footsteps quiet. When he got to the kitchen door, he pressed his ear against it and listened for a few seconds. The only sound he heard was his own heart thumping. He suddenly became aware of how much adrenaline was pumping through his body. It gave him a moment's pause.

The truth was he had much less confidence that he could control the situation than he had let on to Jazz. Osbourne was a fighter. He was cold and clinical. He had murdered his daughter to protect his business – for money, to Trench's mind. Then he had held it together and engaged in an elaborate cover up. Trench doubted he would simply roll over and confess. He would continue to fight. The thought made Trench even more convinced he had to get to him right now.

Trench decided he would have to get the upper hand immediately. If he had any chance of getting Osborne to talk, he would have to get him onto the back foot. Get him into a position of weakness, where he'd have to plea or try to bargain his way out. That was when he was most likely to confess or make incriminating statements, which would be captured on tape.

He figured the best way to do that was to get the cuffs on as quickly as possible. He decided he would make a swift, decisive entrance to the study and immediately snap them on before Osbourne had a chance to react. This would also limit the opportunity for Osbourne to go for the gun. He fished the cuffs out of his pocket and held them in his left hand in readiness. Hearing nothing from inside the kitchen, he slowly turned the handle and opened the door a crack.

The lights were on but he couldn't see or hear anyone inside. He opened the door fully and stepped inside. It was empty. He quickly walked across the kitchen to the far door. He listened again for a moment before opening it. Again, the only sound was the rapid beat of his own heart. He opened the door. He had not been in this part of the house before. There was another long corridor in front of him. There was light coming from somewhere at the end of it, but the part nearest him was in darkness. He slipped through the door.

There was carpet here, minimising the sound from his footsteps. But they still sounded too loud to Trench. He felt like a burglar, creeping down the dark hallway. He quickened his pace. He saw two doors on his right, both closed. He paused at the second one. He was sure Krige had said end of the corridor. Second door from the right. Or had he said second door *on the right?*

Cursing, Trench looked at the bottom of the door. He couldn't see any light coming from underneath it, suggesting there was no light on inside. He moved on, reaching the end of the corridor. It was brighter here. The overhead lights were on in the adjacent hallway. He glanced to the right. The second door from the right in the adjacent hallway was only a few feet ahead of him. He couldn't tell if there was light coming from underneath it because of the overheard lights.

He crept over to it. Pressed his ear against the door. At first he heard nothing. Then he thought he heard a faint clink. He pressed his ear harder. Definitely. Louder this time. It sounded like glass on glass. He pulled his head back from the door and raised the cuffs in his left hand. Pushed the handle down slowly, bracing himself for a charge. When the handle reached the bottom, he silently counted to three. He pushed with full force and rushed forwards. The door swung open. He burst into Osbourne's private study.

And immediately realised he'd made a terrible mistake.

# Forty-Seven

 ou!”

Osbourne snarled at him. Trench froze. Osbourne was on the other side of the room, impossibly far away. The room was about half the size of a tennis court. There was no way he would get to Osbourne before he could pull the trigger of the gun he was holding in his right hand.

He held a tumbler in his left hand, full to the brim, ice floating. He was standing beside a drinks cabinet, having obviously just refilled his glass.

“You scum!” Osbourne roared. “How dare you come into my home.”

He raised the gun and aimed it at Trench, a slight wobble in the hand. Trench raised his own hands at the elbows.

“Just calm down,” he said slowly.

“Calm down? *How fucking dare you!*” Osbourne bellowed. “I should shoot you right now.”

He took a large swig from the tumbler then set it on the cabinet. He grabbed the gun with both hands, keeping it pointed directly at Trench.

“You’re trespassing,” he blustered. “I have every right to shoot you. I never gave you permission to be here.”

Osbourne took an unsteady step forward. This was bad. Very bad. Trench tried to think of something to say to calm the situation. He had badly underestimated the size of the room, and hadn’t figured Osbourne would already be holding the gun.

“I’ve been trying to call you,” was the best he could come up with.

“I’m not interested in your bloody phone calls,” spat Osbourne. “I’ve given you people enough! And you dumped her in a field. You filthy bastards. I ought to shoot you right now!”

He took another unsteady step forward, the gun wavering in his drunken hands. Trench calculated whether he could rush him, but quickly rejected the idea.

Osbourne was still about twenty feet away. There was a sofa and assorted coffee tables between them. He'd never make it before Osbourne squeezed the trigger.

"I had nothing to do with that," he said instead. "Just take it easy."

"Don't you 'take it easy' me, you miserable bastard," raged Osbourne. "You told me you'd take care of her. Properly. That was the deal, you son of a bitch. Not...not this."

His voice choked and for a second he slightly lowered the gun. Again Trench considered charging, but Osbourne quickly raised the gun. Trench realised Osbourne's cheeks were streaked with tears. This wasn't just rage. There was sorrow too. Grief. Remorse?

Whatever it was, the alcohol wasn't going to make him any calmer. Trench tried to process what Osbourne had said so far. It was hard to think straight with the gun levelled directly at him, the potential shooter so obviously unstable. He had to think fast. He had to talk him down.

"Doctor Osbourne, I was not involved in any deal," he said, slowly and calmly. "I don't know what you're talking about. I came here because—"

"*Fuck you,*" roared Osbourne, jerking the gun at him. "You think I don't know your type? You're all the same. Here for a quick buck. You're a bloody parasite, like everyone else. Well, you're not getting another penny out of me. I never should've agreed to your charade. I can shoot you right now. You think I can't get away with it?"

The situation was getting worse. Osbourne was getting more animated, more hostile. His train of thought was becoming more dangerous. Thinking he could get away with it. *Knowing* he could. Trench desperately tried to think of some way to interrupt his thoughts, to get him to calm down. In Osbourne's drink-fuelled fury he could shoot at any moment.

"I came here to arrest the man who double-crossed you," Trench gambled. "I'm not part of any deal you made with him. I want to make sure he pays for what he did to Vanessa."

The mention of his daughter's name caused Osbourne to wince. The gun wavered in his hands again. He stared off into the middle distance, mumbling what sounded like her name. Trench didn't move. He wasn't safe yet, but he had gotten through to Osbourne. The rage had momentarily given way to whatever other emotions were gripping him. Trench decided to push in that direction. To keep Vanessa front and centre.

"Can you help me do that?" he said, arms still raised. "To get some kind of justice for Vanessa. She deserves that."

Osbourne focused on him, his aim also becoming focused again.

"Justice?" said Osbourne softly, tears forming and rolling down his face. "There can be no justice. It's too late for that."

Trench nodded.

"You're right. It is too late for Vanessa. But those who did this to her will face justice. I promise you that."

Osbourne stared at him for a long moment. Trench held his stare. He searched for something that would tell him what Osbourne intended to do next. The rage was receding behind the tears, but there was still a hardness there. Still resolve. Still fight.

Trench stared back. He tried to show resolve and fight in his own eyes. He had to give Osbourne a reason not to shoot him. He knew Osbourne was too savvy to fall for any bullshit about a plea deal or mitigating circumstances. And he had already fallen victim to one scamming copper in all of this. It seemed to be the cause of the rage. Maybe Trench could use it.

"I'm not part of any deal," he repeated, slowly lowering his arms. "If you shoot me, then the only person who walks free from all of this is the one who dumped Vanessa in that field. I won't let him get away with it. Will you?"

They stood in silence for another minute. Osbourne holding the gun in both hands, levelled at Trench, who stared back at him.

Eventually Osbourne broke the stare. He glanced around then took a few steps backwards, keeping the gun trained on Trench. He reached around and picked up his tumbler. He downed another large mouthful.

Osbourne lowered the glass from his lips. He took a deep breath, clenched his eyes shut for a brief second. When he opened them they appeared less sure. A weary look crept across his face. Trench had seen the look in countless faces before. The fight was turning inward. Rage and fury deliberately misdirected at the outside world always found its way home. Where it belonged. Where the fight would rage most furiously.

"Just another scam," said Osbourne, shaking his head, almost muttering to himself as if revisiting a previous conversation. "Stupid. I should have known. Half as greedy indeed...but twice as bloody treacherous."

He paused, lost deep in his own haunted thoughts. Trench let a minute pass. Osbourne was close, he could feel it. The moment a suspect knew the game was up. He was teetering, his conscience wanting to bare what his survival instincts fought to suppress. Trench would have given his conscience more time to prevail, but he knew time was running short. He let another minute pass, but Osbourne showed no signs of snapping out of it.

"Another scam?" he prompted.

Osbourne looked up at him.

"That's right," seethed Osbourne through gritted teeth. "You lot are no better than that bloody street hustler with his ransom flimflam. Though at least that bandit didn't hide behind a badge."

Osbourne waved the tumbler in a dismissive gesture, drink sloshing over its side.

"I should've known better," said Osbourne in a heavy, resigned tone. "You police are just like your bloody paymasters in parliament. My whole damn career, backhanders and bungs. One hand on your shoulder, the other in your pocket. All the bloody same."

Trench needed to get him to focus, to clearly confirm what had happened, before he was totally lost to drink-fuelled rambling. Anything he said after that could more easily be dismissed by a defence lawyer. Time was running out.

"How did he scam you?"

Osbourne looked directly at him again.

"He said he'd make it right. I would have to live with myself anyway, but at least I could spare her mother from knowing what I'd done. Spare her brother and sister. It'll destroy them...I was trying to protect them. Protect them from what I had done."

Trench thought he heard the faint sound of a door opening behind him. Somewhere out in the hall. The Armed Response Unit. They must be closing in. Osbourne still had the gun pointed directly at Trench. Trench watched him but he showed no sign of having heard the noise.

If the Unit entered at that moment they wouldn't hesitate to shoot Osbourne. Trench's eyes shifted to the windows behind Osbourne. He knew the Unit would try to approach from all sides. He squinted but it was too dark outside. All he saw in the windows was the reflection of the room in which they stood.

Trench replayed their conversation, thinking about the voice recording. Did he have enough? He didn't think so. He needed clarity. He needed Osbourne to confirm the whole story. He needed the name. He had to get him to say more.

"Why would he do that? Why would he 'make it right?'"

"Why do you think?" scolded Osbourne, sounding annoyed at Trench's apparent stupidity. "Money, Detective. Always bloody money."

"What was he going to do?"

"He said he could make it look like someone else had…someone else was responsible for what happened to…my daughter."

"Who are you talking about? Who did you give the money to do that?" pressed Trench, desperate for him to say the name.

Osbourne looked at him with utter contempt. He crumpled his face in disgust. He jerked the gun at Trench as he spoke.

"Your man," he spat. "The detective."

"Detective Callow, is that who you mean?"

"Yes, goddamit. That smug wretch who took over the investigation at the weekend. He came back here after he figured out the ransom money I gave him was just paper. He said he knew what I'd done and threatened to arrest me, but then in the same breath offered me a way out. A bargain compared to a ransom, he said. Cheeky bastard. I've had a thousand men try to shake me down and I told every one of them where to get off. But what could I do? He knew. And I had to protect my family. He had me over a barrel."

Trench had the whole story.

He had no doubt Osbourne would later retract it, deny everything. They always did. But that would be a damn sight harder after this. And for Callow, there would be no way out. He wouldn't have the luxury of a retraction or a plea deal or a phalanx of world class lawyers. The brass came down hard on bent coppers. The courts even harder. He was going away for a long, long time.

But at that moment Trench felt no satisfaction. He felt sickened by Osbourne's attempts to portray his actions as somehow protecting his family. The sheer arrogance of it was repulsive. He had no doubt Osbourne had simply tried to save his own skin. He struggled to even say his daughter's name. There were tears, but Trench knew they were only for himself, not for the daughter he had killed.

"Why?" he said. "Why did you kill Vanessa?"

Osbourne jolted, looking almost surprised by the question. But his shield of self-denial had cracked. His eyes dropped to the floor, though they were miles away.

"Do you have children, Detective?" Osbourne said, putting the glass down and picking up a decanter.

Trench nodded.

"Then you'll know that they can make you crazy," said Osbourne, topping up the tumbler. He raised it and took another long swig before continuing. "I never meant to hurt her. I just...she wouldn't listen...she could be so stubborn," he said, tears trickling again. "I knew she'd be seeing Powers that night at the dinner. We had fought about it at the weekend, when she'd confirmed there was something going on with Powers. I told her she had to stop. Powers! Of all the people...I always knew Vanessa would marry well, but Powers..."

Osbourne was shaking his head, in disbelief or remorse. After a minute of silence he showed no sign of continuing. Trench prodded him.

"What happened that night?"

"I was at my office. I'd been drinking, heavily. Believe it or not, I very rarely drink."

He looked down at his tumbler as if seeing it for the first time. He took another long gulp.

"The head of our bid had told me someone in government had told him our bid was likely to fail. I was shocked. It was her fault, Detective. Vanessa had interfered and ruined it. She was always such a busy girl, despite my best efforts" he said ruefully, shaking his head.

"I thought I could get her to speak to Powers. Tell her to forget the interference had ever happened, and just walk away. I went there, to the dinner. I waited outside. I wasn't even sure what I was doing there. I was about to leave but I saw Vanessa come out alone. She started walking. She walked right past where I was. I got out and she was shocked. At first she was annoyed. She thought I was following her.

Which I was of course, although I didn't even know it myself. I think we were both a little shocked. We hadn't spoken since the weekend. It was happening more and more, our rows. Oh, that stupid girl. Why couldn't she just listen to what I told her?"

The more he spoke the more distant he became. The last few sentences were said almost to himself. As if saying them out loud, to explain them to the world, would somehow lead to redemption. He had become more emotional again, tears dripping off his face.

But to Trench, he was just wallowing in self-delusion. Self-pity for how *his* life was about to change. He'd seen it a thousand times. An arrogant, self-centred killer trying to justify his actions by blaming his victim. Killers came in all shapes and sizes. From all walks of life. But in many ways, they were all just the same.

"And you fought again?"

Osbourne nodded.

"She got in the car and we started arguing again. Right there on Park Lane. She was drunk, angry. I'd never seen her like that before. It was like she was possessed. Wild-eyed, so agitated…She said terrible, dreadful things. Things no-one ever said to me before. I suddenly felt an overwhelming anger. I shouted at her to stop but she wouldn't. It was like she was enjoying it. I…I reached out to put my hand over her mouth. Just to stop the things that were coming out…I only intended to shut her up…"

Osbourne paused, his eyes wide. He was seeing things he would never unsee. That he could never run from. He continued in a daze, a startled look on his teary face.

"She pushed my hands away and hit me. Hard. With her phone. I've never been hit before in my life. I just…I grabbed her. Started to squeeze. It stopped the hate pouring from her mouth, so I just…I didn't let go. Even when she gave up, I didn't let go. I kept squeezing and squeezing...

"Then suddenly I stopped. Whatever had come over me just disappeared again, just like that. I recoiled in my seat. I tried to wake her, but I couldn't. She wouldn't move. I screamed at her to wake up. I grabbed her, shook her, but she just flopped down in her seat. I panicked. I started driving. I was going to take her to the hospital. That's where I was going. To take her to the hospital," he said, trying desperately to convince himself. "But it was too late. I knew it was. If I took her there, they would just blame me. They wouldn't understand. They wouldn't know what she had done."

He looked up at Trench, eyes pleading. Seeking desperately for exculpation. For understanding that he was sorry, that it wasn't his fault. He didn't find any. His eyes dropped to the floor again.

"Where did you take her?" said Trench.

"We drove," was all he said.

Trench thought back to the briefing.

"What did you do with her phones?"

"Yes," said Osbourne. "You're right, she had two. I knew they could be traced so I put one under each wheel and reversed over them. A few times."

"And then you drove..." Trench prompted.

Osbourne nodded.

"Eventually I pulled in somewhere. Regent's Park, I think. I moved her. I put her...I placed her in the boot. I needed time to think. I wasn't going to leave her there, you understand. I just needed time to think. I went back to my apartment at the office. I must have passed out. When I woke I thought it was a dream. Just a bad dream. My head was pounding. When I got in the car, I still wasn't sure whether it had happened. I was on my way home, but I diverted and pulled in. I had to check the boot..."

He flinched, almost buckling. Trench waited but he was lost in his thoughts. But Trench had to press him.

"Is that where she's been this whole time?"

Osbourne nodded.

"I didn't know what to do. I couldn't just...dump her. Just toss her aside like...like..." the anger flashed back across his face. "Like your detective has done."

Trench felt an intense disgust for Osbourne. His own daughter. Now spouting off in self-pity and blame at anyone but himself. Refusing to take responsibility for his own terrible deeds. Instead directing his anger at others. At Callow, even at Vanessa herself. It somehow made the crime even more egregious.

He glanced down at the cuffs in his hand. They were too good for him. He looked at the windows again, but there was no hope of seeing anything beyond the reflection. He listened for any movement behind. Nothing. He looked back at Osbourne, still pointing the gun at him but lost in the middle distance.

The gun. A thought suddenly occurred. Why had Osbourne already been holding the gun when Trench burst in? What was he planning to do with it?

Trench stepped forwards. The movement broke Osbourne out of his requiem. Osbourne looked at him. Trench took another step forwards. He slowly brought up his hand. Raising the cuffs. Osbourne looked at them. Then at Trench. A sneering smile cracked his face, but there was no joy in it. Resignation. Defeat, maybe. Certainly some spite.

"Are you here to arrest me, Detective?"

Trench continued to stare directly into Osbourne's eyes.

"Yes I am."

Osbourne let out a derisive snort.

"You think you can put me in jail?"

"You, and anyone who helped you."

Osbourne raised the tumbler.

"It's too late for that too," he said softly, before emptying the rest of the glass.

His left hand dropped the tumbler. His right swung up under his chin. His head tilted back. Eyes glared at Trench. A flicker of fear in the final split second. He closed his eyes.

The deafening blast made Trench flinch. The top of Osbourne's head exploded open, red mist and splatter shooting up. It lingered momentarily like a cloud above his body as it crumpled to the floor. Then slowly drizzled down onto the lifeless body.

A burst of shouts behind Trench. Stomping boots and cries of 'Police! Police!' Trench raised his arms again, his feet staying rooted to the spot.

"Clear!" someone yelled.

Men dressed in black swept around him, Heckler and Koch MP5's held up in front of their faces.

"One down! Floor beside the window."

Trench remained stock still, arms raised, eyes gazing at the crumpled remains of Clarence Osbourne. Inventor, billionaire, father.

Murderer.

"Trench! You okay?"

Jazz was beside him. She turned and followed his gaze, seeing Osbourne's body.

"What happened?" she said.

Trench didn't take his eyes off Osbourne's body as he replied.

"Justice," he said.

# Forty-Eight

They waited until they were alone in the car before playing back the recording. They both stared at the phone while it played, its dim backlight casting them in a pale glow against the evening darkness. Despite being muffled in parts, almost all of the conversation was audible enough to be heard clearly. When it finished, they sat in silence for another minute, staring at the phone.

"Part of me didn't believe it until now," said Jazz. "I think part of me didn't want to believe it."

"You're not the only one," said Trench.

He opened Whatsapp on his phone as he spoke.

"What are you doing?" said Jazz.

"No-one else is going to believe it without this. I'm sending it to Campbell."

Trench attached the audio file to the message, then hesitated for a moment. He wasn't sure what to type in the accompanying message. Eventually he decided to add nothing. The recording spoke for itself. He hit send.

"He can't put us off now," he said as Jazz started the engine.

"Put us off what?"

"Callow. He kept telling me to drop it. Not anymore."

"We're going after him, right?"

"Bloody right," said Trench, as he opened the car door. "Hang on."

He jumped out of the car and ran up to the house. He was inside for less than five seconds, before dashing back to the car. Jazz gave him a quizzical look.

"Gates," he said by way of explanation. "I think I know where he's going. But we've got to hurry."

"Where?" said Jazz.

"He's got the money, right. Osbourne said he already gave it to him. And he knows we're on to him. That means he's going to make a run for it. He'll try to leave the country. His mug is going to be on every screen in the country in a few hours. But if he's carrying all that cash, he can't just catch a plane somewhere."

"Drive on? A ferry. Or the Eurostar."

"Too risky. They do spot searches. Especially single men alone in a car."

Jazz thought for a moment as she hit the accelerator.

"His boat," said Jazz, putting it together.

"Got to be. Now we just need to figure out where he keeps it."

"Essex, somewhere. I know that much," said Jazz, flipping the blues and twos.

"Right, let's head that way. But there'll be tonnes of marinas out there. I'll call Barton, tell him to check Callow's desk. Maybe we'll find a receipt or something giving us the name."

"Try Five Burgers first," said Jazz. "If anyone knows where it is, it'll be him."

Trench looked sceptical.

"He's not answering, remember."

"Worth a try. Here, use my phone," said Jazz, taking out her phone and handing it to him. Noticing a blank look on Trench's face she shrugged. "You never know. He's not always in the mood for intense..."

The car hands free picked up the signal and it rang over the car's speakers. They exchanged a surprised glance when it was answered on the second ring.

"Hello," said Burgess.

"Burgess, it's Jazz. Where are you?"

"I'm at home, Jazz. What's up?"

"Really, you sound like you're in a car?"

"I'm sitting by the window. What can I do for you? Oh, by the way, I missed a call from Trench earlier. I was tied up but meant to call him back. I forgot until now. Tell him sorry."

"Is Callow with you?"

"Like I said, I'm at home, Jazz. No, Callow isn't at home with me," he said, sounding bemused.

"Any idea where he is? His phone is off."

"No idea, sorry. Anything I can help with?"

"Actually, yes. Do you—"

"Sorry, maybe I do know where he is," interrupted Burgess. "We're off duty tomorrow and I think he said he was going out on his boat. He usually goes down the night before when he's going sailing. I'm pretty sure that's where he'll be tonight."

"Do you know where that is?"

"It's moored at a marina in Essex. I'm pretty sure it's on Canvey Island," Burgess said, sounding like he was thinking. "Yeah, I've been there a few times, it's definitely Canvey Island."

"Any idea what it's called?"

"What, the boat? It's called *Captain's Caper*, I remember that much."

"Not the fucking boat, Burgess. The name of the marina," said Jazz.

"Oh, sorry. No, I can't remember. I'm pretty sure it's called 'small' something. Small Creek maybe. Something like that."

"Do me favour. Google it and text me the name when we hang up, okay."

"Sure."

"One more thing. What time did you last see him?"

"A few hours ago," said Burgess, confusion beginning to enter his voice. "Why all the questions, Jazz. Is everything okay?"

"Fine," she said curtly. "Thanks for the info. Text me, okay."

"Is he okay?" pressed Burgess. "He's been a bit off the last couple of days. Why are you looking for him?"

Jazz looked over at Trench, who shook his head. He was Callow's partner. The bond between partners trumped almost any other relationship a cop had. A fact countless ex-wives and husbands could testify to. Even if Burgess wasn't involved, he would almost certainly tip off his partner that they were looking for him. And quite probably anything else they told him.

"Off, how?" she said instead.

"Just a bit scorpy, you know. Ever since the drop went to shit and we got kicked from the case. I think he's taken it pretty hard. He wouldn't normally let that bother him, but this time it seems a little different, is all. Especially considering we pretty much solved the Osbourne case this morning."

"What do you mean 'solved'?"

"The jewellery," said Burgess, perking up. "Didn't you hear? We found Vanessa Osbourne's jewellery at Chapman's lair this morning. She was there, Jazz. In his torture chamber."

"Right, yeah, the jewellery," said Jazz noncommittally. "I gotta go. Text me the name of the marina, okay."

"Sure," said Burgess.

Trench killed the call and immediately Googled marinas in Canvey Island. One of the first ones he found was called Smallgains Creek. Just as he said the name out loud, Jazz's phone pinged with a message from Burgess, which gave the same name. He put the postcode into Google maps. They both groaned in frustration when the estimated time to get there was shown as over an hour.

"He's already got a few hours on us," said Jazz. "What are the chances of him hanging around down there?"

"Only one way to find out," said Trench.

His frustration was growing. A few hours head start. Surely it was more than enough time for Callow to make his escape. Trench had no idea about the protocols involved in scheduling a small boat to set sail, but he doubted there was much to prevent someone from simply setting off. Especially if they were on the run. He started thinking about calling the Coastguard, instructing them to pick Callow up. Whatever it took.

Jazz pressed the accelerator but there was only so fast they could go on the mostly residential streets, some of which had a speed limit of twenty miles per hour. At times they barely even made it that fast, even with the lights flashing and siren wailing.

Trench had his head out the window, in the middle of an expletive-laden rant at a bus that had failed to pull over enough to let them past, when the high-pitched buzzing interrupted him. He glanced at the screen and put the window up as he answered the call he'd been expecting.

"Trench here," he said.

"Where are you?" said Commander Leroy Campbell.

"You get my message?"

"I got it. I've just listened to it. Osbourne is dead?"

"He's dead," confirmed Trench.

"Jesus," muttered Campbell.

"Yeah, well, it's not the worst outcome. Did you listen to the whole thing?"

"Where are you now?" repeated Campbell, ignoring the question. "I can hear the siren."

"Following a hunch," said Trench, reluctant to tell Campbell where they were going.

He had a bad feeling Campbell would try to stand him down from going after Callow.

"Listen to me, Trench," said Campbell firmly. "I have just ordered a squad to pick Callow up from his home. Rest assured we'll put the allegations to him and get his side of the story. I am ordering you not to go anywhere near it. Do you understand me?"

"Get his side of the story? We have the whole story. Osbourne confirmed his involvement. You heard him."

"Actually what I heard was you saying the name and Osbourne seeming to agree," said Campbell. "But he also sounded distressed during the whole exchange. And clearly he was not of sound mind, if he was planning to imminently shoot himself in the head. It looks bad for Callow, I know that. But we must follow due process here. He must have a chance to explain himself. He's one of our own, after all."

Trench threw Jazz a sickened look. When he didn't say anything, Campbell spoke again.

"I'm ordering you not to go near his home, do you understand me?"

"Roger."

"Don't fuck with me, Trench. I'm serious. I know you have history with him. Stay away from this."

"Ten four."

"Stop fucking around," growled Campbell. "One suspect is already dead on your watch. I don't want you anywhere near this one. That is an order."

"Fine," said Trench. "I give you my word I will not go anywhere near his home."

"Okay," said Campbell, sounding mollified. "Tell me what happened today. How did you get Osbourne to confess like that?"

Trench switched off the siren and spent the next ten minutes bringing Campbell completely up to speed. The Commander stayed mostly quiet throughout. But he couldn't contain his own swearing when Trench explained how they'd found the body of Vanessa Osbourne. Trench made sure to state definitively that Callow had dumped her there overnight.

When Trench finished his update, Campbell was silent for a long moment.

"Jesus. He certainly has a lot of explaining to do, no doubt about that," Campbell said eventually. "Who else down there knows it's Vanessa?"

"Danny Kenner, the CSM, is the only one. I've told him not to tell anyone. Not even his own crew."

"Okay, good. Keep it that way. In fact, send me Kenner's number when we're done here."

"Right," said Trench, but he was getting distracted.

They had just turned onto North Circular Road. Finally a dual carriageway, after crawling through the residential streets. Jazz wanted to make up for lost time. She put her foot down and swung into the outside lane. She made a motion to hit the sirens again but Trench indicated she should hold off until the call was finished.

"Anything else?" said Trench.

"Not for now," said Campbell after thinking about it. "You've done good work on this, Trench. I'm very impressed. We'll talk more about that when it's appropriate.

But for now, you can stand down. I'm going to lead the interviews with Callow myself. His treachery, if proven, will earn him a very hefty penalty indeed. That will be for the IPCC – or more likely the courts – to decide."

Trench moved his finger to the switch for the siren, ready to go as soon as Campbell hung up. There was a moment of silence, causing Trench to tune back into the conversation, wondering if he was supposed to say something.

"Okay," he said, just to hurry the call to an end.

"Right," said Campbell, sounding a little weary. "I'll speak with you tomorrow then."

As he hung up, Trench couldn't help wonder about the Commander's reaction. He seemed shaken by the conversation. Usually a master of hiding any form of emotion, he'd seemed unable to keep a jaded, dispirited tone out of his voice. As he considered it, Trench realised Campbell was probably already thinking about the huge damage this case was going to do to the Met's reputation.

Trench hadn't given that a moment's thought. He had followed the evidence. He had no regrets. But he knew Campbell was now part of the governance of the whole Met police force. With that came politics. PR. Brand management. All of which might even be of greater priority to the governors than policing itself.

Fuck that, he thought. Let them deal with it.

He understood the need for the Met to have its own people like Campbell, ready to manage the message sent out to the world. Especially in the age of fake news and media lies, fired from every direction into every device now glued to the hand of every citizen. The Met certainly had its enemies, ready to strike, ready to attack. Ready to set up a parallel police force. In all of that, Trench was firmly on the side of the Met.

But policing itself would always come first.

# Forty-Nine

Jazz flipped the siren and stepped on the accelerator. Right up the arse of the cars in front until they got out of the way. They made good time, even getting past the perennially jammed turn-off for Ikea's flagship London store relatively quickly. Traffic near Woodford got heavier so Jazz made the decision to hit the motorway rather than go out through East London. It was a good choice. Traffic on the M11 was relatively light and the turn off onto the M25 was smooth.

Once on the M25, she floored it. The blue lights carried further in the evening darkness. Cars up ahead quickly cleared the outside lane. After barely fifteen minutes they turned on to Southend Arterial Road. Another long, straight dual carriageway that would take them deep into Essex.

"Looks like there's hundreds of boats out here," said Trench, who had been studying his phone.

"There must be a clubhouse or something," said Jazz. "Someone with a map of which boat is where."

"There's an office, but this says it closed at six o'clock," he said, looking up from the screen. "We'll figure it out. We've got the name. *Captain's Caper*. We'll find it. If it's still there."

Fifteen minutes later they crossed through the Canvey Marshes onto Canvey Island. They were quickly into firstly commercial, then residential areas, so Jazz killed the lights and siren. Google maps led them onto Point Road. They followed it all the way to the end, clearly heading toward the sea. But then the road ended, a barrier blocking the way onto what looked like a gravel track.

"Let me see that," said Jazz, picking up the phone.

She hit the 'satellite image' option on Google maps. After studying it for half a minute, she stuck the car into reverse. She turned around, slowing as they went back down Point Road. There were numerous warehouses and business to their right. As far as she could read from the phone, the marina was behind these buildings. She slowed as they passed a factory, then a warehouse that had been converted into a gym. There was an alley running between them. Jazz turned the car and drove slowly into the alley.

Sure enough, at other end of the alley was the entrance to the marina. Two heavy steel tracks in the ground led back towards the warehouses they had just passed between, a testament to their previous life. There was no sign of any track-bound heavy machinery now, but the tracks continued ahead out through wide gates, onto what they assumed was the pier. Jazz slowed to a crawl and continued through the gates.

At first it looked more like a boatyard than a marina. There were lines of boats to their right and left, the water straight ahead. All the boats they could see were on hoists or huge trailers. Some were under awnings or corrugated iron structures. Almost all had obvious repair work either under way or badly needed. None were in the water.

"Which way?" said Jazz.

"Right," said Trench, after a moment.

As far as he could see, the boats to the left looked in worse shape. Some looked old and rotten, barely seaworthy even to his layman's eye. The ones to the right looked in marginally better condition.

"Let's walk from here," he said. "We need to check every one of them. Assuming we find some actually in the water."

As Jazz pulled the car in, they noticed that one of the rusty iron structures had a café sign above a wooden door. It was too dark to tell if it was still operational, but it looked well-kept enough. Jazz parked in front of it. They both got out of the car.

It was dark here, there were no streetlights. The wind was strong and cold, gusting in hard off the sea. It blew a deafening cacophony as hundreds of ropes clanged violently off masts. Evening gulls screeched out manically. They couldn't see them, but they could hear them. Thousands of them.

Trench retrieved their torches from the boot. He handed one to Jazz. She took it, after zipping up her heavy coat. She pulled the hood up to further protect against the icy wind, stamping her feet as she did so.

"Let's go," said Trench, having to raise his voice to be heard above the din.

They walked quickly out onto what turned out to be a jetty, rather than a pier. They soon saw there were indeed lots of boats in the water. Boats stretched off in front of them for at least a hundred yards. Wooden panels rattled in hinges as the sea wind battered the boats. Somewhere a canvas flap smacked angrily off the tether from which it had broken loose.

They found all kinds of vessels, each in its own mooring. Pleasure boats, fishing vessels, sailboats of all sizes, cruisers. Even a few house boats. They scanned each one in turn. They ran their beams over each boat from a few yards away, searching for the name. Most names were prominently painted, either on the back or side of the boat. They came to one where they couldn't find the name. Trench held up a hand. They halted as the evening howled around them.

They directed their beams onto the deck. It was a white power boat, about thirty feet long. A blue tarp covered the driver's seat and steering wheel. The rest of the deck was uncovered. Jazz pointed silently. There was a door next to the driver's seat, obviously leading down into the boat's interior. They killed their torches and stepped forward, but then hesitated.

There was no light from the interior below. If they shone their torches directly into it, they would alert anyone down there. But it wouldn't be safe to try to clamber aboard in the darkness. And even if they did clamber aboard, surely their weight would cause the boat to rock more than from just the wind, also alerting anyone inside. They stood for a moment in silence.

"This isn't it," Trench said, having to speak louder than felt comfortable given their need for stealth.

"You sure?" Jazz semi-yelled back.

"He's a sailor, right? This isn't a sailboat."

"You're right."

They turned their torches back on and moved toward the next one.

"What's the plan anyway," said Jazz. "How're we going to get on without him knowing we're here?"

"I'm not sure," admitted Trench. "We might just have to be quick."

"Okay," said Jazz, sounding underwhelmed. After another few paces she said, "You think he's armed?"

"Let's hope not," he said loudly, before adding. "Yeah, we definitely need to be quick."

They moved steadily down the line of boats, quicker now they were focusing only on sailboats. Soon they could see the end of the line, only a dozen or so boats ahead. Trench felt an immediate pang of disappointment. It seemed to confirm his worst fears. They'd missed him.

Jazz grabbed his shoulder.

"There!" she exclaimed. "That's it."

It was the next boat. A rush of adrenaline shot through Trench.

He hadn't clocked it because he'd looked up at the end of the line. They both immediately switched off their torches and wordlessly retreated back. They instinctively dropped to their hunkers, peeking out from behind the previous boat. They searched for any sign of activity. They saw none. They listened intently for any sign of life. Nothing.

The boat was about thirty feet long. It was dark blue on the underside, the name *Captain's Caper* clearly visible in large gold letters on the stern. There were no sails evident. The mast was bare. The boom protruding from it was secured fast by rope. The deck was a mix of white and dark brown wood. Short bench-seats ran along either side of the open rear deck, enough for two or three people to sit on each side.

Beyond these seats was the helm, and beside that the cabin. There were a couple of steps down to its door, which had a glass panel at the top. The door was closed. A blind or curtain was pulled down inside the glass panel. It obscured any view inside. But they could tell there was no light on inside.

Trench suddenly felt confused. Much as he'd hoped to find the boat, he hadn't really expected to. He was sure Callow would have bolted. But here it was. More confusing still, it appeared unoccupied. He ran through the possibilities in his head. He came up empty.

"Why's it still here?" he said out loud, though trying a hushed tone.

"Maybe he hasn't got here yet. Doesn't look like anyone's on board."

This caused them both to glance back over their shoulders, toward the entrance to the marina from which they'd just come. They didn't see anyone.

"Let's go the other side," said Trench.

They stood and hurried quietly past the *Captain's Caper*, instinctively making a wide arc away from it as they passed. They initially went behind the next boat, but then scurried further down the jetty. They could still see the *Captain's Caper*, but could also see far enough back down the jetty to watch for anyone approaching. They hunkered down again.

"He's had hours to get here," said Trench, doubt creeping into his mind. "What could he possibly have to do that was worth delaying his escape?"

"Maybe he's gone off to get supplies," offered Jazz. "He might be out there for a while. How far can that thing sail anyway?"

Trench nodded but didn't answer. He had no idea how far it could sail. They both thought for a moment. Then something else puzzled Trench.

"Did you see his car back there?"

"No," said Jazz. "But if he's gone off to get supplies, he'll need it. I didn't see a shop within walking distance."

The wind continued to howl. The gulls bawled and screeched. Trench felt exposed. If he was gone to get supplies then he would be returning any minute. The jetty was too open for them to hide and wait. No matter where they went they would be spotted from a distance. He examined the boat beside where they were crouched. It was another power boat, but smaller than the previous one. The whole deck area was covered by a tarp, cinched tight. There was nowhere to hide.

He looked at the next boat, but knew it wasn't going to work. Even if they found somewhere, it was too cold to linger for long. The frigid wind was already working on his wet clothes. He could feel his feet and hands begin to numb again. He knew Jazz was feeling the same. He could think of only one option. He motioned for Jazz to follow him, further down the jetty away from the boat. He turned to her about ten yards down.

"We've got to go aboard," he said, straining against the wind's roar. "We can't hang around out here. Nowhere to hide and it's way too cold."

"How're we going to open the door?"

"We'll have to jimmy the lock," he said, but noticed Jazz's sceptical look. "Or smash the lock off if we have to, I don't know. We'll check it out. If we can't open it easily or without it being obvious, we'll go back down to the entrance and wait for him there."

Jazz nodded her agreement. Trench felt determined they had to open the door. He was uneasy about the prospect of leaving the boat and waiting back at the entrance. There might be another way onto the jetty. They could miss him. They scouted back down the jetty. Still no-one approaching. They crept right up to the back of the *Captain's Caper.*

There were loud sucking and gushing noises as the sea lapped between the boat and the jetty. They heard wood rattling and glass shuddering. The boat bobbled only gently in the water, despite the strength of the wind. The ropes mooring it to the pier were pulled taut. The protective buoys barely moved. They stood for a brief moment at the back of the boat. They used their phone light rather than their torches, because the light was much less bright.

At the same time, each put one foot on the stern. Trench raised three fingers, then silently dropped them one at a time. On three, they both hoisted themselves aboard. The boat made a definite lurch downward at the back, though it wasn't as exaggerated as Trench feared it might be. They stepped gingerly down into the open deck area. Jazz first, quickly followed by Trench. They rapidly made the few steps to the door. And immediately saw why wood was rattling and glass was shuddering. The door was ajar.

A wooden slider panel at the top of the door was loose. It was clearly part of the door's locking mechanism. It would be pushed forward to allow the door to be opened. It wasn't pushed fully forward, but was not secured in place. It meant the door was clanking in its hinges, the glass panel rattling. They exchanged questioning looks. Trench didn't know what it could mean. But he didn't like it.

Trench pulled out his torch but didn't turn it on. He stepped squarely in front of the door. He gently pushed the sliding panel all the way forwards. But he realised the noise and feel from the wind would notify anyone inside that it was being opened. The element of surprise was gone.

He quickly pushed the door fully open. He clicked on his torch, pointed it down. He saw just a few steps down inside. He took the first two quickly then just dropped down. This was the moment of maximum risk. It was a bigger drop than he thought. He landed heavy but righted himself quickly. It was pitch black down here. He rapidly swung the torch up to take in his surroundings.

The light bounced around off dark wooden panels in the cramped space. Straight ahead, his torch illuminated two doors, closed. Before heading for them, he swung the torch to the left. Cushioned seating, a fold away table. A radio bolted to the wall. He swiftly swung the beam to the right. More seating, black boots. Trousers. They weren't empty. What the fuck? He swung the torch beam to his immediate right. Bloodied mess of hair and face. Gaping brains, crimson mush.

"*FUCK,*" he yelled, recoiling away from it.

The space was too small. He couldn't back away. Less than a foot from him. He turned and grabbed the handrails. Hoisted himself up the steps. He dropped his torch as he pulled himself up.

"What is it?" yelled Jazz. "Jesus, your hands! What happened?"

She was shining her torch at Trench's hands. They were covered in blood. Trench rubbed them on his thighs.

"Fuck," he uttered again.

"Are you hurt?" shouted Jazz.

"No. I'm fine," Trench shook his head, regaining his composure. "Just a fright. Shit. Wasn't expecting that."

He felt a moment's embarrassment at his reaction, but it passed quickly.

"I dropped my torch," he said, as if to divert.

"What is it, Trench? What's down there?"

"A body. He's dead. Half his face is missing."

"Callow?" exclaimed Jazz.

"I don't know, I couldn't tell. Black hair. Maybe," he said, the images jumping back into his mind. "Yeah, I think so."

They both turned and looked at the door.

"I'm going back down," said Trench. "Can you shine your torch through the gap in the top there."

He moved back to the stairs as Jazz moved to the opening where the slider had been before being pushed back. As he descended the stairs again, Trench could now see the blood splattered around on most surfaces. He realised he was contaminating the scene, but he had already unwittingly done that. He wanted to take another look. He had to know if it was Callow down there.

He reached the bottom and picked up his torch. He slowly turned the beam to his right again, this time prepared for the ghoulish scene. Even so, it took some effort not to recoil again.

Not quite half the face was missing. Just the upper left quarter of it. The head lobbed at an awkward angle, toward the cabin wall. Trench shone the beam directly at the face. He leaned in closer. The familiar jowl. The new beard. The hair colour. Though the remaining eye was closed, and what was left of the face had a freakish twist, he knew who it was. There could be no mistake. This hideous mess of skin and brain and bloody tissue was what was left of Detective Chief Inspector Nigel Callow.

Trench straightened up. For a moment he just stood there. He didn't know what to think.

"Is it him?" Jazz called down.

Trench nodded.

"Trench, is it him?" she repeated.

Trench realised she couldn't see his nod.

"It's him," he called back up to her. "Call it in."

"Fuck," he heard her say, in surprise as much as anything else.

Trench quickly got over his own surprise. He scanned the rest of the body, looking for any evidence of what had happened here. He found it on the floor, beside his feet. A pistol, right below where Callow's arm draped down from the seating on which he lay. Trench crouched down for a better look. He wasn't a firearms expert, but knew enough to believe he was looking at a Beretta nine millimetre. He left it where it was.

He stood back up and ran the torch beam around the rest of the cabin. Slowly this time. He was about to start moving carefully toward the closed doors when the beam picked up something that caught his attention. A canvas hold-all on the floor near the doors. Trench swept the beam across the rest of the floor. Some blood spatters where he was standing but nothing else. He stepped forward.

With one hand, he pulled gently at the hold-all. It wasn't fastened closed. He easily pulled it open and peered inside. Money. Lots of money. Bundles of tens and twenties held together by plastic bands. He pulled the bag open just enough to see even more bundles. Nothing else in bag. Just piles of money.

Trench let go of the bag, letting the flap close. He stood up. His mind was flooding with questions. He turned where he stood and focused the beam again on Callow's mangled face. So many questions. But now he'd never get answers. One question came to the fore. The one Trench knew would puzzle him forever.

"Why?" he said out loud.

*

Jazz went back and retrieved crime scene tape while Trench waited by the *Captain's Caper*. They taped off the area around the boat then went back to their car. Trench taped off the entrance to the jetty as well. When the others came he'd ask them to tape off as far back as the warehouses too, in case any members of the press turned up. They then sat in their car, occasionally running the engine to power the heaters. It was an hour before anyone else arrived.

In addition to Forensics Units, Trench figured others would come. It was a huge development in the case. And a huge development for the Met. All of it bad. Officers from across the force would come if they could. They would be drawn to ground zero, even if there was little they could do to help. They would come either to see for themselves or to gather with colleagues for what was certain to be a dark hour for the Met. Human instinct, safety in numbers.

But when the first car arrived and the door opened, he was surprised to see it was Detective Chief Superintendent Lewis who stepped out. Lewis looked around, then spotted where they were parked. He started walking toward them. Trench decided to flip on the full headlights. He could claim it was to help light his way rather than to bug his eyes.

"It'll be interesting to hear what Private Pyle has to say for himself," said Jazz.

"I have no interest in anything he has to say."

"Want me to intercept him?" said Jazz, zipping up her coat.

"Sure, if you're willing to take one for the team," said Trench. "Thanks partner, I owe you one."

Trench watched as Jazz got out and walked over to the approaching Lewis. He kept the headlights on. Jazz was obviously briefing him, pointing occasionally down to where the boat was. Lewis gesticulated in that direction and Jazz began walking that way. Lewis stopped and said something to her, then turned and headed toward Trench in the car.

"Fuck's sake," he grumbled to himself.

He realised that if Lewis wanted to talk to him, he might get in and sit down. It would make it more difficult to walk away from him. After all that had happened that day, the last thing in the world Trench wanted was to listen to petty bullshit or whining from Lewis. He wasn't sure he could contain himself.

Trench opened his door and got out. He kept the lights on and met Lewis just in front of the car. He looked at Lewis but didn't say anything. Lewis looked around for a few seconds before meeting Trench's eyes.

"I heard you found him," he said.

He said it almost too quietly to be heard above the gusting wind and the din from the gulls. Trench didn't say anything.

"Jazz said the money is there too," Lewis continued, slightly louder.

Trench thought he saw a searching, almost pleading look in his eyes. He didn't respond. Lewis glanced over at Jazz, then the ground, then back at Trench. A marked police car with lights flashing emerged from between the warehouses and pulled in by the gates. Its arrival seemed to spur Lewis on to getting to the point. Thankfully.

"Uh, look Trench, I know I made a mistake. Maybe more than one. And I owe you an explanation."

Trench didn't respond.

"And probably an apology," Lewis added laboriously.

When Trench still didn't respond, Lewis became a little more animated.

"You're a difficult man to manage, you know that," he said ruefully. "I know I fucked up but Jesus Christ, you don't make it easy. He told me you planted that gun. Callow. He told me he'd already searched there, but ten minutes later you found it in the exact same spot."

Trench gave a slight nod. He probably would have figured that out if he'd given it any thought.

"And I believed him," Lewis said. "It made me wary of you. I wasn't sure I could trust you. Obviously I know that was wrong now. He played me to a tee. He played the whole squad, I suppose. But he did a real job on me. All his other games. I knew he was trying to play me when I arrived. Whispering in my ear, always first to come in and let me know what was going on in the squad, even bringing me the coffee. Of course I knew. But shit, what else could I do? No-one else in the squad was making it easy for me. Even you barely kept me in the loop on anything. I had to chase you every few hours for your reports. So I had no other option. I had to rely on him until I broke in with the rest of the squad…"

If it was an apology, it sounded more like he was saying sorry to himself. But Trench didn't feel anger or animosity towards him. He felt nothing, nothing at all for Lewis. His head was playing over images of Vanessa Osbourne's corpse in a ditch. Her father blowing his brains out in front of him. Callow's brains already blown out, a foot from his face. And this man was talking about petty squabbles and needing reports every few hours. He didn't get it then and he didn't get it now.

"Look, Trench, what I'm trying to say is, I know I messed up," Lewis was saying, as another two police vehicles arrived in the background. "It's not been the start I'd have wanted. But I'm determined to work even harder to make it right. The Commander seems a bit pissed off with me at the moment. There'll probably be a review. Not just into me, but the whole case. Everything about Callow, from even before I got here. We all made mistakes, right? But some of it will involve me. My handling of the Osbourne case. And of Callow, of course.

"What I'd like is uh, to know I can count on your support during the enquiry. I've noticed he values your word a lot. Especially now, probably. You know I've got the best interests of the squad at heart, right? I'm convinced we can turn it into a real crack outfit. A proper functioning team, that can deliver huge improvements in our stats. I want to continue what we've started. And you'd be an integral part of that obviously. So if anyone asks, especially the Commander, I'd like to know you'll let him know how it is."

At another time, in another place, Trench would have told him exactly what he thought. That his head was way, way too far up his own ass to ever be safely recovered. That the Titanic stood a better chance of being raised from the murky depths of the deep, dark ocean. That not knowing this, and somehow convincing himself that asking Trench to vouch for him was a good idea, was all the evidence needed to prove the point.

But Trench was tired and drained and too frazzled after the intensity of the day to try to get through to Lewis's irrecoverable head. More importantly, he had already tried to do so on numerous occasions. The chance for a free education was gone.

"Good luck to you," he simply said.

Lewis looked at him uncertainly. Other officers were approaching. Lewis glanced over his shoulder then back at Trench. Again the pleading look, but maybe realisation was creeping in too.

"Hey guv," called one of the officers, only a few feet away now. "Where're we going?"

Lewis looked at Trench for another moment. Trench looked back, not hostile, just neutral. After another second, Lewis gave a brief nod. Realisation maybe finally breaking through. He stepped away, motioning to the other officers.

Watching him walk away, Trench mulled what it said about a man who tells you he owes you an apology but then never apologises.

# Fifty

Trench arrived at the station later than usual the next morning. It was nearly seven thirty by the time he got there. After they'd left Canvey Island to the Crime Scene and Forensics Units the night before, he'd picked up his bike at the station and gone straight home to take a long, steaming-hot shower.

He could dump his ruined suit in the bin at the station. He could wash the mud and blood and dirt and grime off his body. But he couldn't easily erase the day's brutal, indelible images from his mind. That would take time, he knew. For now, he was destined to process and deliberate and mull all aspects of the case until his mind somehow managed to make peace with it all. It always happened this way.

After he'd dressed he rode over to Vivian's house. He had missed Milo's bedtime, but he needed to see his son. Although calling unannounced, Vivian seemed to read the mood. A rare occasion when she didn't even try to start a fight. Trench had gone straight to Milo's bedroom. He pulled the wicker chair over to the bedside and watched his son's peaceful breathing. The centurion tuft of black hair at the top of his head was sticking bolt upright as always. His mouth hung open, lopsided as half his face was lost in the pillow. He did sleep the same way he did everything else. Maximum intensity.

The thought brought a smile to Trench's face. After another while, he could feel the harder edges of the day's memories begin to blunt a little. They always did when he spent time with Milo. They would stay with him for a long time, but he was grateful for the respite. Eventually calmness came. He closed his eyes and wondered if maybe he'd be able to get a couple of hours sleep tonight after all. His mind began to wander.

He thought back to the very beginning of the Vanessa Osbourne case. Of the moment they got the call to lead on it, when they'd found the body of what turned out to be Savannah Diaz in Oldbury Woods. Of the next few days of the increasingly desperate search for anything that would point them in the direction of the missing Vanessa. Of the feeling of hope when they discovered she had a secret flat. Of the whole ransom saga.

Yet all the while Vanessa had been long dead. Her body lying in the boot of the car at Blenheim. Just yards from where they'd been numerous times during the early hours of the investigation. He briefly wondered if he should have suspected Osbourne earlier. But the depressing truth was that it didn't matter. She was dead by then anyway. Trench shook his head, trying to ward off a deep and growing sense of vexation. It had all been for nought.

Or had it?

The chain of events had ultimately led to Callow being exposed for what he truly was. And to paying the penalty. A high price indeed, but Trench found he had little sympathy for Callow. The man had initially tried to rob the ransom money, even at a time when that may have resulted in harm befalling the 'kidnapped' Vanessa. When he discovered the ransom was fake, and put it together that Osbourne was responsible for her disappearance, his immediate reaction was to extort money from Osbourne. The only time he even considered Vanessa was when he came up with the abominable plan to dump her body in the field simply to cover his tracks.

Trench blew out his cheeks. It was almost too much to understand. How could Callow have been so far gone? And should Trench have spotted the signs earlier? He'd despised the man, so kept him at arms' length. He wondered if maybe he should have acted sooner. If he should have seen the signs and done something about it. But what could he have done? And more importantly, what were the signs? How do you spot them in the often blurred space where police operate, between the letter of the law and reality on the street?

Trench knew there were bent coppers. Hell, if bent included giving a mate a warning rather than a roadside breath-test, or taking a few quid from a dealer or pimp to look the other way, then maybe half the force was bent. The thin blue line spanned various shades, he knew that. But this? No, what Callow had done was different. It was darker. It went beyond whatever the acceptable level was. He had to believe that.

But instead he found some doubt in his mind. He couldn't say exactly why, but the thought process was making him uncomfortable. Who was he to say where the line was? And where was he on it? He had never done anything even remotely comparable to what Callow had done. And he knew he would never desecrate a victim like that. Not in a million years.

But what of bribery? If he had discovered Osbourne's crime before anyone else knew, and Osbourne had offered him a huge pay off to look the other way, to make it disappear, what would he have done? He would have said no.

But then Osbourne would have increased the amount of money. Was there an amount of money that would tempt him? Vanessa was already dead. Nothing he could do would change that. Osbourne was unlikely to be a danger to anyone else in future. Howard Chapman deserved to be locked away for the rest of his life. Adding another victim to his tally would only help to ensure that.

He looked down at his sleeping son. The thought persisted. Should he secure the financial future for his son? A better standard of life, never having to worry about money again, a nicer home, university fees taken care of, a house when he was ready to move out, mortgage free...his whole life put on a firmer footing. A better life than he would otherwise have. As Dad, was it his duty to put his son first?

Trench told himself no. He wouldn't do it. He'd never do it. No matter what the circumstances. It was irritating him that he was even thinking this way.

But the doubt was insistent. He could tell himself that, but did he really believe it? Did he really know?

Annoyed with himself, Trench finally leaned over and kissed the top of Milo's head. Vivian had already gone to bed so he let himself out and went home. When he got into bed the same thoughts returned. He tossed and turned but he couldn't escape them. Images from the day flittered through his mind. They settled on Callow's obliterated head. Maybe this was how he felt just before. He had found the answer for himself, but it wasn't the way he thought it would be. It had eaten at him. The only escape was via a Beretta nine millimetre.

Trench eventually slipped off to a couple of hours of numbed agitation that would have to pass for sleep. When he got out of bed for the day, he felt sluggish. Lack of sleep and the fact both cases were solved meant he felt no urgency. He took a longer shower than usual then sat with his coffee in the living room before getting dressed.

Amongst the fog of the night's brooding, he still felt bothered by his failure to answer the question definitively for himself. But he also felt bothered at the thought that Callow had grappled with it so much that he had blown his own brains out. As the dust was settling on all the drama and torsion of the past week, he realised that this was emerging as the most jarring aspect of it all.

*

When he walked into the squad room, Jazz was already at her desk. They exchanged 'mornings' and Trench logged on to his computer. He opened his email and scanned the inbox. The first thing that caught his eye was an email from Kevin Johnson, the psychological profiler. It started with an apology for the delay, then an apology for the relatively cursory report, attached.

"Day late and a dollar short," he mumbled to himself.

He moved on without opening the now redundant attachment. He was in the process of deleting most of the other unread emails when he spotted the door to Lewis's office opening. Lewis trudged out, head down, face puce and twisted in a scowl. He marched straight for the squad room exit. He glanced up at Trench as he passed. Trench looked back at him, then his eyes went to Lewis's hand. He was carrying his jacket. He looked back at Lewis's eyes, but Lewis looked away. Then he was gone out the door.

For a moment, Trench continued to gaze at the space where Lewis had just been. He wondered if he'd just witnessed Lewis experiencing the harsh bite of reality. The thought had barely formed when he saw another figure emerge in the doorway of Lewis's office. Campbell looked like he was about to call out, but then spotted Trench was already looking at him. Instead, he curled a finger at Trench and walked back inside. Trench walked over and went inside.

"Close the door, Trench," said Campbell, taking a seat in Lewis's chair.

Trench did so, then pulled out a chair from the small table and sat down. He looked at Campbell, who looked back without saying anything for a long moment. Always the same.

"I'm going to take a risk," Campbell said eventually. "Although, maybe it's less of a risk now than it would have been previously."

He shot Trench a look, seeming pleased with himself for being cryptic enough for Trench not to know what he was talking about. Trench didn't say anything. Campbell eventually went on, perhaps a little disappointed Trench hadn't risen to the bait.

"The events of the past week have been truly…remarkable," said Campbell. "I've experienced very few weeks like it in all my decades with the Met. As I reflected on it, a few things became obvious to me. The first is that we are facing some potentially very, very dangerous circumstances. We have been badly exposed, on numerous fronts. My priority – our priority – is to protect the force from these threats. We must do everything we can to achieve that. All of us. I presume that goes without saying?"

Trench nodded.

"Good. That starts now. And in this case, the person with particular responsibility for this is of course you," he said, nodding and raising his eyebrows at Trench.

Trench wasn't surprised. He knew this was coming given his level of involvement in both cases. He had even prepared a response. He would take a back seat and let Campbell and his PR flunkies engage with the press. That was fine with him.

"Understood," he said crisply. "And I'm happy to defer all media interest to you, sir. I'm sure you're much better at dealing with them than I am. All yours."

Campbell was nodding now.

"Yes, indeed. I'll be handling all media briefings, of course," he said. "But I want you to hear it first. I don't want you uh, wrong footed later. I'm sure you have your own media contacts, Trench. I know you're smart enough. But it's important we are all joined up on this one. It's absolutely vital that we're all saying the same thing, through whatever channels we have to the media."

Trench's suspicion perked up.

"Show me your phone," said Campbell, holding out his hand.

When Trench didn't move, Campbell repeated the request.

"The recording of your conversation with Osbourne," he said. "Show it to me on your phone."

Trench's immediate instinct was to say he didn't have his phone on him. But that wouldn't do anything more than buy a little time for a conversation he may as well have now. He reached inside his pocket and took out his phone, but held it in his hand.

"Give it here," said Campbell, leaning forward and gesturing with his hand. "Who else has heard the recording?"

Trench fumbled with finding the recording to delay for a moment. He suddenly realised what was going to happen. His gut reaction was to reject it, though he'd prefer some time to think it through. But he knew Campbell wasn't going to give him that time.

"Uh, no-one," he said.

"Come on, Trench. Who do you think you're talking to?" said Campbell almost jovially. "You've played it for Jazz obviously. Who else?"

"No-one," said Trench truthfully. "You and Jazz are the only people who've heard it."

"Very good. I'll speak with Jazz later. I know I won't have to worry about her. I suspect she's a lot smarter than you are," said Campbell. "Give it here."

Trench got up and handed him the phone, then stayed standing beside him. He watched Campbell press play to make sure it was the right recording, then stop it and hit delete. Campbell then opened Whatsapp and found the message of the recording sent to himself. He deleted the message. He handed the phone back to Trench, a satisfied smile on his face.

"You're taking a risk alright," said Trench.

"No, no, that's not the risk I was talking about. That's just…house-keeping," replied Campbell, almost beaming now. "The risk I was talking about is you, Trench. Despite the fact you're a stubborn, obstinate pain in the ass at the best of times, I think this past week has shown just how capable you are. Going forward, we need the best people we have in positions where they can make the most difference. That's another thing that became obvious to me following this whole debacle.

"Lewis, for example, was wildly out of his depth. In retrospect, I made a mistake appointing him as my successor. I've just relieved him of his duties as Detective Chief Superintendent at CID. There'll be a process to follow of course, but it's effective immediately. And I'm going to risk making you the new Chief Super. Congratulations, Trench. You deserve it. I've had my doubts in the past whether you're truly capable of putting the Met ahead of your own juvenile pig-headedness, but I think this affair has allayed my doubts."

Trench let the words sink in. This was not something he'd seen coming. Cogs started clicking into place.

Then he saw it. Campbell's full play.

It didn't stop at erasing the evidence of Osbourne's confession. It was the whole lot. The whole story. Campbell, ever managing the damage. This time he was roping Trench in. Quid pro quo. You scratch my back…

"So Callow's the hero cop haunted by his own failure to save Vanessa?" he said, his voice dripping in scepticism.

"Hero might be overstating it. He hardly deserves that, after all. Maybe flawed cop who just couldn't hack one more failing," said Campbell, waving a hand dismissively. "A few carefully chosen words with the right reporters can sort out the detail. But that's not the important thing."

"Right," said Trench. "The important thing is that there's no bent copper. And Osbourne's just the innocent, bereft father who also killed himself after learning his daughter had been abducted and murdered by the deranged serial sadist?"

"It's a better outcome for everyone," shrugged Campbell. "Think of the family. Do you want to be the one to tell Mrs Osbourne that her husband killed her daughter? To tell her brother and sister? What possible good can come from that?"

Trench pictured that image in his mind. Campbell didn't give him any time to dwell on it though. He pressed on.

"And anyway, who'd believe you?" he said, shrugging again.

"Other people know," said Trench. "It'll leak."

"There'll be rumours of course," said Campbell calmly. "But there's always rumours. It's just a matter of getting the official story out there first. Then it'll just fade away, like everything else. When was the last time a story got more than a few days' worth of media coverage? After that it'll just be backroom gossip and conspiracy theories by cranks in the nether regions of social media. Like everything else.

"Everyone complains about social media and twenty-four hour news. But you know, I quite like it. It's given the public the attention span of a gnat. Always leaping to the next salacious scandal and conspiracy theory. Makes it easy to bury a story. All you have to do is brazen out the first forty-eight hours."

Trench just stared at him, his face beginning to frown as he considered everything that Campbell was saying. It felt wrong. It felt dirty. But he couldn't quite pin down exactly why. Maybe what Campbell was saying had merit. Less collateral damage. For the Osbourne family and others, as well as for the Met. What was to be gained by the world knowing what Osbourne had done? What Callow had done?

In his head he was seeing a fuzzy blue line again. Acceptable bends versus unacceptable breaches. He realised he was still struggling to see where the line was. Where he stood on it. Still failing to answer these questions.

Seeing his frown and his silence, Campbell seemed to think Trench needed more persuasion.

"Come on, Trench. There's really not that much to think about," he said. "It's a win-win-win. The best way to salvage anything from a truly dreadful episode. For some people, like the Osbournes, it just makes a tragic situation a little less bad. For others, it ends quite well. Like you, for example, with a promotion."

"You're assuming I'm even interested."

"Aren't you?" Campbell shot back.

That was one question Trench did know the answer to. Nothing about the past week had changed his view on that. But he decided not to answer yet. It felt like he should at least take some time to reconfirm his view. He probably wouldn't get offered the position again for a long time, if ever.

"I'll think about it."

"Fine," said Campbell, a little put out. "But don't take too long. I'll give you twenty-four hours. Word will get out by then that Lewis is gone."

Trench nodded and stood up.

"But the story, Trench," said Campbell, wagging a finger. "That starts right now, you understand. From the minute you walk out of this office. That is the reality now. Understood?"

Trench paused, then nodded.

"Good. I'll see you tomorrow with your answer, if not before," said Campbell. "Oh, and one last thing. You get to bring the good news to the Met Police Benevolent Fund. They'll be nearly a quarter of a million pounds better off after this. Let's call it a dying wish from Callow, ay."

Trench rounded on Campbell.

"What did you say?"

"The money. I can't think of a more fitting end to this whole debacle. Don't you agree?"

"A quarter of a million pounds?" repeated Trench.

"Nearly," nodded Campbell. "They'll be delighted. You deserve to make that call to them. You've earned that right."

Trench spun around and left the office. What Campbell had said hit him like a freight train.

His mind was racing. What had Osbourne said? He searched for the words. "…*'a bargain compared to a ransom' he said...cheeky bastard...*"

Trench turned right. He marched over to the middle row, more of Osbourne's words echoing in his head. "…*half as greedy but twice as treacherous…*". The desks were empty. "…*half…*" as greedy as the ransomer, Osbourne had said of Callow.

That's what had put it in Trench's mind. He couldn't recall whether Osbourne had actually said he'd given Callow a million pounds, but that was certainly the conclusion Trench had been left with. "*Half*" as greedy as a two million pounds ransom.

He stood at their empty desks. Then he remembered what Burgess had told him last night. That he and Callow were off today. He moved around to Burgess's desk and began searching through the papers on it. He opened the drawers in turn, looking for anything with his address on it. As he rifled through the papers, he found an electricity bill with Burgess's name on it. He took a photo of it.

He turned and ran toward the squad room exit. Jazz wasn't at her desk. He decided to go anyway. Maybe he was mistaken about the million pounds but he doubted it. He bounced down the steps three at a time. He replayed Osbourne's words. He recalled Jazz telling Burgess last night on the phone that he sounded like he was in a car, Burgess claiming he was at home. He heard Campbell's words *"…nearly a quarter of a million pounds…"*

No chance. Why would Callow accept such a small sum when he knew Osbourne was good for vastly more than that? He ran to his locker and grabbed his helmet and jacket. Suddenly the notion of Callow shooting himself in remorse seemed utterly ludicrous. It had jarred with him last night. Now he knew why.

# Fifty-One

He sped toward Vauxhall, South London. The address he'd discovered for Burgess was in one of the capital's newest residential skyscrapers, the St George Wharf Tower. Trench had never been inside but knew it by reputation. Knew that most of the flats were owned by foreigners, many of whom controversially had never set foot in them. A few Russian and African billionaires owned penthouses or whole floors of the fifty-storey structure. The flats affordable on a copper's salary were presumably a million levels below those.

Trench ripped across town, making it to the Tower inside ten minutes. He pulled onto the promenade right beside the building. He did a lap of the base of the Tower at crawling speed, only then realising the entrance was accessed from the road. He veered back out onto the road and sped around the Tower. Stopping at a tall iron gate, he was searching for a buzzer when he noticed an adjacent gate opening. He watched as a silver Bentley with blacked-out windows emerged through the gate.

He sped through the open gate, racing up to the revolving door and jumping off his bike. He stuffed his gloves inside the helmet and hung it on the bike. He urgently rummaged for his ID as he pushed through the door. He emerged into a lobby with black velvet sofas and crystal chandeliers. Before he could get his bearings a doorman who looked about sixty years old, replete with bowler hat, strode briskly over to him. Another similarly dressed doorman sat at a desk behind him.

"May I help you, sir," he said sternly.

"Met Police. You're with me," he barked, holding up his ID.

"I beg your par—"

"Do you have access to all the flats in here?"

"Sir, you're going to have to—"

"Do you see what this is?" Trench interrupted, pointing at his ID. "I am Met Police. Do you understand what that means?"

"Yes, sir," said the man, peeved. "But I don't think—"

"That's good, don't think. Just listen, then answer. I'm after a man who lives here. Are you able to open the door to his flat if he won't let me in?"

"No, sir," said the man resolutely.

"Not even in an emergency?"

"No, sir."

Trench didn't believe him, but he had no time to argue.

"Fine," he said. "Like I said, you're with me. Which floor is this flat on?"

He held out his phone with the picture of the address. The man grudgingly looked at it.

"This *apartment* is on the eighth floor. Sir."

"We'll take the lift. Lead the way," said Trench, spotting the lifts and dashing to them.

"Let's go," he hollered at the man, pounding the lift's call button.

The doorman shrugged to his colleague then followed Trench. They stepped inside the lift. The doorman used a fob to activate the lift then hit number eight.

"What's your name?" Trench asked him as the doors closed.

"Harold" said the man, then after a slight pause, "Harry."

"Well Harry, I'm DCI Trench Chambers of Met CID. I appreciate your help here," said Trench, figuring now was the time to get the man fully onside. "What I'm going to need you to do is to knock on the man's door. Tell him it's a security matter or something. Just make sure you get him to open the door, then step out of the way, fast. Can you do that?"

Harry looked at Trench. When he spoke, he dropped the showiness he had clearly been putting on in the lobby, in case any of the residents happened to be watching.

"Yeah, I can do that. What's he done, anyway?"

"I can't tell you that, sorry."

"But you're CID, right? Not just Old Bill?" said Harry.

Trench nodded. Harry had been around the block a few times.

"Must be serious then," said Harry. "Can't say I'm surprised. Bunch of Berkshire Hunts in here anyway, you ask me. You know, there's almost no registered voters living in this whole building? Not a single taxpayer in the whole fackin eyesore. I pay more tax than the rest of 'em put together."

They arrived at eight as Harry started shaking his head. "Whole place is almost always empty. Like a ghost ship at night, it is. Crying shame, mate."

Harry pointed to the left. Burgess's flat was halfway down the ornately decorated corridor. Trench clocked the door's peephole, as he'd expected. He stood with his back pressed against the wall right beside the door, as Harry stood square in front of it. He signalled to Harry, who banged hard on the door. For a moment, nothing.

Trench thought he heard footsteps. They grew louder, unmistakable. A gentle thud on carpet inside the flat. Then a groggy, croaky voice answered from behind the door.

"Who is it?"

Definitely Burgess.

"Good morning, sir. It's Harold from the front desk."

"What do you want?"

"Uh, sir, there's been an incident in the building. I need to check your residency. Can you please open the door."

"What incident?"

"I just need to see your fob please, sir. We're checking every apartment in the building. There's been an unauthorised entrance," said Harry.

"My fob?" came the mumbled reply. "Just a second."

The footsteps retreated from the door. Harry stole a glance at Trench, then winked. He seemed to be enjoying himself. The footsteps returned a moment later. Trench heard the latch being turned. The door opened a crack. Trench lent forward, ready to pounce. But then he heard the unmistakable sound of a chain. The door opened only a few inches. A hand poked out through the gap, a fob clearly visible. But Trench could see a chain on the inside of the door. Harry spotted it at the same time.

"Uh, thank you, sir. Could you please open the door so I can see your face?" Harry ventured.

"Huh? What do you want?" said Burgess.

"I just need to check it's definitely you, sir," pressed Harry.

"What the …" grumbled Burgess.

Trench could see his shadow on the wall inside the door. Then he caught the top of Burgess's head. From where Harry was standing, he could see Burgess's eyes. This was it. Now or never.

Trench sprang forward, jamming his foot into the small gap in the door.

"What the fuck!" yelled Burgess, catching the movement.

He tried to slam the door but Trench's foot blocked it.

"Burgess, it's Trench. Open up!"

"Trench?" said a stunned Burgess. "What…"

Burgess broke off. He suddenly started barging into the door from inside. Pain shot through Trench's foot. He leaned back slightly then rammed his shoulder hard into the door. It didn't open but gave some relief to his foot.

"Open up, Burgess. Don't be stupid. I just want to talk."

Trench rammed the door again. Next thing, Harry did the same. He half hit the door, half hit Trench. His bowler hat flew off and rolled down the corridor.

"Sorry," mumbled Harry, but then rammed it again, this time missing Trench, hitting just the door.

"I'm not opening, Trench!" shouted Burgess. "I've done nothing wrong."

"Then let's talk. Just open the door."

"I didn't kill him," said Burgess desperately. "He did it himself."

"Just open the fucking door and we can talk, Burgess."

"I'm not going to prison," said Burgess, emotional now. "He got what he deserved…"

"I can't help you if you don't open the door," said Trench, trying to sound calm.

"Help me?" cried Burgess. "You think I believe that. It was self-defence. I had nothing to do with his deal with Osbourne. I just…It was all his idea. He was going to just leave…"

Stalemate. There was no way Trench could force the door with Burgess on the other side. He had to try to get Burgess to open the door.

"I believe you. I know what he's like. I know what he did. But you have to open the door."

"*I'm not going to prison!*" shouted Burgess. "You think I'm stupid? You all think I'm stupid. I am not going to prison for this."

Trench heard the footsteps retreat into the flat. He stepped back from the door then smashed his foot against it. He put all his force into it. A slight splintering sound. He reeled back and smashed it again. A definite crack. Once more he reeled back and smashed with his foot. He aimed higher, putting everything into it. The door flew open, a huge bang as it crashed into the wall and bounced back.

"Do not come inside," Trench bawled to Harry. "Go back downstairs. Now!"

Trench stepped inside. He pushed the door closed behind him. He moved slowly. Burgess had already killed one cop. The first door to his right was the bathroom. He poked his head inside. Burgess wasn't in there. The next door was open. The bedroom. No sign of Burgess. Trench felt a gust of cold air.

"Fuck," he gasped, running the next few steps. He was in an open plan kitchen and living room. It was tiny. Burgess was standing on a chair at the end of the room. One foot on the chair, the other on the ledge of the open window.

"Don't do it, Burgess," said Trench, holding up his hands in a calming gesture.

Burgess was sobbing uncontrollably. He was staring down at the ground outside.

"Don't do it," Trench repeated, slowly walking forward.

"Don't move!" screeched Burgess. "I'll do it. I'll jump. I am not going to prison for this."

Trench stopped in his tracks.

"No-one's going to prison," he lied. "We can work this out."

Burgess looked at him through saturated eyes.

"Huh, you think I'm stupid, Trench. You always have. You all have. I'm not going to jail. That prick got what he deserved," he wept.

"No-one thinks—"

"*Shut the fuck up!*" roared Burgess, hoisting himself further up onto the ledge.

Trench looked around the room, searching for anything he could use. Instead he saw a large sports bag on the sofa. It was open. He saw the same bundles of cash inside. It was much bigger than the hold-all bag on the *Captain's Caper*. Burgess glared around, spotted his gaze.

"That prick," sobbed Burgess. "He bribed Osbourne. I had nothing to do with it. When I got suspicious he eventually told me what he'd done. He told me he'd give me ten grand. Ten fucking grand! To take the rap while he fucked off. Stupid prick. Always treated me like shit. Got all the rest of you to treat me like a fucking leper. I never chose to be his bloody partner!"

"Don't say anymore," said Trench, determined to convince him to step away from the ledge. "I didn't hear any of that. Just come down here and we can work it out."

"He had me drive him out to his boat," Burgess continued, ignoring him. "I stood by while he burnt out the car, then dropped him to the boat. He said the money was there. The ten fucking grand. He thought I'd just walk away. When I told him I wanted more, he started telling me to go with him. Said we could both go off on his boat. I knew what he'd do. Get me out to sea then chuck me overboard! I'm not fucking stupid. Yeah, I knew what he'd do. I was prepared. I'd taken that gun from his car. His own gun, stashed there ages ago. He always had a gun handy in case he needed to plant it. He'd forgotten it, but I knew where it was. When I saw the amount of money he had.....ten fucking grand! No way. Not after all he put me through..."

Burgess seemed emboldened, recalling his sudden bout of bravery with Callow. He looked up at Trench.

"You didn't think I could do something like that, did you? Didn't think I had it in me," he said accusingly. "Just stupid old Five Burgers."

"Burgess, listen to me. We can fix this. Nobody else needs to die. It's not your fault. I know what he was like. Everyone does."

"Bullshit, Trench," whimpered Burgess through tears, shaking his head. "Bullshit. They're going to want to lock someone up for all this. Everyone else is dead."

"No-one else knows, Burgess. I swear to you. Not even Jazz knows I'm here. They're going to cover it all up. They want to protect the Met. They care more about that. Pin Vanessa's murder on Chapman and say Osbourne killed himself out of grief. Same with Callow. A burnt-out cop who couldn't handle it, so topped himself as well. Think about it, Burgess. You staged it well. How could they prove it?"

"Bullshit, Trench, you fucking asshole," Burgess sneered. "You really think I'm a fucking fool, don't you. How could they…it doesn't matter. I'm not going to prison. I swore that to myself, if they found out what I did. No fucking way."

At that moment, Trench realised that Burgess really was too stupid. He didn't know how it worked. He'd never believe the Met would stage a cover up to protect its reputation. He couldn't see it. Nothing Trench could say would make him see it.

Burgess shuffled closer to the window. He looked ready to hoist himself fully onto the ledge. Trench realised the only way was to make a lunge for Burgess. He was about fifteen feet away. He'd have to be quick.

"Okay, Burgess," he said softly, inching closer, ready to launch himself. "You're right. Why don't you—"

He dived forward, launching off his legs, arms outstretched. His hands landed on Burgess's tracksuit bottoms. He grabbed two handfuls, pulled hard. They sprung loose, too light. Trench looked up, just in time to see a vacant stare on Burgess's face. It tumbled forward, out. Then it was level with Trench's eyes, upside down. Then his feet. Then nothing. No sound, just wind blowing. A distant, almost imperceptible thud.

Trench scrambled up to the ledge, shock beginning to numb him. He looked out and down. Burgess was there, at the bottom. Red splattered out from him like bugsplat on the windscreen. A bigger pool crept outwards, engulfing the splatter.

"Oh Jesus," groaned Trench.

He stared for another few seconds then turned around, slumped down with his back against the window.

"Jesus Christ," he winced, burying his face in his hands.

Thoughts rushed through his head. Another one dead. Another one twisted and bent. First Osbourne, then Callow, now Burgess.

"Fucking hell. This case is cursed," he uttered.

He raised his head, staring into the living room of his now dead colleague. His eyes came to rest on the sports bag. He stared at it for a long moment. A funny sensation came over him. He leaned forward, crawled over to it.

He pulled it open. Piles of money. The bag full to the brim. He pulled some of them out. Filled his hands with them. Held them. Over three quarters of a million pounds.

He froze.

Three quarters of a million pounds. That no one else alive in the world knew existed.

He stared down at the bundles in his hands.

Then he smiled ruefully to himself. Maybe amidst all this murder and death and corruption, he could at least extract some good from it all.

All his tossing and turning. His failure to answer the question. To know where the line was. To know where he stood on it. To know how he'd react.

Now he knew.

With absolute certainty.

# THE END

# Acknowledgments

First and foremost, thanks very much to you, the reader. I know it's a leap of faith to spend your money and – perhaps more importantly – time, on a debut novel. I truly hope you feel it was worth the investment of both.

Thanks to Mom and Dad, for giving us everything needed to get out there and always give it a helluva shot.

Thanks to Paul, Catherine, Yvonne, Helen and David, for so much. But right now, most of all for your incessant pedantry…

Thanks to my, ahem, editorial team. To Paul, Helen, Ado, David and Susan. Thanks for incisively crafting an endless jumble of words into a story.

Thanks to David, for unlimited access to both sides of your remarkable brain.

Thanks to Tony P, for applying reality and professional fine tuning to the more speculative aspects of my imagination. And of course, for providing integral input into the investigation – they may never have cracked the case without it.

Thanks to Barra, for perdurable support and counsel through the ages.

Thanks to Darcy Dolan, for believing long before I ever did.

And most of all, thanks to my son. To Oscar. I am the luckiest man alive. I've known it from your very first moment, and every moment since. DLY, S.

Colin Doyle, May 2021.

# If you enjoyed *The Dark Side of Blue*

## Please leave an Amazon review

I'd be extremely grateful if you could please leave a review of the book on Amazon. Reviews are the lifeblood of books these days, so every single review is absolutely invaluable.

I know most of us tend to think our own single review won't make a difference, or that enough other people will leave a review. But the opposite is true – each and every review really is ***extremely*** important, and most other people are unlikely to leave one.

Please take a moment to leave a review – or even just a rating.

Thank you very much.

## Have your say

I am currently writing the second book featuring Trench and Jazz. To learn more about its progress and target release date please visit my website.

You can also sign up to the Mailing List to receive the occasional email with progress updates on new releases and related information.

I would love to get your thoughts or feedback on what you think could improve future books. By signing up to the Mailing List you can also reply to emails. I guarantee to read every email and aim to reply to all of them.

www.colin-doyle.com

Printed in Great Britain
by Amazon

72672674R00260